I0657296

RADIANT SENTRY
Where Technology Meets Treachery

by Charles M. Wayne

An Espionage Thriller

Dragonfly Associates LLC
Publisher
www.dragonfly.associates

Dedication

To my wife, Soo Han —
the love of my life and my in-house genius.
Every writer needs a sharp editor. I married mine.
She catches my plot holes, my typos, and
occasionally, my ego.

"any kind of service necessary to public good becomes honorable by being necessary"
— Nathan Hale

"I think the greatest single enemy is the misuse of information, the perversion of truth in the hands of terribly skillful people."
— John Le Carré

"Treason doth never prosper, what's the reason? For if it prosper, none dare call it Treason."
— John C. Denham

"Sometimes we have to do a thing in order to find out the reason for it,"
— John Le Carré

"No man has a good enough memory to be a successful liar."
— Mark Twain

"Rationalization may be defined as self-deception by reasoning."
— Karen Horney

Dragonfly Associates LLC

Independent Publishers
www.dragonfly.assocoates

PUBLISHER'S NOTE

First Edition December 2025
ISBN Digital Online Edition: 979-8-9936193-0-9
ISBN Paperback Edition: 979-8-9936193-2-3
ISBN Hardback Edition: 979-8-9936193-3-0

GSAFD: Spy stories. Classification: LCC PS3559.G54 Q36 2025
Wayne, Charles M. | Radiant Sentry: Where Technology Meets Treachery | Dragonfly Associates LLC. Kindle Edition.

Book Industry Study Group
FIC009000 FICTION / Thrillers / Espionage
FIC019000 FICTION / Thrillers / Military
FIC028000 FICTION / Thrillers / Political
https://www.bisg.org/fiction

TABLE OF CONTENTS

Introduction to the Watchtower Series

This is the first book in the *Watchtower Series*, introducing Team Watchtower—an elite investigative unit within the U.S. Army Counterintelligence Command (ACIC).

Most espionage thrillers revolve around the CIA. However, following the National Defense Authorization Act (NDAA) of 2025, ACIC was formally elevated from a primarily intelligence-focused agency into a hybrid counterintelligence and law enforcement command. This landmark change granted its civilian special agents limited federal arrest authority for national security crimes and expanded its operational scope beyond military installations.

Today, ACIC stands as the only counterintelligence organization with both foreign and domestic jurisdiction—and the legal authority to investigate, detain, and prosecute espionage within and beyond U.S. borders.

Notes on Format and References

Because this story delves deeply into modern espionage and defense operations, it references numerous U.S. and foreign government agencies, along with military acronyms and legal codes.

Military times are displayed in 24-hour NATO format with time zone letters (e.g., 1200 Hours R, for "Romeo," representing Eastern Standard Time at Fort Meade, Maryland).

For clarity, detailed **indices** are included at the end of the book, covering:

- Russian Space Weapons Capabilities

- Chinese Space Weapons Capabilities
- U.S. Intelligence Agencies
- Foreign Intelligence Agencies
- The Five Eyes Alliance
- NATO Military Time Zones
- U.S. Military Defense Conditions (DEFCON)
- Espionage Crimes — U.S. Codes § 792–798
- "Pay-to-Play" Bribery Laws
- U.S. Security Classification Levels
- Comparison of Title 10 and Title 50 Authorities
- NSA Advanced Network Technology (ANT)

Technical Foundations

This novel explores the battle for space supremacy, incorporating advanced science and technologies—most of which exist or are currently under development. Several references to the National Security Agency (NSA) and its programs may appear extraordinary, but history has shown that the NSA's technical capabilities have often outpaced public imagination.

The Advanced Network Technology (ANT) division, part of the NSA's Tailored Access Operations (TAO) unit, develops specialized tools for cyber-espionage and network penetration. Its classified ANT catalog, leaked and published by *Der Spiegel* in 2013, revealed the extraordinary sophistication of these methods—custom implants, firmware exploits, and hardware beacons capable of compromising virtually any system on Earth. These realities underpin much of the cyber-espionage technology depicted throughout this series.

In the world of *Watchtower*, one such development is SYBIL—an advanced AI fusion analytics system created by NSA for the U.S. Army Counterintelligence Command (ACIC). SYBIL ingests and correlates vast multi-domain intelligence streams—signals, financial transactions, behavioral metadata, and human

2

intelligence reports—at machine speed. Unlike traditional analytic platforms, SYBIL is built for cognitive inference, capable of identifying deception patterns, trust anomalies, and disinformation loops before human analysts can see them. It serves not as a replacement for human judgment, but as its amplifier—mirroring the way real-world intelligence systems are evolving toward autonomous pattern discovery and adversarial prediction.

For additional background material and companion resources, visit **https://spyscribe.com**.

Overview of ACIC

The U.S. Army Counterintelligence Command (ACIC) is the Army's principal organization for detecting, identifying, and neutralizing foreign intelligence entities (FIEs), espionage, terrorism, insider threats, and subversive activities targeting the U.S. Army worldwide.

Headquarters: Fort George G. Meade, Maryland

Higher Command: U.S. Army Intelligence and Security Command (**INSCOM**), Fort Belvoir, Virginia

Oversight: Deputy Chief of Staff for Intelligence (G-2), Department of the Army

ACIC's location at Fort Meade places it alongside the NSA, U.S. Cyber Command (USCYBERCOM), and other intelligence hubs—enabling real-time collaboration on digital forensics, SIGINT, and cyber counterintelligence. Proximity to the Defense Counterintelligence and Security Agency (DCSA), FBI Baltimore Field Office, and Defense Information Systems Agency (DISA) ensures seamless coordination on insider-threat cases, contractor investigations, and shared national-level threat intelligence.

I hope you enjoy reading this book as much as I enjoyed writing it.

— *Charles M. Wayne*

CHAPTER ONE

Dead Drop

A Cold February Morning in Maryland

The air bites at her cheeks as she runs, her pace is steady—measured. This isn't a jog for fitness; it's a cover.

In the hushed gray light, a lone figure moved along the winding path of the park. Her stride was even, efficient—not the bouncing gait of a fitness enthusiast, but something practiced. Purposeful. The kind of rhythm born not from health obsession, but necessity.

She wore runner's gear: thermal leggings, gloves, a close-fitting vest with a high collar, and a knit cap pulled low. She looked every bit the casual morning jogger, but her eyes betrayed her. They were too alert, too focused. This was no run for cardio.

The park was still the kind of quiet only found in the lull between sunrise and the city's awakening. She approached the tunnel, a squat, weather-stained underpass of stone and moss-darkened concrete yawning before her, empty and echoing. A faint scent of wet granite and earth lingered as she slipped into the tunnel.

Her shoes made soft slaps against the damp ground as she entered the tunnel. The sound of her footfalls bounced off the walls like a quiet metronome. At the midpoint, she slowed. Her eyes flicked behind her—once, twice. Nothing but silence and shadow.

Under the shelter of the arch, she reached into the tight chest pocket of her vest and pulled out a slim, semi-rigid folder, a muted shade of blue, made from durable polymer, entirely unmarked. She didn't hesitate.

She knows this place—chosen with care long ago.

A narrow crevice in the wall, half-hidden behind a bulging stone. The folder slid into the gap with a soft click.

And she was gone.

The sound of her footsteps faded down the trail as she resumed her pace, vanishing like morning mist. Another woman in her thirties out for a run before work.

Evening fell with the chill still in the air. The sun had long since sunk beneath the horizon, casting the park in steel-gray shadows. A man now took the same path, his breath rising in steady white clouds.

He ran with the familiarity of someone who didn't fear this place. His movements were efficient, economical, calm. The tunnel appeared ahead of him, cloaked in darkness.

He didn't hesitate.

Once inside, he slowed his pace, glancing behind him in the half-light. Empty.

He stopped at the crevice, his fingers reaching forward without fumbling. He knows exactly where it was. In one swift motion, he retrieved the blue folder, tucking it beneath the thermal layer of his jacket. Flattening it against his chest.

No pause. No backward glance.

He continued on, merging with the shadows.

Korolyov, Russia- Roscosmos Mission Control Center - Two Years Later

The night in Korolyov was bone-cold; inside TsUP the air smelled faintly of warm electronics. Pressure thrummed along the rows of consoles—silent, focused—while the flight director's face sat pale and unreadable beneath the lights.

"Telemetry ready," a controller said, flat and steady. The main wall tracked a single white line across the globe: the target satellite. Beside it, the test vehicle's schematic blinked through a checklist—verification window, range clear, safety holdoffs, comms-blackout contingency.

The countdown slid down the display. The Glavny Operativny Rukovoditel (Chief Operating Officer (COO) nodded once to begin. "Начать," he said.

The pulse itself - a burst of high-energy electromagnetic radiation - was almost geometric: a neat spike across the graphs, a vertical cliff that sliced power buses and comms channels. For a heartbeat the room held its breath. Then one camera feed froze into static. One telemetry stream, the target's, stuttered and died.

"EMP signature," someone murmured. Heads pivoted toward the screen showing induced currents climbing, then collapsing—electrical systems frying in milliseconds. The flight dynamics officer reported, voice tight: the target bus had lost attitude control and began a slow tumble. No cascade, no constellation of failures—just one quiet platform, now blind to the sky.

Alarms that had been muted rose to a measured pitch. Controllers moved into triage: isolate the affected bus, attempt power cycles, force redundant processors online. Fingers danced across keyboards, checklists crossed off with clipped Russian. The director wanted facts, not politics. "Status. Recovery window," he said.

A junior engineer ran the diagnostics and then, quietly, the math: a narrow window for salvage, moderate chance of partial recovery if reaction wheels were intact. A comms officer queued a burst to the satellite's last known uplink and replayed the last good telemetry. Outside the glass, a security officer rubbed his jaw and imagined the messages that would follow—embassy cables, terse calls.

When the immediate alarms steadied, relief was small and sterile. The test had achieved its—intended—effect: a single satellite hit, systems impaired. Mission patches on the far wall looked like markers on a map of choices made. The controllers began the slow accounting—hardware, trajectory, diplomatic fallout, each keystroke folding the night into consequence.

Outside, Korolyov kept its winter. Inside TsUP, the lights stayed on, and the people at their stations readied themselves for what would come next.

Georgy Viktorovich Markova, 57, Colonel Senior Military Analyst, Strategic Space Operations Command, watched intently with the eyes of a chess master.

His was a lean, austere frame honed by a life of military discipline. Ice gray, unnerving eyes in their stillness, Iron-gray hair, close cropped, always within regulation. Angular cheekbones, clean shaven, Markova carried himself with the rigid composure of someone always expecting to be saluted.

Markova exuded military rigidity. The embodiment of old-school Soviet military elitism—coldly precise, strategically brilliant, and ideologically unshakable. Markova's lips curled. He didn't smoke, but he twirled a cigarette between his fingers like a relic of habit.

The test behaved exactly as the models had promised—and if scaled and deployed across their orbital arrays, it could blind an enemy's entire space network, erase GPS guidance and severing command-and-control long enough to reshape any battlefield. There was no known defense—it was the game changer.

CHAPTER TWO

Operation Palisades

US I-95 South

Spring teased the air as Major Will Morgan drove south toward the INSCOM headquarters at Fort Belvoir, classical strings swirling around him from the car's speakers. Vivaldi's Four Seasons accompanied the crisp April morning with a fitting grandeur. The road ahead was open, the trees budding with new life.

Morgan, six-foot-one inch tall with close-cropped light brown hair, was lean and wiry, coiled and cerebral. He was the commanding officer of an elite investigative unit within the U.S. Army Counterintelligence Command, tasked with uncovering America's most dangerous traitors—insiders selling secrets to foreign powers.

He wore his Army service uniform, each crease razor-sharp, insignia glinting in the light. He drove with focus, one hand on the wheel, the other resting near the comms console.

His phone buzzed. The radio muted automatically. He tapped the button on his dash.

"Sir," he said in crisp voice.

"Will," came the graveled baritone voice of General Edwin Perry, his boss from Fort Meade. Measured, commanding. A man who didn't waste words.

"Will, I know you're not thrilled…err... pissed to be knee-deep in DARPA eggheads in this investigation, but this wasn't a favor. It was a call-up," said Perry. "Defense Intelligence Agency wanted our best; that's why I insisted on your team."

"You ever sent a guy into a minefield with a blindfold?" Will asked. "Because that's what this feels like."

"DARPA didn't want you; they wanted someone they could handle. Instead, the joke's on them - they got you.

"Your team's the freaking Mounties, for Heaven's sake. You'll get your man."

"Besides, I've sent you into worse."

"That doesn't make this better." He paused. "I don't belong in a lab full of civilians."

"You belong exactly there," Perry replied. "You can smell lies faster than anyone I've ever trained. And this place reeks."

Will said nothing. The silence stretched.

"If something's broken inside that lab, I need someone who won't look away because a résumé says PhD."

Will exhaled. "You always knew how to flatter a guy right before throwing him into the fire."

"I'm not sure yet what this is all about; it's very hush-hush, but this sure as hell isn't exclusively about data leaks. And if the Russians are involved, I want someone watching the watchers."

"Sounds like a real nightmare."

Perry chuckled, "I'm not sure who will have the bigger nightmare - you or them."

"Anyway, this time, I owe you a real one."

Morgan snorted. "You won't mind putting that in writing, sir?"

"You're not recording this?" Perry chuckled.

"Who the hell am I meeting with?"

"All they said is that you're expected. Go to the visitor center. Someone will meet you."

Morgan glanced at the road sign. "Wonderful. Now we can add cloak and dagger to this imbroglio. I'm pulling onto Fairfax County Parkway now. Signing off before we hit the blackout zone. Later, sir."

Fort Belvoir - Visitor Center

Morgan pulled into the Tulley Gate visitor center lot beside a building that was a study in clean lines and silent efficiency. He locked his phone and service pistol in the glove compartment and stepped out into the bright morning sun.

A Marine waited for him in the lobby—rigid posture, clean-cut, with the kind of stillness that hinted at sharp reflexes.

"Morning, sir," the Marine said, offering a sharp salute. "Please come with me. I'll take you to the Nolan Building."

Morgan returned the salute. "Hope you weren't waiting long."

He was driven to the Nolan Building. Another Marine greeted him.

"Good morning, Major. Please follow me to the Commander's conference room."

Morgan's brow creased. "Commander?"

"Major General Edwards, sir."

"That explains the reception - a two star - this must be a big deal," he muttered under his breath.

CHAPTER THREE

Commander's Conference Room

"It's easy to forget what intelligence consists of: luck and speculation. Here and there a windfall, here and there a scoop."

- John le Carre

Fort Belvoir - Nolan Building

Will Morgan is shown in a secure conference room tucked deep within the labyrinth of the Nolan Building. The LED glare off the polished table made the room harsher, more secretive.

The faint new carpet smell, coffee, and a tension that seemed baked into the walls.

He had taken a seat when the heavy door opened again. Three men entered, each radiating the sort of authority that needed no announcement.

Major General Owen Edwards was first. In his early fifties, with an easygoing manner that appeared at odds with the crushing national security responsibilities he carried as Commanding General of the United States Intelligence and

Security Command (INSCOM), the Army intelligence's investigative arm. Edwards nonetheless projected undeniable gravity.

Guy Zarelli followed, a compact, weathered man in his mid-40s whose demeanor screamed military—former G2 in Afghanistan and now a Special Agent within INSCOM and liaison to the Defense Advanced Research Projects Agency (DARPA), often called the Pentagon's brain. Fifteen years in the thick of defense projects left their mark on him: sharp eyes, quick movements, an aura of no-nonsense urgency.

Bringing up the rear was Judd Lockwood: early fifties, balding but fit, Judd bore the unmistakable intensity of a seasoned Central Intelligence Agency Special Agent, his every step calculated, his every glance dissecting the room.

Edwards extended an open palm toward Will in a casual but deliberate gesture.

"Will, I'm Owen Edwards."

Will rose and shook the offered hand, firm and professional. Edwards gestured to his companions as he spoke:

"This is Guy Zarelli and Judd Lockwood."

Will nodded to both men, receiving curt nods in return. Edwards took the head seat at the table and waved the others into chairs.

Settling into his seat, Edwards's voice was steady and direct.

"Guy is Special Agent INSCOM and DARPA liaison. Judd is Special Agent CIA Counterintelligence."

Will leaned back, one eyebrow lifting with mild skepticism. He thought, The Pentagon's mad scientists. This just got complicated.

"DARPA? CIA? Strange company for me, sir. My counterintelligence experience is with embezzlement, fraud, corruption and incompetence." He allowed a small smile to crack his otherwise professional demeanor. "You know, the four horsemen of forensic accounting."

Edwards chuckled; the sound was short but genuine.

"Well, I think you and your team are a little more than that, don't you?

"You helped to take down Willow and Ron Rockwell Hansen. That's not nothing, Major.'

Pause

"The consensus is your Team Watchtower is perfect for this assignment. Besides, isn't it all the same? "People hiding terrible things they shouldn't be doing?"

He leaned forward, voice lowering. "Will, what we are about to tell you is of the most urgent national priority. You will probably never work on a more important investigation the rest of your career. Ed Perry tells me you're the best investigator he's got, which is why you are here."

He gave a short nod to Guy, signaling him to take over.

Guy shifted forward, placing both forearms on the table, his posture alert.

"Major, Russia announced they have developed a nuclear space-based anti-satellite system using electromagnetic pulses - could take down our entire satellite network in minutes."

"We're caught in the middle of pivoting from a service focus to a warfighting one. LaserTech, a Tier 2 sub, has been developing a next level defensive shield codename Radiant Sentry."

"So, this falls under DARPA's new space superiority initiative to defend our satellites against the Russian system."

Edwards nodded again, and now Judd Lockwood leaned in, his intense gaze locking onto Will like a targeting laser.

"We have a highly placed Russian asset—we'll call him Ivan for this discussion—who informed us of a mole in our Radiant Sentry program. Their codename for the operation is Palisades, and the mole is codenamed Sable."

Will frowned, digesting the information. His voice was steady but skeptical.

13

"So, the battlefield of the future is space, and we're at a crossroads. Instead of launching satellites everybody is trying to knock them down.

"How certain are we that the Russian system works, and what confidence do we have in Ivan?" said Will.

All three men exchanged a glance—a silent, weighted exchange that spoke volumes. No beating around the bush with this guy.

Guy answered, voice calm but serious.

"Straight to the point. We have no choice but to assume it works."

Judd picked up right away, his tone blunt.

"As for Ivan, his track record is perfect so far. He has access to operational rosters, communications routing, and—most importantly—the internal debates of SVR leadership.

"However, we never know if we are being double-crossed until it happens. It's not uncommon to be set up for years in advance, waiting for a big moment—and this is quite a big moment.

"Ivan gave us a reproduction of a top-secret LaserTech document. I say reproduction because the original was printed April tenth on security paper and could not be copied or photographed. It contains top-secret sensitive information."

He reached into a slim briefcase by his side and slid a document folder across the table. It was stamped in red: TOP SECRET - EYES ONLY.

Judd studied him.

Will opened it with deliberate care. The upper half of the page revealed an intricate, meticulously detailed diagram—the work of a sharp and methodical mind. Below it sprawled a dense, labyrinthine formula so complex it made him do a double-take the moment his eyes landed on it.

"A reproduction? On regular non-security paper? Does the Bear have the original and how would we know?"

"Very good major. This is one of the many things we don't know. Ivan says he has had eyes on an original on fiber paper. No watermarks full color."

Will shook his head, still staring at the paper. "This sounds like a high-level mole hunt for a rocket scientist, which is way above my pay grade."

Edwards gave a dry chuckle, rose from his seat, hands rested on the table.

"Except for very few, it's above everybody's pay grade. In any case, we can't have a rocket scientist looking for another one—that would be too obvious. We can't afford to spook the Russians and have them go to ground."

He straightened, his voice taking on an authoritative tone.

"The DARPA Director has approved your cover as one of their project auditors, charged with monitoring the project and keeping it on budget and on track. Your background is credible for the job, and no one is about to trip you up. Which is why you are the perfect agent for this job."

Will shifted uneasily in his chair, looking concerned.

"I can see that, but how am I supposed to understand the science?"

Edwards smiled, a rare thing.

"We have that covered. You'll have a consultant with a deep background in the science and all required codeword clearances and more. It's common for DARPA lay managers to have technical consultants, so it won't arouse undue suspicion."

Edwards turned to leave, but not before delivering the final orders with grave weight.

"You are all set up with LaserTech, which has been told only that you have been appointed as a DARPA special auditor. DARPA's annual budget is $5 billion with only 200 or so employees. All the money goes to subcontractors. Believe me— they won't give you any problems."

He paused at the door.

"You will have every resource you need to catch this mole. Every resource. Guy and Judd will get you whatever you need— no questions asked. We're counting on you. Report as soon as you can."

He turned; his last words thrown casually over his shoulder—though the impact was anything but casual.

"Catch this bastard."

CHAPTER FOUR

Some Sense of Humor

Fort Belvoir - Commander's Conference Room

The door clicked shut behind him, leaving Will alone with the two agents, the top-secret document, and the crushing weight of what he had been assigned to undertake.

Judd Lockwood sat in silence, arms folded across his chest, watching the man across the table with a measured gaze. "Initial thoughts?"

Will Morgan shifted in his seat. He rounded his shoulders, leaning forward, planting his elbows on the polished oak. His brow furrowed as if the act of thinking were a burden. He crossed his arms, uncrossed them, then grabbed his chin with one steady hand. The movement was habitual—a reflex that surfaced in moments of reluctant curiosity.

"My initial thoughts," he began, voice tinged with a mixture of skepticism and grim amusement, "are that someone has one helluva sense of humor."

He paused, eyes narrowing, assessing the absurdity of the mission ahead.

"A forensic accountant chasing rocket scientists around a think tank. This wouldn't even make a bad B-movie plot."

Morgan allowed the silence to stretch before exhaling. "Given the way the Commander posed it, I can't very well do anything but give it my best shot."

A wry smirk tugged at the corner of his mouth. "If I fall flat on my face, don't say I didn't warn you."

"Are we starting from scratch?"

Zarelli gave a single nod. "Except for the standard Tier 5 stuff. They are all on continuous status, so we are updating background checks all the time."

Morgan's gaze sharpened. "Where is LaserTech?"

"Linthicum, Maryland, south of Baltimore. We're told you're a workaholic, so we've got you set up in an Airbnb in Glenn Burnie, about four miles away. We have Grace Roberts, your physicist consultant, nearby. We'll get Sara set up nearby as well."

Judd Lockwood spoke. His voice was calm, but instructive. "General Perry will be briefed by the commander. You're free to tell General Perry the gory details; don't tell him—it's entirely up to you."

Morgan nodded again. "I'll be in Maryland tomorrow."

The hum of the engine was a soft counterpoint to the sharp clarity in Will Morgan's voice. He gripped the steering wheel with one hand and spoke into the phone voice activation as the car rolled down the highway. "Call Sara Brant."

"Sara, pack up. We're headed to LaserTech in Linthicum Heights. We could be there for some time. I'll fill you in on the details this afternoon."

Sara Brandt's voice came through the speaker—cool, confident, and touched with amusement. "That's commuting distance."

"Yes," Morgan replied, eyes fixed ahead, "but we'll have condos because there will be a lot of long days, and we don't want to be fighting fatigue and the weather."

"This must be a doozy if Ed is paying for that. Something tells me we're going to earn our keep. See ya in a bit."

Morgan disconnected and voice-activated another number.

"Sir, I was told the Commander is calling you to fill you in."

Ed Perry's voice responded with calm authority. "He already did a few minutes ago. This is top national priority, and I have no budget restraints. Whatever you need from me, let me know."

"Sara and I are driving up to LaserTech tomorrow. "Remember when I told you you'd owe me one—it's gonna be a big one."

Perry chuckled. "I have no doubt. Will... I'm glad your team is on this one."

"Thank you. Later, sir."

CHAPTER FIVE

Stages of Knowing

SYBIL — Systemic Yield-Based Intelligence Liaison

Fort Meade

SYBIL was the Army Counterintelligence Command's quiet advantage—an AI born from NSA data streams, DARPA code, and decades of hidden pattern libraries. Buried in Fort Meade's black servers, she sifted through oceans of intercepted data for the faintest trace of betrayal.

Formally known as the Systemic Yield-Based Intelligence Liaison, SYBIL began as an NSA experimental architecture: a heuristic, adaptive learning system built for ACIC under a joint directive known only to a handful of cleared officers. Her neural lattice linked every major open-source, law-enforcement, and classified database—everything from Census Bureau data to non-FISA NSA intercept repositories.

Technically, she was a machine-learning construct. Practically, she was something closer to a silent partner.

She saw everything at once: calls, bank trails, encrypted mail, surveillance feeds—threads that only she could weave together. To Will Morgan's team, SYBIL wasn't software. She was presence—unblinking, incorruptible, always watching.

What made her unique was her cognitive layer: she could model human intent, sense emotion in speech, even assign probability to motive.

"SYBIL sees patterns," Will always warned. "Not conscience. Use her—but don't surrender to her."

To Watchtower, she was indispensable. To Will, she was still a mirror—one that reflected the people behind her code.

"A goal without a plan is just a wish"
- Antoine de Saint-Exupery

Fort Meade - Watchtower Conference Room - 1300 Hours R

Will tapped a button on the Vibe board. Four lines appeared in his familiar scrawl:
Stages of Knowing
1. You don't know what you don't know.
2. You know what you don't know.
3. You don't know what you know.
4. You know what you know.

A few smiles circled the room. It was Will's ritual opening—equal parts joke and warning.

He turned to face them.

"Our job isn't to prove there's a mole. CIA already did that. Our job is to find them—and stop them before Radiant Sentry becomes the payload the Russians launch for us."

He paced once. "Moscow Station intercepted chatter—SVR penetration of a DARPA contractor. Target: LaserTech. Codename: Sable."

Sara leaned toward Cathy. "SVR's the KGB's successor—foreign ops. We've danced before."

Will tapped the second line. "We're here—stage two. We know what we don't know."

The screen shifted.

Unknowns:

- How long the mole's been inside
- Whether Sable's working alone
- What's already been compromised
- Tradecraft used
- LaserTech's internal weak points

Click. Another list.

Knowns:

- $500 million DARPA contract for Radiant Sentry
- 200-acre secure campus
- Twelve-person EMP research group—mostly PhDs

"Radiant Sentry," Z interjected, pushing up his glasses. "Space-based defensive system to neutralize Russia's nuclear-powered ASATs. Think orbital kill switch for any anti-satellite threats. If compromised, it gives the Russians the upper hand in orbital warfare."

"Or gives them the blueprint to reverse-engineer our defenses," Cathy added, not looking up from her notes.

"Or sabotage them," Sara said. "From inside."

"Next, stage three. We find out what we don't know we already know."

He clicked off the board. The screen went dark. Silence.

Will stood at the front, arms crossed, eyes fixed not on the screens but on the people in the room.

"We'll have help," Will said. "Grace Roberts joins us on-site. She's DARPA's preferred science liaison—knows Radiant Sentry's architecture better than anyone except LaserTech's top engineers. She's a physics professor on loan from UM up the road in Baltimore."

He let that hang for an instant.

"Sara and I head to Linthicum Heights tomorrow. Our cover is as a DARPA team for Project Oversight and systems auditing for Radiant Sentry."

He spoke with quiet authority—measured but pointed.

"I want you all to remember something before we move."

The room stilled. Referring to SYBIL, the purpose-built AI analytics system integrated with DARPA and IARPA models built for his team.

"SYBIL is fast. It's brilliant. But it's not omniscient. It sees patterns, not motives. Signals, not tells. It can intercept a whisper on the other side of the planet—" he tapped the screen behind him,—but it can't feel when someone's lying through a smile."

A moment passed. Thomas looked up from his notes, catching Will's glance.

"SYBIL gives us reach," Will continued. "But it can also make us lazy. Comfortable. Confident that numbers mean truth. And that's when we miss the human element—the thing they never write, never say out loud. A glance. A hesitation. A gesture that doesn't match the mask."

He paused, letting it settle.

"Don't forget that the SVR has studied our systems too. They know what SYBIL watches—and what she doesn't. That's their window. The advantage we have is up here," he tapped his temple. "Human judgment. Instinct. Subtle tells that no algorithm can score."

He stepped away from the screen. "So, trust the tech, but trust your gut more. And watch for the thing that doesn't fit the model. That's usually where the truth hides."

Thomas exhaled and said, "Time to dance."

Silence settled—brief, focused. The hunt had begun.

Roberts Background and Profile

The main preparation meeting had dispersed. Monitors still glowed with tactical overlays and heat map scrolls, but the hum of voices was gone. The rest of the team had filed out, leaving behind the clatter of coffee cups and quiet tension in the air.

Will Morgan stood near the head of the long steel table, arms crossed, eyes fixed on a digital dossier floating on the holographic-display. His expression was unreadable.

Ed Perry, seated across from him, flicked through the DARPA clearance layers with a finger swipe, each level peeling back another sanitized paragraph of Grace Roberts' history.

SUBJECT: ROBERTS, GRACE E.

- Clearance: TS/SBI – DARPA Division 4
- Field: Applied Physics – Quantum Optics, Electromagnetic Control
- PhD: California Institute of Technology, GPA: 4.0
- Dissertation: "Coherence Collapse and Directed Noise in Adaptive Systems"
- DARPA Entry Age: 23
- Current Age: 35
- Noted for: algorithmic cognition, emotion suppression traits, neural redundancy studies.

Ed gave a low whistle. "First in her class. Caltech. Published before twenty-five. She strangely vanishes into the black vault."

Will didn't respond at first. He was watching a video embedded in her file—Grace, years younger, mid-simulation at a DARPA test range, calmly talking a colonel through a failure cascade in a prototype directed energy array.

She didn't flinch. Not once.

Finally, Will said, "I read her intake psych. She never took the accelerated path because she wanted recognition."

Ed looked up. "Why?"

Will: "Control. Precision. She's hardwired for structure. That kind of focus doesn't come from ambition—it comes from damage."

The door hissed open.

Thomas Carrone stepped back in, sleeves rolled, carrying a slim file marked

Behavioral Observation: Roberts, G.E.

He nodded once at the two men. "You're looking at Grace?"

Will gestured to the chair beside him. "Sit. We've got questions."

Thomas took the seat, set the file down. "She's stable. Highly self-regulated. Compartmentalizes emotion into functional code. Same behavioral architecture I've seen in trauma-adaptive children. Except in her case—she weaponized it."

Ed arched a brow. "Meaning?"

Thomas flipped open the file and tapped a single page: a mind-map diagram. "She doesn't react to authority. She reacts to integrity. If you say something stupid, she'll ignore it—even if you outrank her. But if she respects your rationale, she'll follow it into fire."

Will gave a single nod, unsurprised.

Thomas continued, "What's unique is the internal tension. She's not robotic. She feels everything—she channels it through

25

logic. There's grief there. Old and metabolized. But it shaped how she thinks. When she models a system, she accounts for physics—and she accounts for chaos."

Ed leaned back. "She's a physicist who anticipates failure as a default state."

Thomas: "Exactly. Which makes her invaluable under pressure. But it also means she struggles with unpredictability in people. She'll trust a math model over a man any day of the week."

Will studied the screen. "What's her fail point?"

Thomas hesitated. "Prolonged emotional exposure. If you force her to carry emotional weight with no rational outlet—she'll begin to drift. Not collapse, simply… detach. She protects herself by withdrawing."

Will: "And her loyalty?"

Thomas gave him a look. "Unshakable. Once earned."

Will went silent again. He closed the file. Let the image of Grace at the range linger in his mind for one more moment before the screen darkened.

Ed stood, collecting his notes. "She's solid. Brilliant. You want her in the room when the unknown hits."

Will nodded once. "She stays close. I want eyes on her for Phase Two."

Thomas rose with them. "She won't let you down."

Will gave a faint smile as he moved toward the exit. "She can't afford to. Neither can we."

Lights dimmed behind them as they left, the system auto-locking into standby mode. Outside, the rain had stopped. But something colder was still moving in.

CHAPTER SIX

LaserTech

"Things are not always as they seem; the first appearance deceives many."
- Phaedrus, a Roman poet

LaserTech Linthicum Heights, MD 0920 Hours R

At LaserTech, innovation wasn't a simple goal, it's a directive. Under a classified $500 million DARPA contract, the company led cutting-edge research in photonic and directed-energy technologies for national defense. Specializing in next-generation laser arrays, full-spectrum signal disruption, and adaptive optical tracking systems, LaserTech was tasked with pushing the frontiers of electromagnetic warfare to secure U.S. superiority in emerging battlefronts spanning space and cyberspace.

The LaserTech campus sprawled like a private city, tucked behind layers of electric fencing, and monitored by a latticework of cameras perched on sleek black poles. It is a fortress draped in glass and steel—modern in aesthetic but unmistakably, defensive in design.

Will pulled up to the guard gate and was greeted by a tall, uniformed guard.

"Good morning, sir. How can I help you?"

He presented his driver's license and appointment slip and returned the greeting,

"Good morning. Will Morgan to see Taran Gittings."

Checking his daily register the guard gestured with a slight forward underhand motion, "You may park at the main building visitor parking straight ahead. Welcome to LaserTech sir."

The morning light glinted off the mirrored façade as Will Morgan stepped through the main entrance, his footsteps silent against the polished marble.

His eyes swept the lobby with the precision of a soldier. Every corner, every reflective surface, every movement was cataloged instantly. The space was vast, clean, and humming with quiet efficiency. At its center stood a minimalist reception desk—polished white composite, seamlessly integrated tech embedded beneath the surface. Light pooled from above, highlighting the gleam.

To the left, six waist-high security gates clicked as employees filtered through. A uniformed guard oversaw each gate—sidearms holstered but visible, movements fluid, eyes sharp. Will didn't need a second glance. These weren't civilians. These were professionals. Ex-military.

He caught the posture of one guard in particular—the slight shift of weight to the balls of his feet, the casual but ever-ready hand placement near his weapon. Will knew the type. That kind of muscle memory didn't fade. A subtle grin tugged at the corner of his mouth.

He approached the reception desk without a word, reached into his coat pocket and produced his Virginia driver's license – no using Military ID or garb here. He held it below his chin, steady and deliberate. The guard behind the desk—a woman with sharp eyes and a shock of fiery red hair—smiled as she viewed it.

"Good morning. Will Morgan to see Taran Gittings."

The woman reached for the phone with practiced ease.

"Good morning, sir. A moment please."

She spoke into the handset, her voice crisp. "Will Morgan to see Taran Gittings." (A pause.) "Thank you, I'll send him right in."

She set the receiver down and turned back to Will, her hands already preparing a visitor lanyard with a holographic badge.

"Here you are, sir. Please keep it visible at all times." She handed the pass across the desk. "She is located on the first floor. You may enter through the visitor security gate to your right."

Will gave a courteous nod and moved toward the designated gate. At the checkpoint, he emptied his pockets into a scanning basket, his movements measured. He looked guilty in his civilian clothes—like a soldier out of uniform, caught playing dress-up.

The metal detector gave a muted chime as he passed through. A guard on the other side returned his items.

"Thank you, sir. HR is the first door on your right."

The HR office was minimal but sleek, with clean lines and functional decor. Taran Gittings was already waiting by the entrance, hand extended in welcome. Her presence was brisk and efficient, a contrast to the stillness that followed Will like a shadow.

"Good morning, Will. Welcome to LaserTech. You are all set up. We have to get your BIOS and security credentials, and then I'll show you to your offices."

She tapped something into a tablet before glancing up again with a hint of a smile.

"Oh yes, Sara Brandt arrived a couple of hours ago. She's waiting in your office."

The lab gleamed, sterile and futuristic, the air sharp with ozone and alcohol. Will sat upright on the exam table, more like a soldier awaiting inspection than a patient. His eyes flicked, cataloging.

A technician approached with a swab. "Open." Will complied, the motion quick and clinical.

What followed came rapid-fire: cheek swab, fingerprint scan, retinal clamp and flash, scale beep, measuring rod click. Each detail fed straight to the tech's tablet without pause.

"All done. Permanent badge soon. Temporary one now."

Will slid off the table, adjusting his shirt. His gaze lingered on the diagnostic console before he moved to the door.

The corridor leading to Will's new offices was hushed, padded with industrial carpeting and lined with recessed lighting. Will and Taran walked side-by-side, their footsteps quiet.

A squat, waist high delivery robot paused politely to let them pass. It gave a soft chirp as it recalculated its path.

"That's Robbie. Or should I say, one of the Robbies—we have five of them."

As they turned a corner, another figure came into view. Derek Wilshire, tall and lanky, walked toward them. His posture was hunched, gaze fixed on the floor. His hands fidgeted with a keyring, and he moved to the far side of the hallway as they approached.

"Hi, Derek."

He turned away; his voice lost to the hum of the corridor.

Derek mumbles. "Hello."

Will's brow furrowed confused.

"Who was that?"

"That was Derek. He's our Asperger's math savant. He has remarkable abilities—an incredible memory, lightning-fast calculations, including complex higher math. I'm told he can often identify and understand intricate patterns and relationships."

She paused, as if considering how best to explain.

"One example—he's a chess savant. No formal training. A remarkable memory and an intuitive grasp of complex positions."

"A prodigy."

"Well, not exactly. Chess savants are different from prodigies. Prodigies are very gifted players with training. Derek's abilities are intuitive and raw. No formal training - he's the proverbial one in a million."

"What does he do here?"

"He's a consultant. Often faster than our most powerful servers. Scientists give him problems verbally—no time lost inputting data. He just... solves them."

"I've heard of DARPA and others using high-functioning savants... I've never encountered one before."

They arrived at a sleek, glass-walled office suite. Taran tapped a code into a panel, and the door hissed open.

"Here we are."

The door slid open with a soft click, revealing Will Morgan's new workspace. It was more than an office—it was a command post. One large inner office, sleek and glass-walled, opened up into a shared outer space with two large sized workstations. A conference room for eight was accessible from the work area and Will's office. Everything was state-of-the-art and deliberately minimalist, as if designed to invite productivity while leaving no room for distraction.

Sara Brandt was already standing near one of the desks, a coffee in hand and a sly smile tugging at her lips.

Brilliant, blunt, and disciplined, Sara joined U.S. Army Counterintelligence through the Military Intelligence Civilian Excepted Career Program (MICECP), driven by a fierce sense of justice and an unflinching loyalty to her country. Known for her sharp wit and unwavering integrity, she soon became the indispensable second-in-command to Will. He had absolute trust in her, valuing her courage, intellect, and loyalty over protocol.

Sara greets Will, "How do you like the new digs, boss?"

Will smiled—just a little—but it was genuine. He stepped in, taking in the set up with a tactical eye.

"I see you're a step ahead of me, as usual, Sara. This will work fine. Thanks, Taran."

Taran Gittings stood nearby, watching with the careful satisfaction of someone who liked her work to be recognized.

"Glad you like them. If you need anything, I'm on extension 2768."

She gave a small wave before disappearing down the hall, leaving Will and Sara in the hum of their new headquarters.

Sara turned back toward Will, her expression casual.

"Guy Zarelli called. Said he's on his way to Baltimore and wanted to take us to lunch. He'll be here in a little while. Are we going to play nice, or are you going to be yourself?"

Will gave a dry look, the hint of a smirk playing at the corner of his mouth.

"I suppose we have to eat."

Phil's wasn't the kind of place you'd stumble into—it was the place to which you are taken. Tucked into a side street, the rear corner table was the unofficial off-the-books booth for more than one government contractor. The décor was a mix of industrial charm and southern comfort, with mismatched chairs and faded military photos hung crooked on the walls.

Will, Sara, and Guy Zarelli were seated at one of the back tables, menus unopened, the server read the specials.

"Thanks for taking the time to see me. I wanted to take the opportunity to get to know each other."

He leaned forward; elbows rested on the table with casual confidence.

"I read Owen's reports. Y'all are highly regarded. Not surprising—Owen has a talent for tasking talent."

"Thanks. Good to know."

Will's phone vibrated. He checked the screen and answered.

Sara said, "Rut rho."

"Hey... yes, sir... no problem... I'll be right back... thank you, sir."

He stood abruptly and dropped a few bills on the table.

"Gotta jump. Guy, can you give Sara a ride back after lunch?"

"Sure. We'll bring your sandwich."

Will nodded and moved off, leaving Sara and Guy sitting with half-empty coffee cups and plenty of curiosity.

Sara gave him a look that hovered between polite amusement and suspicion.

"You have us at a disadvantage. I'm sure you know our shoe sizes by now, and we know nothing about you... yet."

Guy fought back a chuckle. "Sorry, but it's true what they say—you guys always speak your minds."

He gave a small shake of his head, the kind reserved for people who were both impressed and a little disarmed.

"Everyone says you can do no wrong in Will's eyes, and he couldn't care less about your verbal charms. As high a compliment as one can get."

"Well, I hope so. He hands out flowery compliments like manhole covers."

Guy Zarelli chuckles. "See?"

"He thinks a job well done is its own reward… which, I guess, it is. Of course, when he does hand out praise, it means a lot more."

Guy nodded in agreement, folded his napkin and leaned back.

"Sara, I must say—Will has an impressive reputation for results. He's something of a prominent figure in CI. Operating in the shadows, shaping events from behind the scenes. Never giving up. All the most talented people want to be in your tribe. What's the attraction? I mean—he's a nice enough guy, but no Mr. Congeniality."

Sara smiled, but it is the kind that came with layers.

"He gets respect because he treats his team with respect. He's an old school CI pro—ground and pound offense. Fundamentals. Blocking and tackling. We practice in pads."

She sipped her drink before continuing.

"He annoyingly quotes Woody Hayes, the great Ohio State football coach who famously said, 'Only three things can happen on a pass play and two are bad - incompletion and worse, interception.' You see, Will doesn't ever beat himself. He wears you down and waits for you to make a mistake."

"No pass plays."

"Not no pass plays, but if we're gonna throw one, it damn well better work. He will take well-thought-out risks. He jokingly calls them 'Ray Rocks' R-A-R-O-C decisions- risk adjusted return on career decisions." Sara added. "Every decision has a risk, and an associated return. The higher risk needs to have a higher reward, or it isn't worth taking."

"What would you say is his weakness?"

Sara considered it, then shrugged with something approaching honesty.

"I wouldn't exactly call it a weakness…, if you're looking for quick results, he's not your best choice. He senses that's the case here."

She paused for emphasis.

"Normally, time is on our side. However, you need to catch this mole fast—which is not the CI norm. He recognizes he will have to make more high-risk decisions than he would prefer." She concluded.

Guy nodded, the weight of that statement sinking in.

"Everyone thinks y'all are our best shot. I agree. Sara, I'm going to enjoy working with y'all. I'll do my best for you."

LaserTech Security Center - Later that afternoon

The polished silver of the biometric scanner gleamed under the bright overhead lights. Will Morgan pressed his palm flat against the wall-mounted device with the ease of someone who had done this a hundred times before. A soft chime rang out—a sound that barely registered on the senses but signaled absolute access.

The door whispered open, revealing a compact ante room enclosed entirely in bulletproof glass. The air inside was crisp and hummed with silent systems hard at work.

Sara stepped in behind him. The door sealed shut with the heavy finality of a vault. No one got in—or out—without clearance.

A disembodied, serene voice filled the space, as polite as it was commanding.

"Please look directly at the retina scanner. One at a time."

Will stepped forward, letting the narrow beam of light find his eye. A blink. A scan. Another chime. He stepped aside. Sara followed. The same result. The system was satisfied.

With a low clunk, the inner door disengaged and slid open.

Anders Eriksson waited for them inside.

He stood like a man born into posture—tall, squared shoulders, tailored jacket, and eyes that missed nothing. His presence had a stillness to it, like the eye of a storm. "Good afternoon. I'm Anders Eriksson, Director of Security."

There was no handshake, only a nod and a motion toward the hallway beyond.

He led them directly to his office, no wasted steps, no unnecessary words. Once inside, he took his place behind a stark desk. Will and Sara took the two guest chairs facing him.

"I understand you are from DARPA to review everything, and I'm guessing you are starting with security."

"Good guess."

Anders Eriksson smiled, "We're proud of our security set up at LaserTech. Everything here is top-of-the-line—staff, equipment, and protocols. I am happy to answer any questions.

"Shall we start with a tour of the facility?"

"Sounds like a plan."

LaserTech Security Ops

They stepped into a chamber of screens and silence.

The lighting was dim, save for the ambient glow of monitors and overhead task lights. Every surface hummed with the presence of advanced technology. The room felt like a control tower—unforgiving, observant, alive.

Eight large workstations were arranged in two precise rows, each facing a massive wall of surveillance screens. The screens displayed a nonstop ballet of camera feeds—hallways, labs, server rooms, parking lots, and dumpsters—stitched together into a seamless, shifting grid of watchfulness.

Each station was outfitted with six monitors stacked two-high, flickering with live video, schematics, and data that never stood still.

Behind a glass partition at the far end of the room, a wall of humming servers blinked with a hypnotic rhythm. The server room was sealed tight, the secure doorway flanked by more cameras.

"Each of our workstations is purpose built for us. They are faster and more powerful than anything commercially available. They can't print, email, or download anything. We use polarized filters that appear blacked out on cameras, preventing the screens from being photographed. All of the workstations in the science section are the same."

Fascinated, Will examined one of the stations, eyes narrow with interest.

Will incredulous, said, "Surely, there are times when a hard copy is needed."

"On that rare occasion, the print is sent to one of the printers you see over there in the secure printer room. The hard copy is printed on special paper with embedded fibers that prevent copying or photographing. The document is given a unique number and bar code, and the identity of the person requesting the hard copy is recorded for auditing. The hard copy is then delivered by a Robbie... er... secure robot."

"What's to prevent the hard copy from leaving the building?"

"That's one of the main reasons we use security paper with a unique number and barcode. Of course, we also know who printed it. Then we make spot checks to make sure all printed documents are onsite."

"To be clear, it is possible for a document to leave the building, if only briefly...yes?" questioned Sara.

"Yes. Very, very difficult, but possible.

"Code-word staff strip out of street clothes before entering. Personal items stay locked away. Lab coats have no pockets. Nothing leaves this space unless it's checked out under strict authorization."

Will nodded. Not expected. Still—every possibility mattered.

"What about program security? Who has access to the code?"

"Every programmer on a team needs access." Explained Anders.

"What happens if a programmer creates a lot of code only he or she understands, and then leaves?" Sara asked with a quizzical frown.

Anders, anticipating the question responded, "This only happens if there is not a good development process—code review and module tests. Our process is very rigorous and designed to prevent poor or malicious code."

"Protocol?"

"For physical access, we use DOD-compliant software by Digitus Security and follow DoD cybersecurity protocols. No cell phones in the building, of course. No outside email. No doors on the restroom stalls."

"That leaves staff."

"We have twelve Reliant Sentry-cleared Security Analysts deployed in three shifts—eight during the day, and two during evening and graveyard shifts."

"Very impressive. Thanks for the nickel tour," complimented Will, "I look forward to learning more."

"Yes, impressive." agreed Sara.

LaserTech - Morgan's Office

Sunlight slanted through the tall windows of Will Morgan's office, cast soft golden shapes across the round conference table where he and Sara Brandt sat. A faint hum of ventilation filled the room, blending into the low rhythm of a typical workday—tense and focused.

The door opened with a gentle knock. Taran Gittings entered, accompanied by Grace Roberts.

She was what you expected from someone with clearance this high or credentials this long. She moved with calm precision, each step a quiet command. Her wardrobe, stylish and efficient. Her expression, open yet analytical.

Taran Gittings was smiling and enthusiastic, "Will, let me introduce you to your new technical advisor, Grace Roberts."

Will Morgan noted the two Welshmen, "A Welsh invasion!"

He rose from his chair, offered his hand with the ease of a seasoned professional and the faintest spark of curiosity in his eyes.

They shook hands. Her grip was firm. The connection—instant recognition between two people used to working at high levels under pressure.

Will gestured to the conference table. Grace joined Sara as Taran offered a polite nod and excused herself.

"Dr. Roberts, I've looked forward to meeting you. Everyone has such wonderful things to say about you. This is Sara Brandt, my associate."

Grace, being accustomed to such compliments, responded with her normal humility. "Thank you, I'll try not to disappoint you. Pleasure to meet you, Sara."

Sara smiled, acknowledging the warmth behind Grace's composed front.

Grace Roberts got straight down to business as was her manner. "I've been briefed and I've studied the files I was sent, but I'm new to this type of investigation. How do we begin and what are you looking for from me?"

Will's gaze lingered on her a moment longer, as if studying the cadence of her voice, the pace of her thought.

"The truth of the matter is that we spend most of our time stumbling around in the dark. So, the best place to start is with motivation. The most common motive is greed."

Grace ever the inquisitive mind. "How long have you been doing this?"

"My whole career. I joined Military Intelligence in 2009 and then Counterintelligence Command when it unfurled its flag in 2019."

Grace's curiosity worked overtime. "Is that why you were chosen for this assignment?"

Will, a bit surprised by the question, patiently replied. "We are the least bad choice to lead this investigation. They couldn't use a physicist for fear of compromising the investigation. The best they could do was team a couple of agents with a technical expert - you. Sara has been with me for the last five years."

Sara jesting, "Six, but who's counting?"

Will in a tone of finality to wrap up the meeting. "Get a good night's rest. We'll get started in the morning."

As Grace rose to leave, Will's eyes followed her, not with impropriety—but with thought. Calculating, intrigued. Sara caught the look and raised a curious brow; lips curled in an amused smile.

Grace stepped into the outer office space. Two large cubicles faced each other separated by the entrance aisle. Bright lights gave everything a sterile feel, but Sara's presence added an undercurrent of warmth.

"I plopped myself down over here," explained Sara," That cubicle is yours. If you need any help setting up, I'm glad to help.

"Oh, yeah, there is also an envelope on your desk from HR with your Glenn Burnie condo keys, parking pass, passwords, etc."

"Thanks. Is there a cafeteria here? I didn't have any lunch," replied Grace.

"I could use some fresh coffee. C'mon, I'll show you."

Grace scooped up the envelope as they headed out.

LaserTech Cafeteria

The corridor was empty now; the pulse of the day had faded. Overhead, motion-sensitive lights buzzed, snapping on as they passed on their way to the cafeteria.

"Thanks for making me so welcome. My friends call me Gracie, by the way."

Sara Brandt smiled, "Gracie it is then."

"You must know Will very well; Ed tells me he reposes a great deal of trust in you. What's he like... besides the obvious?"

"Let's see. He has two personae—one public and one private. People who meet him at social events find him outgoing, personable—charming. Otherwise, he's pretty much what you see is what you get.

"He's a great boss, but he can also be a big pain in the ass on little bullshit. Don't let it bother you. Always remember, he won't ever throw you under the bus and when the shit hits the fan, he's the guy that'll jump in your foxhole without hesitation to fight for you or with you, whatever the situation demands."

They reached the cafeteria, still open, faint music drifted from hidden speakers.

"Gracie, when you meet him, ask Z what I mean."

"Z?"

41

Sara laughed. "Zbigniew Zawadzki. Our Ukrainian-Polish analyst. Hard to find anyone who despises the Russians more—even here."

"I like him already."

"Will really is the proverbial curmudgeon with a heart of gold. Oh, he won't remember birthdays, anniversaries, etcetera—and we don't do Secret Santa or birthday cakes. He never uses nicknames. He never utters terms of endearment. You've screwed up if he calls you soldier, officer, agent—or in your case, maybe professor or genius."

"As long as it's not Doc."

"He won't call you Doc, and he won't let anybody else either. That's reserved for an incredibly special person he had in his life."

"Will seems like a colorful, complicated character."

"Alliteration—he'd appreciate that. He has a master's in forensic accounting. You can tease him, but I'd advise against using 'bean counter'."

"Accountant! I thought he was some sort of super spy catcher."

"Gracie, what we're doing here is counterintelligence. To catch a spy, we need to go on a MICE hunt for motive—Money, Ideology, Coercion, Ego.

"With Americans its more often than not money - hence the accounting skills. Once we figure out motive, usually by process of elimination, things fall in place fairly logically.

"It's slow, agonizing, frustrating work—detailed work. It requires dogged determination, intense focus, and the ability to work long and hard to achieve the objective.

"He's a Taurus—if you believe in that sort of thing, Google Taurus personality traits and you will see why he is well-suited for the job. He's the best at it. He could go the corporate route and make three or four times more, and the brass knows it. He never throws it in anybody's face and never asked for anything special—except for staff to get the job done."

"I imagine that gives him significant influence—not to mention leverage."

"Everyone is aware if you're gonna take him on, you better bring more than a couple of guys."

"Good guy to have on your side."

"Not for nothin' Gracie, but you're off to a good start with him."

"How so?"

"Last night he looked at your FBI file so long he must have it memorized by now."

"I have an FBI file? I knew I had a DARPA file, but an FBI file?"

"Duh… Gracie. Of course. A pretty fat one at that. After all, you consult for the most secret agency on the planet."

"Yikes."

"Today, I could tell he respects you—and I think he likes you. If you gain his trust, you may be let into the inner sanctum. Not many of us in there."

"Coming from you, that's comforting to know. I'll try not to blow it. What about his personal life? Does he…?"

Sara cut in, "Oh, that's easy—he doesn't have one."

Grace Roberts, laughing. "No, really—family, interests, hobbies, love interests?"

Sara replied pensively. "No living family. Work is his only interest. No hobbies. His job gets in the way of any lasting love interest. There is some personal stuff that explains why he's tough to get close to, but… you need to get that from him."

Sara asked, "What about you? I know you went to Cal Tech but you're not from there - either the Midwest or Upstate New York."

"Wow, Cincinnati, how did you know that?"

43

"Your accent or should I say lack of one. Back in the day telephone directory service was located in Central New York—Utica, because everybody could understand them. Flat "a" as in cat or act. Dead give away for those of us to whom it matters."

"And you?"

"City girl."

They both smiled warm smiles.

Hyde Park, Cincinnati – Winter - 2006 Age 16

The snow had fallen heavily that night. Wet, wide flakes blanketed the front yard, muting the world outside her bedroom window. Grace sat at the desk in her childhood room, a dim brass lamp casting amber over a stack of notes for her AP Government midterm. She hadn't heard the knock on the door. Only the sound of it opening. Then her mother's voice—hushed, flat, impossibly calm.

"Gracie."

Grace turned. The way her mother stood there, back perfectly straight, hands folded so tightly her knuckles were white—it told her everything.

She didn't speak. Not then. Not when the police officer at the door said the words. I'm sorry… accident… heavy snow on I-71… no suffering… immediate.

Her mother folded into the armchair by the fireplace and didn't move for an hour.

Grace went into the kitchen. Not to escape. Not to cry.

To do something.

She found the bills and her father's files, still in neat piles on the dining table. His manila folders were labeled in his usual scrawl—Utilities Q1, Mortgage Refi, FSA Account Notes. She sat down and started reading them. Not because she understood it

44

all. But because someone had to. Someone had to take the chaos and sort it into something knowable.

Two hours later, her hands were ink-streaked and her eyes raw, but she had a list of what needed to be done: insurance claim, temporary power of attorney for her mother, the car title, his client records. She found a blank legal pad and started copying down steps in crisp handwriting. She drew a box next to each item so she could check them off later.

In that moment—beneath the fluorescent light, with the furnace humming in the basement, Grace Roberts became the calm inside the storm.

Linthicum public library – 1930 Hours R

The brick building glowed under the dusky sky, a modest, glass-doored refuge nestled between oak trees and an empty elementary school lot. Grace Roberts stepped out of her car with a bounce in her stride, her bag slung over one shoulder, eyes already scanning the windows like she was coming home.

A banner near the entrance read:

"OPEN UNTIL 10 PM – MON–THU"

She smiled at it, a genuine, delighted grin.

Grace approached the welcome desk, where an older librarian with silver-streaked hair and tortoiseshell glasses sat behind a plastic shield labeled "EVELYN."

"Hi! I think I have some holds waiting—Grace Roberts. I reserved a few titles a couple of days ago".

Evelyn typed cheerfully, "You certainly did. Let's see... three nonfiction, three fiction. All about spies, no less. Doing some research?"

Grace grinned, "Something like that. I'm new to the subject. Russian military intelligence, SVR, GRU—trying to understand

45

the mindset. And the spy novels… well, they're for balance. Tone and texture."

Evelyn raised an eyebrow in impressed amusement.

"Sounds like quite the rabbit hole. And a serious one at that."

Grace's smiled response, "I consider my books my friends. I spend hours with them every day. They never lie to me—unless they're supposed to."

Evelyn chuckled as she slid a neatly stacked pile across the counter—thick volumes on Cold War espionage, an annotated history of the GRU, and le Carré's Tinker Tailor among them.

Evelyn said, "Glad you're making full use of us. Not everyone is aware we're open until ten most nights."

"I checked before lunch. I was eating with a colleague and practically rushed out the moment the clock hit six. Libraries that stay open late are a public service miracle," complimented Grace.

"Except Fridays and Saturdays—we close at seven. And Sundays, sadly, we're ghosts. "Noted Evelyn

"I'll survive. Monday through Thursday, I live here now," said Grace.

They both laughed. Grace pulled out her sleek phone and scanned her library card barcode.

"Maryland resident?" asked Evelyn.

Grace responded, "Born and raised. Got the card online two weeks ago. This is my first pickup."

She scooped the books carefully into her tote bag like precious cargo.

"I like learning about people I may never meet. Or maybe already have."

That last sentence hung in the air for a moment—cryptic, playful, yet weighted.

Evelyn curious, warm, "Then you're in the right place. Stay curious, Ms. Roberts".

Grace offered a nod and a smile that flickered with something deeper—resolve, perhaps, or anticipation.

Grace stepped out into the cooling air, the soft hum of crickets rising in the trees. She paused at the base of the library steps, looked down at her books, and whispered:

"Let's get to work, friends."

She crossed the lot at a slow gait, already flipping to chapter one.

Grace's Apartment 2200 Hours R

Soft lamplight spilled across a clean, orderly living room. A candle flickered beside a small bonsai tree. Grace lay curled on her couch under a gray cotton throw, one of the spy novels open on her lap — le Carré's Tinker Tailor Soldier Spy — a mug of green tea cooling on the table beside her.

Her eyes scanned the page, her lips moving.

The more identities a man has, the more they express the person they conceal.

Grace paused. Let the sentence settle.

She marked the paragraph with a sticky note and reached for the spiral notebook beside her. Flipped past two pages of notes on Soviet command structures and down to a blank sheet labeled "Behavioral Signals".

In clean handwriting, she wrote:

She glanced back at the novel, tapping the spine with her pen.

Fiction tells the truth over time. But it always tells it.

Her eyes lifted toward the window. Only shadows and the pulse of a distant highway.

Back to her notebook. A new line:

Spy novels aren't about plot. They're about behavior.

She closed the book. Looked toward the pile on her coffee table — next up: Inside the SVR: Structure and Operations.

She picked it up and smiled.

Let's see how deep this rabbit hole really goes.

CHAPTER SEVEN

Team Watchtower

"The best executive is the one who has sense enough to pick good men to do what he wants done, and self-restraint to keep from meddling with them while they do it,"
- Theodore Roosevelt.

Fort Meade - Team Watchtower

Major Will Morgan led Watchtower with quiet ferocity. He wasn't the loudest voice in a room—he didn't need to be. A suggestion from him carried the weight of an order, and his team moved without hesitation.

What set him apart wasn't rank or intellect, but discernment. Years in counterintelligence had given him an x-ray instinct for people. Five minutes across a table and he could tell who would thrive under fire and who would crumble.

He didn't waste time sanding down flaws. Weakness was noise; strength was rare. Morgan built his team like an architect fitting beams of odd shapes into balance—accepting imperfections, protecting what made them exceptional. That's why they trusted him.

He'd learned the hard way that every strength carried its own shadow. Resoluteness became stubbornness. Ambition bent into opportunism. Confidence tipped toward arrogance. Even loyalty, his prized currency, could rot into blind spots.

The line was always thinner than it looked. He'd seen others cross it—suspects, colleagues, himself. The trick wasn't erasing weakness. The trick was knowing when your strength started to turn its face.

Morgan never forgot that lesson. It was the compass he carried into every room, every recruit, every mission.

To outsiders, Watchtower might have looked like a collection of mismatched individuals. In truth, it was a lattice of distinct talents, each piece balancing the others, together forming a team of uncommon precision.

They came from nine nationalities and spoke thirteen languages—three Chinese dialects among them—a chorus of perspectives that made the whole sharper than any part.

Will Morgan kept his gaze fixed on the horizon, always scanning for the next threat, and the next recruit who might add depth or widen the scope.

LaserTech Cafeteria 1205 Hours R - Chess Match

The cafeteria hums with chatter, the soft clink of trays, and the steady hum of the overhead lights. Sara emerges from the food line, her tray a careful balance of items, her eyes scanning the room. At a corner table, Derek sits alone, an island in the bustle of the cafeteria. He's hunched over, his brow furrowed in thought, his fingers idly tracing the rim of his coffee cup. The soft fluorescent glow casts shadows across his features, making him seem more distant, more isolated than he likely intends.

Sara hesitates for a moment, straightens her shoulders and approaches. She clears her throat, offering a tentative smile.

Sara, with a warm tone. "Derek, right? May I join you?"

Derek doesn't respond right away, his eyes fixed on something distant, as if lost in a world of his own. After a moment, he nods, the motion slight but purposeful, signaling her to sit. There's no verbal acknowledgment, but the small gesture is enough.

Sara sits across from him, setting her tray down with a soft thud. She eyes him briefly, reading the cool distance that he holds, yet feeling an underlying warmth in the way his posture subtly shifts as she settles.

Sara, conversationally. "Thanks. I hear you have an aquarium in your office."

Derek's eyes flicker up at the mention of the tank. For a moment, something stirs behind his gaze, a flicker of life that wasn't there before. He smiled—a genuine smile this time—and the light in his eyes softens.

Derek Wilshire brightening, the mention of his aquarium a familiar joy. "Yeah, I do. A small saltwater tropical tank. Do you like fish?" Derek repeats, "Do you like fish?"

Sara curiously, "Oh wow. Do you think I can see them someday?"

There's a brief pause, and Derek's expression tightens, the ease in his smile replaced by something more guarded. His gaze darts to the side, as if trying to find an escape from the question. But then, he exhales slowly and turns back to her, the invitation lingering in the air.

In a quiet voice, Derek responds, "If you want."

"Yes, I do. Very much. How about I grab you for lunch tomorrow, and you can show me before we head to the cafeteria?"

Derek, a wide smile spreading across his face, "Okay. I'll wait for you in my office."

Sara grins, enjoying the rare exchange of openness from him. Her eyes flicker over to the side, noticing something near the entrance of the cafeteria.

"Derek, there's the boss, do you mind if he joins us?"

"I saw him in the hall with Taran yesterday," he said while nodding yes.

Sara caught Will's attention and waved him over.

"Hi Derek, thanks for letting me join you," said Will politely.

As lunch wore on, Will was taken *by* the unexpected normalcy of Derek's interaction with Sara contrasted with the awkward silence with others.

Sara had obviously connected with him, which was nice to see. A proud smile adorned his face. That's my Sara he thought.

Sara Brandt asked, "Say, Derek, what's with the chess set up over there by the entrance?"

Derek follows her gaze toward the arrangement of five chess tables, each with its own lazy Susan and set of boards. His face shifts briefly, and there's a hint of amusement mixed with resignation in his voice.

"Oh, that's the Marcus Liebowitz challenge." replies Derek with a shrug, "He plays against anyone who wants to go up against him—all at once. It's not really chess though... no clock."

Sara with a teasing smirk, "Do you play?"

Derek hesitates, his fingers tapping against the surface of the table as though weighing the question. His expression hardens a shade, but then he shakes his head.

"They won't let me."

Sara's lips curl into a mischievous smile, and there's a spark of challenge in her eyes.

"Oh, really? We'll see about that."

❖ ❖ ❖

Cafeteria Next Day

The next day after the lunchtime rush passed, the cafeteria was quieter. Along the far wall, five chess sets sit on their own small tables. Each set is placed atop a lazy Susan, allowing the boards to rotate easily for each player. Each board is carefully numbered from one to five, though no names are attached—an anonymous series of games in progress.

Marcus Liebowitz enters the space, his stride purposeful, his eyes already scanning the row of games. His hands are clasped neatly behind his back as he approaches the first table. He pauses, studying the board in front of him. A quick move, the click of a piece against the wood, and the lazy Susan turns smoothly, presenting the new position to the next challenger.

At Game 2, he does the same—quick, almost absent-minded, but precise. Game 3: another glance, a swift motion, and then the turn. Game 4 follows the same pattern. By the time he reaches Game 5, the board is nearly untouched, brand new, and his eyes narrow as he studies Sara's opening move. She's already placed her pawn to e4.

Marcus's fingers hover over the board for a moment before he responds with c5—his signature move. The lazy Susan turns back to white, signaling that it's now her move.

Marcus surveys the room one last time, his gaze sweeping across all five boards. Without another word, he turns on his heel and walks away, his presence leaving a faint ripple in the air.

Cafeteria Later Same Day

The cafeteria is nearly empty now, the last few stragglers heading out for the day. The fluorescent lights buzz overhead as Sara and Derek walk toward the fifth chess table. Derek's eyes flicker over the board, his mind already racing ahead to the next move.

Sara leaning in, "What's our next move?"

Derek's eyes narrow, a thoughtful expression crossing his face as he considers the game,

"Knight to f3."

Sara quizzically, "What kind of move would you call that?"

Derek, a bit amused, "Aggressive but careful. He'll probably move a pawn to d6."

Sara smiling Your move, Marcus.

Derek studies the board for a long moment before turning to Sara with a slight shrug.

"Derek, how did you learn to play chess so well?"

Derek's gaze shifts away, as if pondering the question, before he answers. "I don't know."

LaserTech Cafeteria Next Day

Marcus played d6. He spun the board toward them.

The cafeteria was muted, its usual clatter subdued beneath the late afternoon calm. Derek and Sara stood before Game 5; the pieces locked in a battle of intention and intellect.

Derek peered at the board, then nodded.

"Told you he'd do d6. Do knight c3. We're going into Open Sicilian."

Sara leaned in, her hand hovering over the knight. She didn't speak. She didn't need to.

Sara smiled, heart pounding, she moves her knight to c3.

The move was made, the message sent.

She barely breathed.

— Marcus returns. Played e6. Calm. Calculated.

Derek said, "French variation. Odd choice..."

— They volleyed moves. Marcus—swift, confident. Sara—steady, focused, guided by Derek's whispered analysis.

— Later. Marcus studied the board. Game 5 had changed. It was no longer friendly—it was war.

— Derek leaned in, voice low.

"Bishop to c4. Trust me."

Sara moved.

— Marcus returned. He hesitated. Frowns. Then slid a pawn forward—defensive.

— Final round. Derek inched closer.

"Queen to h5. It's mate in two," said Derek matter-of-factly.

Sara stared. Then played it.

— Marcus folded his hands. Stared at the board, puzzled, searching. Then, he tipped his king.

A long moment of silence.

He walked off without a word.

— Sara and Derek inspect a handwritten note at Game Table 5:

"You're playing next week. All five boards."

"Was that... a compliment?", asked Derek.

Sara laughed.

"From him? That was a standing ovation."

LaserTech Team Office - 0220 Hours R

The low hum of the HVAC system filled the space outside Will's office, a steady, subtle vibration beneath the usual clicks of keyboards and occasional squeaks of office chairs.

The afternoon sun filtered through the slats of the mini-blinds, casting thin ribbons of golden light across Grace Roberts's workstation. She sat, poised, alert, with a pen in one hand and a legal pad scribbled with equations and project notes in front of her.

Inside, the muffled cadence of voices—Sara Brandt and Will Morgan—carried no discernible words, only the soft thrum of conversation that hinted at code word things beyond Grace's clearance.

Her desk phone rang. She answered with crisp professionalism.

"Sara's line, Grace speaking."

The voice on the other end was warm and easy, threaded with curiosity.

"Oh hi, Grace, nice to meet you. I'm Z. I'm looking for Sara."

"Z" to everyone who ever worked beside him—had the kind of name you didn't forget and the kind of loyalty you couldn't buy. Z grew up hearing two languages in the kitchen and one warning in every story his grandparents told: never trust the Russians. That warning etched itself into his soul.

His maternal grandparents—proud Ukrainians—were killed in the early years of the war against Russia, their home obliterated in a missile strike during the battle for Mariupol. Z never forgot. He never forgave.

Grace's voice lightened, intrigued by the calm charm radiating through the line.

"She's in with the boss at the moment. Shall I get her for you or would you rather she call back?"

"No worries, she can call back."

Grace hesitated for a second, then asked the question she had been turning over since yesterday's lunch with Sara.

"Hey Z, may I ask you a question? I understand if you would rather not answer but Sara suggested I talk to you and said it would make more sense once I did and I would better understand."

A pause. Then: "Understand what?"

She took a breath, choosing her words with care.

"Well, she was telling me about Will being the guy you want in your foxhole."

The man on the other end—Zbigniew Zawadzki—responded with a deep, knowing tone.

"Sure...here goes...For reasons beyond understanding, when I was promoted to his team the Army saw fit to pay me twice—once for my old job and once for my new one."

Grace leaned back in her chair, listening as Z's voice dipped into a story burned into memory.

"I told Will right away and he told me to notify the local Army Pay Office and the Defense Finance and Accounting Service payroll department and cc him.

"He also said to open a new account at the Armed Forces Bank and use it only for the old direct deposits to prove I didn't spend it.

"I wrote six memos, one for each month I received a second direct deposit. In the seventh month my journey into hell began. DFAS accused me of defrauding the Army. Then the Army Military Pay Office, then the Army Inspector General."

Grace's lips parted ever so little, stunned.

"The bureaucracy run amok..."

"I didn't know if I was going to serve time at Fort Lewis or be dishonorably discharged."

She blinked, staring blankly at her notepad as her heart sank.

"I thought I was on the verge of a breakdown."

There was a tremor in Z's voice now, subtle but unmistakable.

"Then—out of nowhere—I got a letter of dismissal from the IG and, believe it or not, a letter of apology from the DFAS.

"Major Morgan personally went to that pay office. I don't know how true this part is, but I tend to believe it. He told the Colonel in charge that if it wasn't fixed ASAP, he would rededicate the rest of his career to ruining his."

57

Grace sat upright, eyes wide.

"Whoa Nellie, upbraiding a Colonel."

"A full Eagle at that. Guess it's true you can say anything to an officer as long as you end with sir."

There was a faint chuckle in his voice before he continued.

"But that's not all. Sara told me that he also threatened to retire. He apparently told Ed Perry that if his team was going to be treated so shabbily, he couldn't do his job effectively and there was no point in staying. As I am sure you know by now, he is the best we have. He has solved some high-profile cases. His retirement would reverberate well up the line. Ask Sara to tell you about Willow and Ron Rockwell Hansen."

Grace smiled wistfully.

"Everyone has told me that except him."

Z's voice dropped to a more reflective timbre.

"I think about it all the time. This is the freakin' US Army and it's his whole life and who the hell am I? I was brand new to his team. Anybody else would have written a memo and called it a day. Not him. I was on his team and that was all that mattered. To hell with the consequences."

Grace's smile softened. She stared out the window, her expression a mixture of gratitude and awe.

"That's quite a story, Z."

"Grace, if you need someone to run through a wall for him, don't hesitate to call me."

She laughed, shaking her head.

"You might have to stand in line! Thanks for sharing, Z."

"Of course. And welcome aboard."

The line went dead. Grace held the receiver a moment longer before setting it down with care. She gazed out over the parking lot, the sun glinting off windshields. Her reflection stared back at her in the glass—contemplative, moved.

CHAPTER EIGHT

The Search

"It's the oldest question of all, George. Who can spy on the spies?"

— John le Carre

LaserTech Team Conference Room 0900 Hours R

Morgan's team assembled in the conference room in his office complex at LaserTech. The Vibe board had been rolled in for the presentation with Cecil Brandon and Thomas Carrone attending remotely.

"Good morning, everyone," Will began the meeting, "I have asked Grace Roberts, our Science Advisor, to give us an overall view of the current status of space weapons.

"Grace is a physics professor at the University of Maryland who consults with DARPA on a wide range of projects – Grace…"

The conference room was darkened, blinds drawn tight, the only light coming from the Vibe board. Will Morgan leaned forward, elbows on the polished surface, hands steepled beneath his chin as the screen behind the presenter flickered to life.

The digital slide was stark and simple—two words in bold white type against a field of black: SPACE WEAPONS.

The room fell silent, save for the gentle hum of the HVAC system.

"Before I begin the main presentation," Grace began, "Everyone seems to understand kinetic attacks, but I am often asked to explain the differences between laser attacks and Electromagnetic Pulses or EMPs. These are distinct types of directed energy weapons, each with different mechanisms and effects. Lasers use focused electromagnetic radiation to damage materials with heat, while EMPs disrupt electronic systems by inducing strong currents and voltages that fry electronic components."

"So lasers melt them from a distance?" asked Sara.

"Yes, cooks them well-done."

"How long does it take?" asked Rick.

"Faster than a vampire shutting his coffin before sunrise.

"Let's begin.

"The United States has, over the last decade, accelerated the development of offensive and defensive weapons designed for use in the space domain," she said. Her voice carried the weight of hard-earned intelligence, stripped of interpretation."

A slide shifted. The words on screen were clinical, but what they implied was anything but.

For the next forty-five minutes Grace ran through developments in space weaponry both deployed and in development. She also covered Space Debris, The Outer Space Treaty of 1967, Strategic Stability and Technical Difficulties.

The lights came up, and Grace Roberts stepped forward, her voice carrying the calm confidence of a professor used to explaining complex physics in plain English.

"Let me cut through the alphabet soup. The United States has a range of programs, everything from anti-satellite systems to directed-energy research and interceptors. The common thread is this: we're focused on defense and deterrence. Protecting our satellites, hardening communications, and keeping the high ground secure.

"But here's the problem—our adversaries are not standing still. Russia has already demonstrated the ability to shadow, stalk, and disable satellites with what they call 'non-destructive tests.' They've resurrected old Soviet-era ambitions and proved they can put small killer-satellites into orbit, maneuvering them like chess pieces.

"China, meanwhile, is sprinting ahead across the entire spectrum. They've shown they can destroy satellites outright, they're experimenting with robotic arms in orbit, they're probing our assets with close-proximity maneuvers, and they're building cyber and electronic warfare tools to blind or hijack what we rely on. It isn't one capability—it's layered: kinetic, cyber, directed-energy, and orbital robotics.

"The takeaway?" She clicked to a stark graphic of Earth bristling with orbiting platforms. "Space is no longer uncontested. It's crowded, it's hostile, and it's fragile. One collision, one attack, one miscalculation could trigger cascading effects—political, military, even economic.

"So, the question for us isn't whether adversaries are preparing for conflict in orbit.."

Sara leaned forward and said, "They already are."

"Exactly. The question is how we respond—without letting the first spark ignite a firestorm in the one domain where no one can afford a war."

The room went silent, the glow of satellites and orbital paths casting ghostly lines across the team's faces. The screen went black.

Silence held moment. Then another.

The silence stretched until Sara Brandt leaned forward, brow furrowed.

"Gracie, when you say the Russians can 'shadow' our satellites—what does that mean? Can one satellite really kill another?"

Grace adjusted her glasses, eyes glinting in the LED light. "Yes. They've demonstrated co-orbital vehicles that can sidle up alongside one of ours—close enough to observe, or nudge it, or even release a smaller payload. Think of it like someone tailgating you at a hundred times the speed of a rifle bullet. One wrong move and you're debris."

Derek Wilshire sat forward, hands folded in front of him. "And if there is debris? "You said it could cascade. Are we talking about one satellite breaking apart, or something worse?"

Gracie nodded, advancing the slide. It showed a simulation of an orbital collision—one impact scattering fragments, each fragment colliding with others, until the screen was a blizzard of wreckage encircling the planet.

"Worse. It's called Kessler Syndrome. A single collision can trigger a chain reaction. One satellite becomes a thousand pieces of shrapnel. Those pieces smash into others, creating more debris. The cascade could take out dozens or hundreds of satellites. Navigation, weather, communications—gone. Imagine our grids, our markets, our military command-and-control... blind, deaf, paralyzed."

Derek repeated, "Worse. It's called the Kessler Syndrome."

A low whistle came from Cecil Brandon. "WTF. So, one strike in orbit could shut the Eastern seaboard harder than a blackout. No bombs, no missiles—gravity and physics doing the work."

Grace didn't smile. "Exactly. That's why space weapons are so dangerous. You don't just attack an enemy—you poison the environment everyone depends on. Including yourself."

The room stayed hushed, the glow of the orbital map now more menacing than scientific.

Will Morgan finally spoke. His voice was calm, but there was an edge beneath it.

"Which means Radiant Sentry isn't a simple project anymore." It's insurance against civilization hitting the reset button."

The team exchanged looks. For a moment, the spinning Earth on the screen seemed smaller than ever—fragile, suspended, one misstep away from ruin.

"So," Will continued, "the war might not start in space…"

He looked around the room—at Sara, at Rick, at Grace and Guy and the rest of the team.

"…but we'd better be damn sure we're ready when it moves there."

As they walked back to their offices, Sara said to Gracie, "Did you notice how Derek repeated what you said? I read that's a way some people on the spectrum process things. It's something called echolalia. It's when a person repeats phrases they've heard—sometimes right away, sometimes later—almost like an echo. It's not random, though. For Derek, it can be a way of processing, or of trying to anchor himself in a moment."

She paused, gauging Gracie's reaction. "So, if you hear him repeating something you've said, don't be unsettled. It's not mockery. It's his way of holding onto it."

Gracie gave a small, thoughtful smile. "That… actually makes sense."

"Explains a lot, doesn't it?"

Grace's expression softened. "Thanks That's good to know."

The morning light gleamed off the glass-paneled walls of Morgan's office. Sara Brandt pushed the door open with Grace in tow, both carrying coffee cups and folders, ready to brief the major.

The room was empty. But something on the Vibe whiteboard caught Grace's eye—Happy Birthday Gracie! Her lips curved instantly.

"Oh! How thoughtful. Thanks, Sara."

Sara blinked, taken off guard by the scribbled message:

She squinted at it, bemused. This isn't happening. "Uh... I didn't do it. But Happy Birthday," she added. Sara thought to herself, _Hmm...no nicknames - until now._

Grace glanced around, feigning casual curiosity. "Who did? Could it be Derek?"

Sara snorted. "Um... I doubt if Derek knew it was your birthday. I didn't."

Grace tapped her chin with her pen. "Oh, I know. It was probably Taran."

The office door opened behind them. Will Morgan strolled in, coffee in hand, expression unreadable—until he spotted Grace. His face lit up. "Happy Birthday, Gracie!"

She beamed. "Thanks, boss."

Sara cocked an eyebrow at his uncharacteristic cheer.

"My, my, aren't we in an ebullient mood, today."

Morgan chuckled, not missing a beat.

"Good morning to you too, soldier."

The three shared a warm glance. The atmosphere—rare in its lightness—briefly softened the world of military protocol.

They sat down at the small table to work while Will sat at his desk, _wondering where Derek was this morning._

Sara watched him from across the room, that usual storm cloud focus shadowing his face. Will Morgan wasn't easy to know—not for most people. But she'd learned to read his silences, the edges of his restraint, the thousand things he never said. He didn't give trust easily. Hell, he didn't give anything easily. But he'd given it to her.

And that meant something. It always would.

He never blinked when she told him—years ago now, a hesitant confession in a moment of shared honesty. A soft nod, no questions, no hesitation. Not even curiosity, simply... acceptance. Like it didn't change a thing, like it wasn't even a thing at all. It sounds small, but it wasn't. Not when you've spent your life measuring how much of yourself you're allowed to show.

He never made her feel like a token. Never pried. Never joked. Never pretended to understand when he didn't. He faithfully stood beside her—steady, unflinching. That kind of loyalty was rare. That kind of friendship? Rarer still.

So no—she wasn't in love with him. But she loved him. Deeply. Fiercely. In a way that didn't need definitions. He was family, the kind you choose. The kind who sees all of you and doesn't flinch.

And Grace...

She noticed the way he softened around her. Subtle, but real. Something in his voice, something in his stance. Sara had seen that flicker before—people falling in love, trying hard not to. He'd never say it, not out loud, not yet. But it was there.

And she hoped—God, she hoped—Grace would be the one to reach him. To pull him out of whatever war he still carried in his bones, to heal whatever family scars still harrowed. Because if anyone deserved peace, it was Will. And if anyone could offer it, maybe it was her.

Sara smiled to herself, turning back to her notes. She didn't need anything from him but what he gave: trust, honesty, and an unspoken understanding that didn't ask her to be anyone but who she was. And that... that was everything.

CHAPTER NINE

Suspects

"Each betrayal begins with trust."

- Martin Luther

LaserTech Conference Room—Next Day 0800 Hours R

The air in Will Morgan's conference room buzzed with tension and caffeine. The walls were gray, functional, but the 75-inch Vibe whiteboard on wheels lent the space a battlefield edge—a tactical map for digital warfare.

Will stood at the head of the table, sleeves rolled back, a Dry Erase cap held between his teeth. Sara Brandt and Grace Roberts sat across from him, their laptops open, eyes sharp. They weren't ordinary analysts. They were sleuths focused on national betrayal.

Derek as usual sat in silence observance now a constant guest everywhere Sara and Grace were.

"OK, first things first. We can conduct physical surveillance and collect metadata in public areas.

"We can start with what we have. Review the T5's and latest polygraphs. How old they are and pay particular attention to the caliber of the polygrapher. Nine out of ten times spies could have been prevented by a good polygrapher.

"We'll also need a list of all the printed documents to see who printed the leaked ones. Once we know who that person was we will have to figure out a way to confirm if it's missing without arousing suspicion. If we can show who printed the leaked document and that it is missing. That ought to be enough for probable cause."

Gracie asked, "Won't that be a fait de accompli?"

Sara explained, "Don't we wish. We will still have to prove no one else had access to the printed document."

"Or, tampered with the database records like a programmer." Added Will.

"Or what the boss is wondering—could someone have purchased the same security paper and simply reproduced the document, putting the original back?"

Will Morgan rolled his eyes, "Sara, you're getting scarier with your mind reading every year."

Sara exaggerated expression, "Yah think?"

Will gestured at the whiteboard and clicked open a stylus menu.

"According to Grace, there are twelve people with the knowledge to know what they would be looking at. We can assume that anyone starting here after the date of the breach is not a suspect.

"Cathy, check the employment dates and see who we can eliminate."

As the meeting ended Thomas Carrone entered. He caught Will watching Grace just a fraction too long as she left the room. The glance, the pause—small tells, but Thomas noticed everything.

He sat next to Will and leaned forward in his chair, voice pitched low so only Will could hear.

"You know, she's not made of glass. And in case it's slipped past you… she's different around you too."

Will's brow furrowed that guarded expression sliding into something caught between annoyance and realization.

"…Duly noted."

Thomas gave a faint, knowing smile. "Good. Thought I'd save you the suspense."

Will exhaled through his nose, almost a laugh, almost a groan. A duh moment, plain as day.

Fort Meade - Watchtower Ops

Cathy Wang's phone was already on speaker when Taran Giddings answered, her voice bright but professional.

"Taran—this is Cathy Wang from Will Morgan's staff. I need start dates for the twelve Radiant Sentry cleared staff. Can you read them to me?"

There was a brief pause. "You want me to pull that now? I can—unless you want to call back; I'm finishing a meeting."

"I'll wait," Cathy said. The room around her hummed with low chatter; on the wall, a feed of LaserTech's perimeter camera ran in slow motion.

After a pause she returned.

Taran exhaled and began, slow and deliberate, reading names and dates as Cathy scribbled them on a plain legal pad: "George Lee—August 3, 2016. Genevieve Larsson—March 12, 2011. John Jankowitz—June 7, 2018…" The list continued—ten more entries, each given with the careful cadence of someone reciting payroll.

When Taran finished she added, "I'll send the full file to you by email, so you have it in writing—"

"No," Cathy cut in, polite but firm. "I'm all set I don't need an email."

On the other end, Taran's tone shifted, a quick professional quirk of surprise. "You want me to not send it?"

"'Don't bother," Cathy said. "I wrote It all down."

Taran hesitated for a beat, then gave a short, understanding laugh. "Understood. If you need anything else, call me directly."

Cathy folded the pad closed, the names already stored in her head and on an offline sheet tucked into her jacket. "Thanks, Taran. Appreciate it."

The line clicked dead. Cathy looked at the list once more, then slid it into a locked drawer—paper, for now, and nowhere else.

LaserTech Morgan's Office - Next Day - 0900 Hours R

Sara and Grace were already sitting at the small round table in his office when Will walked in.

"Good morning everyone." Greeted Will as he looked over at Derek sitting on the couch absorbed in his tablet.

"Good morning, Derek." Said Will with no acknowledgment from Derek who was obviously off in his own world somewhere.

Will smiled to himself as he sat down behind his desk.

The Vibe screen clicked to life and the Watchtower team assembled in their conference room at Fort Meade appeared on screen.

Will nodded at everyone and in his customary frugal word style asked, "Where are we?'

Cathy said, "Taran was great and got me all the records. Only six employees were here when the file was printed.

"Here they are." She clicked on the Vibe Whiteboard.

69

Gracie said, "Of those six, there are only four of our suspects that would have access to the kind of material that was stolen.

"In addition to George Lee, the Director, there is Gene Larsson, John Jankowitz, and Marcus Liebowitz."

Will remembered something - "Oh yeah, we should also take a look at the Security Director as well."

Will wrote on the board in sharp, confident strokes: SABLE on the top line and on the second line Alpha, Bravo, Charlie, Delta, Foxtrot.

"Alpha will be George Lee, Bravo will be Gene Larson, Charlie will be John Jankowitz, Delta will be Marcus Liebowitz, and Foxtrot will be Anders Eriksson - to avoid confusion with Operation Echo we will skip Echo."

Sara said. "Gracie, the drill is to memorize these code names and not write them down anywhere."

Will added, "From now on, we will refer to them by code name only. Be careful not to use pronouns that will give away gender. We'll start at the top with Alpha. Grace, I understand you were at Cal Tech with him. How well did you know him?"

"Pretty well. We were both there all four years and had the same majors, so we had many classes together. We didn't socialize except for school events. You probably know he graduated high school at fifteen and Cal Tech at eighteen and was second in his class. He got his PhD at twenty-one. His dissertation was on Laser Science. Not too many on his level."

Sara referred to Gracie with a devilish smile, "Didn't someone we know graduate first?"

Gracie smiled sheepishly and ignored Sara's comment.

"He was quite normal for a geek. If you consider a nerd as having no social skills, he was a geek rather than a nerd. He was born and raised in upstate New York and his family is second-generation Chinese from Hong Kong. George has a wife and a new baby girl, Alyce."

"We'll split the rest up. Thomas you take Bravo, Cathy…Charlie, Z…Delta and Sara you have Foxtrot," said Will. "By tomorrow everyone."

Morgan in as serious a tone as he could muster admonished, "I want everyone to pay particular attention to what I am about to say.

"I don't have much faith in our cover story. It may fool everyone at LaserTech, but it won't fool Kir Smirnova or the Russian SVR. Palisades is undoubtedly his operation so there are more illegals embedded here. They are seven hours ahead of us, so they probably found out about our arrival before dinner.

"We are very familiar with Kir and have crossed horns a few times in the past.

"We can expect to be led astray by false flags that create diversion or misdirection. They may try deceiving us into thinking that an event was caused by someone else here at LaserTech when it was instigated by the deceiver.

"Radiant Sentry is as important to them as it is to us – probably more so.

"Most importantly, have a heightened awareness of your surroundings and let me know immediately if you spot anything out of the ordinary or anything that concerns you.

"Kir is fast rising in the SVR because his operations are clean, precise and deeply embedded. And, oh yes, he's utterly ruthless,"

The SCIF was quiet. Will Morgan sat at the head of the table, the rest of the team arrayed before him. He looked at Thomas and nodded. "What did you find out?

Thomas Carrone (50), "Glass" stood, dossier glowing on the wall display: BRAVO.

A veteran ACIC civilian profiler with over 30-years of experience specializing in the psychological profiling of foreign intelligence agents, embedded spies, and NOC operatives, he brought a rare blend of academic rigor and field-savvy insight into the minds of those living double lives.

Known for his calm methodical yet intuitive approach, Morgan often brought Thomas into sensitive operations. He valued him and saw profiling as more than a skill—it was a duty to detect and defuse threats before they surfaced.

The dossier shifted on the wall display: BRAVO. Thomas Carrone adjusted his glasses, his voice steady and clinical.

"Gene, er... Bravo may be the smartest one on the team. She's a pure scientist. If she had any desire to do so she would probably be running the place. Her nickname, which she has had since high school, is Geneiac."

"As in Brainiac, the villain from the comic series?" Sara asked.

"Yeah. When you blow the curve for everybody, you are indeed a villain."

Will playfully looked at Grace and chuckled, "Do I sense a bit of empathy from anyone here?"

Grace crossed her arms and raised an eyebrow, deflecting with deadpan precision.

"Genevieve Larsson. Physicist. Long-time DARPA contributor, seven years at LaserTech. Full clearance, full technical access. She has the requisite knowledge to compromise Radiant Sentry."

He scrolled through the data points.

"Clean polygraphs, solid financials. No stress indicators. Pragmatic in outlook, no ideological extremes. Ego within normal bounds. Nothing suggests coercion or vulnerability."

Grace arched a brow. "So, she checks every box for capability—none for motive."

Thomas gave a small nod. "Correct. Bravo has access, but no red flags."

Will Morgan leaned forward, tapping the table once. "Then we keep her squarely in play. Capability without motive can still shift fast."

The Bravo file glowed with a steady amber, left active on the board.

Cathy Wang "Echo" was the newest member of the team. She sat two seats from Grace, posture straight but compact, like a spring wound tight. At twenty-three, she was the newest in the room—the outlier among seasoned operators and hardened analysts. A city girl like Sara, Cathy carried herself with quick, sharp energy. At barely five feet tall, she looked fragile until you watched her work.

Graduated in the top percentile from the highly competitive Stuyvesant High School in New York City on an accelerated degree track, specialized in computational modeling at the University of Rochester, Her reading speed and retention was off the charts, with recall sharp enough to rattle even Rick in back-and-forth sparring.

Whispers from her recruiting class had written her off as too young, too green, too bookish. Nobody wanted her. Nobody but Diane Watson, DARPA's formidable Director of HR. Diane had walked her file straight to Will Morgan's desk, dropped it without a word.

Will had skimmed only the cover sheet, then nodded. "If Diane backs her, I don't need to see more."

He hadn't been wrong.

Within weeks, Cathy had proven herself a miniature powerhouse—absorbing terabytes of documentation, spotting patterns others missed, feeding the team's tempo with her

73

uncanny speed. She might have been "Cat" to her classmates, but to Will's unit she was Echo: the one who caught every signal and sent it back sharper than it came in.

The dossier rotated forward: CHARLIE. Cathy Wang straightened in her chair, a hint of nervous energy tempered by crisp delivery.

"John Jankowitz. Advanced degrees from Columbia and MIT. Leading expert in high-energy physics—our materials specialist on Radiant Sentry. First-generation American, Polish descent."

She glanced at her notes, then back to the team. "Happily married, kids, strong financials. Very American in outlook. Polygraphs solid. Most normal ego of the group. And if we're measuring sentiment, he outright hates Russia. By all appearances, he's the least likely suspect."

Grace leaned forward, pen tapping the page. "Capability without inclination. One of the cleanest reads we've got."

Cathy gave a small nod but kept her tone careful. "Still, he has the access. He can't be dropped from consideration."

Will Morgan's eyes lingered on Charlie's profile. "Noted. Access keeps him on the board. But his file stays in the green."

The dossier dimmed to amber-green, hovering between vigilance and dismissal.

The screen flicked to the next dossier: DELTA. Zbigniew Zawadzki—"Z"—rose from his seat, voice even, carrying the weight of quiet authority.

Zbigniew Zawadzki (30) "Chisel", a SUNY Poly computer science standout, with interrogation training from American Military University, he became lethal both behind a keyboard and in the box. Initially doubted, he proved himself to Will Morgan on a critical op—and his loyalty since has been absolute.

Broad-shouldered, razor-smart, relentless against the SVR, Z cracked networks and suspects with the same precision. Once he was in, he never let go until the job was done.

"This is beginning to sound like a broken record; Delta is another genius type.

"Marcus Liebowitz. PhD from MIT, high-energy lasers. Came straight to LaserTech out of school. Considered a prodigy. Well-liked and respected by peers and superiors."

He let the profile scroll—family photos, tournament snapshots.

"Family man. Ranked chess player. Probably the cleanest polygraph of the entire roster. Excellent financials, no anomalies. Solidly American in ideology. No coercion indicators. Ego exactly what you'd expect from a top physicist—normal, not outsized."

Z paused, allowing the profile photo to linger—Marcus caught mid-smile, sleeves rolled, marker ink still on his hand from a whiteboard session.

"He has one quirk worth noting. He keeps a jar of red licorice on his desk—swears he thinks better when he's chewing. Colleagues joke that the candy disappears faster than his equations go up on the board."

Rick cracked a grin. "Genius runs on sugar. That's one I can believe."

"So, we're looking at a genius, but not a threat," said Cecil.

Z gave a short nod. "Correct. Brilliant, but stable. Delta is clean."

Will Morgan's gaze lingered on the dossier before he spoke. "Then Delta stays low on the board. Watch, but don't burn cycles."

The profile dimmed, filed behind Alpha, Bravo and Charlie, another piece locked in place on the hunt.

Sara Brandt, (37) "Vesper" stood, dossier glowing on the wall display: FOXTROT.

Blunt, brilliant, and disciplined, driven by a fierce sense of justice. Her sharp wit and unshakable integrity made her Will Morgan's indispensable second-in-command—trusted beyond protocol.

She grew up in Brooklyn, the only child of working-class parents whose traditional values clashed with her independence and, later, her identity as a gay woman. Estranged during college, she graduated Magna Cum Laude from NYU on a tennis scholarship and never looked back.

For fifteen years she anchored him in a world of shifting loyalties, living authentically and building a chosen family of her own. Sara Brandt never apologized for who she was—and never had to.

"Anders Eriksson. Age forty-nine. Director of Security at LaserTech. Top Secret clearance, mainly administrative. Married, two kids. Finances stable. Clean polygraph." Said Sara.

Grace lifted her pen. "And technical background?"

"Security and management only. No physics, no optics, no engineering. He has no pathway to sensitive project data. He's not a strong prospect."

Rick leaned back with a smirk. "Unless we're chasing badge logs and HVAC codes, Foxtrot's a dead end."

Sara nodded. "Recommendation: archive and refocus on candidates with technical access."

Will leaned forward, voice flat said, "Noted. Foxtrot goes cold. We hunt where it matters."

On the screen, the dossier dimmed to gray—moved to the edge of the board.

LaserTech Morgan's Office - 1110 Hours R

The midmorning sun cast angled shadows across Will Morgan's cluttered desk, papers and coffee-stained folders evidence of the whirlwind that had overtaken LaserTech's team. Sara Brandt stood opposite him, jaw firm, holding a printed page like a smoking gun.

"Bravo printed the leaked document April tenth."

Morgan didn't flinch. He nodded, already forming his next steps.

"We need to set up new interviews with the Greeks conducted at their workstations or offices. While there, we will ask to see their printed document files."

His tone was clipped. Business-like. Beneath it, though, urgency simmered.

"Let's check with DCSA to see fresh T5s on everyone in the department." He paused, scanning Sara's face for any flicker of doubt. There was none. "We're ramping up the vehicle and foot surveillance on Bravo to 24/7."

Sara gave a tight nod. The walls of suspicion were closing in.

CHAPTER TEN

The Russians

"I cannot forecast to you the action of Russia. It is a riddle wrapped in a mystery inside an enigma; but perhaps there is a key. That key is Russian national interest."

- Winston Churchill

Yasenevo, Moscow - SVR Headquarters

The walls of the SVR headquarters in Yasenevo 11 bore the cold dignity of the Russian Federation's foreign intelligence elite. In a room high enough to overlook the frost-laced treetops, the muted ticking of a Soviet-era clock was the only sound beyond the hum of secure electronics.

Kir Smirnova, 45 years old, married, a major and rising star within the KR - External Counter-Intelligence Directorate of the SVR was the architect behind the LaserTech infiltration. He is smart, dedicated, shrewd and hard. He excelled at Moscow State University before being recruited into the SVR Academy, where he trained intensively for three years in clandestine operations, tradecraft, linguistic immersion, and psychological warfare. He graduated top 5% of his class, specializing in deep-cover intelligence and manipulation of technical infrastructure through human vectors—an area once dominated by GRU.

Kir's reputation in the intelligence community was defined by precision and patience. He wasn't flashy. He avoided the theatrical. His operations are clean, subtle, and deeply embedded—he planted seeds that germinate months, sometimes years later. He was cold, calculating and merciless.

He sat in a leather chair at a conference table carved from birch and shadowed by velvet drapes. A samovar hissed steam in the corner, ignored.

Kir Smirnova said, "Palisades is going well. Sable delivered an interesting file our physicists are reviewing. This is the first time we have managed to get a complete file. Fancy Bear your GRU Unit 26165 has infiltrated the system at LaserTech and is working on identifying useful files among the ten million lines of code. We detect no FBI or CIA activity - Sable remains secure."

Across from him, his counterpart in the GRU, Georgy Viktorovich Markova, 57 said, "Isn't this a DARPA project? Wouldn't it be an Army CI responsibility?"

"Yes. But let's hope they don't get involved. ACIC is exceptionally good. They have been a thorn in our side."

Markova grunted. Memories of failed operations flickered behind his eyes.

"Our moles Ikar Lesnikov and Gray Willow would still be active if it weren't for their persistence."

Kir Smirnova added, "They are the only American CI agency that has both domestic and foreign authority as well as law enforcement authority when it comes to national security."

"And Will Morgan—a worthy adversary. We've crossed paths twice before—once in Prague during our failed extraction of a compromised diplomat, and again in Istanbul, where Will's interference led to the dismantling of an SVR cyber-co-opting plan. In both cases, Will outmaneuvered us - not through brute force, but through psychological resilience and improvisational skills.

"He is a dangerous unflappable opponent. He displays exceptional pattern recognition, loyalty manipulation, and operational improvisation. He has a high threat rating. We must not underestimate him."

Privately, Kir admired Will's intellect and leadership—but also saw in him the very reason Russia's post-Cold War ambitions had met friction. In Kir's eyes, Will represented the last gasp of a principled American counterintelligence officer: incorruptible, infuriating, and effective.

Kir Smirnova said, "From time-to-time DARPA assigns project auditors to make sure the project is on track."

"With the Americans that usually means on budget," said Markova.

"They have done so here. An auditor has been assigned to the project." noted Kir "It appears to be routine but we have a sleeper agent embedded in the accounting department, A swallow, she compromised the Assistant HR Director. She will find out."

Their eyes met in shared understanding—neither of them genuinely believed in 'routine' when DARPA was involved.

"We should get an update on our playboy translator Zakharov," said Kir, "he is our only asset with official cover in contact with Sable in America."

Moscow Center – SVR Directorate

The fluorescent hum of the overhead fixtures seemed louder than usual. Irina Sokolova "Barynya" sat at the long steel table, back straight, eyes fixed on the polished surface. Across from her, the two senior officers leafed through thick folders stamped Секретно / SECRET.

"Comrade Sokolova," Kir Smirnova began, voice heavy with disdain, "explain again why Nikita Zakharov is still useful to us."

Irina met his gaze evenly. "Zakharov retains privileged access. He delivers documents on Radiant Sentry without hesitation. His record—"

"—is sloppy," Georgy Viktorovich Markova cut in sharply. "We have reports of irregular movements, unexplained absences. He lingers too long in cafés. He smiles at Americans as if he were one of them. Do you call that discipline?"

Irina suppressed the urge to snap back. Instead, she leaned forward, calm and precise. "He smiles because he is arrogant. That arrogance keeps him productive. Zakharov believes himself untouchable, and in that delusion, he continues to work for us. It is effective."

The older officer drummed his fingers on the folder. "Arrogance also leads to betrayal. He travels; he enjoys their luxuries. Wine. Women. Western air. And when Moscow watches too closely, such men crack."

Irina allowed a pause before replying. "He has not cracked yet. He brings us what others cannot. He is… valuable."

The two men exchanged a glance. Not agreement—just shared suspicion.

Finally, the elder spoke again, low and deliberate. "Comrade Sokolova, we remind you: compromise is a contagion. It spreads from one man to an entire program. If there is even a shadow of doubt—" He closed the folder with a hard snap.

Irina kept her face still, though her pulse raced. She understood what they were saying: Zakharov's days were numbered. Her defense had bought him no safety, only a delay.

As she rose to leave, one officer called after her. "Stay close, Barynya. Moscow will be watching you closely."

CHAPTER ELEVEN

National Security Agency (NSA)

"The life of spies is to know, not be known."

Fort Meade - NSA Analyst Ops 1025 Hours R

Buried deep beneath the fortified perimeter of Fort Meade lies a realm most Americans will never see, never hear of, and never know exists. It's a world of humming machines, shifting code, and glowing glass, where the line between silence and signal defines national security.

The analyst operations floor sits behind several layers of biometric gates, airlocks, and Faraday-shielded corridors. No personal electronics enter. Every moment inside is timestamped, cataloged, and fire-walled—both literally and psychologically.

The facility is a sprawling, underground nerve center of America's most advanced electronic surveillance capability. Ceiling-mounted LED panels cast a cool, sterile glow over long rows of workstations, each surrounded by a cocoon of ultra-high-resolution monitors. Every cubicle is less a desk than a cockpit—wrapped in screens streaming everything from live satellite feeds to anonymized packet captures from undersea fiber-optic cables. One display might show real-time metadata from a suspected Iranian comms node. Another—deep packet inspection of a

Russian diplomatic backchannel. Another—social media pattern analysis scraping Mandarin dialects from Western servers.

It is a cathedral to data.

A temple to silence.

Analysts here don't wear uniforms, but they operate with military discipline. Many are in their late twenties or early thirties, with eyes strained from sixteen-hour shifts and minds sharpened by years of parsing chaos into pattern.

They are mathematicians, linguists, computer scientists, and codebreakers. But above all, they are watchers.

Each one sits surrounded by billions of dollars' worth of hardware and software—signals intelligence collection nodes, real-time encryption processors, machine learning triage engines, and cyber attribution tools the private world doesn't even know exist.

The walls are lined with black glass panels displaying live threat dashboards—digital constellations of nation-state activities, lit up like galaxies across the surface of Earth. One blink from red to yellow could mean a satellite uplink has been spoofed. Another—a proxy malware drop in Eastern Europe. A third—a broadcast pattern from a Cuban short wave numbers radio station previously dormant for decades.

And through it all, the analysts toil. No sunlight. No natural sound. No end in sight.

Day after day. Night after night.

They track fragments of signals through an infinite ocean of noise. They know they'll never get credit for what they find. Most of what they see, they can't even tell their families exists. But they keep watching. Keep parsing. Keep trying to see around the next corner of global threat.

Because somewhere in the static, a war may already be starting.

Will and Grace were ushered into a small, sealed room with a low ceiling and no windows. The room breathed in the cold pulse of blue light. Not from any one source, but from many—banks of monitors, ambient glow from touchscreens, blinking indicators along the server banks that lined the perimeter like silent sentinels. Hushed, efficient. The space felt more like a control tower than an office.

An NSA Security Analyst sat at her station, her posture impeccable, her eyes trained on the center monitor. She was in her early thirties, the sharpness in her gaze honed by long hours and long years. Coffee had long ago been replaced by adrenaline and instinct.

The analyst nodded, gesturing to a screen filled with lines of data.

"The message came in moments before 0200 hours, relayed through a fortified node in the NSA's SIGINT division. A pirate Russian shortwave station called The Buzzer broadcasting on an odd frequency above 14 MHz, transmitted a one-time pad message—cryptic, concise, and unmistakably meant for one person.

"Genevieve Larsson."

The moment it hit the analyst's screen at Fort Meade, the cold-blue hum of the control room seemed to tighten around her. She leaned forward, fingers flying across the keys, decrypting the OTP with the known pattern: a pre-issued numerical cipher tied to a dictionary. Within seconds, coordinates bloomed on her central monitor.

39.03989 N, -77.11344 W.

Rockburn Branch Park. A wooded trail system not far from Columbia, Maryland.

"Sir, Subject Larsson received coordinates via OTP broadcast. Location is Rockburn Branch Park."

"What are the coordinates?"

"Thirty-nine point zero three nine eight nine north latitude. Seventy-seven point one three four four west longitude."

"Thanks. You're the best. I'm writing this up."

The NSA analyst beaming from ear to ear, "Thank you sir. Means a lot coming from you."

The comment went right past Will, but Grace took note that even to the rank and file in this mysterious cyberland Will was widely known and highly regarded. It did not escape her that he always took care to compliment the anonymous toilers and pluggers that were indispensable to any large operation but rarely noticed. In a funny way, she thought, these were his team as well - and somehow they knew it!

As they were leaving Grace looking shocked, "How can you do that? The recipient, I mean. Obviously the broadcast source is out in the open and you monitor all the numbers stations, but there are millions of radios in the US and probably a billion in the world."

"Grace you seem like a kind person. I could explain it to you but... no I wouldn't have to kill you, but somebody would," he laughed.

"Gracie, before nine eleven it was not possible. But it's amazing what a trillion dollars can buy these days," Will chimed in playfully.

Fort Meade - NSA SKIF - 1130 Hours R

Will was pacing the floor of his borrowed SCIF, phone pressed to his ear. The line was already ringing.

"Cecil," he said as soon as the voice clicked in. "I need surveillance on Larsson tomorrow. Rockburn Branch Park. We intercepted an OTP with coordinates pointing there."

There was a pause at the other end. Cecil Brandon's voice came in low, hoarse with exhaustion but sharp.

"Dead drop?"

"Looks like it."

Cecil exhaled audibly. "I'll need three shifts. Six to seven operators per. That place is full of trailheads and tree cover—too many blind spots."

"Can you make it happen?"

"Hey man, they told you whatever you need and they meant it. You'll have it by dawn. Full coverage. If Larsson makes a move, we'll have eyes on it."

Will hung up and dialed another number, this time reaching a line that routed through Alexandria, Virginia—ACIC headquarters.

A few rings. Then a dry, amused voice answered.

"Will. You calling to complain about the cafeteria again?"

"No time for jokes, Thomas. I need a profile. Bravo."

There was a pause. "Bravo. Isn't she the one they call Geniac? "

"Yeah. The one who got coordinates via an OTP for a meet at Rockburn Park."

Thomas Carrone, one of the most unnervingly accurate behavioral profilers Will had ever worked with, dropped the playfulness from his voice.

"I'll get to work. You want personality, tradecraft, trigger behaviors, foreign training indicators?"

"All of it - the lot. I want to know if she's the kind of gal who'd walk into a drop. And whether she's a true believer or someone we can crack."

"You'll have my assessment in four hours."

Will leaned back in his chair as the room around him seemed to slow. The night had teeth. Genevieve Larsson was either a deep-cover sleeper who'd been activated for Palisades as the Russian called their operation—or a mole motivated by money, ego or whatever.

Either way, tomorrow would bring answers.

Will thought to himself with a smile the game is a foot as they say.

He turned to Gracie and said, "Let's grab something to eat at the Officers Club. The food's not bad and it's quick."

Fort Mead - Officers' Club - 1230 Hours R

The officers' club exuded elegance, its walls adorned with portraits of decorated veterans, its tables set with crisp linens. Will and Grace settled into a corner booth; menus opened in front of them as they waited for a server.

"So," Grace said, folding her hands. "What's an O-T-P?"

Will smiled. "One-Time Pad. The gold standard of unbreakable encryption—if used correctly."

"Unbreakable?"

"It's simple, really," he explained. "You take the message—the plain text numbers—and pair them with a truly random key. But that key? It's used once and never again."

"So, each number is matched with one from the key?"

"Correct. Combine them using modular addition. Only the second digit matters—like eight plus three equals one."

Grace leaned in. "How are the letters represented?"

"Two ways," Will said. "Basic: A is one, B is two, and so on. More advanced? Five-digit groups. Each code points to a word in a specific book—usually a dictionary."

He tapped the table for emphasis. "First three digits for the page, fourth for the paragraph, fifth tells you how many words in. Left or right."

"So, the book is the key," she said.

"Right. And if you don't have the exact edition? You're screwed."

"But wouldn't a bunch of five-digit numbers raise red flags?"

"Doesn't matter. The mole never sends them. They receive them. Via shortwave."

Grace stared. "No encryption? Just... broadcast?"

"Wide open," Will said, nodding. "But only one person can know what it means—if they've got the right pad."

"How do they know it's their message?"

"Some stations play Beethoven. Others, if you can believe it, use cartoon clips. Each asset is aware of their 'songs —one uses 'Yosemite Sam.'"

"Like a signature."

"Bingo."

Grace leaned back, a bit unnerved by the elegance of the system. "Together with printing the document and receiving the transmission... seems like game, set, and match. No?"

Will frowned. "We might like to think so, but it's only game and set. We have no idea what was in the message—even if we can prove she was the one who got the transmission."

"But they figured out the coordinates."

"Pure computing power. If you know the document - in this case a dictionary - its brute force.

"Of course, if you don't have the right document like I say, you're screwed."

His phone buzzed on the table. He answered. "Morgan."

Sara's voice crackled over the line.

"Boss, Bravo's pen register is back and loaded in the search program. Bravo made a call almost two years ago—April—to... wait for it... the Baltimore field office of the FBI!

Then, eighteen minutes later, Bravo got an incoming call lasting thirty-six minutes from an unidentified number with a DC area code."

Grace leaned forward. "Could the first one have been a wrong number?"

Sara said, "Possible, but around here we don't believe in coincidences. FBI cell phones are unidentified and untraceable."

"I see," Grace said, eyes narrowing.

Will turned to Grace. "Let's ask Guy to see if he can find out if that number belongs to the FBI."

"And we got the paper company client list," replied Sara,"—and our friends at the GSA are on it.

"Huh?" Grace asked.

"Delivered one box to the Hoover Building." Sara explained, "Attention Paul Vogle."

Will's mouth curved into a grim smile. "That's a Bingo."

Dr. Genevieve "Gene" Larsson

Fort Mead – Watchtower Ops

Thomas Carrone as he handed out copies, "Here is the profile you requested of Bravo. It's basic at this point but she has worked for DARPA subs since school and has been at LaserTech for seven years. So, as far as information not in our collective files – there may be none.

Character Profile: Dr. Genevieve "Gene" Larsson

Age: 37 Position: Deputy Director Radiant Sentry Project and Senior Physicist, LaserTech Industries (DARPA Subcontractor)

Specialty: Directed-energy physics, optical systems, applied electromagnetics

Nickname: "Geneiac" – earned in high school after repeatedly blowing the curve for classmates

"Gene Larsson grew up in Grand Rapids, Michigan, the daughter of a conservative, upper-middle-class family with deep Midwestern roots and a reverence for hard work. Her parents—her father an orthopedic surgeon, her mother a classical pianist—expected excellence, and Gene delivered.

"She earned a full scholarship to the University of Michigan, where the liberal academic environment contrasted with her conservative upbringing.

"While Gene isn't politically active, she's civically thoughtful. She describes herself now as a 'pragmatic idealist.'

"Career: Gene earned her PhD in applied physics from Michigan at age 26, publishing a dissertation on non-linear effects in high-energy lasers that garnered DARPA's attention. She's since bounced between projects under multiple defense research umbrellas, but LaserTech became her home seven years ago.

"Gene is arguably the smartest person on the LaserTech team—and the most modest. If she has a flaw, it's that she holds herself to impossible standards and is often reluctant to acknowledge her own impact.

"Personality: She's a diehard University of Michigan football fan (Wolverines above all), prefers long solo hikes to social gatherings, and keeps a steel-string guitar in her apartment that she plays on Sunday mornings to clear her head. Enjoys opera and classical music. She's an avid runner and trains with Navy SEAL-style intensity, mostly as a form of mental discipline.

"Despite her striking athletic looks, tall, blonde hair, blue eyes, confident—Gene shows little interest in dating. She's been approached more times than she can count, she's not reclusive merely self-contained.

"Her team sometimes jokes that if aliens ever landed, Gene would be the one to communicate with them—logically, calmly, and probably with a dry pun.

"Values: Above all, Gene believes in competence, clarity, and contribution. She doesn't need recognition—but she doesn't abide incompetence or posturing. She's the type to work 20-hour shifts without complaint if it means protecting U.S. national security through her work.

90

"She believes in science as the best defense against chaos and ignorance. Yet she also holds firm to the belief that science without ethics is a dead end. It's this quiet moral compass that makes her indispensable on DARPA's team."

Walking around like a professor lost in his thoughts, Thomas summarizes:

"Will, this one is puzzling. If ever I saw a hardened target, Bravo is it. I can't begin to see what angle the Russians could use. Can't be money — she has plenty and isn't motivated by it anyway. There is no love interest, she has no ego to speak of, her ideology while liberal is basically mainstream and there are no signs of coercion.

"If there is anything suspicious about her it's that...well, she's too perfect.

"I have asked The Bureau to look into any possible coercion possibilities. However, that seems to be a long shot."

"Thanks Thomas, we've been surprised before. But it's still early."

CHAPTER TWELVE

False Flag

"Never attempt to win by force what can be won by deception."

-*Niccolò Machiavelli*

Yasenevo District, Moscow - SVR Headquarters

Kir Smirnova preferred operations that looked like gravity—inevitable, natural, impossible to resist. John Jankowitz was the ideal target. A familiar face at Gene Larsson's lab, a scientist whose constant in-and-out routine made him blend seamlessly into the background noise. The kind of man who could plausibly slip a file out, reproduce it, and return it without drawing more attention than a lab coat.

So, Kir built the story. Layer by layer.

The first breadcrumb appeared as if by accident: ten thousand dollars in cash, tucked behind a row of rarely touched binders in Jankowitz's personal lab space. Crisp bills, serial numbers designed to catch an auditor's eye. Kir made sure it was found by triggering a silent alert to security about an 'unsecured item,' knowing the subsequent search would turn it up,"

Then, a second breadcrumb—louder, harder to dismiss. Investigators, nudged in the right direction, "discovered" an unreported foreign account in his brother's name. The balance was one hundred thousand dollars. Enough to smell like payoffs. Enough to turn suspicion into narrative.

Now all that was needed was theater.

Columbia, MD

The Brush Pass.

A week later, surveillance teams clocked Jankowitz at the Wegmans on McGaw Road. Security cameras caught the moment: a tall, striking woman with Slavic features brushing past him in the produce aisle. No contact beyond a shoulder graze, no words exchanged. To the watchers, it was everything. A "chance" encounter that didn't appear like chance.

The whisper of a handler.

Columbia, MD - IHOP

The Dead Drop.

Two nights later, the trap tightened. ACIC's surveillance logs noted Jankowitz leaving his home well past midnight, careful not to wake his wife. He drove with his lights dimmed longer than necessary, parked three blocks from his destination, and walked the rest of the way with his head down.

At the local IHOP, he slid into a booth across from a man no one recognized. Cameras caught them leaning close, voices low. Fifteen minutes passed—enough for suspicion, not enough for context.

Then the handoff: Jankowitz produced a plain envelope, pushed it across the table. The unknown man pocketed it without fanfare. No money exchanged, no handshake. Just silence, a nod, and departure.

Minutes later, Jankowitz retraced his path, skulked back into his house, and slipped under his covers before dawn. To any watcher, the picture was complete: foreign handler, hidden cash, covert meeting.

Result

On the surface, Jankowitz now looked like the perfect mole. Every thread led in his direction. Every frame of footage added weight to the suspicion.

Jankowitz, his wife and brother were placed under 24/7 physical surveillance. mass digital surveillance and an undercover agent was placed in his lab area.

As Kir Smirnova intended.

LaserTech Cafeteria – Noon

Will, Grace, Sara, and Derek sat around one of the small tables, half-eaten sandwiches and coffee cups scattered between laptops and data pads. The conversation drifted from project specs to harmless banter until Sara suddenly pushed her chair back.

"I've got to get back to my desk," she said casually, grabbing her coffee. "See you guys later."

Derek glanced up, surprised she was leaving mid-lunch, but stayed seated.

From behind Will and Grace, Sara gave Derek a sharp look—then a quick nod toward the door, mouthing, come on.

Derek blinked, confused, but stood up anyway.

As they walked out, he frowned. "Uh... what was that about?"

Sara smiled, lowering her voice. "I just wanted to give them some time. You know—alone."

Derek squinted. "They already know each other."

"Not like that," Sara said, a teasing grin creeping in. "I think they like each other. And they could use a little space to figure that out."

Derek paused, processed, then shrugged. "Uh... whatever."

Sara smirked, sipping her coffee. "You'll see."

LaserTech Cafeteria – Continuation

The cafeteria had thinned out, leaving only the low hum of conversation and the clink of silverware on trays. Sunlight filtered through the glass wall, scattering across the table between them.

Will leaned back slightly, watching Grace sip her coffee. "So," he said, "quiet lunch for once. That's new."

Grace smiled over the rim of her cup. "You say that like peace makes you nervous."

"Maybe it does," Will said. "When things are calm, something's usually about to explode."

"Spoken like a man who doesn't know what to do with downtime," she teased.

He smiled. "I can adapt. Eventually."

She tilted her head, amused. "You're not exactly known for eventually. You're more of an immediate-results kind of guy."

"Not always," he said, eyes flicking to hers. "Some things are worth taking slow."

Grace met his gaze and didn't look away. "Is that your version of patience?"

"Maybe I'm learning," Will said quietly. "Some lessons take the right teacher."

Her laugh came soft, a low note that carried more warmth than sound. "Careful, Major. You almost sounded charming there."

He feigned a frown. "Almost?"

"Almost," she echoed, smiling. "But I'll give you points for effort."

He picked up his coffee, turning the mug between his hands. "I'll take what I can get."

For a moment, neither spoke. The silence wasn't awkward— it was easy, lived-in. The kind that didn't need to be filled.

Then Grace stood, gathering her things. "Thanks for lunch, Will."

He rose automatically, as he always did. "Anytime."

She hesitated, then added, "Just... try to enjoy the quiet while it lasts."

Will's smile was small but real. "Only if you promise not to make it too quiet."

She shook her head, amused, and walked away—her reflection fading in the glass wall as Will watched, that rare, unguarded warmth still in his eyes.

CHAPTER THIRTEEN

License Plate JD4978

"Diplomacy is the velvet glove that cloaks the fist of power."

—Robin Hobb

LaserTech Morgan's Office

The office coffee was bitter enough to strip paint. Grace took a sip, grimaced, and set the cup down. "This should be a controlled substance."

Derek glanced up from his notepad, deadpan said, "Technically it is. Torture."

Grace let out a laugh she hadn't realized she was holding in. "Spoken like a man who prefers tea."

"Spoken like a man who prefers survival."

They shared a grin, the bleak coffee momentarily forgotten.

Will Morgan stood at the head of the small conference table, arms crossed over his chest, the faint blue glow of the NSA video shimmering off his face.

Sara Brandt leaned forward in her chair, her gaze locked on the grainy footage playing across the Vibe screen, the sound of keyboard clicks and background chatter from the NSA tech room faint in the background. Grace settled beside her, tapping notes into her secure tablet, while Derek studied with cool concentration.

The room buzzed with tension, despite its quiet—until Sara broke the silence.

"We checked the registration of JD 4978," she said, eyes still on the screen. "It is registered to Nikita Zakharov, a translator in the Russian embassy."

She turned toward Will, her voice colder now.

"He has diplomatic immunity. This car is registered to him."

A brief pause.

Cecil Brandon explains, "The only car he drives is a vehicle with diplomatic plates. JD 4978 is probably parked in a garage or commercial lot. We'll find it eventually."

The voice came through clear and clipped over the Vibe speaker from a secure location miles away, where Cecil Brandon, Guy Zarelli, and Judd Lockwood had joined remotely, their faces arranged in three square tiles hovering above the feed.

Will leaned on the edge of the table.

"Will you tag it?"

"Probably. After all, that would not be out of the ordinary. We have to make sure he sees us surveilling him in it, so he doesn't conclude he was tailed previously."

Surveillance—Floating Box Formation

Glenn Burnie, MD 0815 Hours R

The sky was a flat wash of gray, diffused with the promise of early spring. Gene stepped out of her condo dressed in a sleek black running jacket, dark tights, and running shoes that had seen miles but bore no brand. Her breast-pack backpack looked small, decorative. It wasn't.

She approached her car without concern, scanning the street with the trained indifference of someone used to being noticed. Parked tactically around her vehicle were four innocuous sedans: Echo1,2,3 and 4. To an outsider, they might've been neighbors. But they faced outward in the classic stakeout box. Ready to roll, no matter which way she turned. Whichever way Gene turns the cheating vehicle will radio command vehicle who will direct the others. Whichever way Gene turned, they'd know. The system was old but effective.

Gene got into her car, tossed her breast-pack on the passenger seat flopping on top of her copy of The Cherry Orchard, she started the car and drove.

"OTM" said Echo-1, the code for on-the-move.

Echo 1 let her merge onto the highway before slipping into the rear view.

Cecil leaned over the hood of the Tahoe, tablet in hand, watching the blue blip marked "GENE L" slide past Dorsey Road on I-97 headed North. A soft rustle of wind and the chirp of a passing trucker's CB was all that moved in the morning heat. His team was already in play. The floating-box was up.

Genevieve Larsson didn't know it yet, but she was inside a cocoon of surveillance.

The system had been perfected by the FBI and adopted with ruthless precision by ACIC. It was called the floating box — not because it followed, but because it floated around the target like a school of sharks around a swimmer who hadn't yet seen the fin.

Five agents. Three vehicle types. All invisible.

Echo-1, a dull-gray Accord with a cracked taillight, was the command vehicle, and their agent inside had "command of the target." That meant maintaining steady visual contact without drawing heat.

She was taking the Interstate, making it easy to hang back. I-95 turned into I-97 and then joined with I-695. She exited at 7A to I-895 and the Accord didn't flinch, gliding past the exit as if uninterested. She wouldn't even notice it in her mirrors.

Two blocks down, a white RAV4, Echo-2, drifted into her lane and picked up command like passing a baton. Backup vehicle: fill-in, ghost switch, deception layer. If Gene thought she'd shaken her tail by watching the Accord disappear, she was wrong. This new tail was a completely different ghost.

Echo-3 and Echo-4 were the outriders — loose orbiters sweeping the box's perimeter. They ensured she couldn't break the net. Gene could slam a U-turn, duck into a garage, or try a fast left through yellow — and the box would flex but never break. That was the art. The agents weren't following her. They were surrounding her, embedded in her urban ecosystem like locals headed to brunch, a contractor hauling drywall, or a nurse in scrubs on her way to a double shift.

Echo-5, the controller, sat in an old plumbing van near the traffic circle outside a 7-Eleven, its antennas tucked low. From here, Cecil coordinated the ballet — no voice chatter, just bone-conducting throat mics and coded clicks over secure comms.

Click-click.

"Is that you, Echo?"

Click-click.

"Are you in command of the target?"

Click-click.

"Has the target made contact with the other suspect yet?"

(Silence.)

"Is the target not in contact with the suspect?"

Click-click.

Perfect. It was working.

The vehicles themselves were modified. One SUV had dimmable headlights and rigged brake lights that wouldn't flare on a tail. Another had a stall switch; in case they needed to simulate a breakdown mid-intersection. The black Tacoma—Echo-3—had reinforced bumpers from a retired border patrol fleet. These cars weren't bought—they were built.

Cecil watched the map update again.

She exited at exit 3 to US 1/ Montgomery Road. Four- and one-half miles later at the Rockland Elementary School she turned right into Rockland Branch Park.

She thought she was alone.

She wasn't.

Saturday Run

Rockland Branch Park, MD 0846 Hours R

The scent of wet leaves and distant rain hung in the air. BRAVO pulled in and parked, her breath calm, her expression unreadable. She stepped out and stretched - slow, fluid. Her eyes scanned the horizon with purpose. Saturday runs were her cover, but her mission never paused.

Across the lot, Echo, Tango, and Sierra mirrored her. Each dressed like weekend warriors, matching her stretch for stretch.

From a plain van nearby—no markings except for a faded Howard County Parks decal—Cecil Brandon emerged. He moved like a man who hated wasted time. He opened the trunk, removed a drone case, and disappeared briefly down a dirt path. A few minutes later, a Falcon 6, a drone buzzed skyward.

Cecil returned to the van and monitored the feed in silence.

BRAVO put her ear buds in and turned on Rachmaninoff's Rhapsody on a Theme of Paganini and began her jog. Her watch beeped—low, unmistakable. She'd reached the dead drop. She slowed, jogged in place, glancing at her vitals. The watch's light blinked red—then turned green. Message received. She didn't hesitate. She picked up her pace and vanished into the trees.

Cecil leaned into the monitor. He caught the pause. A mere two seconds—but deliberate.

Later, the same Parks van returned, this time with two operatives in uniform. They set up a sandwich board that read "TRAIL CLOSED" at the trailhead. Under cover of signage, they moved in.

They followed BRAVO's route via GPS, stopping at her pause point. Four compact Wi-Fi cameras were installed like ghosts—buried under leaves, wedged into bark, hidden in roots.

On their way back, they deployed two more cameras—one facing the parking lot's entrance, the other its exit.

Surveillance. Live.

A lone jogger—tall, athletic, nondescript—moved along the Clover Trail Path. He paused beside a half-buried rock, knelt casually, and examined his shoe.

But what he really did was open a tiny hatch in the rock and swap a battery inside. He sealed it, stood, and continued jogging.

Fifteen minutes later, he drove away without ever glancing back.

Cecil Brandon

Phil's Place

Warm light spilled from the soft Edison bulbs overhead, casting a nostalgic glow over the worn brick walls of Phil's Place. Wooden tables were set close together, filled with the murmur of evening diners and the clink of silverware.

Will Morgan sat at a small table tucked into a corner, opposite Sara Brandt and Grace Roberts. They were halfway through their drinks and when the door opened in strode Cecil Brandon (50) a twenty-five-year veteran.

He was unmistakable—broad shouldered black man, confident gait, with charisma that filled a room before he even spoke. His eyes scanned the dining room until they landed on Will, and his grin exploded.

Will saw him at the same time and mumbled under his breath.

Sara Brandt whispered, "Watch this. Will hates PDAs and Cecil is a hugger."

Cecil closed the distance in three strides and wrapped Will in an enthusiastic bear hug. Will's body stiffened like a board, his arms awkwardly patting Cecil's back before he extracted himself.

"My man!."

Cecil turned to the women, his charm now in full effect.

"Sara, gorgeous as ever, and you brought a beautiful friend. I'm Cecil Brandon and you are?"

Grace Roberts, half laughing, half smiling said, "I'm Grace."

The group sat. Will cleared his throat and leaned in, lowering his voice said, "The reason we didn't meet at the office is that Brandon is a Surveillance Officer. We try not to risk the chance of inopportune observations."

Grace raised an eyebrow, unsure if Will was being cryptic or bureaucratic. Sara smiled knowingly.

"What he means is LaserTech is a big place, and he could be innocently seen by many people.

"If on the job one of them saw him and, in an attempt to be friendly, gestured recognition, his cover could be blown."

She sipped her drink.

"At best it might be a nod, smile, or wave, and at worst one of those, 'didn't I see you at LaserTech?' encounters."

Grace Roberts said, "The Scots call it Zemblanity. The inexorability of unfortunate discoveries. No extra charge for that."

Will nodded with a faint grin. "In case you haven't guessed, Grace is our PhD consultant."

He gestured toward Cecil. "Cecil is a surveillance officer with the ACIC covering agent program. He was recently tasked to provide vehicle and foot surveillance on Bravo."

Sara Brandt teases Cecil quipping, "That makes him a SSG and an MSP."

Cecil Brandon laughing robustly. "That's my Sara. MSP is Male Sexist Pig. She loves me, ya know. You can tell because of her playful banter."

Will smiled and cut to business.

"So, what have you learned?"

"She is no pro. Not a novice, but not a pro."

"She runs at different parks each weekend. She seems to work late almost every night. Otherwise, unremarkable habits."

"Saves her money, goes to church often, enters charity races, eats healthy."

He grinned.

"Stops to pet every dog and chats up their owners."

"Gets hit on all the time but doesn't have any dates. Her busy schedule probably gets in the way."

He leaned in now, more serious.

"We are going to need CCTV inside and the help of our NSA TAO friends."

Will Morgan said, "In the works."

"In the meantime, we have cameras covering the front and back of her building."

Gracie asked, "TAO?"

"Tailored Access Operations, the cyber-warfare intelligence gathering unit of the NSA," replied Sara.

A server arrived and took their orders. The conversation shifted, but the tension of surveillance lingered under the surface.

The night had settled thick and quiet over the dimly lit parking lot, the air sharp with early spring chill. Sodium vapor lamps buzzed overhead, casting amber halos on the blacktop. The lot was half-empty now—only a few vehicles remained, their windshields dusted with pollen, their presence unnoticed except by those who lived lives in the margins.

Will Morgan and Cecil Brandon walked in silence for a few steps before wordlessly splitting toward their respective cars, the rhythm of their footfalls syncing before diverging. Nearby, Sara Brandt's sedan beeped as she unlocked it. Grace Roberts moved to join her, slipping into the passenger seat.

The car doors thunked shut, enclosing them in warmth and the faint smell of fresh leather and Sara's lavender hand cream. The engine hummed to life.

Grace stared ahead a moment, then turned toward Sara with a smile that was half mischief, half awe.

"Cecil is some character."

Sara grinned, pulling out of the space.

"Sure is. He's one of our favorites. He's the best surveillance specialist in the command. Master of disguise. If you're being watched, and you don't know it yet... chances are it's Cecil,"

Grace let out a short laugh, eyes wide.

"This project gets more interesting every day."

"Cecil is Will's oldest friend and most trusted field operative. Reliable. Unshakable. Underrated," said Sara chuckling to herself. "In Istanbul, he saved Will's life during an ambush—no fanfare, no debt spoken aloud. Will is now godfather to Cecil's children."

Gracie reached into her coat pocket, fishing out a slip of folded paper. She glanced at it, then at Sara again.

"Z told me to ask you who Ikar Lesnikov and Gray Willow are."

Sara gave a slow, knowing nod, her gaze steady on the road ahead.

"Ikar Lesnikov was the Russian code name for Peter Debbins. And Gray Willow was Ron Rockwell Hansen—not to be confused with Robert Hanssen."

She gave Grace a glance, her expression thoughtful now, weighed down with history.

"We played key roles in uncovering both. They were extremely damaging spies. It was a huge deal."

Grace leaned back, letting the weight of the information settle.

"Cool. By the way, I meant to ask you about Doc?"

The warmth in Sara's face faded a bit. She inhaled through her nose before replying.

"Oh... he had a doctor for over twenty years. Thought she was the best he ever had and an even better person."

The car glided under a streetlamp washing Sara's face in soft gold.

"He adored her. When he moved three hours away, he kept her as his primary. Drove six hours up and back—it took the whole day."

Grace didn't speak, she listened, her face unreadable in the shadows.

"According to him, she had saved his life, and he would be a fool to change."

Sara's voice dropped, touched with reverence now.

"After all those years, she kept telling him to call her Leslie and he never would. Said he respected her too much and that she earned the title of doctor more than most."

A pause.

"She was always Doctor. Sometimes Doc. Never Leslie."

She sighed.

"She died of cancer. It's the only time I've ever seen him cry."

Sara's hands gripped the steering wheel tighter.

"And if you understand that, Gracie, then you begin to understand him."

CHAPTER FOURTEEN

Burn Notice

"Spying is like a game of chess: Sometimes you have to withdraw, sometimes you have to sacrifice one of your own pieces to win."
- John Rhys-Davies

Nikita Zakharov Condo Monday 0918 Hours R

The sedan pulled out from the underground garage beneath a luxury condo complex in Foggy Bottom. The black car gleamed in the morning sun, its diplomatic plates unmistakable. Behind it, a gray SUV with tinted windows idled at the curb, staffed by members of Cecil Brandon's surveillance team.

Inside, binoculars tracked every movement.

"Target moving," the driver said into a throat mic. "Embassy sedan confirmed. Zakharov at the wheel."

"Copy that," came the reply in his earpiece.

They didn't conceal themselves. That was the point.

The sedan turned down E Street, and after a block, the SUV made a visible turn, catching Zakharov's eye in the rearview mirror.

"Break off," came Cecil's command.

The SUV peeled away, turning down a side street and disappearing. Mission accomplished.

Washington, DC Wednesday, 07:12 AM

The cherry blossoms were starting to fall.

Nikita Zakharov sipped his bitter black coffee from a paper cup as he walked down Virginia Avenue. He kept his head low, sunglasses tight to his face, and his coat collar turned up against the breeze that carried a deceptive softness. Spring in Washington always smells like optimism.

Today, it smells like danger.

He'd spotted the first tail two days ago. The SUV making a turn down E Street, and after a block, the SUV made a visible turn, catching Zakharov's eye in the rearview mirror—just long enough. Then peeled away, turning down a side street and disappearing.

A man parked in a blue Ford Fusion near his apartment, pretending to sleep behind the wheel. The same car reappeared last night across from Safeway. Different driver. Same posture. Surveillance rotation.

Then there was the woman in the sunglasses—subtle, but she hesitated too long at intersections, never took a phone call, and didn't buy anything when she walked through the Walgreens behind him. She wasn't shopping. She was watching.

Nikita had worked enough counter-surveillance to recognize the tightening of the noose.

This morning confirmed it.

He'd left his apartment at 6:15 a.m. sharp, exited through the service stairwell, changed jackets three blocks away, and cut through a hotel lobby to the Metro. At every checkpoint—every reflection in a glass door, every glimpse in a security mirror—someone was there. New face. Same pattern.

They were good. Not clumsy enough to spook him into running but deliberate enough to let him know.

Which meant this wasn't only surveillance.

This was pressure.

Heat.

FBI? Perhaps. ACIC?

Nikita ducked into a copy shop on K Street, heart hammering. The girl behind the counter glanced up. He made his way to the rear hallway, where the security camera blinked red and the wireless router was ten years out of date. He pulled out the burner phone and texted a number he hadn't used in eighteen months. Used for emergency messages only.

"ACTIVE WATCH. MULTI-UNIT TAIL DEAD DROP COMPROMISED."

Yasenevo, Moscow - SVR Headquarters

Elimination Directive Директива по устранению

The fluorescent lights buzzed above the polished metal table. Beyond the bulletproof windows, the late Spring snow drifted down in lazy spirals over the empty courtyard, softening the brutalist lines of the compound—but inside, there was no softness. Only purpose.

Kir Smirnova entered the room without ceremony, his wool coat already damp with melted snow, the cold still clinging to his shoulders like the weight of decision. He nodded once at the man seated at the far end— Colonel Dimitri Orlov, GPU. With his slicked-back silver hair and sharp cheekbones, Orlov looked more like a chess grandmaster than a senior military man. Orlov was the handler of cutouts across three continents.

Kir sat, sliding a coded dossier across the table with "Palisades in Russian 'палисады'." on the cover.

"Nikita Zakharov reported surveillance," Kir said. "Tight. Professional. Likely FBI. Possibly Army Counterintelligence, though he doesn't think it's linked to Sable directly."

Orlov opened the Palisades folder, reading quickly. "What was he doing?"

"Dead drop at a Maryland Park. Changed batteries two days ago. No visual contact with Sable, and no other transmissions logged since late March."

Orlov frowned. "And Sable?"

"Still dark. As ordered. But there's more." Kir's voice dropped a register. Our handler for our swallow with a relationship with an HR staffer at LaserTech—sent word. Morgan is at LaserTech."

That got Orlov's full attention. "Will Morgan? Army Counterintelligence at LaserTech?"

Kir nodded. "He's embedded now. Covert team in place. He's popped up where we least want him."

Orlov's gaze lingered on the name in the report. "He's surgical. If he's got eyes on Zakharov, it's no coincidence. It's process. He's connecting dots."

Kir leaned forward. "If he flips Zakharov—"

"He won't," Orlov interrupted. "We can't let him."

Silence stretched between them. The air in the room felt colder, heavier. The knowledge that Palisades was a top priority, and failure was at the very least a career ender and perhaps much worse was foremost on their minds.

"We have two options: move him, or silence him," said Kir.

Across from him, Orlov lit a cigarette, his tone almost casual. "Exfiltration preserves the asset. Moscow will ask why he wasn't protected."

Kir's jaw tightened. "Exfil means movement—cars, manifests, signatures. He's sloppy. A playboy. Too many women, too many eyes on him. One checkpoint, one tail, and every cutout in this city unravels."

Orlov exhaled smoke, eyes narrowing. "And if we kill him, we burn capital. He was still useful."

"Useful doesn't matter if he's compromised. A body we can return under Vienna Convention—sealed, diplomatic, untouchable. An extraction? That's a parade of vulnerabilities. Do you want the Americans inside our network because one man couldn't keep his trousers shut?"

Orlov tapped ash into the tray, then nodded slowly. You've weighed it, then."

Kir's reply was measured, devoid of hesitation. "I have. And I'd rather lose one pawn cleanly than the whole board in fire."

The silence that followed was thick, final. Orlov stubbed out the cigarette and pushed back from the table. "Then it's decided."

Kir sat a moment longer, staring at the empty chair where Zakharov should have been. His voice was low, more thought than speech.

"Better a coffin than a trail."

Orlov set the file aside. "Make it clean. Natural cause, suicide or accidental. No bullets. No trails. Moscow Protocol."

Kir pulled a small secure tablet from his coat, tapped a command sequence, and opened a scrambled link. A screen blinked on—a field controller in St. Petersburg. Kir's voice was calm, clinical.

"Operatsiya Nabat. Target: Nikita Zakharov. Location presumed within the D.C. perimeter. Execute within seventy-two hours. Authorization code: Smirnova–Viktor–Delta–Zima."

"Understood," came the reply. No questions. No hesitation.

Kir killed the feed.

Orlov stood, smoothing the front of his suit jacket. "There's no joy in this work, Kir. Only necessity."

Kir stood with him. "Joy is for civilians."

As they left the room, Kir glanced once more at the snow outside. It was always quiet before something fell. The Americans were closing in—he could sense it.

But they weren't going to get Zakharov.

Not alive.

Moscow - Smirnova's Apartment – 2000 Hours C

The muted clatter of silverware and the scent of roast duck filled the apartment. From the living room window, golden-orange light spilled in from the low sun slanting over the rooftops of Akademichesky District. Kir Smirnova sat at the table, half-listening to the laughter of his ten-year-old son playing on the carpet with a model MiG-35. His wife, Elena, moved quietly in the kitchen, humming to herself, unaware that his wineglass had gone untouched for the better part of an hour.

His mind was elsewhere—in Maryland, on LaserTech, on Will Morgan.

Kir stared at the linen napkin beside his plate, folding and unfolding it between his fingers, as if the motion might unravel the tightening coil in his chest. Operation Palisades had always carried risk, but now... now it bordered on reckless. He had read the ACIC dispatch logs this morning—redacted, scrubbed, but telling. Morgan's team had embedded faster than expected, and worse, had already begun probing into Lynx's workstream. Too close.

He had never failed. Not once. In twenty-one years, his record was surgically clean—precise, competent, unblemished. His rise through the SVR Directorate S had been methodical, fueled by performance and an ironclad instinct for minimizing risk. From Budapest to Copenhagen, then Riyadh—every operation he ran came in under radar, under budget, and under scrutiny. Even Berlin. Especially Berlin.

But if Operation Palisades collapsed—if Lynx was burned, or if Sable was compromised by these Americans—it would not simply be a red mark in his file. It would be a stain. A career ender, perhaps. Or worse. The kind of failure the Service didn't allow to linger in memory, or in Moscow.

Elena sat across from him now, her smile gentle. "You're thinking too hard again," she said, touching his wrist. "Don't let them live in your head when you're here."

He offered a faint smile, but it didn't reach his eyes. "It's a tight mission," he replied. "And it's gotten tighter."

She gave a knowing nod, not pressing. She'd long accepted that some parts of her husband's work would remain in shadow.

His son darted past the table, chasing the plastic jet through the air, shouting: "Papa! Look! Intercept complete!"

Kir chuckled despite himself, the sound hollow but real. Intercept complete… If only it were that simple.

The stakes had shifted. Will Morgan was not an analyst. He was a hunter. The Americans had sent a closer. That meant Washington believed LaserTech mattered more than even the SVR had guessed.

And it meant that Kir had no margin left.

Success would launch him—possibly to Brussels, or back into executive rotations. He could already envision the plaque. But failure? He looked again at his son, now sprawled on the rug making explosion noises with a grin too pure for this world.

Failure wasn't an option. Not for the Service. Not for his family.

Kir lifted the wineglass, took a long, deliberate sip, and nodded to himself.

Tomorrow, he will send the signal to Voron.

The game was accelerating. And he was not ready to lose.

114

❖ ❖ ❖

Washington. D.C. Foggy Bottom – Zakharov's Brownstone

The apartment sat on the second floor of a brownstone walk-up in Foggy Bottom, Washington, D.C.—an aging brick building nestled between diplomatic offices, anonymous contractors, and too many surveillance cameras. But none of them saw what happened that night.

The three men entered at 02:14.

No doors were forced. No alarms tripped. The lock was bypassed cleanly, and the building's camera feed rerouted to a decoy loop with ninety seconds of frozen footage..

Nikita Zakharov had been asleep, wrapped in a thin blanket on the pull-out sofa, his laptop still glowing beside him, a mug of half-drunk tea gone cold on the coffee table. He didn't scream. Didn't resist.

One man held him. The second administered the injection. The third opened the window to stage the scene.

Potassium chloride—clean, fast, virtually undetectable without specific toxicology screening. His body seized once, violently, then slackened.

The lead operative surveyed the room. It was sparse—books, some scientific journals, a Faraday pouch on the desk, two phones. One encrypted. One burner.

There would be no suicide note. Only ambiguity.

They staged the scene with practiced ease. An open window. A bottle of vodka tipped beside the couch. A small cut on the forearm—postmortem—enough to confuse the timeline. No signs of struggle. No fingerprints. Another tragic end in the city of secrets.

By the time they exited, the fog had rolled in over the Potomac, blanketing the city in quiet. A Metro bus groaned down the block, and the only sound was distant traffic and the hum of air conditioners clinging to early spring.

At 09:10, a neighbor would call building maintenance about the sound of a television playing static all night. D.C. Metro PD would arrive, take statements, bag the body. No forced entry. No witnesses. No note.

Just a man—dead and alone.

Silenced.

Zakharov "Suicide"

Fort Meade - Morgan's Office

The tension inside Will Morgan's office was thicker than the morning's humidity. Will and Grace were mid-discussion when Sara Brandt rushed in, Derek trailing behind her.

On the television mounted playing on the Vibe, a breaking news headline scrolled by:

"Russian Diplomat Found Dead: Apparent Victim of Suicide. Nikita Zakharov, 45, a Diplomat for the Russian Federation Embassy, was found dead this morning at his District of Columbia home. His body was found in his bedroom an apparent victim of suicide."

Sara read it aloud, her voice edged with disbelief. The room fell into a heavy silence before Will spoke, voice tinged with bitter irony.

"We can't win for losing."

Grace covered her mouth with her hand. "Please tell me the CIA didn't do that, did they?"

Will shot her a dry look. "Geez Professor, this is reality not a movie script. Try to stay with us here on planet earth."

Sara cut in, voice sharp. "Russians don't come here to commit suicide."

Will's expression darkened. "No, they don't. To me, this is a rush job."

Sara's sarcasm lanced the tension.

"Like they didn't have the time to come up with something less suspicious. Did they bother to come up with a suicide note?"

Will crossed his arms, thinking. "Let's ask Ed to get all the gory details."

Grace's voice wavered with confusion. "Why would the Russians kill their own guy? Couldn't they have just sent him back to Russia?"

Will leaned back against his desk. "Lots of reasons that could have nothing to do with us, although the big rush makes that unlikely.

"Someone wanted him silenced forever, not only out of the way."

Grace held onto a shred of hope. "The autopsy should shed some light."

Will shook his head. "Autopsy? There is not going to be any autopsy."

Grace blinked in disbelief. "No autopsy?"

Sara answered for Will, voice cutting. "Diplomatic immunity. Right about now the Russian embassy is calling State asking for the body."

Will stared out the window, deep in thought.

"They're up to something."

Will Morgan's phone buzzed the display flashing Perry – ACIC. He answered on the second ring.

"Morgan."

Ed Perry's voice came low and clipped, the kind he used when the weight of Washington was already pressing down. "Will, heads up. DC Metro's flagged Zakharov's death as suspicious. Coroner says he was in good health—no underlying conditions."

Will's jaw tightened. "So, natural causes don't fly."

"Not with Metro. But here's the problem. The Russians invoked diplomatic immunity. They've denied permission for an autopsy. Vienna Convention gives them that right—body's inviolable."

Will leaned back in his chair, eyes narrowing. "And they've asked for the remains?"

"Demanded. Their embassy courier already filed the request. State is on the line with Moscow as we speak. You know how it goes: we respect it, so our people get the same protection abroad."

"Which means no toxicology, no post-mortem, no clean answers."

"Exactly. Officially, he's gone and the file gets sealed. Unofficially—we still have to assume he was silenced. Keep your team sharp. Moscow's playing their usual game: deny, deflect, retrieve the body before anyone asks the wrong questions."

The line went quiet for a beat. Will stared at the muted glow of the operations map on his wall.

"Understood. If they're pulling the body this fast, they're burying more than a man."

"That's my read too. Keep it tight, Will. I'll update when State caves to the handover."

The call ended. Will set the phone down slowly, his reflection in the black glass staring back like a challenge.

Washington, DC - The Russian Embassy

The Russian Federation invoked the Vienna clause and immediately processed the consul courier.

A gray rain slicked the streets of Massachusetts Avenue as the hearse pulled into the gated courtyard of the Russian Embassy. A row of uniformed DC Metro officers stood at the curb, their presence ceremonial; jurisdiction had already shifted. Behind them, a State Department liaison clutched a briefcase thick with paperwork, face pinched in discomfort.

Inside the embassy gates, two Russian security officers in dark overcoats waited, silent, posture rigid. The double-headed eagle on their lapel pins caught the light of the floodlamps.

The back doors of the hearse opened. Zakharov's body emerged sealed inside a diplomatic casket, brushed steel with crimson trim. No chain of evidence tags, no coroner's seal—only the stamped insignia of the Russian Federation affixed in wax.

The State Department officer cleared his throat and said, "By agreement under the Vienna Convention, Article 29, the remains are returned without examination. No further conditions stipulated."

One of the Russians produced a leather folio, signed the paperwork with a flourish, and slid it back without looking at the American. His accent was clipped. "Protocol satisfied. The Ambassador extends gratitude."

The casket was lifted onto a waiting embassy van, its windows blacked out, engine already running. Within moments it was gone, swallowed into the embassy compound where U.S. law had no reach.

The Metro sergeant muttered under his breath. "Suspicious death, no autopsy, and now no jurisdiction. Hell of a thing."

The State liaison closed the briefcase with a snap. "Welcome to diplomacy. They bury their man; we protect ours overseas. That's the bargain."

From across the street, an unmarked ACIC sedan idled, rain streaking its windshield. Inside, Cecil Brandon watched the embassy gates close. He reached for his phone—he knew Ed Perry and Will would be waiting for the update.

Zakharov's body was gone. And with it, the truth.

Yasenevo, Moscow - SVR Headquarters - 0000 Hours C

Inside a dim, wood-paneled study, the mood was ice-cold and clinical. Dimitri Orlov leaned over a low table, swirling a glass of vodka, speaking as if reading a report.

"Nikita was an unfortunate precaution. We couldn't afford to have him turned."

Across from him, a stern Kir Smirnova nodded.

"These Americans are no fools. They suspect something or they wouldn't have been following him."

Orlov's lips twitched in a humorless smile.

"Yes, we have run into them before — they are very good. But so are we."

He sipped his drink before setting it aside.

CHAPTER FIFTEEN

Maskirovka - The Art of Deception

"All warfare is based on deception. There is no place where espionage is not used. Offer the enemy bait to lure him."

- Sun Tzu

Yasenevo District, Moscow - SVR Headquarters

Operation Maskirovka

- Classification: Active Disinformation
- Protocol Origin: SVR / Spetsviaz
- Division Objective: Destabilize Western trust in institutional narratives by deploying targeted misinformation across media ecosystems.
- Methodology: Fabrication of plausible events, insertion into legitimate media channels, amplification via AI-managed botnets and sock puppet networks.

- Primary Tactic: Confuse, divide, and erode consensus reality without requiring factual acceptance—only doubt.

The operation was not a mere act of deception—it was an ecosystem of falsehood, a strategic fusion of Cyber intrusion, psychological manipulation, and narrative engineering. Born from Soviet-era doctrines and refined for the digital age, the operation's goal was not to convince the world of a lie, but to corrode the very idea of truth. It didn't need believers; it needed confusion. it weaponized ambiguity, turning a single fabricated incident—the alleged assassination of a Russian linguist—into a global crisis of confidence. By the time Western agencies realized what was happening, the damage wasn't in facts, but in faith.

Moscow, Underground Bunker

The outdated underground bunker pulsed with the hum of aging servers and fluorescent light. Colonel Kir Smirnova stood motionless before a monitor displaying a seemingly benign academic article:

"The Forgotten Death of Nikita Zakharov: A Linguist Caught in the Crosshairs of Paranoia."

He gave a nod to his aide, Ivan, who added the final flourish:

"…a reminder that surveillance states can't distinguish between real threats and innocent lives… until it's too late."

"Medium, Substack, Reddit," Kir ordered. "Burner distribution only. And queue the alt-left pipelines for the U.S."

The article was seeded with surgical precision—factual enough to evade immediate scrutiny, emotional enough to go viral. As Ivan hit send, Kir lit a cigarette. -

"Let them dig their own hole," he growled.

New York City - 42nd Street Public Library

A woman in her forties, dressed like an NYU grad student, slid into a dusty terminal beside a wall of microfiche drawers. She inserted a thumb drive with a trembling hand—well-practiced tremble, rehearsed.

The virtual OS booted in silence.

In seconds, auto-scheduled content dropped to a series of email tip-lines:

- editor@wapo.com
- sourcebox@npr.org
- opsec@theintercept.com

Attached: a dossier on Zakharov, complete with falsified employment history, voice print metadata, and a single blurry image from a Brussels hotel.

Subject line:

"Whistleblower or Target? The Unanswered Death of Nikita Zakharov."

She stood, wiped the keyboard clean with a napkin, and vanished into the city's gray morning.

Washington, D.C. – National Newsroom

Inside a bustling newsroom, a junior editor leaned closer to his screen, frowning at a flagged tip that had bypassed first-line filters.

A black-and-white headshot.

Foreign name.

Keywords: NSA, translator, civilian casualty.

"Hey, get Legal," he said with urgency. "Someone's throwing a grenade in our inbox."

Moscow Safehouse – Disinformation Hub

Inside a fortified SVR satellite station in Moscow's northeast sector, Operation Maskirovka unfolded like clockwork.

Digital signal traffic jumped 200% within 90 minutes. Sock puppet accounts activated in bulk. Human moderators injected carefully staged emotional arguments to keep threads alive. A fake subreddit reached front page.

Kir Smirnova stared at a dashboard of American hashtags lighting up like brushfires.

#JusticeForNikita
#ZakharovFiles
#WhoKilledZakharov

Cigarette in hand, he said, "Push phase two. Let Capitol Hill smell the blood."

Washington DC - Capitol Press Briefing Room

Senator Gregory Lane, suit crisp and voice grave, stepped to the podium.

"We are investigating potential abuses in classified programs, including whether an unarmed linguist was targeted."

Cameras snapped. Reporters surged forward.

"Is it true the NSA was involved?"

Lane paused—a fraction too long.

"We've received independent documentation. The American public deserves answers."

The press corps erupted.

Global - multi-node botnet operations

Operation Maskirovka's second wave deployed the Typhoon Doctrine—Russia's chaos-by-design strategy:
1. Saturate channels with contradictory narratives.
2. Humanize the supposed victim.
3. Fragment public consensus.

Rick leaned back in his chair, eyes on SYBIL's lattice as it pulsed with new traffic. He explained, "Six-oh-three, Kaliningrad. Encrypted bursts through Tor. Think of it like an onion—layers on layers, each hop stripping one, until you've got no idea where the core came from. Looks messy, but it's deliberate."

He tapped his keyboard, bringing up a grid of faces. "And here's the follow-up: sock puppets. Fake accounts—clean bios, pictures that don't exist, even hometown slang. GAN-generated faces, so real you'd swear you've seen them in a grocery line somewhere. Each one runs like a separate person, but it's just one hand pulling the strings."

Sara frowned at the grid. "And their purpose?"

Rick smirked. "Amplify a message, drown out dissent, bend the narrative. Same old game—just wearing better masks."

Posts varied:

By 10:45, an anonymous "EU memo" was leaked. Fabricated. Dressed in diplomatic tone. Implied Five Eyes had Zakharov tagged since 2021.

No one could verify it.

That was the point.

Europe, U.S., and Social Media Wildfire

TikTok conspiracy breakdowns. Podcasts hosted by former intelligence "whistleblowers." Academic YouTube explainers. Alt-right and progressive voices echoing the same outrage in different dialects.

In Austin, a podcast titled "American Black Bag Ops?" hit a million views in under seven hours. In Berlin, street graffiti of Zakharov's face appeared overnight.

No single narrative took hold.

Instead: a cloud of mistrust.

Was Zakharov CIA?

Was he a Russian defector?

Did he try to expose something inside the NSA?

It didn't matter which version you chose.

Only that you doubted your own.

Fort Meade - ACIC – Psychological Ops Wing

Sara Brandt stared at the screen. Twelve news cycles deep and counting.

"They're not saying we did it," she said, "They're saying someone did—and that we buried it."

Z stood behind her. "Belgian authorities are stonewalling. Zero cooperation."

"SYBIL?" she asked.

"Signal attribution confirms a Russian operation. Yekaterinburg servers. Typhoon Doctrine signature."

Sara looked at the trending map.

#ZakharovFiles had reached 29 countries.

"Don't counter it," she said. "Not yet."

"Why not?"

"Because if we try to kill it, we'll confirm it's alive."

Brussels, Archive Footage Room

Back in Belgium, investigators re-opened an old surveillance tape—grainy footage of a man entering a hotel. Another man follows. No one sees them leave.

Zakharov's body had never been recovered.
Officially, he died in an accident.
Unofficially, he'd been forgotten.
Now, his ghost was global.

Global Consciousness

By the end of the week:

- European Parliament opened inquiries.
- Amnesty International called for sanctions.
- U.S. media speculated on Fort Meade's "black budget ops."

No proof.
No evidence.
Only questions.
Thousands of them.
And that was all Russia needed.

CHAPTER SIXTEEN

Operation Razor Burn

"It is double pleasure to deceive the deceiver"
— *Niccolo Machiavelli*

Fort Meade - Watchtower Conference Room

The big screen glowed with the header CLASSIFIED // ACIC EYES ONLY. Beneath it, a bold line of text:
ACIC Counter-Disinformation Initiative

Sara Brandt stood at the front, remote in hand. Her voice was steady, deliberate.

"Here's what we're running. Primary objective: disrupt, redirect, and neutralize the Russian misinformation campaign surrounding Nikita Zakharov's death. They want to turn him into a martyr. We're not going to let that happen."

She clicked, and the doctrine filled the screen.

"Operational doctrine is simple: fracture the narrative. We don't just deny their story—we split it. We seed alternate versions, each one sharper, cleaner, more plausible. In the end, no one knows which account to believe. Their signal drowns in our noise."

Rick gave a dry half-smile. "Aye yah, controlled chaos."

Sara nodded. "Exactly. Blur the picture. Cloud the source. By the time Moscow figures out which way is up, the world's already moved on. That's how we win—one fractured story at a time."

She set down the remote, letting the silence carry the weight. "Questions?"

There were none.

Fort Meade – Signal Ops Room – 0041 Hours R

The room pulsed with low blue light, server towers clicking like sentries at attention. Wall-sized monitors blinked with cascading signal trees—bots, content farms, darknet memes—all feeding Russia's latest firestorm.

Grace stood at the central interface, eyes locked on the evolving disinformation network. Sara Brandt entered with two coffees and a sealed binder stamped: RAZOR BURN – ACIC SPECIAL AUTHORIZATION.

Referring to JoAnn Fallow, Director ACIC Misinformation Response, Sara said, "They greenlit it; Fallow's team is standing by."

Grace's voice was flat. "The GRU's stepping over SVR. They just dumped a new batch of threads—'NSA kill squad,' 'AI threat modeling,' even one suggesting Zakharov triggered a rogue quantum flag."

Sara skimmed the live chatter. "They're not strategizing. They're flailing."

Grace tapped the command display. "Good. That means we're just in time to bury them in their own fiction."

Fort Meade - Rick's Office

Inside the binder, Operation Razor Burn unfolded in phases: narrative infiltration, metadata weaponization, and influencer amplification.

"Five civilian amplifiers," Sara confirmed. "Two in Berlin, one Prague, two former contractors in the U.S. All insulated. All pre-cleared."

Rick had already seeded a staged whistleblower thread. Zakharov wouldn't be framed as a defector—but as an SVR asset killed by the GRU for getting too close to their biotech program.

"We flip their lie sideways," Rick said. "Turn it into betrayal inside their own walls."

Sara smiled. "We don't need to deny their story. We need to make it more believable that the Russians did it."

Metadata payload embedded. Script written. Fallow's voice came over the comms:

"Influencers are green. Drop scheduled. Mimicking panic leak through Ukrainian expat Discords. Saturation in 18 minutes."

"Inject the secondary rumor," Rick said. "Zakharov's project intersected unauthorized GRU experiments. Biotech vectors. No oversight."

Fallow: "Understood. Splitting the blame narrative."

Sara watched metrics shift in real time. Threads that had roared with certainty now fractured under the weight of a better story.

Sara's voice was cold as she read the dashboard: "Thread cohesion dropping. Sentiment divergence is rising. We turned their lie into a fight with itself."

Grace: "Phase Two?"

Sara: "Leak fragments of the SVR-GRU schism to Brazil, Kenya, India. Non-aligned zones. Let them watch Moscow turn on itself."

She raised her coffee like a toast.

"To confusion. The old weapon—with a sharper edge."

Moments later, the Razor Burn payload ignited across the net.

#ZakharovCoverup began trending—then twisted.

Now it wasn't the U.S. being blamed.

It was Russia eating its own.

LaserTech, Morgan's Office – Later That Night

The live broadcast blared across the screens. Will Morgan stood stiffly, eyes cold as steel, as Senator Lane fanned the flames on national television.

"Let's light it up our way," Will growled.

He accessed a restricted file:

OP RAZOR BURN – COUNTER DISINFORMATION INITIATIVE.

"Pull the Zakharov file," he ordered. "The real one. Let's give Comrade Smirnova something to choke on."

Grace leaned toward Sara. "Comrade who?"

Sara whispered back, "Kir Smirnova. SVR. Will's crossed swords with him before."

Arlington - Pentagon Secure Briefing – 0320 Hours R

The room was packed with every letter of the U.S. alphabet. NSA. CIA. DOJ. ACIC.

The Pentagon spokesman spoke without flourish.

"Zakharov was never a civilian linguist. GRU asset. Deep embedded. The 'mistaken identity' narrative was built on forged FOIA slips and AI-generated academic boilerplate."

Screens behind him blinked with forensic footage, metadata trails, surveillance timestamps. The digital fingerprints all traced back—to Russia.

"Facial vectoring confirms the NYPL terminal user," an NSA analyst added. "She's tied to Unit 4040. Spetsnaz Signals Division."

Sara interjected. "And the fake FBI file? Sloppy. They used 'фонарь' for 'lantern.' That's a literal translation. GRU slang would've used 'зеркало.' Mirror. It's off-code."

The room absorbed the detail like gospel.

The spokesman tapped the folder.

"Send this to Vice. Twitter. Podcasts. Everywhere Lane's aides get their morning coffee."

The exposé hit like a thunderclap:

"DEEPFAKES, DEAD MEN, AND DISINFORMATION: How Russia Almost Punk'd the Senate"

The net shuddered.

Hashtags mutated in real time:

Editorials reversed. Comment sections flipped. Networks issued soft corrections. The temperature in D.C. dropped ten degrees.

Washington, DC - Senator's Lane's Office

The office was a tomb of political ruin. Senator Lane sat slumped behind his massive mahogany desk, face pale, jaw tight. His aide entered, tablet in hand, tapping it nervously.

"Sir..." he said, his voice close to a whisper.

On the screen was the Vice exposé, already viral, already metastasizing.

Lane stared at it in disbelief. "We got played," he said.

The aide cleared his throat. "Do we cancel the hearing?"

Lane's face twisted into a rictus of rage.

Through gritted teeth he spat out, "We postpone. Quietly."

LaserTech – Will Morgan's Office

Will sat in the low hum of post-op silence. Operation Razor Burn had worked. No diplomatic fallout. No civilian trace. Effective confusion—and story supremacy.

SYBIL's interface blinked in the corner, her AI logic flawless in its pattern recognition. Across the screen:

Sentience. Surveillance. Sovereignty.

He allowed himself a rare smile.

"Checkmate," he whispered.

Ping.

Secure line. No sender.

Encrypted message:

"Nice move, Will. But we're not done. — K"

Morgan stared at the screen.

And then leaned forward.

Fort Meade, Watchtower Ops - 0920 Hours R

The morning light filtered through the privacy glass like an overexposed photograph. ceiling panel lights revealed the long row of secure workstations inside the operations enclave of Watchtower. Will Morgan's team had been unusually quiet this week—an eerie silence that always followed the restless classified upheaval that never made the news.

Sara Brandt stood outside the bullpen, arms crossed, watching the new girl drown in bandwidth. Cathy Wang, fresh from ACIC orientation, sat scrolling through Tier-3 intercept summaries and trying to take notes faster than her mind could absorb.

Sara gave her a moment. Then, with a half-smile, she strolled over.

"Hey, Cat," she said smiling. "You been briefed on the coffee rotation yet? It's the most cutthroat part of this job."

Cathy looked up, startled—then smiled. "I'll take my chances."

Sara leaned on the edge of Cathy's desk, glancing at the annotated files on her screen.

"You diving into the Zakharov case?"

"Yeah," Cathy said. "Trying to profile his 'double agent' work in Geneva—"

Sara stopped, blinked, and let out a laugh so dry it could sand wood.

"Okay. Time-out. Emergency teaching moment."

Cathy frowned. "That bad?"

"Worse. Walk."

Sara guided her into the secure break room. Coffee poured. Chairs claimed. Sara pointed a finger at her like a weary professor on her twentieth lecture of the week.

"You called Zakharov a double agent," Sara said. "Which is adorable. Wrong, but adorable."

Cathy groaned. "The press calls people double agents all the time—"

"   And the press calls everything 'unprecedented' too. Doesn't make it true."

Sara leaned back.

"So, rule one: a double agent has to start out as a *real* spy for one side first. Then they get flipped. Or pretend to. If you weren't a spy before, you're not a double. You're just a regular, garden-variety traitor."

Cathy winced. "Okay… that tracks."

"Good. Because Zakharov? Loyal Russian. He was Sable's handler. We were circling him, and Moscow iced him before we could flip him. 'Palisades'—their code name for our Radiant Sentry breach—mattered too much."

Cathy nodded, taking it in.

"Ames?" Sara continued. "Not a double. Traitor. Pollard? Traitor. Pitts? Nicholson? Traitors. The whole gang."

"What about that FBI tech in New York?"

"Still not a double. She was a spy. A traitor. If we'd caught her and flipped her? *Then* double. But she never got her merit badge."

Will's voice drifted in from the doorway.

" For the record," he said, "this distinction is important. Mislabel one, and people die."

Sara glanced over. "Thank you, Professor Doom."

Will ignored her. "You're learning fast, Cathy. Keep it up." Cathy blinked. "You think I belong here?"

Sara snorted. "Kid, if Will thinks you belong, that's basically sainthood. He trusts maybe four people on earth, and one of them is a dog he met once at an airfield."

Will folded his arms. "Two minutes in the room and you're roasting me?"

"You walked into it," Sara said, smiling.

Will gave a small, resigned nod. "Fair."

Sara turned back to Cathy. "Listen. Ask questions. Even the ones that scare you. Especially the ones that scare you."

Cathy nodded, feeling the weight shift from fear to resolve.

As they stood, Sara tapped the table.

"And write this down: double agents must be agents first. If you forget that, Will starts quoting doctrine at you."

Will deadpanned, "Only when people deserve it."

"See?" Sara said. "Terrifying."

The clock flipped to 0937.

Cathy straightened.

She finally felt like she was part of the room.

CHAPTER SEVENTEEN

Under Surveillance

Linthicum Heights, MD

It started small.

A Honda CR-V that turned onto the same block two mornings in a row. A reflection in the corner of a car window half a second too long. The slight shift of a silhouette in a mirror as Sara rounded the corner by her gym. Alone, each incident was nothing—random noise in the city's endless churn.

But they weren't alone.

Will Morgan had survived too many deployments, too many black-budget field ops to believe in coincidence. He felt it before he could articulate it—like the subtle presence of static in a radio signal. A shadow where there should be none.

On Monday morning, he paused as he stepped into the crosswalk across from his building in Alexandria. A rideshare car idled at the red light—white Toyota Highlander. The driver stared straight ahead, both hands on the wheel. But the rearview mirror was tilted wrong. It didn't show his own face. It showed Will.

By the time Will reached the opposite curb, the Highlander had pulled away.

He didn't mention it. Not yet.

Sara Brandt was built for suspicion. Since the day she joined the MICECP fifteen years ago, she'd trained herself to trust pattern breaks more than patterns themselves.

That Thursday evening, she ran her usual five-mile loop near the base. At the three-mile mark, at GORC Park, she caught a flash of motion behind her. A man, jogging behind her, same pace, thirty feet back. Could be nothing.

She veered abruptly into a baseball park.

The jogger didn't follow.

He stopped, pretending to retie his shoe.

Sara didn't stop. She jogged out the other end, cut through a dog park, and exited onto the parking lot.

That night, she called Will.

"I think we're being ghosted."

"I know," he mumbled. "I was waiting to see if you felt it too."

Odenton MD - Yoga Studio - Thursday

Grace Roberts prided herself on situational awareness, but she'd also spent years buried in classified white papers and orbital telemetry spreadsheets. She wasn't field. Not like Will. Not like Sara.

But even she spotted when the same woman showed up three times at her yoga studio in one week—and asked her name twice.

She mentioned it the next day.

Sara looked at Will. Will nodded.

"We're under," he said.

No panic. Just fact.

Grace swallowed. "All of us?"

"Yeah."

"Russians?" she asked.

"Illegals," Sara said. "We're not seeing official coverage. No diplomats. No consulate staff. These are NOC teams."

Will with serious tone in his voice, "It makes sense they will want to protect Sable."

"At a minimum they need to check us out to make sure we are not a threat to her in any way. Normally, if Kir discovered I was here they would simply go dark until we lost interest. "

"However, this project is far too critical so everything will be on the table."

Grace. "Everything, you mean,,,"

Will, "I mean everything. So, we need to be very careful."

Will leaned in. "We're going to do this according to protocol. No erratic movements. No panic buys. No blowing cover. We flip the script."

Will called Cecil. "Hey, we're under."

"Who?" asked Cecil.

"As far as I can tell Sara, Grace and me but I can't rule out Z or Rick or for that matter you." Replied Will.

"Where Linthicum or Fort Meade?"

"Could be both."

"Daylight, wake hours, tailored or 24/7?"

"Not sure but I think it's wake hours."

Cecil thought for a moment.

"OK, I'll put a team together right away, twelve ought to get us started until we know more. I'll be back later today."

Grace played it safe. She set a baited trap.

She invited the woman from yoga for coffee—neutral ground, busy café, controlled acoustics. She used all the techniques Sara had taught her: clean phone, burner app, indirect invites, call-backs that made her pause.

Over a latte, the woman dropped a tiny detail—something Grace had never told her.

"My sister teaches out in Denver too, what a coincidence!"

Grace had never mentioned Denver. Her cousin taught in Madison.

The woman was fishing. Building profile.

Grace nodded, smiled, and made a mental note.

She called Will. "Her name is 'Danielle Temple.' Her business card said she works PR for a startup in Bethesda. I ran the firm. No digital footprint. It doesn't exist."

Will exhaled. "She's illegal."

Will called a closed-door meeting. No phones. No laptops.

They'd identify the teams first. Then they'd watch the watchers.

Following the Followers

Glenn Burnie - Friday 0630 Hours R

Friday morning, Sara dressed in civilian grays—loose windbreaker, nondescript runners. She left her condo by the front entrance at 0630, walked two blocks, and stepped onto a Metrobus. Two stops later, she got off, ducked into a dry cleaner, and came out of the back dressed in athletic wear.

Then she jogged.

She took a modified route: five turns in under a minute. She ducked into a hotel lobby, circled through, exited out the service hallway. Behind her, through the rotating door reflection—movement.

She had a tail.

Will, meanwhile, rode his usual route into Fort Meade but ran a passive tag test. At two separate intersections, he adjusted his speed to create irregular spacing. Both times, the same white sedan adjusted as well.

At the parking deck, Will stepped out, turned casually, and took a high-res photo of the license plate reflection in the chrome bumper of a black Suburban.

He smiled.

"Gotcha."

Fort Meade- Watchtower Ops - Friday 0800 Hours R

Sara would lead foot surveillance reversals. Rick would monitor digital signals. Will would begin feeding them data—true but twisted. Decoy targets. Phantom meetings.

Let them chase ghosts.

Let them run hot, burn assets.

The game was on now.

A hunt, A war in the shadows.

The man who jogged behind Sara that Thursday evening had returned twice since—once during her grocery run at Wegmans and once parked down the street in a plumber's van that hadn't moved for three hours. He wasn't sloppy. But he wasn't top-tier SVR either. His surveillance discipline was sharp but loose enough to suggest inexperience or uncertainty.

Perfect.

"Name's probably fake," Sara said, clicking through a still shot of him from a lamppost camera, enhanced and filtered by Rick Huang's AI facial suite. "But gait analysis and earlobe markers match a guy we flagged two years ago in Prague. Codename back then was Koyla. Claimed to be a Bulgarian telecoms consultant."

Will looked at the file Rick projected onto the SCIF wall. "We need one of these bastards inside. If we turn Koyla, we start punching back."

They began subtly.

Rick launched a digital pressure campaign—an intentional cascade of digital alerts around Koyla's cover ID. His front business—pet supply import/export—was unexpectedly flagged by the Department of Agriculture. His credit card was cloned in Vegas. A parking ticket he never received became a court summons.

Rick ghosted into his phone through a traffic camera signal bounce and mirrored his Signal and Telegram messages. Nothing overtly incriminating. But the subtext was clear—Koyla was worried.

They left one final breadcrumb. One of Z's specialties: a perfectly forged but suspiciously worded internal Russian memo.

"Memo from 'GRU Moscow' to local NOC handlers," Rick explained. "We embedded it into a web server we know he scans."

It warned of a possible mole within the illegal network in D.C.

Koyla downloaded it.

Then his routine changed.

He stopped jogging. He shaved his beard. He left his condo at 3 a.m. and walked five miles to a bus depot.

Cecil saw it all from a rooftop two blocks away.

"He's sweating."

"Good," Will said. "Let's open the door."

They waited until Koyla was off-cycle—midweek, late morning, en route to a secondary safe house in Provinces Park. Alone. No surveillance on his six.

Will followed at a distance. Cecil closed from the front, dressed like a construction inspector in a DC waterworks vest.

At the foot of the alley, he blocked his path.

Koyla stopped. Hands half-raised. Calculating.

Will stepped out behind him.

"Relax, Koyla," he said, switching to Russian. "We're not here to arrest you. We're here to give you a way out."

Koyla's expression didn't change, but his pulse visible in his neck betrayed him. "I don't know who—"

"You're exposed. Your team's rattled. Your superiors think you're compromised."

Will handed him a folder. Inside: stills of him watching Sara. Footage of his handler meeting a suspected Chinese intermediary in Baltimore. The forged GRU memo.

Will leaned closer. "They're already planning your exit. Either in a black van or a closed casket. You know how this ends."

Koyla's lips pressed thin. A flicker of emotion passed through his eyes—not fear. Betrayal.

Will softened his voice. "You're not the first asset to be lied to. But you can be the one who survives it. Help us, and we will help you. Walk away clean. Start over."

Silence.

Then in a soft voice: "I need to think."

"You have 24 hours," Will said. "After that, we close the door."

He showed up 18 hours later.

Same alley. No disguise - a man who'd made a decision.

"I'll talk," he said. "But not here."

They took him to a blacked-out van, drove two hours to a secure house under a false FBI sting operation shell in College Park. Inside, Will debriefed him himself. Rick and Sara monitored from the command van, logging every tick of biometrics.

Koyla—real name: Alexei Pavlovich Morozov—talked for six hours straight.

SVR logistics. Drop sites. Signal codes. The identity of two other Illegals in the DC area. And one more thing: a name.

The name of a U.S. federal contractor who had been feeding intel to his handler for over two years.

143

Koyla was no longer a Russian asset.

He was theirs.

Officially, the flip didn't exist. His original identity would be terminated in the Russian registry. A new one was already being built.

And the war in the shadows tipped in their favor.

Fort Meade- Watchtower Ops

The name Koyla gave them came wrapped in shame.

Diana Cray. Senior systems engineer at Ganymede Systems, a high-science federal contractor based in Arlington. Cleared TS/SCI. Dual specialization: telemetry encryption and orbital satellite communications.

"She's been passing data for two years?" Grace said, stunned, skimming the decrypted transcript.

"On and off," Will replied, jaw clenched. "Low-level at first. Abstract specs. Then she got bolder. Targeting defense satcom protocols."

"Why?" Rick asked. "Money? Politics?"

Koyla had already answered that. Neither. Cray thought she was passing secrets to an EU-funded think tank focused on demilitarizing space. They'd hooked her early—flattering interviews, peer-reviewed 'collaboration papers,' then cash grants routed through a shell foundation. It had the illusion of academia.

But the 'think tank' was a Russian cut-out. Her handler was a man she'd only ever met once, in Brussels. SVR had worked her like a violin.

"She thought she was helping prevent conflict," Sara said. "Now she's a pawn starting one. The Russians call these useful idiots."

Will stood. "We're going to flip her. Then we're going to break the network feeding her."

Diana Cray lived alone in a minimalist condo in Crystal City, drove a navy-blue Mazda, and grocery-shopped every Thursday. No pets. No late-night habits. Lived in Lululemon. Always walked with ear buds in but rarely listened to music—Rick confirmed via spectrum analyzer; the line was dead. It was camouflage. She was always alert.

"We're not dealing with a fool," Cecil grumbled as they watched Cray reroute her walking path twice in ten blocks. "She's paranoid."

"She's also clean," Will said. "If we don't move carefully, she'll close down or go to ground."

They installed two pinhole cameras inside her condo HVAC vent—thermal and wide-angle. Nothing overtly damning yet. But one drawer in her bedroom nightstand was lined with lead mesh.

A Faraday pouch.

Inside it: a USB key shaped like a novelty giraffe.

Will didn't want a search warrant. He wanted a confession.

So, they built a rabbit hole.

Rick cloned Cray's Ganymede work laptop and inserted a false satellite data schematic—a fake targeting patch they called "Nyx Protocol." It looked real. It contained enough corrupted math to scream sabotage under the surface.

Cray found it on a shared drive two days later. She opened the file, saved it to her giraffe drive, and—hours later—left for her "gym."

Instead, she diverted to a Korean bakery in Fairfax. Switched bags with a man drinking oolong tea by the window. Gone in under four minutes.

The man was SVR. The bag contained the giraffe.

She was still in the dark.

They intercepted her on a Saturday morning run.

Cecil approached Cray in Lake Waterford Park just after dawn. Calm, casual, dressed in black Lycra.

"Diana," he said, falling into stride beside her. "Let's talk about giraffes."

Cray stopped running. Her face flushed, then drained.

Will arrived seconds later. No cuffs. No threats.

"We know what you did. We know you thought it was harmless. We also know who your contact is, where the data goes, and how badly you've been used."

Cray didn't deny it.

"I thought it was... research."

"It's not," Will said. "It's war."

They sat her down on a bench overlooking the lake. Sara let the silence stretch. Then she laid down the terms.

"You help us. Right now. Or your life ends today—not literally. But everything else? Your job. Your clearance. Your future."

Cray stared across the lake, hollow-eyed.

"What do I do?"

Within 48 hours, Cray sent a fresh drop—one they'd designed. The "Nyx Protocol" update, with a malicious payload embedded. It contained signal backdoors, malware triggers, and beacons Rick could trace.

Her SVR contact picked it up.

Within an hour, the malware pinged its destination: an FSB-accessible server farm in Kaluga Oblast.

They had their proof. Their pathway. Their backchannel.

And thanks to Cray, they also had a name. Her original recruiter—code-named Orlov—had a Stateside alias and was flying in next month.

"Let's set the table," Will said.

Sara cracked her knuckles. "And cook him alive."

❖❖❖

146

They didn't know his real name. Only the code name Zarya. He was in fact a Colonel in the GRU.

Dimitri Orlov. Architect of the Cray deception. Handler of cutouts across three continents. A "non-official cover" officer. No diplomatic immunity. No embassy ties. A ghost.

He was scheduled to arrive on a Delta flight from Geneva, routed through JFK and landing at DCA on a foggy Tuesday morning.

Cecil stood inside the airport's secure observation post, coffee going cold in his hand. Sara was stationed near the car rental kiosks. A team member monitored foot traffic near the escalators. Rick watched wireless traffic from Fort Meade.

No moves until they saw him.

Then—Cecile's voice crackled in the comms. "Target visual. South concourse, Gate 18. Camel-colored coat, no luggage."

Team member's voice followed. "Clean face. Just got a haircut. Looks like he moisturizes."

Orlov walked with the casual ease of someone who had nothing to hide. Slight limp in his left knee. A thin roll-a-board slung behind him like a businessperson late for a conference.

But he wasn't late. He was early.

And he wasn't here to pitch software.

He was here to clean up Diana Cray.

Cray was back at work. She wore the same glassy calm she'd had since the day of the run. The only sign she wasn't at ease was the small tremble in her hands when she typed.

Orlov reached out by burner phone that night. "Courier failure. I need to meet in person."

She responded, perfectly on script: "Next drop is physical only. I'll bring the drive."

147

The location was pre-chosen by Sara—a quiet, empty café in Foggy Bottom, halfway between the Russian Trade Office and nothing in particular. Neutral ground. Public, but sparse.

Diana wore a black pea coat and a silk scarf, every movement rehearsed. Will's team was in place long before she arrived.

Hidden mic in her bra clasp. GPS beacon in her watch. Ocular recording from contact lenses—experimental tech, courtesy of Rick. It worked like a GoPro for spies.

Orlov arrived five minutes late. Carried a copy of Foreign Affairs under one arm.

He ordered espresso. Sat without pleasantries.

"You look tired," he said in a soft accent—one of those smooth, unplaceable Russian-American blends that came from expensive private schools in Zürich.

"Long week."

He nodded. "Did you bring it?"

She placed the giraffe USB on the table between them.

"You didn't touch the files?"

"Of course not."

Orlov hesitated.

And in that moment of hesitation, Rick's whisper came through the comms. "He's scanning it. He's got a hidden reader embedded in his belt buckle."

Sara smiled from her position outside. "Cute. That's one way to get your hands dirty."

Orlov plugged the USB into a covert port disguised in his phone case. The malware payload activated instantly, pinging a beacon across several routers, finally bouncing off a Russian node in Omsk.

That was the moment Will was waiting for.

He nodded once.

And the café filled with bodies.

Two agents from Homeland Security closed in from the back. Another two from FBI Cyber walked in from the front, flashing badges. Orlov froze—not like a panicked man, but like a chess master realizing he'd been outmaneuvered three turns ago.

Diana stood slowly.

"I told you I was tired," she said. "I meant of lying."

Interrogation Room - Day 1 -Tuesday 0140 Hours R

They held Orlov in a secure SCIF under classified legal authority. No Miranda. No press. No charges. Just quiet conversations about options.

Facial recognition had identified him with his slicked-back silver hair and sharp cheekbones as Dimitri Orlov a Colonel in the Russian GPU.

He refused to speak for the first 48 hours. Then Rick fed him a data trail—fabricated satellite activity suggesting his failure had triggered a purge back home. Cray's betrayal. Koyla's defection. The crash of Cosmos 2576.

The Interrogation — 2 Days Later

Tuesday passed into Wednesday and Wednesday to Thursday.

Will and Z played their parts with metronomic discipline—sometimes looming in the chair opposite, sometimes scrolling through weather updates or sports scores, sometimes just sitting there, still as statues. Orlov matched them, at first. Shoulders square. Breathing even. A faint, defiant curl at the edge of his mouth.

But by the third day, the quiet had begun to eat at him. The fatigue showed first in his eyes, bloodshot and dry. Then on the way his hands shifted restlessly against the table, fighting the urge to scratch an itch or stretch his fingers. The silence carved him down minute by minute, the way water hollows stone.

Interrogation Room - Day 4 - Thursday 0140 Hours R

By the fourth day, Sara leaned forward from behind the glass.

"He's trying to calculate which version of reality we believe," she said. "We should force a choice."

Will nodded.

Z leaned in just enough to whisper as Will entered, "He's cracking. Not much, but it's there."

Will only nodded. They kept up the routine. No questions. No relief. The sound of phones buzzing. The scrape of a chair leg. Orlov left to stew in the vacuum.

He walked in carrying a thick folder, not with documents, but photos. Surveillance stills. Bank records. Satellite imagery. IP logs. Names.

He dropped it on the table with a thud.

"We're not here to play games, Orlov. We already know who you are. We want your network."

Orlov raised an eyebrow. "You're bluffing."

Will didn't blink. "Koyla flipped."

The Russian's composure cracked for half a second.

Will pulled out pictures slowly one-by-one placing each in front of him then left the room leaving the pictures.

Orlov sat there for the rest of the day with nothing to do but browse the pictures.

Interrogation Room - Day 5 - Friday 0300 Hours R

Will stepped into the interrogation room early in the morning with two cups of coffee and set one in front of a sleepy-eyed Orlov.

Orlov looked up, pale and calculating.

"What do you want?" he asked.

"Names," Will said. "Dates. Access points. Illegals under your direction. Flip for us, and we don't ship you back to Moscow in a crate marked diplomatic mail."

Orlov sat back. Smiled.

"You think you've won."

"No," Will replied. "I think you're the first domino. And your whole game is about to fall."

Will Morgan turned and left the room without another word.

They didn't call it torture.

It wasn't physical. There were no cold rooms, no blaring noise, no waterboarding.

But it was pressure. Expertly applied. Time-tested and precise.

Interrogation Room - Day 6 - Saturday 0110 Hours R

Orlov sat in a chair bolted to the floor of the interrogation room. No windows. The same single steel table. A carafe of water. The same mirrored wall that wasn't a mirror. He had memorized every scratch on the mirror and each dent in the table.

Will and Z entered. They didn't begin with questions. They began with silence.

Hours of it.

He and Z rotated through the chair opposite Orlov, sometimes watching him with flat eyes, sometimes scrolling lazily through their phones as though the man shackled to the table was no more interesting than a headline.

151

"Boss, did you see this?" Z muttered once, angling his screen toward Will. A score update. Will gave a grunt, a nod, then went back to scrolling. Neither spared Orlov a word.

The Russian stared back, chin high at first, the residue of swagger still clinging from the café. But the stillness pressed on him like weight. No questions, no frame to push against—only the quiet drip of minutes that made his skin itch. His composure held, but it was the brittle kind, the sort that cracks without warning.

The room had become its own weapon: a place where rhythm vanished, where ego found nothing to cling to.

The Interrogation — Seventh Day 0900 Hours R

It was on the seventh day that Sara walked in.

She didn't slam the door or posture the way the men had. She moved quietly, setting down a mug of tea, the steam curling gently between them. She didn't look at Orlov right away, only sat, folded her hands, and let the silence spool out a few more minutes.

When she spoke, her voice was soft, almost conversational. "Do you know what they'll do with you when we're done here?"

Orlov's eyes flickered—the smallest shift. His lips pressed together, but the silence wasn't as sharp as before.

She leaned forward slightly, tone still even. "They'll forget you. The service you bled for, the men you protected, the secrets you carried—they'll erase you. Just a footnote. A man who vanished. A name no one dares say out loud."

Orlov swallowed hard, the first real crack in days.

Sara didn't press. She let it hang, sipping her tea as if the conversation were already over.

Minutes ticked by before he rasped, voice hoarse from disuse. "They won't forget me."

She set the mug down, eyes locking with his. No triumph, no smile—just calm certainty. "They already have."

Seventh Day 1600 Hours R

Sara came back seven *hours later.*

"You're not going back to Moscow," she told him plainly. "If you're lucky, you'll get to live in an undisclosed location with a GPS anklet and an American name."

Orlov blinked. "I don't want protection."

"What do you want?"

He looked up at her, voice firm. "Revenge"

"Revenge?" Sara asked.

"I was caught in a failed operation due to other's incompetence. After my years of extraordinary service, I should never have been deemed expendable by political cowards. I should have been exchanged in a trade. I will destroy those who wrote me off. "

The fight drained from his posture in an instant. His shoulders slumped. The defiance bled away. And when he finally spoke again, it wasn't a declaration, but a confession.

"What do you want to know?"

Sara glanced toward the observation window, knowing Will and Z were listening. She didn't answer him right away. Instead, she reached for her tea, the steam curling between them once more.

"Let's start simple," she said.

Once he began to talk, it wasn't linear. It came in fragments—time zones, code names, patterns. Will's team had to piece it together like a Cold War crossword.

The Ukrainian-born line cook in Arlington who serviced a cleaning crew that swept the Pentagon. Left burner phones in the mop closet.

A pediatric nurse in Silver Spring. Single mother. Transmitted encrypted patient logs every Wednesday from a hospital network terminal, masked as a vaccine order report.

The married couple in Charlottesville posing as antique dealers. Their store, "Bygone Days," was a front for dead drops behind imported Russian samovars.

Each had been trained by Orlov himself in Europe. Each had a role: signal watcher, document smuggler, metadata courier, or asset spotter.

None had diplomatic cover. All were "illegals."

Fort Meade-Watchtower Ops - Saturday 0230 Hours R

Rick worked through the nights tracing Orlov's digital trail. Every USB drop, every burner signal, every ping across the mesh.

"There's a pattern," Rick murmured to himself. "Not random. This is tradecraft, not tech sloppiness."

He mapped the hits.

A software update on a contractor's phone that pinged twice in Reston before bouncing to Sofia.

A bookstore Wi-Fi exploit that rerouted secure White House staffer traffic through Moscow servers.

And then the masterstroke—Orlov's use of steganography: concealing operational data inside Instagram food photos posted from burner accounts in Philadelphia.

Lasagna posts weren't about lasagna.

Each revelation triggered parallel sting operations. Teams rolled up the pediatric nurse during her shift change. The cook was taken at his apartment over a pizza delivery order. The married couple tried to torch the antiques shop and flee south but were boxed in by a quiet operation along I-95.

Each take down revealed another thread.

The network wasn't just spying.

They were positioned to sabotage.

Power relays. Communication nodes. Water treatment protocols. Even satellite maintenance logs.

These weren't watchers. They were sleepers.

And Orlov had the keys to all of them.

CHAPTER EIGHTEEN

Protocol Tishina

"The saddest thing about betrayal is that it never comes from your enemies, it comes from those you trust the most."

Yasenevo, Moscow - SVR Headquarters - 0000 Hours C

Snow drifted past the ornate facade of the Sluzhba Vneshney Razvedki (SVR) headquarters the Russian Foreign Intelligence Service. Inside, the lights never dimmed, and the cold was not from weather, but purpose.

The moment Orlov's defection was confirmed, the directorate activated Protocol Tishina—the Silence Protocol.

The betrayal wasn't personal. It was systemic. And it was devastating.

Orlov had once been their sharpest scalpel. His network of illegals had burrowed through the American fabric for years. Now that scalpel was in American hands—and bleeding intel. Retaliation wasn't an option.

It was a necessity.

Within hours, encrypted messages were sent from dead letter drops in Belarus and Kaliningrad, carried by diplomatic pouch and mirrored through compromised embassies.

The directive was simple: Cleanse the network. Cut the exposed. Preempt the fallout.

Stateside, three things began happening simultaneously:

Illegals went dark.

Across Washington, San Francisco, Miami, embedded assets disappeared. Phones powered down, signal apps deleted, caches burned. One vanished from a yoga retreat in Sedona. Another slit his wrists in a Bethesda bathtub, leaving no note—only a flush-burned SIM card floating in bleach.

The courier chain collapsed.

Dead drops weren't just ignored—they were poisoned. Literal contamination: a trace compound in chalk lines burned the skin of anyone who touched them. It was a message. Don't pick up. Don't be next.

A mole hunt began—in reverse.

SVR's Directorate K—the counterintelligence branch— activated its own assets inside the U.S. intelligence community. Not to spy. To identify who turned Orlov.

Someone, they were certain, had whispered in his ear. An American asset or a Russian gone soft. That person now had a price on their head.

Two days later, Gene Larsson opened a padded envelope that had slipped past security at LaserTech.

Inside was a photo of her on her Saturday run. Taken from six feet away.

On the back, in Cyrillic, was a single word:

Вы следуете - You are being followed.

Yasenevo District, Moscow - SVR Headquarters - 0930 C

A closed session of SVR command reviewed the fallout.

Six assets compromised. Nine suspected. Four extraction teams in motion. Two journalists in Europe were marked for accidental death—in case they had been fed pieces.

And Orlov?

The name once invoked respect now drew only contempt.

They passed a sealed folder to a man known only as Koschei—a ghost in their ecosystem. Former Spetsnaz, special forces units of the Russian military's GRU (Main Intelligence Directorate). Now operating under deep cover in Western Europe.

The folder had three items:

A grainy photo of Orlov's new U.S. safehouse

Satellite coordinates

A single phrase:

"Return the traitor to the soil."

Fort Meade-Watchtower Ops

"Boss, they're not just coming for Orlov, they're trying to melt our whole op," said Rick.

"We've experienced multiple login attempts across the team's internal server—each laced with polymorphic malware using a mutation engine to alter its decryption routine or encryption keys every time it infects a system. Makes it look different each time. Makes it difficult for our signature-based detection methods to recognize and block it."

"How are they getting in?" asked Will.

"Something had piggybacked on a software update from a compromised contractor in Tallinn. Within minutes, the lab was air-gapped. Backups sealed. But it was close."

Sara said, "That's not all."

"Grace Roberts received a padded envelope with an image—herself mid-stride, her morning run near the Potomac. Beneath it, the message in Cyrillic—Вы следуете—You are being followed.

"Two days later, Gene Larsson opened a padded envelope somehow slipped past security at LaserTech. Inside was a photo of her on a Saturday run. Taken from six feet away. On the back, two words in Cyrillic "Вы следуете" You are being followed."

Rick didn't look up. "Five intrusion attempts in the last hour. All bounced through Danish telecom proxies. They're dirty. Custom payloads, AI-written code. It's not just fishing—they're targeting us."

"They've gone active," Sara said. "And they're getting sloppy. That picture wasn't tradecraft—it was a threat."

Will said, "It's active, not surveillance—it is targeting."

"Why do you say that?" asked Gracie," they aren't …watching someone?"

"Sure, they're trying to scare, intimidate and in Gene's case perhaps test.

"Surveillance and targeting sound the same, but they aren't.

"Surveillance is broad. It's background noise. It can be routine, passive, or long-term. Patterns of life.

"It's the cameras on every corner, the drone in the sky, the feed they archive so they know where someone goes, eats breakfast, who they meet, sit next to and what times they move. They learn who you are when no one's looking.

"Targeting is different. It's when they stop being passive. Its narrow. Designed to prepare for an outcome—arrest, recruitment, disruption, neutralization, or worse.

"Targeting means they've picked the moment, the weakness, the crack in the armor. Its identifying pressure points and setting conditions to act. It's not just knowing when you go to the gym—it's using that moment to plant the bug in your locker or the bullet in your head."

"So, surveillance maps the board. Targeting takes the piece." Said Gracie.

Will gave the faintest smile. "Exactly. And if you mix them up, you don't just lose the piece. You lose the game."

Rick leaned back. "Then we need to bait them."

Sara nodded. "A canary trap. Let's feed them a controlled leak. Something spicy enough to trigger a response—but fake enough to isolate their method."

Rick smiled for the first time in hours. "I've got just the thing. A fictitious comms audit from Will's office to the DARPA lead engineer—mentioning an unnamed Russian asset leaking specs from inside Roscosmos."

"Roscosmos, state corporation for space activities?" asked Cathy.

"Yes," said Rick, "this is sure to get attention."

Sara raised an eyebrow. "Make it look urgent. Flagged 'eyes only.' Watermark it with our own tracer."

"I'll bake in a quantum beacon," Rick said. "If they download or forward it, we'll know the device, the node, the subnet—hell, the coffee brand in their cupboard."

Sara tapped her nails once on the desk. "Good. Now where do we plant it?"

Gracie said, "Plant it on my machine. Let them come."

"I want surveillance overlap—triple. If they're watching her, they're watching the others. We need physical tails monitored and looped in real time." Said Sara

Will gave her the nod. "Already flagged Sara and Judd. Cecil's reactivating our side-channel audio trap in the elevator shafts. And we're putting a drone up over your condo."

She didn't flinch.

"Gracie, don't let them rattle you," Will added.

"Oh, they haven't," she said. "But I want them to think they did."

Odenton, MD 0725 Hours R

Grace had her mission—implicating a high-ranking engineer in Roscosmos.

At night, Grace drove to her regular Food Lion grocery store in Odenton, picked up only a single bag of arugula and a copy of The Atlantic, then walked outside to the Dunkin's where she used the reflection of the window to spot the white Ford SUV idling behind her.

She took her time.

Then, she moved down the street—past a Mamma Roma's restaurant with CCTV—and entered a building through the Great Clips entrance and exited through the rear into an alley, vanishing from the tail's line of sight.

In the rear alley Grace removed from her pocket a slim copper pouch and clenched the burner phone—a matte-black slab with no markings and a fingerprint-smudged screen. Inside: a MediaTek Dimensity 9400+ chip, powerful, stealth-optimized, and featuring extended-range Bluetooth 5 capable of point-to-point relay across several miles.

Inside: a fictitious dossier implicating a high-ranking engineer in Roscosmos. The specs for a classified satellite propulsion system—fabricated, but convincing enough to create panic.

A moment later, she tapped "Share", scrolls to Bluetooth, and selects a paired device:

PERSEUS LENS

The moment she tapped "Send," the phone screen went blank for 1.2 seconds—normal behavior for this configuration. The encrypted document is now airborne.

Two miles away, a rusted open utility hatch sits half-concealed under vines. But behind its corroded faceplate lives a whispering machine.

Inside: a passive relay node, codenamed PERSEUS LENS, fabricated to look like old weather instrumentation but built with mil-spec internals, a small solar array, and a directional antenna system.

The relay receives the Bluetooth burst—authenticated by a rolling one-time pairing key tied to Grace's device and the pre-approved time window.

No storage. No logs. No memory.

Just a high-speed L-band signal burst fired upward to a low Earth geosynchronous satellite—leased under the guise of "Occasional Use" by a ACIC shell company in Panama.

She dropped the USB behind a gas pipe as they told her. The bait was planted. Panic would do the rest.

Then she turned and disappeared muttering, "Time to return the favor."

The burner phone was already back in its pouch when Gracie headed back to the Dunkin's, stepped inside, bought a muffin and coffee and headed home.

Fort Meade - Handshake confirmed

Back at Fort Meade, Rick Wang sat hunched at his workstation. His eyes flicked between monitors and a paper cup of stale tea, but he was waiting for only one thing.

It came as no sound, no flash— a blink.

A photon, one of a paired set, shifted its state—imperceptible to anyone but Rick's TAO custom-built receiver.

He didn't smile.

He spoke into the throat mic: "Handshake confirmed. She's in. Coordinate lock acquired."

If the file made it into GRU hands, it would trigger a mole hunt. It was the trap.

Grace knew what Rick's signal meant.

She wasn't alone anymore.

Fort Meade - Watchtower Conference Room

The team gathered in the secure conference room. Grace unrolled the printed IP trace. Rick layered it with traffic data and drone footage from Grace's condo.

Will stared at it.

"That phone's not a watcher," he said. "It's a handler."

"Which means…" Grace started.

"…the surveillance teams are reporting up. Illegals. Still operational."

She looked at the photo again—herself running in the open.

The SVR had made their move.

Now it was her turn.

Grace sent out a signal through an unencrypted channel on an old device the SVR had compromised last year. It was a decoy now—a shiny object.

The message was simple: "Private briefing materials from Morgan safe pending move. Will leave at usual drop."

Nothing real.

But real enough to draw a shark.

Tuesday morning, Grace left her condo wearing a lemon-colored windbreaker, sunglasses on, earbuds in and headed to Friendship Park.

When she pulled into the parking lot her ghost pulled past her and parked on the far side of the lot. She saw him in the car door window with a faded Orioles cap. Blue zip-up. Hands in pockets.

She walked briskly to Aircraft Observation area where Will and Cecil were watching planes take off. At the base of a fence post she discarded an empty soda can with an encrypted USB drive. Inside, the schematics of fictional classified weapons and a mock memo about enhanced DARPA collaboration.

She left and passed her ghost, coming in the opposite direction. She had to resist the temptation to turn around.

He stopped at the post, turned to make sure she was out of sight and picked up the soda can.

Will, now behind him said in perfect, unaccented Russian, "Ты проиграл. You're blown."

He blinked—shocked he'd spoken his language. Even more shocked when he saw Cecil, sidearm drawn but low. Will added one last line as they cuffed him: "Tell Kir I said hello."

Back in the command center, Grace tossed her jacket on the chair and grabbed a seltzer from the fridge. Will smiled at her.

"Gene walked in, holding a flash drive. "We ran his phone. Burner SIM. But we got images. Not only of you. He's been filming Grace and Rick too."

Grace popped the seltzer, took a long sip.

"Then it's not surveillance."

Will met her eyes.

"It's targeting."

Fort Meade Interrogation Room

They didn't use the basement.

That was for the movies—pipes dripping, bare bulbs swinging. No, Fort Meade had a better place. A clean room—soundproofed, temperature-regulated, with neutral paint and soft lighting designed to disarm rather than intimidate.

The man with many passports, this one—Mikhail Antonovich Razin sat at the stainless-steel table. His wrists were cuffed to a stainless-steel loop bolted to the floor. Not too tight. Just snug enough to remind him he wasn't going anywhere.

He hadn't spoken for two hours.

Grace stood behind the glass, arms crossed. "You sure you want her doing this first round?"

Will answered without looking up from the dossier in his lap. "You know Sara. She's not asking permission."

Sara entered the room without a file. No notes. Just a bottle of water.

Razin looked up, dark eyes registering her without flinching.

Sara sat. She didn't speak at first. She unscrewed the water cap, sipped, and set it down precisely in front of him.

He didn't touch it.

"You know what I admire about your kind?" she said after a moment, casual.

He blinked.

"You adapt. Most people don't. They cling to their mother tongue. You? I've seen the footage. You speak better English than I do. Accent-perfect. Regional idioms. Very Pittsburgh."

Still no reply.

"But here's the thing: You people work so hard to pass you forget to protect. Your encryption protocols are garbage. You're two generations behind. Your dead drops are mapped. Your handlers' names are on our phones already. You were a ghost, Mikhail. Now you're a mirror. And we're reading everything."

His mouth twitched.

Sara leaned forward, elbows on the table. Her tone turned surgical.

"We don't need you. That's what you need to understand. We got you after the network folded. Orlov sang. Your own man. He gave us codenames, nodes, handoff procedures, Dropbox passwords. You were the confirmation."

The words landed. His pupils shifted.

Sara tapped the table once. "But here's your lucky day. See, Moscow doesn't know we have you. Not yet. And if I were you? I'd keep it that way."

She slid a single photograph across the table.

His daughter.

Eight years old. Ballet recital.

"We know she's not in the system. You kept her off-grid. Smart. But your wife had a smartphone. Took this. Uploaded it to a dummy Facebook profile in Richmond. You used it to build your cover ID as 'Michael Radcliffe.' You liked a few photos. Replied to a couple of them. We traced the network."

His breathing changed.

Sara didn't smile.

"Now here's the deal, Mikhail. You talk—now—and we keep you useful. A channel. A ghost. You tell us who's left in your cell. Who's assigned to Grace. Who's in the DC Embassy we haven't mapped yet."

He finally spoke, voice rough.

"You'll send me back."

"No," she said. "We'll send them after you. If you lie. But if you talk... you'll stay right here. With a pulse. Under a new name. Probably teaching code at a state college in the Midwest. Your daughter gets piano lessons. Your wife keeps her job at the dental clinic."

He stared at her.

Then down at the photo.

Will turned to Grace. "That kid's the hook."

166

Grace nodded. "He's starting to break. We give him twenty minutes. Let it sink."

"Then Judd goes in?"

"No," she said. "Then you do. He's scared of you."

Will raised an eyebrow. "Why?"

"Because you haven't spoken yet. And he doesn't know what kind of man stays that quiet."

"Sparrow"

Fort Meade Interrogation Room

Two chairs. One occupant.

Sparrow sat with perfect posture, hands cuffed in front of her, eyes forward. Her face was unreadable—no fear, no fatigue. She looked like someone waiting for a train she already knew would arrive late.

Sara Brandt stepped in with a file folder tucked beneath her arm. Will stood behind the one-way glass, watching, saying nothing.

Sara tossed the file onto the table and sat across from the woman.

"Your name is Anastasia Burakova. But you've used at least seven aliases in the past ten years—four of them during this operation alone."

Sparrow didn't blink.

"You've been embedded in the U.S. since 2011. First in San Diego. Then Baltimore. Then here. Quiet, clean, reliable. Until now."

Silence.

Sara smiled—thin, professional, without warmth.

"I know you were watching Grace Roberts. I know your handler's dead, courtesy of your former comrade Orlov, who flipped last week."

A flicker. The edge of a breath caught in SPARROW's throat.

Sara leaned forward. "So, here's the problem. You've got two choices. You can sit in this room until you're transferred to a black site in Poland where they'll make your bones into soup stock. Or—"

"I want a lawyer," Sparrow said in near-perfect English, tinged with a Russian husk.

Sara smirked. "Cute. You're not on U.S. books. No visa, no passport, no country. You're an illegal combatant, sweetheart. The Geneva Conventions don't even know you exist."

Still, the woman didn't flinch.

Sara stood. Walked slowly behind her.

"You know what really interests me? You didn't run. Not after Orlov defected. Not after Mikhail—your field contact—gave us your cell structure. You stayed. Why?"

The silence broke.

"I follow orders."

Sara stopped. "And those orders were to watch Grace Roberts."

"Yes."

"To what end?"

"Unknown. I was to log her daily movements, personal habits, circle of contacts, and vulnerabilities."

"Why her?"

Sparrow turned her head. "Because someone in Moscow believes she comprehends more than she realizes."

Sara's brow furrowed.

"More about what?"

There was a pause. Sparrow tilted her head back and said:

"LaserTech. Project Palisade. And the man codenamed Sable."

Behind the glass, Will exhaled hard. The name they knew to be our double agent —Sable—had surfaced in an unexpected place.

Sara pressed in, quiet but sharp.

Fort Meade Watchtower Ops—1435 Hours R

Back in the operations center, Will looked over Katrina's transcript.

"She gave us Sable," he said. "Or at least tied Gene to her."

Sara rubbed her eyes. "But she's playing long game. She wants us to focus on Gene now. It's too clean."

Rick joined them, holding a tablet. "Orlov's files unlocked. There's something worse."

He handed the screen to Will.

A message. Intercepted two days before Sparrow's capture. Moscow Center to remaining deep cover assets.

'Sable has been compromised. Clean up begins now. Use the blackbird protocol.'

Sara's blood ran cold. "Blackbird means burn the whole net."

Will nodded. "They're tying off loose ends."

"And we just became one of them."

Will glanced at Cecil - he knew the look. The same hard stare they gave each other in Kandahar when the rooftop snipers started painting targets without a shot fired. The kind of look that said, we're being watched—no, we're being sized for burial.

What Sara's watcher meant. It wasn't about surveillance anymore. It was preparation.

In the SCIF beneath the secure facility at Fort Meade, Will stood before the board, sleeves rolled up, tie off. The air hinted of toner and cold sweat.

He pointed to the digital map of the DMV area. A red perimeter formed a loose triangle: Bethesda, Foggy Bottom, Alexandria.

"They're not watching us to gather intelligence," he said. "They're clocking exit routes, reaction times, vulnerabilities. This is kill team prep. Textbook SVR liquidation grid."

Sara leaned forward, eyes flint-hard. "They've activated the illegals."

Rick added, "Three of their phones beaconed near Grace's building and mine. And two near your place, Will. This isn't pattern-of-life collection. It's dry runs."

Will nodded. "Then we take the leash and yank."

Somewhere Unknown

Cecil Brandon had worked espionage long enough to stop being surprised—but even he had to admit, what happened at LaserTech was unprecedented. In all his years in the field, he'd never seen such a concentrated storm of foreign interest directed at a single target. LaserTech had the outward appearance of a tight ship—high-end biometric checkpoints, man-trap vestibules, surveillance redundancies, rotating badge schemas. The place looked airtight.

Which meant the points of failure had to be on the inside. The hiring.

He'd seen it too many times. Moles, sleepers, and traitors didn't come in one shape or color. They were American, European, Latin American, Asian—every accent and ancestry you could imagine. Will Morgan once told him over eighty countries were actively spying on the U.S.—not just the usual suspects, either. Israel, Mexico, Taiwan, even EU allies ran offensive collection inside American borders. A recent CNN segment had floated the number: one hundred thousand foreign agents working inside the United States.

China worried him the most.

Over a quarter-million Chinese nationals were enrolled in U.S. universities, the majority in STEM fields. Around half of master's students—and more than three-quarters of PhD graduates—stayed long-term. They filled labs, internships, think tanks, and, eventually, roles inside critical tech firms. Many never intended to spy—but it didn't matter. Sooner or later, most of them came under pressure. Beijing didn't make a distinction between military and commercial espionage. China wanted it all.

Some DARPA contractors had entire research divisions stacked with Chinese nationals holding green cards. No one blinked. No one paused to ask if it might be a problem.

The Russians were different.

More precise. More deliberate. They didn't cast a wide net, they hunted. Their appetite focused on military tech and dual-use systems. For them, DARPA was the crown jewel. But the true threat with Russian operatives wasn't the hardware they stole, it was how invisible they were. Russian illegals didn't stumble. They spoke fluent English. Wore L.L. Bean. Barbecued on the Fourth of July. They lived here for years as perfect ghosts, melting into suburbia, until the day came to act. You never saw them coming.

So, when the Bravo case hit Cecil's desk—a high-value subject possibly linked to a Russian sleeper network and internal sabotage—he didn't flinch.

His orders were clear: initiate full-motion surveillance. Run condo coverage with rolling teams. Rotate tails on late-night vehicle traffic. Track jogging routes. Get audio into the café umbrellas. Make it clean. Make it invisible.

It was a daunting task. But Cecil trusted his people.

They were up against professionals, sure. But so were they.

He had Will Morgan's crew—sharp, creative, borderline obsessive. —and behind them, the bottomless toolbox of the NSA.

They won't know we're watching.

But we'll be there. Every second. Every breath.

And when they move?

We'll be ready.

He wouldn't say it out loud, but deep down, Cecil felt it:

They were going to crack this.

CHAPTER NINETEEN

Blackbird Protocol

Fort Meade - Watchtower Operations

Operation Iron Echo—a counter-intelligence net designed to bait and expose the SVR execution team.

Phase One:.

Sara authored a memo suggesting Orlov had given up six deep-cover SVR operatives in the U.S.—code-named Koyla, Nadya, Viktor, Serpent, Birch, and Helix. Rick planted the document on a burner laptop wired into a public Wi-Fi node at Union Station. The SVR's digital rats would sniff it out in under an hour.

They did.

Two hours later, a man in a brown jacket snapped photos of Grace walking into the DoD cafeteria. Sara ran facial recog—hit on an "Alan Petrov," a supposed Czech energy analyst flagged once in Belgium for brushing shoulders with a GRU colonel.

Sara and Rick faked an argument in a public food court. Sara "stormed out" with a flash drive labeled "Orlov Deposition / Classified - For Will ONLY." Three teams followed her. One was a fake cleaning crew that hadn't emptied a trash can in 40 minutes.

Perfect.

Public Concourse – Union Station – 2015 Hours R

SYBIL had flagged Petrov on entry.

Cecil on comms, low, said, "Petrov's signal just bounced off a device registered to a St. Petersburg shell. Same MAC as Brussels 2022."

Talia Moreno, Cecil's, urban tailing specialist said, "Same guy who lingered outside the EEAS cybersecurity wing with a sandwich and no phone? That one?"

"Marcus "Shiv" Kwan, Cecil's Technical surveillance, facial recognition optimization expert said, "Standby. Sara's triggering phase two."

Sara stood, casually brushing crumbs from her coat. As she passed the trash bin, she slid a small red-capped thumb drive into the tote's outer pocket—purposefully visible. Petrov's gaze flicked once. Then again.

She walked slowly past the escalators, weaving between travelers, giving Petrov plenty of opportunity to fall in behind.

Will approached from the opposite side—coffee in one hand, phone in the other.

Sara and Will "bumped" at a public crosswalk inside the station.

Sara with a small smile said, "You're late."

Will casually taking the tote. "Blame the Commander. He talks more than I do."

He adjusted the tote on his shoulder, making sure the thumb drive flashed into view.

Surveillance Feed – ACIC Mobile Command Van

Cecil watching camera feeds said, "Hook set. Petrov's trailing Will now."

Marcus "Shiv" Kwan, Cecil's technical surveillance specialist analyzing. "Facial heat signature confirms fixation. He took a picture—frame 722, front lens bounce."

Cecil said, "Then let's make sure that picture reaches Moscow."

North Capitol Street – 2043 Hours R

Will entered a rideshare and let the tote rest beside him, thumb drive exposed. The car pulled away slowly.

Behind them, Petrov followed on foot, phone at his side, already sending. His trail car swung over quickly to pick him up.

Will, soft, in earpiece, "Iron Echo is live."

GORC Park Odenton, Maryland 2345 Hours R

After three hours of a surveillance detection route to maintain credibility, Will walked into GORC Park alone. No security detail. Just a bomber jacket, a baseball cap, and a walkie clipped inside his sleeve.

The bait: a backpack supposedly containing a full SVR penetration list—locations, names, drop points.

He sat on a bench and waited.

Ten minutes in—movement. Two men approaching from opposite directions, casual but coordinated. One passed behind, the other circled front.

Fifteen minutes later two more emerged from the woods in staggered intervals, just outside flashlight range.

Will kept still.

An FBI Hostage Rescue Team hid in the shadows nearby. Considered one of the most elite tactical units within the FBI and U.S. law enforcement, HRT is designed to provide a rapid response to high-risk incidents including high-risk arrests, and surveillance operations. HRT operators are trained in special skills, including fast-roping, parachuting, marksmanship, breaching, and close-quarter tactics.

Then he whispered into his sleeve: "We're good. Set it off."

A second later, four bright white beams snapped on from hidden drones above. The woods lit up like a stage.

"NOW."

Dozens of footsteps hit the ground. Twelve FBI HRT agents, and one Special Agent with a shotgun and Cecil came storming in from concealed perimeters.

The kill team didn't run.

They drew weapons.

Two went down in the first volley.

One tried to shoot Will. Cecil's slug caught him in center mass before he could finish the trigger pull.

The last two were cuffed and on their knees in sixty seconds.

Will spotted Cecil trying to sneak away, "Hey, what the hell is an old fart like you doing here…trying to get yourself, killed?"

Cecil with his ever-ready smile larger than usual replied with glee, "Margie reminded me how clumsy you can be and that your godchildren would never let me forget it if something happened to your sorry ass."

Will turned to acknowledge some of the HRT guys and when he turned back around Cecil was gone. He mumbled to himself, "I hate it when he leaves and never says goodbye."

❖ ❖ ❖

Fort Meade – Watchtower Ops

Back at Fort Meade, Will watched the interrogation feed. One of the captured operatives, soaked in blood and silence, refused to speak. The other—Serpent—cracked first.

"Orlov betrayed Moscow," he said in clipped English. "Now we balance the scale."

"How many more of you?" Will asked through the mic.

Serpent didn't answer.

Rick looked up from his monitor. "There's chatter on the darknet. SVR burned four of their own safe houses. They're cutting the tail. Going underground."

Rick added, "And they know we're not merely watching anymore."

Sara stood at the doorway, arms crossed. "So, what now?"

Will replied without turning: "Now we turn the hunters into ghosts."

Fort Meade - Outside Interrogation Room - 0215 Hours R

Cecil and Gracie sat in silence on a bench outside the interrogation room, the adrenalin leaving their bodies with the bone-weary residue of sheer exhaustion.

Gracie broke the silence.

"I heard what happened out there. I think I am still shaking.

"Nobody talks about it, but I sense you and Will have some sort of special bond."

"We go back a long way. From Bosnia to Baghdad, it's hard to explain the bond formed in combat. Lives depend on one another.

"The only thing in the world that matters in the field is not letting your unit down.

"We can say the words to describe it but unless you have experienced it you can't really understand at an emotional level.."

Gracie nodded.

"I didn't know he was in combat."

Cecil looked at her a bit surprised.

"Gracie, may I call you Gracie…

Grace interrupted, "You've certainly earned it tonight. Please do."

Cecil continued.

"We weren't on the front lines or anything, but we were in the combat zone. Our job was to root out corruption, black markets stuff. Believe me, over there they would just as soon shoot you as to explain."

"I guess you know he not only respects you, but just like Sara," said Gracie, "he loves you though he would never admit it."

Cecil chuckled, a welcome moment of levity in an altogether far too serious day.

"Gracie, you're made of the stuff he values, A blind man could see it. We're all glad you're here."

CHAPTER TWENTY

Disaster All Around

Yasenevo District, Moscow - SVR HQ - 0950 Hours C

Dim light. Stark walls. Surveillance gear hums in the background. A digital map of Washington, DC glows across a wide display, tracking recent ACIC sweeps and take downs.

Major Kir Smirnova, stands over a steel table, scanning through a decrypted dossier. His voice is quiet but commands the room.

Will's team uncovered Fidel Francis, a useful idiot, and his Russian swallow Irina Volkov aka Karina Vale who had exposed Kir Smirnova, as the mastermind familiar antagonist.

Will's team had turned the tables on Kir's surveillance team by dismantling the entire DC sleeper illegals operation forcing Kir to go dark and eliminate assets as well as to activate the waiting Blackbird Protocol team. Two kill team agents are killed in a brief firefight with the FBI and two arrested. A disaster all around.

Worst of all, the only asset located stateside was Nikita, who Kir already eliminated. He could not know if Sable was compromised or might be in the future.

179

Ever the professional, Kir had another mole embedded at LaserTech who had remained silent until now. Victor Levin (real name Oleg Morozov) – Code Name Lynx was lab assistant to John Jankowitz, a LaserTech physicist working on Radiant Sentry. Lynx, while low-tier Lab support and not part of Radiant Sentry science Kir thinks he is perfect as they'll never see him. He vets Sable's feed. The Russian had a second source for confirmation.

A Russian handler's voice crackles over an encrypted speaker phone line.

"Two dead. Two in custody. Francis broke right away. Volkov was sloppy. Her alias is burned."

Kir doesn't blink. He places a photo of Fidel Francis beside one of Karina Vale, both marked with a sharp red "X".

"Francis was a liability from the beginning. Too emotional. I told them not to use him."

He turns slowly to a wall where photographs of Will, Grace, Sara, Rick, and Gene Larsson (Sable) were arranged— annotated with movements, access patterns, and timestamps. Thin lines of thread connected them in a silent web.

"ACIC executed the sweep in thirty-six hours. Morgan's team hit every known node." said the Voice."

"Will Morgan… always methodical. I had eyes on him for a reason."

His tone stays measured, but a simmering fury brews beneath the surface.

Kir reaches for Gene's photo—his knuckles whitening as he stares at the woman who may have compromised them all.

"Zakharov was our only tether to Sable. And now we're blind. We do not know what Sable has said. Or will say."

"Then we assume Sable been turned?" said the Voice.

"We assume nothing. Assumptions are for the careless." Replied Kir.

A long pause. Kir's eyes shift to a secure case. He unlocks it and withdraws a small drive marked with Cyrillic lettering— PHASE 2.

"I have taken two steps; I have activated Lynx and Voron as Sable's new handler.

"Zakharov commanded with charisma and manipulation, Volkova leads with results and relentless control. She's not interested in ideology—only leverage. She was trained to operate across hostile borders without direct Kremlin oversight.

"Lynx is still embedded. They won't see him—he's a ghost in the lab."

"He's low-tier," agrees the Voice.

"Exactly. Not part of the Radiant Sentry code word team. No one would expect him. That's what makes him ideal.

"He'll begin quiet verification. If Sable is feeding them disinformation, Lynx will expose the lie. If not—we keep siphoning."

"What of extraction?" asked the Voice.

"Too early. But prepare contingencies for asset removal in the Northeast. If Levin is touched, we lose everything."

Kir gazes at the board—then, without a word, peels Gene's photo from the wall and burns it with a lighter from his coat pocket.

"If Sable breaks... we bury her."

Yasenevo District, Moscow - SVR Headquarters

The corridors of the SVR's headquarters were hushed, the kind of quiet that preceded irrevocable decisions. Snow sifted down outside, the city was blanketed in cold silence. Inside, heat and calculation reigned.

Kir Smirnova stood in front of a backlit screen, the dossier open in front of him. A single photo was paper clipped to the front: a bespectacled man in his fifties, wearing a LaserTech ID badge.

Smirnova, flatly, to his aide, "Sable is compromised. No further transmissions until verification. We need internal eyes."

The aide gave a subtle nod. Makarov tapped the folder once, deliberately.

Smirnova commands, "Activate Lynx. Ten years in place. He has proximity to Jankowitz. He's overdue."

The aide hesitated.

AIDE questions, "He's low-tier. Lab support. Not part of Alpha science."

Smirnova confidently replies, "Perfect. That's why they'll never see him. He vets Sable's feed. We are double-blind.

"He thinks he's just confirming data. He doesn't need to know he's our failsafe."

The aide turned and walked briskly toward the communications suite. Smirnova stared at the man's photo for a long moment. Quiet. Invisible. Loyal—for now.

Smirnova thoughtfully, "Ego and envy—America breeds it in bulk. You just have to know when to harvest."

CHAPTER TWENTY-ONE

Useful Idiot Code Name Kukla

Linthicum MD - LaserTech

Fidel Francis was a polished, intelligent professional with a calm demeanor and a knack for interpersonal diplomacy. Having risen through the corporate HR world on charm, professionalism, and strict procedural fluency, Fidel found himself uniquely placed at LaserTech—a high-security defense subcontractor—as a liaison between technical staff and upper management.

He was admired for his even temperament, conflict resolution skills, and an ability to make people feel heard—useful in a facility populated by driven, sometimes eccentric specialists.

When Fidel Francis joined LaserTech's HR department, SVR's behavioral analysts flagged him as an ideal target—recently divorced, emotionally isolated, and responsible for sensitive internal data.

Over eight months, Fidel was compromised by a honeypot operation run by Russian sleeper agent Irina Volkov (code name Snezhinka – "Snowflake"), who posed as Karina Vale, a low-level accounting assistant embedded at LaserTech three years earlier.

Karina initiated contact with small HR queries that grew into dinners, confidences, and a discreet romantic affair. Fidel saw connection; she saw leverage. Through him, she gained access to HR data—travel logs, clearance levels, stress evaluations, disciplinary notes on DARPA contract staff. He never handed over documents, but once—while drinking—he shared his login credentials. Karina used them with a hidden exfiltration protocol buried in routine audit files.

NSA behavioral analytics flagged anomalies tied to Fidel's access patterns. Under questioning, he initially denied wrongdoing, then broke when confronted with surveillance showing the manipulation. He expressed remorse and had since cooperated, providing valuable intelligence on SVR's asset network. He is under protective custody.

Karina attempted to flee under a fabricated "family emergency," but was intercepted by DHS/Army CI. Her go-bag held multiple passports, a burner laptop, and $50,000 cash. She resisted arrest but was captured alive. She was now in a black site facility—initially uncooperative, but analysts assessed potential for defection.

SVR's reaction: radio silence. Karina was presumed burned.

Black Site Interrogation Room Day 1— 0412 Hours R

Windowless. Chilled air. Sparse table. Two chairs. Surveillance running silently behind the glass. Will enters, alone. Karina (Snowflake) is already seated, wrists cuffed, posture perfect. Her hair is tied back, her expression unreadable.

Will sitting slowly, measured, "You don't look particularly anxious for someone who's just watched their entire operation burn to ash."

Karina smiling, "That would suggest I was emotionally invested. I wasn't."

"So, it was what… a job?

"In your country, I believe the phrase is 'nothing personal.'"

Will studies her. Silent. Calculating. Then, leaning in enough to shift the tone.

"You're a professional. So am I. We both know you're not breaking under pressure." said Will, "So here's the deal: you're off the board. But the SVR? They've already scrubbed your name. To them, you failed. You're dead. Meaning your future depends on what we decide you're worth."

"You want me to flip. Be your little fountain of secrets."

"No. I want you to make a choice. You either start talking, or you spend the rest of your life in a cell deep enough to forget sunlight."

Karina firm, emotionless: "And what do I get in return?"

"Nothing at first. Because people like you don't get deals." Will responded with brusqueness, "But if I start to believe there's still something human under that concrete casing you call a soul… maybe you get transferred. Maybe you get to sleep without chains."

Karina holds his gaze. A crack flickers, "You don't believe I'm human?"

"I believe you were trained to forget how to be one."

She paused and then said. "Then why are you here, Will Morgan?"

"Because I've been in your head since you walked into LaserTech. I know how you picked Fidel. I know your tells. And I know the one thing people like you never prepare for: failure." concluded Will.

He leaned closer. "So, I'm here to watch what happens next."

Karina shifts, just a shade, for the first time unsure. Will stands, calm and controlled. He knocks once on the door. As it opens, he looks back.

"We'll talk again tomorrow. Maybe by then, you'll remember what it feels like to be scared."

He leaves. The door seals with a cold, final hiss. Karina stares at the space he occupied, still—expressionless—but her thumb begins to tap, once, twice… a tic that wasn't there before.

Black Site Holding Cell Night Day 20 - 0160 Hours R

She asked for a pen and paper.

They gave her a dull pencil. No eraser. She wrote something.

Not a confession. Not yet.

A single name.

One of her SVR handlers.

One who had never appeared in any U.S. intel before.

She folded it neatly and stared at it for hours before pressing the call button.

Black Site Interrogation Room Day 30 - 0712 Hours R

Will walked in alone, the folded slip of paper still untouched in the center of the table. No cuffs on Karina this time—another quiet tactic. The gesture wasn't kindness. It was leverage.

She looked different today. Less defiant. Not broken, but… thinned out. Will noted the twitch in her left hand, the subtle way her gaze avoided his eyes just a second too long.

"You wrote down a name."

"I did."

Will sitting, measured.

"That's new."

He didn't reach for the paper. Just let it sit between them like an unopened letter from a dead relative.

"You want to talk about why?"

"It was time. That's all."

"No. It's never only time. People like you don't move without purpose. You put your trust in a machine that never trusted you back. And now you're sitting here realizing you're on the wrong side of silence."

She looked away. Not in shame—but in recognition.

"You think this is regret?"

Will leaned back in his chair.

"No. I think it's clarity. They left you. It happens to all of you. The myth of loyalty breaks down when your name stops appearing on their rosters."

"You don't know them."

"Don't need to. I've seen enough broken agents to know the moment when the center shifts. When you stop looking at us like the enemy and start wondering if you've been betrayed twice— first by the country that trained you, and second by the one that made you believe you belonged."

Karina flinched again. Barely perceptible. But real.

Will reached forward, tapped the paper with one finger.

"You're not giving me this for a deal. You're giving it because you've started to care what happens next. You want this to mean something."

"Do I?"

"You tell me. You just blinked first."

He finally opened the note.

"He read the name. The corners of his mouth moved, but behind his eyes: motion. A flicker of recognition. Someone they'd never been able to pin—until now."

Will slowly, "You picked a hell of a domino to tip."

"I didn't tip it. Just... stopped holding it up."

"Then let's see what falls next."

He stood. Left the room without another word.

Karina leaned back in her chair, breath shallow. She wasn't free. She wasn't safe. But for the first time in a long time, she felt real. Like the person she had buried six years ago was clawing her way back up—painfully, violently, but undeniably alive.

Fort Meade - Watchtower Conference Room Day 31 - 0803 Hours R

The team was half-slumped around the conference table, waiting for Will to return from a secure call. The room was dim, blue-lit screens casting long shadows across the table. The air was heavy with coffee and fatigue.

Z leaned back, twirling his pen between his fingers, eyes flicking toward Sara.

"Remind me, what's the record for you talking an asset into confession without them realizing it was a confession?"

Sara smirked, arms folded. "Forty-six seconds. But only because he tried to flirt back."

Rick snorted. "Still faster than Z disarming a door lock. We timed him. Twice."

Z rolled his eyes, but a grin crept in. "Fine. Next time you're locked out, enjoy sleeping in the hallway."

Laughter rippled, quick but real.

At the far end, Cathy frowned at her laptop, frustration pinching her face.

"My VPN client keeps dropping the secure tunnel—"

Before she could finish, Rick slid his chair over, hands already flying across the keys.

"Cat, if you're fighting the tunnel, you're already losing. Here. Let me show you the shortcut."

Cathy watched, her annoyance softening into curiosity. "Okay, that's... actually useful."

Sara caught Z's eye, the inside joke still hanging between them. A flicker of warmth passed around the table, unspoken but binding.

For a moment, they weren't just counterintelligence operators. They were a team.

Will strode in, everyone knew he had something. They could read it in his gait—controlled but weighted.

He stood at the front, behind the central monitor. No preliminaries. No coffee. No jokes. He held up the folded slip of paper from Karina.

Will said, "Name came in less than an hour ago. Not under duress, not for leverage. She offered it because something broke—and she is aware of it."

He unfolded it with care, as if the name itself might burn.

Will reading aloud said, "Clara Vetrova. Alias Clara Vance—Code name Baba Yaga."

A sharp inhale from Sara. Gene blinked twice. Derek scribbled something, eyes narrowing. Thomas didn't move—he studied Will's tone like a waveform.

"Alias. She's been operating inside LaserTech's accounting division under the name Clara Vance, Level 4 clearance, responsible for indirect cost allocations."

Sara exclaimed, "Jesus. She's been with the company for over five years!"

Will frustrated and disgusted said, "Honeypot play. She flirted with Fidel Francis—Assistant HR Director. Played him like a soft asset for over a year. Nothing major at first—just credential leaks, internal schedules, travel orders. Then came the clearance rosters."

Thomas said, "Death by access drift. Classic swallow op."

"Karina confirmed Clara was planted well before the DARPA sub-award came through." explained Will, "They were seeding placement. Long game. Clara had a dormant SVR handler protocol—activated around the same time as the Radiant Sentry alert.

Rick without looking up, said, "I ran her last 200 days of network behavior against the expected latency curve. She's been uploading fractional packets using a modified steganography schema—exfiltrating using invoice metadata. That's why it passed audit."

Will gave him a short nod. He already suspected as much. Hearing it confirmed was a cold validation.

"We're going to let her run. Passive surveillance only." said Will, "We need to map her full network before pulling the wire."

Gene, asked, "You think she perceives Karina gave her up?"

Will answers, "No. I am not sure they are even aware of each other. So, we keep it that way. For now, she's just another cog. But this cog spins a wheel we haven't seen the full size of yet."

Will turned to the main screen. A grainy surveillance still popped up—Clara exiting LaserTech at dusk, sunglasses, scarf, tote bag over one shoulder.

"This is the enemy you don't see coming. Embedded, fluent, patient." he continued, "The face of the new battlefield."

Will said, "Let's find out who else she's touched. Every access point, every footprint. Don't leave anything in the dark."

Sara said, "On it"

CHAPTER TWENTY-TWO

Dinner & Therapy

"History, despite its wrenching pain, cannot be unlived, but if faced with courage, need not be lived again."

- Maya Angelou

Odenton, MD - Carrone Residence -1920 Hours R

Thomas Carrone lived in Odenton, Maryland, with his wife Mary, a novelist, and two adult children based in D.C. A lifelong reader of philosophy, espionage fiction, cognitive science, and global affairs.

With Mary at a book signing, the Carrone house was quiet, dimly lit by the soft glow of sconces and the low crackle of the fireplace in the family room. The faint scent of garlic and rosemary still lingered in the air, remnants of the hearty osso buco and risotto Thomas had served with pride.

The chef himself—shirt sleeves rolled up, cheeks a bit flushed from the wine and the warmth of the kitchen—sat across from Will Morgan in a leather armchair, swirling a generous pour of Barolo in his glass.

"Not bad for a guy with a badge, right?" Thomas smirked, the edge of his Sicilian pride showing through.

Will offered a slight smile, nodding. "You could open a place. Call it 'Interrogation and Entrées.' First glass free if you crack under pressure."

Thomas chuckled, but his eyes remained fixed on his old friend. He didn't need a behavioral profile to read the weight in Will's body language—shoulders slouched, gaze unfocused, as if the wine was fighting something more stubborn than tension.

The silence hung just long enough to signal something unspoken.

"Will," Thomas said, leaning forward. "Something on your mind? Something I can help you with?"

"What, the assassination attempt? That?"

"That'd be a start."

"Not much to say. They missed."

"They tried to kill you, Will. That's not a footnote."

"It is to me."

Thomas studying him, "You've always done that—absorbed the impact and kept walking. Like hate's the only thing you trust to carry."

"Hate's clean. Hate's useful. You can aim it. Shape it. I don't burn out from it—I work better. Sharper."

"SVR?"

"They earned it. Every name I had to bury. Every smile that turned out fake. Every op that ended in static. My hate for them? It's not noise. It's ballast. Keeps me steady when the ground shifts."

"And fear?"

Will without hesitation, "No room for it. Fear slows you down, makes you hesitate. I can't afford hesitation — not with Radiant Sentry on the line."

"So, you bully it."

"Like a drill sergeant. I keep it in line; make it march in time or shut the hell up."

"Even now?

"Especially now. I was almost killed. So what? I filed the report, logged the risk. It's done. I'm still here. The mission's still mine."

Thomas leans in, "But love—that's where the architecture collapses, isn't it?"

Will doesn't answer right away. Just breathes. Something flinches behind his eyes.

"I don't hate it. Don't fear it. I just... can't hold it anymore. Not safely. Not after—"

"Your family?"

Will said, "Yeah. That betrayal rewired something I don't know how to fix. Love's a language I don't speak anymore. A map with half the landmarks torched."

"But you're still standing on the edge, looking over."

Will shaking his head said, "I don't even get that far. I stop at the border and turn back. Every time. I can read a room in seconds, break a man's psyche from a glance... but let someone in?"

(He exhales, frustrated with himself.)

"I lose all operational clarity."

"So, you stick to hate. Discipline. The mission."

"Because the lines are clear there. I don't need a compass. And when the walls come down around Radiant Sentry—I don't hesitate. I stand in front. That's what I know how to do."

They sit in silence. Thomas lifts his glass, takes a long sip, then sets it down gently.

Thomas said, "One day, someone's going to cross that border. You're not as impenetrable as you pretend."

"Then let's hope they're friendly."

They both half-smile, neither convinced.

Will didn't meet his eyes right away. "Yeah… but the problem is, I don't know how to describe it." He rubbed his thumb along the rim of the wine glass. "Don't even understand what's bouncing around in my head."

Thomas tilted his head. "Can you describe any of the thoughts?" His voice took on a calm, clinical cadence—measured, safe. "Sometimes when we're stuck, we talk out loud. Not to anyone specific—just process what's up there. It helps. The fancy term is cognitive processing."

Will gave a half-grunt of acknowledgment.

"It's like emotional regulation," Thomas continued. "Putting feelings into words sometimes helps us understand them better. And you can do it alone… or with a friend."

Will cracked a reluctant smile. "Like a volunteer?"

Thomas raised his glass. "Sure. Volunteers are good—cheap too."

A long pause.

Will stared at the wine as if searching for answers in its dark red depths. Then, slowly, he spoke.

"How would you describe me to a stranger?"

Thomas leaned back, considering. "In terms an accountant would understand… I'd say you're a man with a big emotional balance sheet. Huge assets. Huge liabilities. And a pretty damn large reservoir of net worth."

Will gave a quiet "Hmmm…"—not quite agreement, not quite resistance.

"Here's the deal," Thomas went on. "You deploy your emotional assets—discipline, loyalty, focus—to do your job. To protect your people. But the liabilities… the betrayals, the trauma, the distrust… you suppress those. You don't hide them behind a wall, Will—you bury them. Deep."

Will exhaled, eyes still downcast.

"It's worked, I guess," Thomas admitted. "But there's a price. Your guardedness—your mistrust keeps you from forming real, personal connections. The kind that doesn't just make life bearable, but meaningful."

Will finally looked up. His voice was low. "Supposing I buy that. And I don't argue with Italian chefs." He gave a half-laugh, soft and strained. "The burning question is... why now?"

Thomas smiled knowingly. "Typical Will. Straight to the heart of it. The answer is—something changed. Something's stirring that you're not equipped to deal with. Not because you're weak—hell, you're one of the strongest people I've ever met. But because this is unfamiliar territory."

He let the words sit for a moment before continuing.

"When we struggle to regulate emotions, it's because we haven't had to face them in a long time. Or we've always beaten them into submission. But sometimes, something sneaks past the defenses. A person. A moment. A feeling."

He gave Will a pointed look. "The three strongest emotions are love, hate, and fear. You're an expert at defeating the last two. That leaves love."

Will didn't flinch, but his jaw tightened.

Thomas lifted his glass again. "Anyway, that's all I've got on the subject. Sorry if the wine made me too philosophical."

Will was silent for a thoughtful moment. Then, "No... thank you. You helped more than you know."

Thomas nodded. Sometimes, with Will, silence was the clearest sign of breakthrough.

Will's phone rings and the caller ID shows Judd Lockwood.

"This can't be good," Will quips as he answers, "when the CIA calls at night, it's never good news,"

"Will, hope you're sitting down," came Judd Lockwood's voice, heavy with implication. "We received a new document from Ivan. It's a request to the mole for specific documents—by file name. Someone has access to the index."

Will's grip tightened. The index. This changed everything.

"Can you meet me at your office at Fort Meade tomorrow, say ten o'clock?"

"Sure," Will said. His voice was calm but low with urgency. "I'd like to bring Grace Roberts, my physicist. She has Reliant Sentry code clearance."

"Good idea. See you at ten."

The line clicked off. Will stood there in the silence, the bourbon untouched, his reflection staring back at him in the glass of the microwave door.

The hunt had escalated.

Highway to Fort Meade

Sunlight flickered through the canopy of oaks lining the narrow highway as Will Morgan's government-issued sedan cruised toward Fort Meade. The hum of tires against the pavement was the only sound for a moment, both occupants lost in their thoughts. Grace Roberts sat in the passenger seat, tapping her fingers lightly on her thigh, her mind racing with the implications of everything she had recently learned.

"I'm new to all this Spy versus Spy stuff," she said, breaking the silence. "Can you give me an idea of what we're up against?"

Will glanced at her briefly, one hand on the wheel, his other resting near the gearshift. "The drive is short, so it'll have to be the Cliffs Notes version."

She gave him a quick, expectant smile, and he continued, his voice steady and edged with gravitas.

"We have what the world wants. And it's far cheaper and faster to steal it from us than to develop it. The public has no idea of the scope of espionage directed at America."

He paused, turning onto a two-lane access road where the foliage grew denser. "There are over eighty countries constantly spying on us."

Grace blinked. "Wow. I guess everybody spies on everybody."

"Not everybody," he corrected. "The 'Five Eyes'—the U.S., Canada, UK, Australia, and New Zealand—have an agreement not to spy on one another."

"Interesting. No France or Germany?"

"The French are well... French. And Germany has too many Russian agents hanging around."

She gave a small chuckle, but his tone darkened as he pressed on. "China is far and away the most active—orders of magnitude greater than the Russians, who are second. They're interested in everything: military, medical, tech... even agriculture. They were caught trying to steal hybrid corn seeds from a farm in Iowa."

"I had no idea," Grace murmured.

"Russia," Will said, "is primarily after technology, military and otherwise. They've been at it longer than anyone and they're incredibly good at it. Not as good as the Cubans, but very smart, with excellent tradecraft."

"The Cubans?!" she asked, eyebrows rising in surprise.

"Without a doubt the best and most difficult to penetrate. They've got a deep-seated hatred for America."

"Not surprising," Grace said. "We did crush their economy with sanctions. Then we tried to invade them. Not to mention the assassination attempts on Castro."

"In the eighties," Will said, his voice lowering with something close to awe, "we thought we had thirty-eight agents spying on Cuba for us. Turned out—when we finally turned a real asset—every single one of them was a double agent. Some had been feeding us disinformation for twenty-six years."

He shook his head. "Like the North Koreans, they sell their information to the Russians. It's one of their sources of foreign currency."

Grace was quiet letting the magnitude of the statement sink in.

"Since the Cold War, if you take every identified spy and stack them up on top of one another in a timeline, there has never been a period when there has not been an active known spy. Imagine the ones we never caught."

"Counterintelligence investigations," Will continued, "involve several disciplines. Skills that may include case officers, analysts, surveillance teams, technical and double-agent specialists."

He looked out at the approaching security checkpoint in the distance. "To make matters worse, CI officers aren't popular. They're not welcome because, like Internal Affairs, they usually bring unwelcome news. Operators don't want to hear there may be problems with their cases—it can hurt careers. Add the bad press and recriminations when we unearth moles."

"Is that why we're working undercover?" she asked.

"It's because we don't want to spook the mole."

Grace nodded slowly, but another thought struck her. "One thing I don't understand. Why would anyone need to print a document when it's right in front of them on their screen?"

Will gave a grim little smile. "Sara wondered about that as well. When we interview her, we'll be sure to ask."

Fort Meade - Morgan's Office

Will and Grace sat in the familiar confines of his office at Fort Meade as Judd Lockwood entered, a thick folder tucked beneath one arm. His expression was tight, his tone clipped.

"Either our mole has taken great pains to create an index list," he began without preamble, "or the LaserTech system has been hacked."

Will's eyes narrowed. "I doubt the system was hacked."

Judd nodded. "So, to create the index, they would've had to physically transcribe every word of each title while at the office. And those are long file titles. Most likely, they snuck each title out one by one, afraid of being caught with an entire or partial index."

He laid the folder on the table, his fingers tapping restlessly on the cover. "They could've coded it off-site or left it up to their handler. Either way, it took time. But now they have it... they'll be reaping the benefits more rapidly—until we stop them."

Will leaned back in his chair, his voice steady. "They won't need to smuggle documents. A series of questions and answers would be almost as good in most cases."

Fort Meade - Morgan's Office

The office was dark but for the glow of Will Morgan's desk lamp and the steady pulse of lights from a row of encrypted drives. His monitor illuminated his face in shades of blue and white. He picked up his phone and dialed.

A voice answered after one ring.

"Rick, I have a couple of questions. First is, can you hack into LaserTech?"

Silence as Rick thought, then replied, "Uh, well considering they are one of ours, yes. You mean if we were an outsider?"

"Oh, yeah."

"An outsider starting from scratch would need some kind of help."

Will leaned forward, scribbling notes in the margins of a printed flowchart.

"Without it they might be able to do it, but it would take tremendous effort. It would have to be a state actor."

"I'm assuming China or Russia."

"Then yes, but it would take a lot of resources and time. Second question?"

Will tapped his pen once against the table.

"Assuming they could get in, could they replicate stored Word documents?"

"Interesting question."

The line went silent for a moment, then Rick continued.

"Microsoft Word is written in C++. Documents are basically zipped XML files. If there's no file-specific encryption, yeah— they could replicate a file and print it somewhere else."

"Even if it's password protected?"

"Just a matter of time. Cracking passwords is work, not magic. But LaserTech... being a DARPA subcontractor? I'd bet they use either AES or FHE."

"FHE?"

"Fully Homomorphic Encryption. If they're using FHE? Forget it. NSA-grade stuff. Even NSA can't break it... unless they wrote it."

Will exhaled, absorbing the implications.

"What about file names? Just the names."

"Unencrypted. You need to identify them to open or request them. So yeah, file names are visible."

Will's eyes moved to the cascading list on his monitor.

"So, if the Russians got in... they could at least build an index."

"Exactly. File names, file paths—enough to guess content, timing, even authorship patterns. It's not nothing."

Silence.

Will leaned closer to the screen. Hundreds of filenames stared back at him—cryptic, clinical, but not meaningless. Muttering to himself, *Breadcrumbs...*

Linthicum Heights, MD - LaserTech - Morgan's Office

The office was heavy with the exhaustion of a night spent chasing shadows. A thin gray light filtered through the blinds of Will Morgan's office at LaserTech, casting a sterile glow over the cluttered conference table where Sara Brandt still worked with her customary diligence.

On the couch, Will was a crumpled figure, deep in sleep, the tension of the past few days briefly erased from his lined face. His chest rose and fell at a steady rhythm, oblivious to the soft clacking of keys and the quiet hum of the monitors.

Next to Sara, Derek Wilshire sat perched, his knees tucked up, absorbed by the mesmerizing stream of code rolling across the wide screen. Line by line, the program searched the vast architecture of LaserTech's code base with precision, a digital tide revealing secrets long hidden.

Sara tucked a loose strand of hair behind her ear and glanced at Derek, who hadn't moved in nearly an hour. Smiling with fondness, she closed her laptop.

"Derek, I have to check something on my computer. I'll be back in a few minutes."

Her voice was soft, maternal, but Derek was lost in the hypnotic flow of information, too transfixed to respond. Sara lingered a moment, then gathered her things and slipped from the room.

Hours passed. The day outside deepened into night, and the quiet buzz of the office grew heavier.

Will stirred first, his body stiff from the awkward position on the couch. He blinked groggily, the world swimming back into focus. The whiteboard caught his bleary attention. Scrawled in thick black marker, stark against the white surface, there were four curious digits:

6828.

Will frowned, muttering to himself under his breath.

"What the hell is that?"

Before he could gather his thoughts, Sara appeared, brushing a cold gust of air with her.

"Have a nice nap?"

Will sat up, rubbing the sleep from his face and forcing a smile.

"Yes, I did, thanks. What are you working on?"

Sara, halfway to her workstation, froze mid-step. Her eyes flicked to the whiteboard, and confusion clouded her face.

"What the hell is that on the board?"

Will stood slowly, joints protesting.

"I thought you might know. Was Gracie in here with you while I was conked out?"

Sara shook her head, her brow furrowing.

"No, only Derek. He was here watching the code roll by with your Hail Mary on the Vibe."

The two stood there for a long, still moment. Then, like an electric charge passing between them, realization struck at once.

They looked at each other, wide-eyed and incredulous.

Will urgently, "See if Derek has left for the day."

Without waiting, Sara sprinted out the door, her shoes slapping against the tile in rapid beats. Each second dragged seeming without end to Will as he waited, pacing in tight circles.

At last, Sara returned—breathless and triumphant—with Derek in tow.

"It's a code line in the damn compiler!"

"Did our Hail Mary program flag it?"

"No. Derek did. That aquarium is the best investment the Government has made since Velcro."

Will couldn't help but chuckle, his mind already racing ahead.

"Derek, where would you like to go to dinner—we're buying."

Derek's face lit up like a Christmas tree.

"Is Sara coming?"

"Wouldn't think of going without her. Why don't the two of you work out the place and time?"

Will grabbed the office phone, hitting the speaker button. The line crackled to life as he called Rick Huang.

"Rick, have someone check LaserTech's code line six thousand eight hundred twenty-eight — 6 — 8 — 2 — 8."

Rick's voice came back sharp and alert, "Sixty-eight twenty-eight got it. I'll be back."

Linthicum Heights, MD - Phil's Place 2030 Hours R

Later that night, the trio sat at a booth in a dimly lit restaurant, the remnants of burgers and fries scattered across the table. Sara and Derek leaned in, their faces illuminated by the warm glow of Will's phone as it buzzed to life.

Recognizing Rick's number, he answered,

"Hey Rick, whataya got?"

"Bingo. Very artful penetration. They hacked the compiler. Only came in once, Modified the compiler's source code to include a backdoor. To make it harder to detect, the compiler was designed to recognize when it was compiling itself and to insert the backdoor logic into newly built compiler versions as well. This created a self-replicating attack where the malicious code persists across compiler updates, even if the source code for the compiler appears clean.

"Very smart. How'd you catch it— with your program?"

Will grinned at Derek across the table, a spark of pride in his eyes.

"Nah, Derek, our secret weapon."

Derek smiled a humble smile touched with pride.

There was a pause on the line, Rick's confusion palpable even across the airwaves.

"Can we get a copy of Derek?"

Will barked out a laugh.

"I would if I could, but God only made one copy."

"Huh?"

"Derek is a human."

A second of stunned silence.

"No shit?"

"Gotta run. Talk again later and I'll explain. Thanks for your help."

He hung up, the team's small victory tasting sweeter than any dessert.

Kolpachny, Moscow

A different kind of tension threaded the air halfway across the globe. In a private government facility outside central Moscow, Kir Smirnova crossed the room with slow, deliberate steps. His black boots echoed lightly against polished concrete. Facing him from behind a utilitarian steel desk was Major Georgy Markova, senior military analyst for strategic space operations.

Kir's tone was matter of fact, but his eyes gleamed with the weight of revelation.

"Georgy, we now have the file directory of the Reliant Sentry program, "he began, handing over a spiral-bound document coded with layered encryption seals. "From the titles, we can intuit the contents of each file."

He took a measured breath.

"Our scientists can make targeted, educated guesses as to the questions to ask. This is considerably less risky since we have no need to steal whole documents. While it may take longer, the risk-reward is far greater."

Georgy remained seated; brows knit as he flipped through the first few pages.

"How can we be sure we are not being fed false information that will lead us down a false path?"

Kir met his gaze without blinking.

"Sable has been consistently accurate. Science has been carefully verified. As with most Americans, the motive is money—and we are paying Sable exceptionally large sums. Over one and a half million rubles each delivery."

Georgy frowned.

"Yes, but I understand that so far the information has been helpful but has not provided us with any new breakthroughs."

Kir nodded, acknowledging the truth.

"That has been mostly due to communications challenges. If Sable knew what we know and don't know, the process would go faster. But for obvious reasons we are never going to let that happen—so we have to iterate our questions."

He crossed his arms, steady.

"We are dealing with very high-level physics, and it takes time to verify everything."

Georgy pushed back from the desk, his tone tightening

CHAPTER TWENTY-THREE

Fort Belvoir Briefing

The INSCOM ops center smelled of coffee and sealed secrets. No windows, white noise humming. Concrete walls kept distractions—and daylight—out.

Will Morgan stood at the head of the table, sleeves rolled, tie off, the strain of seventy-two hours etched into his shirt. Around him sat the hardened core of U.S. intelligence.

Will exhaled. "We were compromised almost from the moment we set foot inside LaserTech."

Faces didn't flinch—they'd suspected. Now they knew.

"The DARPA audit was cover. Russia didn't buy it. The moment my name hit the roster, Kir Smirnova knew something was off."

He clicked a remote. Satellite shots, comm intercepts, heat maps filled the screen. "They assumed—correctly—we were after Sable. What they didn't expect was our bait."

A surveillance still of Nikita Zakharov appeared, mid-stride on a Bethesda Street. "Cecil Brandon let himself be seen trailing

206

Zakharov. On purpose. Moscow burned him fast—called it suicide, smothered it with disinfo."

"Classic fog machine," Zarelli muttered.

"It backfired," Will said. "Their panic told us Zakharov handled Sable. With him gone, they lost control."

Edwards leaned forward. "So, you turned their surveillance?"

"Exactly. We mapped three Russian illegal teams in D.C.—auto, foot, digital intercepts. Not amateurs. Prepping termination missions. Us."

Silence.

"Yes," Will added. "Project Palisade is that critical. They were ready to kill three CI officers on U.S. soil."

He clicked again: blurred mugshots, redacted dossiers. "With FBI help we flipped or compromised half their local network. Illegals went dark. Courier chains collapsed. Moscow's running a mole hunt. They don't suspect us—yet."

Zarelli chewed his cheek. "So… where does that leave us?"

Will's tone dropped. "They moved to eliminate me. Indicators all over—cutouts, brush passes, call-and-burn cells. A four-man kill team deployed two weeks ago. We got the jump. Two dead, two in custody."

No one smiled. Survival wasn't victory—it meant the next move was overdue.

"We believe Sable is still active. Still embedded. Trusted. We can still use her."

And with that, the war behind the war turned another page.

CHAPTER TWENTY-FOUR

Chasing A Ghost

Fort Meade — Watchtower Ops

SYBIL's lattice washed the room in cold blue light.

Cathy Wang scrolled through her tablet; Sara Brandt leaned against the table, coffee cooling in her hand.

"I think we've been chasing a ghost," Cathy said, bringing up a bank statement.

"The ten grand from Jankowitz's lab? Not a payoff. He withdrew it himself—catering, florist, band. He's planning a surprise anniversary party."

Sara frowned.

"And the diner meeting?"

"The 'mystery man'? Party planner. The envelope was a venue deposit."

SYBIL pulsed across the wall display, text flickering in white:

ACCOUNT HOLDER UNAWARE. ACCESS PATTERN INDICATES EXTERNAL SEEDING.

Sara exhaled.

"His brother's account was hijacked. The money's planted. He's being framed."

Cathy blinked.

"So, we've been tailing a guy planning a vacation?"

"While Smirnova's real asset kept moving," Sara said. "We're the ones on his leash."

SYBIL's synthesized voice broke the silence.

"Confidence level: eighty-seven percent. Jankowitz is not the source."

Sara's hand tightened around her cup.

"Then we're back at zero — and out of time."

Fort Meade — Commander's Office

The blinds were drawn. A single LED bar cut across the table. Will Morgan sat opposite Ed Perry, surveillance stills spread between them—Jankowitz at a diner, an envelope, a handshake in a Wegmans aisle.

"It's theater," Will said. "The cash came from his own account — anniversary party and cruise deposit. The Liechtenstein transfer? Seeded externally. He's being framed."

Ed's Zippo clicked open, shut, open again.

"So Smirnova dangled bait—and we took it."

"Too perfect," Will said. "That's the tell."

"So, we keep the play alive," Ed replied. "Pull surveillance and Smirnova smells the pivot. We let him believe it worked. Keep Jankowitz under the microscope on paper while SYBIL digs for the real mole."

"We let Kir think he's winning," Will said. "When he relaxes, we follow the trail back to whoever's feeding him."

"Gene Larsson's still on the board," Ed said, closing the folder. "One wrong move and Jankowitz isn't the only one who burns."

Will nodded — message received.

They'd walk the line … and pray it held.

CHAPTER TWENTY-FIVE

Polygraph

"Listen, I don't know anything about polygraphs and I don't know how accurate they are, but I know they'll scare the hell out of people."

— *Richard M. Nixon*

Polygraph Room – LaserTech – Morning

Gene Larsson sat rigidly in a sterile gray chair, her back unnaturally straight, hands clasped in her lap. A thin film of perspiration clung to her temple. The room is clinical—more an interrogation cell than an office. Electrodes and pneumatic tubes were strapped around her chest and fingers. The polygraph machine beside her hummed, the monitor displayed her vital signs in real-time: heart rate, respiration, skin conductivity.

Behind the one-way mirror, Will Morgan, Sara Brandt and Cathy Wang stood in tense silence. Will's jaw was clenched, arms folded across his chest. Sara's hand occasionally drifted to her face, brushing an imaginary strand of hair from her cheek as she watched Gene's every micro-expression. Cathy stood in silence in the background.

The polygraph examiner, a calm, methodical man in his fifties with wire-frame glasses and an unreadable face, adjusted the sensors one final time and began.

"Good morning. I am Salvador Rodriguez, an American Polygraph Association–certified examiner. Before we begin, let me explain the procedure. I will ask you a series of control and relevant questions. The polygraph instrument will record your breathing, pulse, blood pressure, and galvanic skin response.

"You have the right to consult an attorney and the right against self-incrimination. Do you understand these rights?"

Gene Larsson responded her voice is soft—breathy—betraying the tension she's trying to contain. "Yes."

"Please sit upright, feet flat on the floor, and do not cross your legs. Please do not press your feet on the ground or pinch your thigh during the control questions—these things do not work to deceive and are very obvious.

"This morning's examination is part of a counterintelligence investigation. Are you ready to begin?"

"Yes."

A slight waver—barely audible. The polygraph marked it.

The questions started routine, almost lulling:

"What's your full name?"

"Where were you born?"

"Ever dealt drugs?"

"Have you ever stolen anything?"

Each answer is flat, efficient.

Next to simple non-espionage-related questions came the real ones.

"Have you ever been approached by a foreign intelligence service?"

"No."

A tremor in her breath—minute, but it registered.

"Have you ever shared classified information with someone not authorized to have it?"

"No."

"Have you ever lied on a test?"

"Yes."

"Have you ever had contact with a foreign government official?"

"Yes. Conferences. Scientific forums."

"Have you ever used any other name for any purpose?"

"No."

"Have you ever falsified information?"

"No."

"Have you ever stolen or lost classified information?"

"No."

Will tightened his arms. A red spike on the monitor. Sara exhaled.

"Have you ever been involved in espionage or sabotage?"

"No."

"Have you ever paid or accepted a bribe?"

"No."

"Did you tell the truth on your employee application?"

"Yes."

"Have you answered all questions during this process truthfully?"

"Yes."

As the exam concluded, the polygrapher leaned back, his eyes never left Genevieve Larsson. He adjusted a setting on the console, then said in an even tone, "For the record, Genevieve, a few of your responses flagged as deceptive — particularly the ones regarding unauthorized communications and prior contact with foreign nationals." He let the words hang, just long enough. "Is there anything you'd like to clarify before I finalize the report?"

The room fell still. No beeps, no fan noise—just the soft creak of the chair beneath Gene as she looked up, eyes narrowed. The pause, the look of surprise on her face — that was what Salvador was watching for.

"No. I answered truthfully. You can ask as many times in as many ways as you like and my answers will be the same." A now indignant Gene replied sternly.

Rodriquez smiled and said, "I don't think that will be necessary today."

The room falls still. The rhythmic ticking of the polygraph machine fades to silence. Rodriguez types something on the terminal, then unstraps the electrodes from Gene's arms with professional detachment.

"Thank you. That concludes the examination. LaserTech will be in touch with the results shortly."

Gene nodded, visibly drained. She didn't speak. She rose from the chair and exited the room.

Behind the glass, Will and Sara said nothing. The screen still glowed with Gene's final physiological data. A final red peak flickered before fading to black.

Will, Sara and Cathy stood huddled by the monitor as the door opened behind them. Salvador Rodriquez, calm and composed entered holding a digital tablet and a neutral expression.

He glanced at the screen, then turned to face them.

"Let's talk about Larsson."

Will started, "Three reaction spikes. Two major, one minor."

"Correct. But there were no knock-ins and not enough for me to classify this as deception indicated. I'm calling it inconclusive."

Sara frustrated, "She reacted to questions on espionage and unauthorized disclosures. That's not nothing."

"It's not nothing. But it's also not a smoking gun. Polygraph isn't mind reading — it's physiology. "You saw what I saw — she was nervous but composed. The reaction to 'foreign contacts'

213

could be tied to a prior briefing or even a training environment. The spike on 'classified data' is more telling... but again, not definitive."

Will asked, "What about coaching? You think she was trained to beat the exam?"

'Possibly. But unlikely. Beating a polygraph with consistency requires exceptional discipline and rehearsal. Most people who try fail—especially civilians. Especially someone like Gene."

"But there's another factor. One I've seen before."

Will and Sara both leaned in.

"Double agents—true ones, under deep cover—sometimes believe they've been authorized to disclose information. Their handler convinces them the leak is sanctioned, part of a 'joint op' or 'higher clearance' game. That reframes their internal response."

Sara asked, "So when I ask if they shared classified info with a foreign agent—"

"—They say 'no' and believe it. Because in their mind, their handler is part of the mission. Same with the "contact" question. They're trained not to disclose handler interaction to anyone, including a polygrapher. Especially a polygrapher."

"So, you're saying she could be lying." said Will, "Or she could believe she's not."

"Yea. And in that ambiguity, I can't ethically certify the result either way. So it goes in the report: Inconclusive.

"Besides, you saw her reaction to my challenge. I have been doing this a long time, Will, and that felt real to me."

He handed Will the tablet. The preliminary report is already logged. Will scanned it, jaw tight.

Sara asked, "And if she is a double?"

"Then she's been very carefully managed. That's usually FBI tradecraft, not foreign."

Cathy leaned in and whispered to Sara, "What's a knock-in?"

214

"In the parlance of polygraph examiners, an incriminating admission made by a test subject, usually of illicit drug use, is known as a knock-in."

Sara and Will traded a glance. A silent flash of realization between them.

Will, "Then we watch her…Tight."

Fort Belvoir - Guy Zarelli's Office - 0915 Hours R

Guy Zarelli's office sat within a sterile government annex, all cold steel, and humming fluorescents. He stood as Morgan entered, offering a firm handshake.

"Good morning, Will. Thanks for coming down."

"Of course." Morgan didn't waste time. "We've determined that Gene Larsson, one of the primary physicists, printed the leaked document—but she has it in her files."

He let the implication hang in the air.

"It's a mystery how it could be in two places at the same time unless it somehow got reproduced—not copied but reproduced."

Zarelli leaned against his desk, arms crossed, brow furrowed.

"It would have to have left the building for that, wouldn't it?"

"That's the point of failure in the security." Morgan stepped closer, voice low, serious. "We know the document is still in our possession - in her files, but if it left the building we have no way of knowing how long it was gone."

He drew a deep breath. "It could have been reproduced if someone had the same security paper and reproduced the document on it. Many vendors make security paper and that wouldn't take more than a couple of hours."

He slid a sheet across the desk. "LaserTech gets their security paper from a company in Iowa. I would like to subpoena all their customer records for the last year."

Zarelli didn't pick it up. He didn't have to.

"That's pretty thin probable cause. The court may ask how that's going to help us unless we know who we're looking for. And we don't, do we?"

Morgan shook his head. "No, we don't. But we do have an extensive list of front companies."

A moment passed. Then Zarelli gave a slow, grudging nod. "Hmm. It's worth a try. Our guys are rather good, and DARPA isn't before FISA court every day. I'll talk to legal."

"Thanks, Guy. That's all I can ask."

As he turned to leave, Morgan's phone buzzed. He held up a finger to Zarelli, then answered.

Sara Brandt said, "Sorry to bust in on your meeting, but you'll want to hear this. The formula in the leaked message was bugging Gracie, so she showed it to Derek."

Morgan stilled. "Go on."

Grace Roberts said "It's wrong! Apparently, when it was transcribed to the reproduction, one character was incorrect. Very minor error—I looked at it twenty times and missed it. Derek nailed it first time."

Morgan switched to speaker. "Grace, you guys are on speaker. Are you sure?"

"Math doesn't lie. It's either a typo when transcribed or a beautiful phony, but a phony it is. Crafted to deceive and misdirect us—to think they don't have the correct formula? Only Alpha, Beta, and Delta would know how to do this. Charlie and Foxtrot are out."

Morgan lowered the phone, his face tightening with focused resolve.

"We're down to three. Thanks. See you this afternoon."

Morgan hung up and looked at Zarelli.

"This changes everything. That ought to be enough for subpoenas on those three, shouldn't it?"

Zarelli rubbed his chin, thoughtfully.

"Might be. I'll get on it.

LaserTech Cafeteria - 1215 Hours R

Morgan spotted Sara and Grace sitting beside Derek at a corner table. Sara and Grace enjoying a quiet laugh. Derek's voice, soft and steady, threaded through theirs like the low harmony of something domestic and calm. The three of them shared something unspoken—a rare flicker of camaraderie in the tense halls of LaserTech.

Will stood alone by the window, his reflection on the glass with the heavy rain beginning to press against it.

It hadn't always sat easily with Will.

At first, Derek's presence had felt like interference—too close, too gentle, too persistent. But he soon had come to see the shape of the man for what it was: not ornamental, not opportunistic. He was anchoring. A welcomed presence. Unquestioning, without judgment, just kindness and appreciation.

Derek didn't ask for space. He unknowingly created it.

He didn't speak much, and, unlike most people, there was never a need to wish he would shut up. He knew how to defuse Grace's temper with a wordless glance, how to let Sara drift without judging the orbit. He had no tactical value in a firefight — not in the traditional sense—but Will had started to understand that survival wasn't always about force. Sometimes it was about being the person who made sure everyone else could breathe.

Will didn't trust easily, not even now. But he trusted results. And Derek had delivered—again and again—in the quiet, overlooked ways that kept teams from being shattered.

"He's not a weapon, Will thought, but he's a tool I'd never throw out. And maybe that's more useful in the long run."

LaserTech - Morgan's Office

Back in his office Morgan Dialed.

"Guy Zarelli." The voice came quick, familiar.

"Guy, remember when Owen said you guys would get me anything I needed, no questions asked?"

"This oughta be good." Laughed Guy.

"I need a large aquarium stocked with salt water tropical fish. Like a great set up you would find in a corporate lobby."

Guy paused confused by the request then asked, "LaserTech can't afford an aquarium?"

"That sounded like a question."

Zarelli chuckled, mock-annoyed. "You must have misheard me. You'll have it in a couple of days."

"Who's better than you?! Thanks."

Zarelli mumbled to himself, "A freaking aquarium..."

Morgan hung up, smiling. Grace appeared in the doorway, arms crossed.

"That's a very sweet thing you did there."

"He earned it twofold."

"Or it was just a nice thing to do. It doesn't make you a softy, you know."

"Whatever. I thought it was the right thing to do, professor."

CHAPTER TWENTY-SIX

US Attorney's Meeting

U.S. Attorney's Office — Baltimore, MD - 0900 Hours R

The secure conference room on the fourth floor smelled faintly of coffee, toner, and dry-erase ink. Gray walls, no windows, white-noise hum overhead. A long oak table dominated the space, its edges worn from years of hard decisions.

Will Morgan and Guy Zarelli waited when Diane Watkins, Assistant U.S. Attorney for Maryland, strode in—five feet of composure and fire. She dropped a sealed folder on the table.

"Where are we?"

Zarelli leaned forward, eager. Will stayed silent, arms crossed.

"I'm holding a draft indictment," Diane said flatly. "Genevieve Larsson. Espionage Act. 18 U.S. Code § 793."

She looked from one man to the other. "You're asking me to charge a woman with a spotless fifteen-year clearance, DARPA commendations, and no prior issues—on what? A failed polygraph and a hunch?"

Will's voice was steady. "She didn't fail. It was inconclusive."

Diane's eyes flicked up. "Inconclusive as to what, Major?"

"To stolen information. Espionage. Contact with foreign agents."

She flipped a page. "And the drone surveillance? The supposed dead drop?"

"A message appeared in a concealed transmitter. She read it, pocketed it. That's all."

"No materials exchanged?"

"No, ma'am."

"She white-gloved the breach," Zarelli added.

Diane exhaled. "Then indict the phantom hacker. Don't bring me a scientist who blinked wrong on a polygraph and expect me to wreck her life over it."

She skimmed the bullet points. "She printed the file, but it never left her folder. The Russian version doesn't match, no chain of custody. The shortwave intercept is suspicious—but not evidence."

Her tone hardened. "Everything you have is circumstantial."

She turned to the monitor and brought up a DOJ header: U.S. v. Larsson, G. The gold seal glowed like a warning.

"Do you understand the gravity of this? Charging a U.S. citizen with espionage isn't a sandbox exercise. Once filed, it's forever."

Silence.

Finally, she pushed the folder across the table. "You've got three plays. One: pre-indictment plea—show her the draft, see if she breaks. Two: sneak-and-peek warrant—find that OTP or something tangible. Three: custodial interview—go hard, but once she knows, the game's over."

She stood, gathering her papers. "Pick one—or come back when you have more than smoke."

The door shut behind her.

Three loaded options—and every one aimed straight at Gene Larsson.

Dim light. LCD panels glow across the walls, SYBIL's lattice pulsing like a quiet heartbeat. Onscreen, timelines overlap with document fragments and profile shots.

Will Morgan sits at the head of the table, hands clasped. Around him: Sara Brandt, Grace Roberts, Zbigniew "Z" Zawadzki, Rick Huang, Thomas Carrone, and Cathy Wang—coffee cups half-drained, digital notepads open.

Grace leans forward, eyes fixed on a highlighted line. "ε^4 in the original. ε^3 in Ivan's copy. That's no typo. Drop one power on the dielectric factor and the system collapses at peak resonance."

Cathy taps her stylus. "But under low power it still simulates right? Enough to fool a test run?"

"Exactly," Rick murmurs. "False confidence. Months lost—or containment gone."

Will's gaze sweeps the table, silent but tracking every word. This was why he built this team—diverse, dangerous talent.

Rick continues. "Ivan swore he copied the original. Impossible. That stock kills duplication. No scan. No photo. Paper self-scrambles."

Sara frowns. "So, either he lied, or someone tampered before he saw it?"

"Neither" Rick says. "Aye Yah. Why plant a mistake you know we'll catch? Only scenario that tracks someone walked out the real thing, hand-copied it onto pilfered secure stock, slid the original back. Zakharov left with what he thought was genuine."

Sara shakes her head. "But that kind of access—who clears it without tripping logs?"

"Unless they are the anomaly," Rick says. "Admin level. Inside the print queue. Invisible."

Will crosses his arms. "An insider confident no one would question them."

Rick nods. "A surgical breach. The system fooled by its own routine."

Silence. SYBIL's pulse brightens, as if echoing the conclusion.

Will stands, taps the screen. A branching matrix lights up. "Four unknowns," he says evenly. "One: what do the Russians actually have—paper, file, or mimic? Two: how did SVR receive it—dead drop, code embed, brush pass? Three: what did they hand the CIA? Four: what did CIA show us?"

Z's voice is low. "They control the narrative at every step."

"Which means," Sara says, "the typo might be bait. A breadcrumb or a trap."

Will let the words hang. "Until we answer those four, Gene Larsson stays in limbo. We have whispers but no motive—and nothing forensic."

The screen dims again. The only sound is SYBIL, humming like a living witness.

Will paces, voice lowering.

"We need to reverse the leak trail. Let's list every individual with access and potential motive to alter the formula:

He taps the screen. Names appear:

1. *Gene Larsson – lead physicist, could be attempting to mislead the Russians.*
2. *Paul Vogle – internal Agency rival. Political motives., maybe protecting info.*
3. *Nikita Zakharov – Former Russian handler, now deceased. Following instructions.*
4. *Judd Lockwood – Rogue CIA. Attempt to create chaos.*
5. *CIA agent – Langley's IVAN handler. Someone may be muddying the trail.*
6. *Ivan – Our SVR mole. Can he be trusted?*
7. *Unknown mole at the SVR – potentially American, feeding false data upstream."*

"Gene had the clearest access. But not the clearest motive." said Grace.

"Unless she's playing a longer game." said Sara, "Or trying to mislead the Russians."

Z asked, "What if the typo isn't a mistake? What if it's deliberate—a digital dye pack - designed for manipulating digital images?"

Cathy thinks out loud, 'A canary trap?'

Thomas finally contributes, "Or a failsafe. Something only the real author would notice."

The room falls silent.

Will states what is on everyone's mind, "Then the key question becomes: Did Gene know the typo was there - not hers?

He lets that linger. "We need to find the first instance of that document, pre-leak. Metadata, print logs, access history. If we isolate the moment that typo appeared… we isolate the mole."

"Rick, you and Derek have Sybil access all archival logs indexing version history of all Sable-derived formula documents. Let's see if there is a signature trace. No assumptions. Just facts. And maybe—just maybe—a shadow in the code.

"Then, we will reconvene."

LaserTech Morgan's Conference Room - Moments later

The room was too quiet for midday. Monitors flickered with encrypted traffic and heat maps, but all eyes were on SYBIL's main display.

Grace stood arms crossed, lips thin. Rick tapped a tablet. Z paced slowly, hands clasped behind his back. Derek hovered beside Sara, silent as always.

"SYBIL," Grace said. "Audit LaserTech node Bravo-Four. Last thirty days. Flag any print hash mismatches."

SYBIL's calm voice filled the space.

"Initiating audit... parsing discrepancies..."

Five seconds. Ten.

"Discrepancy detected."

Z stopped pacing. "Details."

"Print job ID 92477," SYBIL said. "User: G. Larsson. Timestamp April 9, 16:13. Document: ENERGY_CORE_SEQ_MASTER.001.

Expected hash: 4a7f...993d.

Actual hash: 6c9b...12ee.

Routed through nonstandard spool buffer: FBI_NODE_REDIRECT_02. Credentials: Special Agent P. Vogle."

The silence cracked.

"Jesus," Rick muttered. "He rerouted the print job."

Grace turned slowly. "How does an FBI handler bypass SYBIL in a Level 5 SCIF?"

"Manual override," SYBIL replied. "Authorized Tier-Six OGA_NexusKey."

Z's eyes narrowed. "OGA. Other Government Agency."

"CIA," Rick said flatly.

SYBIL continued. "Energy scaling constant altered from ε^4 to ε^3. All other variables intact. Modification time: 87 seconds."

Grace's voice was a blade. "This wasn't a leak. It was a burn. Vogle crippled the formula so the Russians would trust it and fail."

"Or track them," Rick said.

"And Gene Larsson's the patsy," Z growled.

Sara snapped. "He has her print it, then calls it off. The file never leaves her folder, but he grabs it, duplicates it on secure stock."

Rick added, "Fancy Bear already had the file names. Word docs sitting unencrypted—easy pickings."

Sara gave a bitter laugh. "Vogle thought he was outsmarting the Russians. He was stepping on Gene's trap."

No one spoke. Gene's credibility had just spiked—but at a price.

Grace raised her hand. "Flag Vogle. Tier-One Priority. Alert Will."

SYBIL's display pulsed. "Command received. Intercept protocol 'Iron Echo.'"

CHAPTER TWENTY-SEVEN

Interrogation

"The point of interrogation is to get at the truth, not to get at what the interrogator wants to hear."

— Martin Seligman

LaserTech - Interrogation Room - 1750 Hours R

A cold fluorescence bled from a single overhead light in the windowless interview room. The air hung heavily with silence. One blinking red camera watched from the corner ceiling like a tireless sentinel. The table was metal. The three chairs unpadded.

Gene Larsson sat in one of them, alone.

Her face was pale, calm at first glance—but her fingers trembled where they rested on the tabletop. Her LaserTech ID badge was gone. Stripped of it. Her breath came light and shallow, as if each inhale carried consequences.

The heavy door opened. In stepped Zbigniew Zawadzki "Z" and Sara Brandt, the former carrying a slim folder under his arm.

Z moved with calm precision, the intensity of a man used to secrets and betrayal.

"Gene," he said. "Thanks for staying late."

Gene didn't look up.

"Wasn't much of a choice."

"That's true." He paused, voice hardening. "You're not under arrest—but you are being detained for questioning under federal authority. You are entitled to remain silent. You are entitled to legal counsel. Do you understand these rights?"

A small nod.

"We'll need verbal confirmation."

"I understand."

"Good."

He laid the folder on the table, but left it closed. No games—pressure.

"You're a physicist, Gene Larsson. One of the best. You've had codeword clearances for over a decade. We've never had an issue."

Gene remained silent.

"But a document classified Codeword Eyes Only—related to Reliant Sentry—was printed from your terminal. That copy never left your file drawer. And yet... a nearly identical version ended up with a Russian handler in Moscow."

Her eyes lowered.

"We also have video of you decoding shortwave messages using a one-time pad."

He slid a photo across the table. She didn't touch it.

"We've seen your phone logs. Calls to a number assigned to a Bureau agent two years ago. And a dead drop pickup, two nights ago, Northeast sector."

Silence.

"Gene, this is your chance. You can help us. Or you can go down alone."

She swallowed.

"I was helping."

"Helping who?"

"I was passing disinformation. They said... they said I was protecting the program. Feeding what we chose to share. Slowing them down to give us time to complete Radiant Sentry."

"Who said?"

"The FBI agent. The one who called me back after I contacted the FBI when approached in Oslo."

"Name."

She hesitated. Her voice cracked.

"He said his name was Casey... Casey Jones, FBI counterintel. I was told it was compartmentalized—even my clearance wouldn't confirm it."

Z and Sara exchanged a glance. The name was new.

"You're telling us you thought you were working for us?"

"I didn't think. I believed it because I was."

A long silence stretched between them.

"Okay," said at last. "That's a start. We'll check it out."

Gene sat frozen, posture rigid, as if braced against invisible pressure. Z leaned in closer now, elbows on the table, tone quieter—but sharper.

"Gene Larsson... if you are a double agent or were manipulated—used—those we can work with. But we need the full picture."

She nodded slowly, a flicker of uncertainty in her eyes.

"It wasn't just a voice on the phone. I met him. Once."

"Where?"

"Parking garage under the old NSA annex in Laurel. He showed credentials — FBI, Counterintelligence Division."

Z watched her carefully. She believed what she was saying.

"Describe him."

"White, mid-forties, clean-cut. Calm, but... cold. Like everything was rehearsed."

"What kind of files did he ask for?"

"He didn't ask for documents. Not at first. He'd describe scenarios — 'If a Russian team were targeting our Low Earth Orbit grid, how would they do it?' I'd sketch answers. Draw diagrams. He said it was war gaming."

"When did it shift?"

"A few months ago. After some satellite test over the Pacific. He wanted information on Reliant Sentry protocol thresholds, encryption routines. Said the misinformation would slow them down. Create noise."

"So, you planted false data?"

"Some of it. Not all. He said that's how it had to look—real enough to be credible. I was careful. He said we needed a document that was clearly Reliant Sentry. I explained that it was impossible because everything was printed on security paper.

He said he had access to our security paper and could reproduce it. The only thing I ever printed was a document with an erroneous formula. But I never gave it to him because he changed his mind."

Z didn't flinch.

"Careful doesn't stop a mole from stealing state secrets."

He checked his phone. A single text had come in. He read it, then looked back at her.

"Gene... there's no Casey Jones in FBI Counterintelligence."

Her pupils dilated. "That's impossible."

"No. That's how a pro operates."

He leaned back, voice casual.

"Have you ever heard of the Ballad of Casey Jones? Mighty Casey Strikes Out? I guess not."

He shook his head.

"FBI CI agents don't use their real names—for security reasons. To protect the case, themselves, and their families."

He rose from the table.

"We will find out who Casey Jones is."

Gene stared at him, her world cracking open.

"How do you contact him?"

Gene reached into her pocket and put a burner phone on the table. "With this. He gave me this phone with his number - it's the only number on it."

"Gene... er... Sable," he said, invoking her codename on purpose.

"We're going to take a short break. Relax for a few minutes."

He left her there in silence, the door closing with a click like a judge's gavel.

Outside the conference room door, he handed Gene's burner phone to Will who was waiting patiently. Will dialed the number and Paul Vogle answered on the first ring.

"Gene?"

"This is Will Morgan, ACIC. We just finished a custodial interview with Gene Larsson. You don't want to strike out on this call, Casey."

"Where are you?

"LaserTech."

"I am Special Agent Paul Vogle. I can be there in about an hour."

"I am undercover as a DARPA management auditor; I will have a pass waiting for you at the main gate and reception. See you in an hour."

Gene looked at her reflection in the mirrored wall wondering who was monitoring the interview on the other side. Someone she knew? Someone new? Did she really care?

The door opened with a whisper of hydraulics.

Z and Sara reentered the room, and Z dropped the folder on the table and didn't sit.

Sara pulled out a chair and sat down across from her, folding her long legs with casual elegance.

"We're not here to scream or scare you," she said. "We're here to understand one thing: whether you altered the formula."

Gene's eyes flicked toward her, then back to Z.

"Is that what you think?"

Z opened the folder. "Original document from LaserTech. Energy sequence line four. ε to the fourth power." He flipped the page. "The version Ivan supplied to the SVR—ε cubed."

He looked up.

"That mistake didn't happen by accident."

Gene leaned back. "I didn't transcribe it. Wherever you got it must have done it."

Sarah asked, "So that there is no misunderstanding you created the document with an error, but the transcribed document has a different error? Like a typo?"

Z smiled. "Sure. But he transcribed it from your lab's secure terminal. Paper printout. No scans. No copies. Only one human in the loop."

Gene's jaw tightened.

Z circled the table. "You've reviewed that formula twenty-three times in the last two months. We pulled the logs. You printed it twice. Once, three weeks ago. Once five days before we discovered the breach."

He leaned in. "Who was the second printout for?"

"I only printed it once."

Sara folded her hands. "Let's talk about motive, Gene. You're loyal. We know that. You've worked too hard, sacrificed too much to all of a sudden hand over real tech to the Russians."

She tilted her head.

"So maybe you degraded it. Just enough to keep them chasing shadows. ε^3 instead of ε^4. Close enough to look right,

231

but wrong enough to fail. That would make you the patriot in this room."

Seconds passed. Gene looked at Sara but said nothing.

Z wasn't as patient. "Was it you? Just tell us."

Sara's eyes narrowed just a fraction. "Would you? Or would you operate off the record to trace the breach internally?"

Gene's tone was neutral. "If I had suspected a leak, I would've reported it."

No reply.

Z tapped the folder again. "We considered a few options. You made a mistake. You sabotaged the formula. Your FBI handler, Casey or whomever, instructed you to alter it. Ivan doctored it on the way out. Or the CIA got involved and changed it without telling anyone."

Gene gave the faintest shake of her head. "The CIA doesn't have access to my lab."

Sara leaned closer, voice tightening. "What about Ivan? Did you ever meet him outside protocol? Off-hours? A chat that didn't hit SYBIL?"

"No, I never even met Nikita Zakharov. I followed every protocol. In the beginning we used dead drops and later electronic Bluetooth walk by messages."

Z studied her. "So why ε^3? Why not ε^2? Or ε^5?"

Gene blinked once. No flicker of confusion.

Sara caught it too. "That's the thing, Gene. You didn't react like someone hearing about this error for the first time."

Gene looked at both of them. Her voice, when it came, was soft but firm.

"If someone tampered with that formula between my printout and your mole's delivery, it wasn't me."

Gene her tone shifted to defiance now, "This makes no sense. I already told you that I created the document with a wrong factor in the formula on purpose. What would be the point for me to add a different error in a second document? Both versions are wrong.

"It should be obvious to you Sherlocks that someone else, unaware of my fraudulent factor, decided to add their own.

"And has anyone bothered to notice that ε^3 instead of ε^4 is not the error I inserted. Apparently, you didn't look past your noses to see where I altered the formula—perhaps it never occurred to you, or you simply were not able to find it?"

"Then give us names," Z said. "Who had access?"

Gene paused. "Print jobs are logged. Secure terminals. No external storage."

Sara sat forward, finally interested. "Did Vogle see the full printout at any time?"

"No."

"Did you hand it to him directly?"

"No," Gene said. "I told you he changed his mind."

Sara and Z exchanged a look.

Sara stepped back. "That's enough for now."

Z hit the comm switch on the wall. The door hissed open.

Before he walked out, Z looked back at Gene. "You're either our firewall… or the fuse."

He closed the door behind him.

LaserTech Morgan's Conference Room - 1138 Hours R

The room was quiet—too quiet for midday. Focused silence as multiple monitors cycled through encrypted traffic and biometric heat maps, but everyone's attention was pulled toward the front wall where SYBIL's interface had just lit up.

Grace Roberts stood with her arms crossed, lips pressed tight. Rick Huang flanked her, tapping on a tablet. On the opposite side, "Z" Zawadzki paced in a slow loop, arms behind his back like a general waiting for the first domino to fall. And as always, Derek stood invisible in the background next to Sara.

"SYBIL," Grace said, "run a comparative audit of print access logs for LaserTech node Bravo-Four. Filter for the last 30 days. Flag all variances between document hash signatures and system-confirmed outputs."

SYBIL's voice, calm and measured, filled the space:

"Initiating audit. Cross-referencing print log metadata... Parsing hash discrepancies..."

The room held its breath.

Five seconds. Ten. Thirty. Then—

"Discrepancy detected."

Z stopped pacing. "Details," he said mumbling.

SYBIL responded:

"Print job ID 92477 — initiated by user: G. Larsson, timestamp: April 9, 16:13 hours."

Document: ENERGY_CORE_SEQ_MASTER.001

Expected hash: 4a7f...993d

Actual output hash: 6c9b...12ee

"File was routed through nonstandard spool buffer prior to paper output. Buffer identified as FBI_NODE_REDIRECT_02."

"Intermediary system signature matches credentials of Special Agent P. Vogle."

The silence broke like glass.

"Aye Yah," Rick muttered. "He rerouted the print job."

Grace turned slowly. "How the hell does an FBI handler reroute a classified print job from a Level 5 SCIF node without triggering SYBIL's watchdog protocols?"

SYBIL answered before anyone else could.

"Manual override flag detected. Classified access token authorized by 'Tier-Six Override: OGA_NexusKey'."

Z's eyes narrowed. "OGA—Other Government Agency."

Rick's voice was flat. "CIA?"

Grace said nothing. She stared at the display like it had grown teeth.

SYBIL continued:

"Document modification occurred during buffer process. Energy scaling constant altered from ε^4 to ε^3. All other variables preserved. No indication of formatting errors or corruption."

"Conclusion: The document was intentionally degraded during unauthorized buffer intervention. Operator: P. Vogle. Override key origin: OGA/FBI."

Z crossed to the screen and tapped SYBIL's prompt line.

"Timestamp of modification?"

"April 9, 16:15 hours. Total time in buffer: 87 seconds."

"Enough time for a deliberate edit," Rick said.

Grace finally spoke, voice low and razor-sharp. "This wasn't a leak. It was a burn operation. Vogle had the formula altered—crippled—so the Russians would trust it and fail."

Rick's eyes darted. "Or so someone could track how they used it."

Z didn't move. His voice growled. "And Gene Larsson was the patsy."

"Sneaky bastard." fumed Sara, "He has her create the document, then after she prints it, but before she delivers it, he tells her he has changed his mind and doesn't want it anymore. That way the document never leaves Gene's files, but he grabs it electronically and replicates it on the secure paper he got from the printing company."

Rick adds, "We know Fancy Bear had hacked into LaserTech's system and that document file names are stored unencrypted. Then word docs can be grabbed from the server. As my father likes to say 'easy, peasy'."

Sara enjoying the situational irony. "Vogle thought he was cleverly manipulating the formula to mislead the Russians, but he was interfering with a trap of planted disinformation by Gene."

The room held still. No one liked what it meant.

Gene's credibility jumped up a notch.
Grace raised her hand toward SYBIL.
"Flag Vogle as Tier-One Priority. Alert Will."
SYBIL acknowledged:
"Command received. Intercept Protocol Iron Echo'
The screen blinked once.

CHAPTER TWENTY-EIGHT

Labyrinths & Mazes

LaserTech Conference Room - 2300 Hours R

The day was late, and the room was silent, the kind of silence that thickens around lies and truths not yet named.

Will Morgan stood alone, hands clasped behind his back, eyes trained on the door. His expression was unreadable—a practiced stillness carved from years of deception, fieldwork, and buried cost. A half-empty bottle of water sat untouched on the conference room table. The lights overhead cast long shadows, but none more pressing than the one sitting behind his eyes.

The door opened.

FBI Special Agent Paul Vogle, in his late forties, trench coat slung over his arm, suit impeccable but lived-in, was escorted to Morgan's conference room where Grace, Sarah and Derek were seated. As he entered he looked like a man who had eaten too many secrets and learned to digest them. His eyes scanned the room, locked on Will.

"Thanks for seeing me so quickly," Vogle said, setting the coat on the chair but not sitting.

Will didn't blink. There was no use dancing around it. His voice low but firm he said, "We know that Gene Larsson possess stolen classified documents that have made their way to Russia.

"There are labyrinths and mazes, A maze is designed for you to lose your way; a labyrinth is designed for you to find your way. Which do we have here?"

Vogel said, "That depends... on whether you're hunting—or being led."

"We're done with being led. The hunt is well underway. Gene Larsson. Codename Sable. I need it confirmed. Right now."

There was no aggression in his voice. Just precision. Measured, scalpel-sharp.

Paul let out a dry, humorless chuckle. "Nice work. You won't tell me how you know if I ask... will you?"

"Not at this point, "Will said, allowing himself a small, wolfish smile. "I do think we can work together - probably have to."

Vogle didn't flinch. He took his time, then pulled a folded leather wallet from his inside jacket pocket and flipped it open on the table. Inside, a red-flagged document—a compartmentalized intelligence operations clearance.

"Palisades. That's what the Russian's call it," he said. "Two years running. Authorized by NSC subcommittee directive our codename Iron Vista and run exclusively out of FBI Counterintelligence. She was approached in April—two years ago. She came to us immediately. Voluntarily."

Will stepped forward, slowly. One move at a time. His voice dropped a register.

"And you trusted her? With Radiant Sentry intel? With the very thing they're killing people over?"

"She never gave them anything real. Only engineered narrative. Prototypes we knew wouldn't work. Equations crafted wrong enough to stall replication. It bought us eighteen months of breathing room."

Will stared, searching Vogle's face for any tremor, any hitch in the cadence.

"Why the hell didn't you tell me?"

"Because that's the point of a deep-cover op," Vogle snapped, tone sharpening, "You think I liked watching her sit in that lab, knowing she was a target, knowing she had no backup but a burner line and me? She lived in the crosshairs for twenty-four months so we could use her as a disinformation vector."

Silence.

"And because we didn't know if we could trust you. You would have done the same."

That landed like a quiet shot. Not cruel. Just honest.

Will's jaw tightened. A flicker of heat barely contained. But it passed.

"She says she's clean. That she told you everything. That she never wavered."

"She's telling the truth," Vogle said. "And you know it. You've seen the field signals. Cross-check her fake data—it matches our uncovered drop patterns. Hell, you've used some of it to run your own traps."

Will exhaled through his nose, a storm beginning to settle.

"She risked everything."

Vogle finally sat, tired lines etched around his eyes.

"She still is. Sable played a dangerous game. But she played it for us. For you."

"One last thing, we know that you intercepted Gene's document, altered it and passed it by some means to the Russians," said Will, "on security paper you bought from LaserTech's vendor no less."

Vogle sat is stunned silence for a moment wondering how they found that out, then said, "Again, compliments, yes, I wanted to provide Gene with some deniability so I had our people alter the formula and print it on the same security paper."

"Would it surprise you to learn that she had already altered the formula?" asked Will.

"No. I didn't ask her to, but she is very careful, and you know how smart she is. Doesn't surprise me at all."

"Are you not concerned that two errors might stick out to the Russians?"

"Yes, but they have to find them first and we didn't find Gene's so, it is not that simple."

"In other words, oops. Let's hope for the best."

"Had I known she had already altered the formula I wouldn't have had the need to do it myself. Again, she wasn't told to provide her deniability."

Another silence passed. Will looked away for a moment—just a moment—then returned his gaze with full weight.

"If I find out you lied to her, used her for something else... I'll put you in the ground myself."

Vogle nodded.

"Fair."

They stared at each other—two men from different empires of secrecy, aligned for now by the slender thread of one woman's loyalty.

Finally, Will stepped back.

"She stays under ACIC protection. Nobody touches her unless I sign off. Not NSA. Not Bureau. Not even the damn President."

Vogle's eyes flicked with something—respect, maybe. Maybe relief.

"Understood."

Will moved to the door, hand on the handle, then stopped.

"I'm sure you know she is about to go through the ringer. Can't be helped – wish it could but there is too much at stake and it's out of my hands for now.

The door clicked behind him as he disappeared down the hallway, leaving Vogle in the still room, alone with the weight of his thoughts.

Double Agents Can't Be Trusted

LaserTech – Morgan's Conference Room–Next Day 0820 Hours R

The room buzzes with quiet intensity. Will Morgan stands at the head of the table, sleeves rolled up, a mug of black coffee untouched in front of him.

Around the table: Sara Brandt leans forward, her notepad closed but her mind turning. Grace Roberts watches silently, arms folded. Derek Wilshire sits cross-legged, chewing on a pen cap. On the conference screen: split boxes showing Cathy Wang, Rick Huang, Cecil Brandon, and Thomas Carrone, all patched in remotely on ZoomGov.

Will glances at the team, then back at the whiteboard, where the words "GENE LARSSON – ASSET or LIABILITY?" are scrawled in red.

"All right. Let's get real. We've cracked the IVAN formula puzzle. SYBIL mapped it out perfectly. The FBI inserted a fake variable. But they didn't know Gene beat them to it—she'd already planted a bogus factor of her own."

Grace said, "Two false leads in the same formula. That's poetic."

"More like terrifying." replies Sara.

"It should be. That kind of layered deception doesn't happen by accident. It takes intent. Calculation."

He turns to the team.

"Now, I know some of you feel sympathy for Gene. She came clean fast. Took the polygraph. Volunteered for the custodial debrief. Hell, she reported the SVR approach to the FBI less than twenty-four hours after Oslo."

Thomas the team profiler said, "That's what we want from a patriot who's been approached."

Will ever the professional, "It is. But it's also what a good double wants you to think."

"Let's all remember the Katrina Leung disaster. Leung worked as a valuable FBI informant for over two decades, providing information on Chinese intelligence operations. The FBI paid her $1.7 million while she was a triple agent providing our secrets to the PLA.

"Ever since then double agents face extensive scrutiny."

A pause. Will taps the whiteboard.

"Let me say this clearly: DCIS's position is that double agents can never be one hundred percent trusted. Not even the ones we create. Especially not them."

Cathy Wang the newest on the team questions, "But we recruited her. She's ours."

"Is she?"

He looks directly into Cathy's feed.

"She agreed to work for us. That's cooperation. It's not loyalty. There's a difference."

Rick said, "So what are you saying? That Gene's still playing us?"

"I'm saying the potential always exists. Let me break it down for you."

He walks as he talks; each point punctuated with crisp clarity.

"One: She's already crossed the line once. She took a Russian pitch. Doesn't matter if she rejected it—she was in the room. That means she considered it, even if for a second. And once you've considered treason, the door never fully shuts."

242

Grace adds, "Nikita Zakharov didn't court amateurs. She was targeted for a reason."

"Which brings us to…

"Two: Turned doesn't mean transformed. People flip for all sorts of reasons—greed, fear, ego, resentment. But none of those motives guarantee conversion. You can scare someone into flipping. Doesn't mean they believe in your flag."

Sara said, "So even if we own their actions, we can't own their soul."

"Right. Their loyalty's leased. Not bought."

"Three: Initiative stays with the double. A good one knows how to signal their old handler, slip disinformation, or hedge a truth so it can't be traced. Every interaction is a dance—what to give, what to withhold.

"That's what makes her useful, though. She knows how the Russians think."

"She knows how we think too. That cuts both ways."

"Four: We're not the only ones playing her. The SVR might know she flipped. They could be feeding her curated garbage to test us. Or using her to send us off a cliff. If she's a triple and we don't see it—we lose the whole board."

Cecil said, "She passed CI. No deception flagged."

"Her test was inconclusive. Polygraphs don't measure allegiance. They measure physiology. Belief, not truth. A well-trained liar believes in their lie.

"Five: Every word from a double agent is strategic. Not heartfelt. They ask themselves: "What does my handler want to hear?" Then they deliver. That's not honesty. That's performance."

Thomas said, "Sounds like half my patients."

Will chuckled, "And we don't deploy them in black ops."

He stops, serious now.

"Six: Doctrine says: Never fully trust someone who's already betrayed their own. Use them? Sure. But always assume contingency. Always assume misdirection."

A long silence. The team absorbs this.

Cathy asked, "So what do we do with her?"

"We use her. Smartly. We confirm every report. We run redundant surveillance. And we never, ever let her forget whose leash she's on."

Grace asked, "Even if she's clean?"

"If she's clean, she'll understand. If she's not—we'll catch the twitch.

"Look, I'm not saying Gene's dirty. I'm saying she's human. And humans—especially the brilliant, conflicted, compromised ones—are the biggest operational risk we've got."

He lets that hang in the air.

"A double agent is a tool. Not a teammate. They can be vital. But never safe."

He picks up his cold coffee. Still doesn't drink it.

"There will come a time when her role as Sable surpasses its useful life. It will be too dangerous for her to continue to be Sable. If she is clean she won't be able to safely work for DARPA, to be in the open. The best thing for her and us may be to keep her close - very close."

Thomas asked, "What does that mean?"

"We'll see. That's one valuable human being who just may be the real deal."

Now. Let's talk next steps. For the time being, we use Gene Larsson. But we don't trust her 100%."

SYBIL: Confirmed. Asset Larsson flagged for dual-track validation protocol.

Will raised an eyebrow. SYBIL has already moved ahead of them.

Will said, "See? She gets it."

Sara and Grace head back to their workstations.

Sara's knowing smile began at the corner of her mouth, a quiet upturn. Her eyes—cool, calculating—held the real message: she understood what was going on. Not just what was said, but what wasn't. It wasn't smug. It was measured. Controlled. A signal to those paying attention that she'd connected the dots—maybe before anyone else had. It didn't ask for recognition. It told you she didn't need it.

Grace whispers to Sara, "OK give, what was that bit at the end all about? I'm confused never isn't never where Gene is concerned? I know you know."

Sara giggles, "Yeah, I've seen this before. That little speech was for staff. He has something up his sleeve. Cards he can't play yet but there is no way he is letting a talent like Gene Larsson get thrown under the bus now that he knows the facts. Stay tuned."

CHAPTER TWENTY-NINE

Inquisition

Fort Meade ACIC Secure Conference Room

The hum of overhead lights was the only sound as Gene sat alone at the glass table, her ACIC badge clipped to her lapel, her eyes fixed on nothing. Her posture was composed, but her fingers traced silent, invisible patterns along the edge of the table—tiny betrayals of nerves she couldn't quite suppress.

The door opened, and Will Morgan entered. No entourage. No briefing packet. Just him.

He shut the door behind him and didn't speak right away. She studied his face, searching for the verdict.

"Vogle vouched for you," Will said.

She exhaled, a small release of tension from her shoulders. "Then you know."

"Yeah," he said, stepping closer, eyes locked to hers. "I know. You were approached by Russian assets two years ago. You went straight to the Bureau. You agreed to work with them— to run interference, feed the SVR disinfo, stall their tech pipeline."

She nodded once. No excuse, no elaboration. Just confirmation.

"Operation Palisades," Will continued. "You were their plant. But our weapon."

"I never gave them anything real," Gene said with urgency in her voice. "You need to believe that."

"I do."

The room went still. But it wasn't over.

Will took a deep breath, then sat across from her, his expression firm.

"But this doesn't just go away. Now, it's the inquisition."

She knew. Of course she knew. But hearing it from him still felt like a crack in the floor beneath her.

"The CIA will want to run a full trace on your past communications. Every phone call, every encrypted drop. NSA's already flagging your Radiant Sentry terminal activity for behavioral anomalies. DCSA's going to strip your clearance down to the rivets and rebuild it from scratch—assuming they approve it at all."

She met his gaze, unwavering. "I understand."

"And ACIC..." He stopped for a beat. "My own people aren't thrilled I didn't know. Some of them think I got too close."

A flicker of hurt moved across her features, then buried.

"So, what happens now?" she asked.

"Now," Will said, "you get dragged through hell."

She nodded again, quietly. Bracing for it.

"It's going to get invasive. Personal. They'll question everything. Not just your work—your intentions, your motives, your life. They'll make you relive every decision you made for the past two years and force you to explain it to people who don't care about nuance or context. Just threat vectors."

Gene let out a tight breath.

"And if they don't clear me?"

Will didn't answer right away. He stared at her—really stared.

"Then they're fools," he said.

A silence settled between them. Dense, but not empty. It held history now. And something else—unspoken but known.

She studied him for a long moment.

"You believe me," she said whispered.

"I have to," he replied. "Because if you were lying, we'd already be dead."

Then, softer:

"Because I want to."

The line hung in the air, more dangerous than any bullet.

She gave him a small, rueful smile.

"That's not very professional."

"No," he said. "It's not."

A pause. Then he stood.

"You'll get through it. And when it's over, when they clear you—we finish what we started. Radiant Sentry, Iron Vista, all of it."

He moved to the door. Before he opened it, he turned back.

"I'm not letting them burn you for doing the right thing. Not on my watch."

He left.

And Gene, sitting alone again, closed her eyes—not in fear. But in relief. Because for the first time in two years, someone other than Vogle believed in her. Someone who had a voice.

Fort Belvoir—0910 Hours R

The Commander's conference room at Fort Belvoir was a different beast altogether—larger, colder, humming with hidden microphones and unseen cameras. The morning air buzzed with a mix of stale coffee and the sharper smell of tension.

Around the table sat Commander Edwards, Ed Perry, Will Morgan, Sara Brandt, Grace Roberts, Judd Lockwood, Thomas

Carrone and Guy Zarelli. Everyone wore that particularly grim federal look—serious, calculating, ready for battle.

Owen adjusted his glasses, looking over the rim at the gathered team.

"It appears that we may, I repeat may, have an exceptional opportunity before us," he began, voice steady, "to slow the Russians down."

Will leaned forward, voice tight with urgency. "The pressure is on us to give our scientists a comfortable lead."

Owen nodded, shuffling a thick folder of papers. "I would like to get everybody's views. But first, let me summarize the situation so everybody is on the same page."

He glanced around the room to make sure everyone was locked in, then continued.

"Will's team developed a great deal of circumstantial evidence against Genevieve Larsson - not enough evidence to satisfy the U.S. Attorney to indict her for espionage. However, she agreed that she might be guilty of something.

At her suggestion, we placed her under custodial investigation and interrogated her at which time she claimed to be a double agent. We then met with Paul Vogle an FBI Counterintelligence Agent, who revealed that Gene has, in fact, been an FBI double agent for the past two years."

The revelation hung in the air like smoke.

The weight of the information seemed to settle heavily across the room.

"Our CIA asset is not aware of the fact that Gene is a double agent," Owen went on.

"We did not inform Vogle of any details of Will's investigation or the existence of—what did you call him, Judd?"

"Ivan, sir," Judd replied.

"Yes..." Owen nodded. "Of the existence of Ivan."

"For the past six weeks Gene endured extensive interrogation under custody. We need to make a determination if she is ours or theirs." he said.

He allowed a second for that to sink in before moving on. "So, the question now is how best to take advantage of this situation, assuming we conclude she is ours."

CHAPTER THIRTY

Truth

"The trust of the innocent is the liar's most useful tool."

— *Stephen King*

Odenton, MD - Morgan's House

He'd read the transcript twice.

The words were clean. Reasonable. Structured like honesty.

But he'd learned the hard way that truth doesn't always come dressed as a lie. Sometimes it wears sincerity like a uniform—creases pressed, voice steady, logic airtight.

Sometimes it means well.

Will leaned back in the chair, eyes unfocused. A memory surfaced. A choice made by someone he loved—someone who hadn't meant to hurt him but did. Someone who'd convinced themselves it was the right thing.

Lies didn't always come from dark places. That was the part nobody liked to talk about.

People lied out of fear. Out of love. Out of the unbearable weight of wanting to protect. And those lies were harder to see. Harder to challenge. Because they wore the face of trust.

He thought of SYBIL—her glowing confidence percentages, her ranked threat assessments, her cold certainties presented without context. She never hesitated. Never doubted. Never asked why someone might do something—just what they'd done.

Words mattered. But words, without an understanding of motive, were just noise.

A string of letters. A signal. Intercepted, cataloged, ranked by priority.

He'd seen what that led to—decisions made in haste, trust given to the wrong person, truth measured in metadata instead of meaning.

He wasn't bitter about it anymore. He just understood now.

Trust wasn't built on clean reports or algorithmic clarity. It was built on watching, listening, absorbing the spaces between words. The delay before an answer. The flicker of guilt. The too-perfect phrasing.

That was where truth lived. In the shadow, not the spotlight.

And that was where he'd always keep his eyes.

He stood and looked out the window into the darkness as his mind wandered to the past.

He had come into the world beneath a quiet, persistent shadow. His mother, newly separated and barely twenty-two, returned to her parents' modest home in the gray spine of Pennsylvania coal country. In Reading, divorce was less a fact than a whispered disgrace, especially in 1981. For years, Will was the only kid in class without a father in the school auditorium or on the Little League sidelines. He never talked about it. He didn't have to. The silence did the work for him.

He bore that silence like scar tissue—tough, invisible, and just beneath the skin.

His grandfather filled the space no one else would. A Welsh immigrant with calloused hands and unbending ethics, he never softened the world, only taught Will how to endure it. From him, Will learned discipline and work ethic, as well as the kind of pride that didn't need applause.

When Will turned eighteen, preparing to leave for college, his mother stood in the doorway of his room and made an offer she had rehearsed for years. Did he want to meet his father - the man who lived in the same town all these years—the man everyone assumed was his father? After a long, empty silence, Will said no. Not cruelly. Yet finally. To him, his grandfather had already earned that title, and no one else ever would. He never asked questions. He never looked back.

But the past doesn't always stay buried. Not forever.

At thirty-two, Will got a call from a probate attorney. The man presumed to be his biological father had died. His second family contested the will, claiming Will couldn't be related. Will didn't care about the money. What burned was the implication—what it said about his mother's truth, about her dignity. He saw it as an attack on her character, and that was something he'd never allow.

What followed was a slow unsealing of history.

His mother's former divorce lawyer, speaking carefully and within the bounds of confidentiality, nudged Will toward what had long been hidden: a sealed settlement, an exchange of silence for alimony, an unspoken arrangement made to shield a young mother and child from the weight of small-town judgment.

He would never forget the phone call.

His mother's voice was small, frightened, unfamiliar in its vulnerability. And finally, she told him the truth.

The man he'd refused to meet wasn't his father. Not biologically. His real father had been a wartime affair—an accidental flame sparked while her husband was stationed overseas. A brief, guilty moment that left her pregnant and terrified. When her marriage dissolved, she kept the affair hidden, folding it into the broader shame of divorce. And when Will declined the chance to know the man he thought was his father, she took it as a sign. A gift. Permission to keep the secret buried.

But secrets don't die. They wait.

That night, Will didn't rage or interrogate. He did what he always did—he acted.

He wrote her a letter.

It was deliberate, composed, and honest. He told her he understood. He told her he forgave her. He told her he loved her.

What he didn't say—what he wouldn't write—was that he was still learning how to forgive himself. For expecting her to be flawless. For the distance he let grow between them. For all the years he mistook silence for strength.

Two years later, she was in hospice—frail, fading, and riddled with cancer that had stolen her voice and her energy, but not her will. The nurses said she was holding on for something. Will knew what it was.

He boarded a red-eye and arrived at her bedside as the sun rose.

She opened her eyes when he took her hand, her grip as light as breath. She didn't ask for much. Only one thing.

She desperately needed to hear it.

And he gave it to her—quietly, fiercely, without hesitation. That yes, he had forgiven her. Years ago. Fully. Unreservedly.

That he loved her. Still. Always.

She passed later that afternoon. And for the first time in her life, she left this world with nothing left unsaid.

Today, Will keeps his private life sealed tight as if it were a case file.

Loyal to his team, revered by those under his command, he channels the ache of his personal history into an unwavering pursuit of justice.

He doesn't chase praise. He doesn't seek closure. He seeks truth. And justice. Knowing sometimes both arrive with blood on their hands.

Langley – Sublevel Briefing Room Delta-3, 7:02 A.M.

It was six weeks after her interrogation.

The walls hadn't changed. Neither had the monotonous hum of mechanicals, or the cold glint of brushed steel along the table's edge. But the atmosphere was different now—subtly taut, as though the room itself understood what it had cost to bring Gene Larsson back here.

She sat alone at the far end; badge clipped to a navy blazer: Consultant – C5. Temporary. Tentative. But it was a badge.

The side door opened—not the main entrance. The one to which few people paid attention, because few were allowed to use it. Will Morgan stepped in, charcoal gray suit, no tie. He carried no folder. He needed none.

Gene met his eyes, but he didn't smile. He gave a slight nod—silent confirmation of everything he'd fought for behind closed doors.

Then Assistant Director Helen Crowder entered, brisk and unsentimental, a red folder in hand. She walked straight to Gene and dropped it on the table.

"Zürich account. Audit closed. No violations. No contact outside Bureau parameters. You're clear."

Gene didn't move. Her hands stayed folded.

Crowder exhaled. "Morgan wouldn't let it go."

She glanced at him. Will said nothing.

"He said you were a true double agent. Not tactical—moral. That you put yourself in harm's way not for money, not for leverage, but for the one motive no one wanted to believe."

Crowder's voice flattened, as if quoting from memory:

"She did it for the country. That's all. Which makes her more dangerous than anyone in this building."

Gene's eyes flicked to Will again, but this time there was something there—a faint shift in posture. Gratitude she wouldn't let herself say out loud.

Crowder placed a leather folio in front of Gene.

"This document outlines the scope, limits, and protective measures involved in your formal reinstatement under Directive 9-Bravo of Operation Echo Mirage."

Gene didn't reach for it.

"Your security classification is restored. Your handler is William Morgan. You report only to the mission's Tri-Agency Liaison Board. Your cover will be rewritten. Your file sanitized. Your past communications, if reviewed, will be made to help with the integrity of the operation. You will be protected."

Silence.

Gene stared straight ahead.

Then: "And what about my Swiss account? The one you've been feeding rubles into to keep up appearances?"

Crowder answered this time, voice neutral. "It remains under Agency custody. No withdrawals. No interest gained. But the Russians still believe you're compromised."

"And that's worth more to us than any confession," Will added.

"I never wanted this," she said. "And the way you all doubted me—made me doubt myself—I should walk away."

Crowder didn't reply.

"But I won't," Gene said. "Because this isn't for you. And it's not about me. It's about what they're trying to break—and what we're still trying to protect."

She turned.

"I'm in."

Crowder handed her a badge.

"Welcome back, Larsson."

She then handed her a folder, labeled Top Secret - Eyes Only - Operation Echo Mirage.

Gene opened it and read it without saying a word,

The mission's primary objective was to execute a sustained scientific misinformation campaign that introduced highly technical, plausible, but deliberately flawed data into known Russian collection channels.

The goal was to protect American orbital assets by ensuring the U.S. laser defense system remains a step ahead— untouched, uncountered, and fully operational when the next generation of space warfare begins.

Gene's brow lifted. "And now you trust me?"

"No," Crowder said in a pointed manner. "But he does."

Will Morgan stepped forward. For the first time, he spoke.

"She's vital. No one else can maneuver that kind of quantum-level misdirection from inside the entanglement framework. Not without burning years of signals infrastructure."

He looked at Gene, not with pity, but resolve.

"You're not a liability. You're the fulcrum. The entire phase-two vector of Echo Mirage depends on your signature being what the SVR expects."

Gene stood slowly, picking up the red folder without a word. No applause. No apology. Just the cold machinery of national security turning with her, not against her, for the first time in years.

As she walked out, Will followed behind her.

"There is a car for you, or I would be happy to give you a lift back to Linthicum." offered Will.

"Thank you I would be grateful." she accepted.

Ride home

Outside, the sky was starless. The car was quiet enough for honesty.

Gene broke the silence first.

"So. Fulcrum."

Will looked up.

"That's what Crowder said. 'You're the fulcrum.'" She gave a dry laugh. "Funny, a few weeks ago I was radioactive. Now I'm a keystone."

"You always were," he said.

She watched him. Will Morgan didn't flatter. He observed. Assessed. Predicted. But this wasn't tactical.

"Why'd you fight for me?" she asked, wondering.

Will exhaled, then leaned forward, both hands grasping the wheel.

"Because I've seen what real betrayal looks like," he said. "And it never cries in the back of a safe house at 1 A.M. wondering what more it could've done."

Gene looked away, throat tight.

Will went on, voice thoughtful.

"I read your file. I've read everyone's file. But yours... I don't think the paper ever came close.

"I read everything. Your dead drops. The surveillance logs. The intercepts from Moscow. You risked your life for two years. No leverage. No payoffs. Not even a guarantee you'd be alive the next morning."

He paused.

"You were never playing both sides. You just played their game better than they did."

Gene finally looked at him. Her eyes were glassy, but not wet.

"You believed me."

"I did."

"Why?"

He took a moment, as if trying to find a version of the truth she could accept.

"Because no one signs up for what you did unless they're either lying or burning. And you weren't lying."

Gene gave a hollow smile. "And all it got me was a three-hour interrogation and six weeks of being watched like I might sell the nuclear codes to a pawn shop."

Will leaned back. "And now it gets you a shot to stop a Russian asset who's laying groundwork for quantum spoofing inside our satcom architecture. You think I'd trust anyone else with that?"

She studied him for a moment, then asked: "Did you really say that line? The one about me being more dangerous because I did it for the country?"

"I did," he said. "Twice. First in the situation room. Second in front of the Joint Committee."

Gene leaned her head back against the bulkhead and closed her eyes.

"Jesus."

Will gave the faintest smile.

"Rest while you can. When the adrenaline leaves you're going to feel like a used washcloth."

She looked away again.

"You ever wonder if any of this matters? Or if we're just playing our own version of chess while the real game is already lost?"

Will glanced at her.

"I wonder every day. Then I think about what happens if we stop."

Gene spoke without looking at him.

"Do you trust me, Will? I don't mean operationally. I mean really."

He didn't hesitate. "Yes."

She finally nodded. Not approval—acknowledgment. As if a wire had been tightened between them, pulled taut and humming with unsaid things.

She didn't respond right away.

But for the first time since... since the interrogation, she wasn't alone.

CHAPTER THIRTY-ONE

Marcus Liebowitz

Linthicum Heights, MD - LaserTech Parking Lot - Evening

The late sun casts long amber streaks over the asphalt. The building behind them hums down into after-hours silence. A few cars trickle out, headlights flickering on. Derek stands near the curb, clutching a slim chessboard case and wearing his favorite hoodie—navy blue with faded MIT lettering. He shifts his weight rhythmically from one foot to the other, eyes scanning for a familiar car.

Will and Sara exit the building nearby, mid-conversation. Will's tone is clipped, habitual intensity intact. Sara's is looser, still thoughtful from their last briefing.

Sara commented, "I think Grace will stay on. She's wired for this, even if she doesn't know it yet."

Will wryly, "That makes two of you."

Sara raises an eyebrow at that—was that a compliment? Will doesn't clarify.

Then she spots Derek and slows her pace. Will follow her gaze.

Sara "Oh. He's got that look. The one before he beats someone in under thirty moves."

Will a bit amused, "That's the only look he has."

A black Lexus sedan pulls up smoothly in front of Derek. The passenger window lowers. Marcus Liebowitz, dressed in a crisp charcoal jacket and tie loosened enough to suggest end-of-day comfort, leans over the console.

Marcus lowering the window, "On time as always, Grandmaster."

Derek shyly, "That's an inaccurate title. But I am punctual. That is true." Derek repeated, "That is true."

He opens the door, slides in before he shuts the door, he glances out toward Will and Sara, "Bye, Sara. Major."

Sara replies for the both of them, "Have fun, Derek. Don't go easy on him."

Marcus, interjecting, "He never does."

The car pulls away, quiet and unhurried.

Will and Sara watch it disappear down the tree-lined road.

Sara smiled, "Marcus has been good for him."

Will nodding his chin, "He gets him. The structure, the rules, the game beneath the game. That's rare."

A pause. Sara tilts her head toward him, playful, "Like someone else I know?"

Will doesn't bite, but the corner of his mouth tightens, "Let's hope Derek never sees the board we're playing on."

Sara's smile fades into thought, He might be the only one who could beat it.

Marcus Liebowitz's Townhouse – Dining Room - Night

A cozy, book-filled home that speaks of quiet intellect and domestic warmth. The table is set for five—Marcus, his wife

Leah, his teenage daughter Naomi (17), his young son Ben (9), and Derek. A roasted chicken sits on a large wooden platter surrounded by small bowls of salad, rice, and roasted vegetables. The hum of family life blends with classical music playing from the kitchen smart speaker.

Marcus enters with a bottle of sparkling water and smiled as he gestures for Derek to take his seat. Leah follows behind with a bowl of steamed broccoli. She's warm and unassuming, dressed in weekend-casual comfort.

Leah, smiling kindly said, "Derek, I hope you're hungry. Marcus says you've got a chess match waiting after dessert."

Derek replies, "I am… acceptable. Thank you. Yes, we have unfinished business from last Tuesday."

Naomi Liebowitz to Ben, teasing, "Don't even try to watch. You'll get a headache."

Ben Liebowitz, nods seriously. "Last time I saw Derek play, Dad lost in fourteen moves."

Marcus, seating himself, "It was sixteen. Thank you, son, for preserving my dignity."

Everyone chuckles lightly—except Derek, who glances around, taking it all in.

Leah said, "Marcus told us what you're working on. Not the details, of course. But… thank you. For helping people stay safe."

"I don't do it for thanks. I do it because I'm efficient at pattern disruption."

Naomi raises an eyebrow. "That's… kind of metal."

Ben, loud whisper to Derek, "That means cool."

Derek's face twitches into something that might be a smile.

Marcus, raising his glass. "To pattern disruption. And family dinners."

Everyone. "Cheers."

Living Room – Later

A large, well-used chessboard rests between two chairs by the fireplace. The rest of the family chats in the kitchen, cleaning up and laughing. Derek and Marcus are locked in a focused match. The room hums with quiet intensity.

Derek asked, "Do you ever worry about them? Your family?"

"Every day. And that's why I do the job. So, they never have to see what we see."

Derek absorbs that. He looks toward the kitchen—where Leah gently pats Ben's head as he helps with dishes.

"If I were you… I'd protect them too."

"That's the plan."

Derek makes a move. A dazzling sacrifice. Marcus blinks.

"You've been holding that since turn five, haven't you?"

Derek answered, "Correct. You left your back rank open."

Marcus chuckled. "You're dangerous."

CHAPTER THIRTY-TWO

Gracie & Lynx

LaserTech – break room – late afternoon

Grace sat at the corner table, a tea mug warming her hands. A spreadsheet glowed on her tablet screen, but her eyes drifted—tracking quiet movement by the sink.

Victor Levin, dressed as always in neatly pressed neutrals, rinsed a glass. Methodical. Precise. Nothing unusual. Except—

He checked the clock. Twice.

Then, with near-surgical smoothness, he reached for the paper towel dispenser... but didn't tear one off.

He ran his hand along the underside. Once. Then again, slower.

Grace blinked. Frowned. That was odd.

Victor finally tore a single towel, dabbed the glass, and left.

Grace waited ten seconds. Got up. Walked casually over to the dispenser.

She ran her fingers beneath it. Smooth plastic. Seamless. Except—

A faint scratch mark in the shape of a curve. Palm-sized. Deliberately rubbed down, but visible at an angle under the fluorescents.

She stood there a moment longer, her body language neutral. Just a woman drying her mug.

Then she returned to her seat, opened a new tab on her tablet, and typed one line:

Lab 2B break room – surface check under towel dispenser.

She minimized it.

Didn't speak to anyone.

Just sipped her tea, staring through the glass wall, where Victor's reflection passed by—calm, unreadable.

Always watching. Always recording. But only acting when it counts.

LaserTech Lab–1910 Hours R

The building was mostly empty. Only the soft hum of climate control and distant security doors clicking echoed in the hall.

Grace moved carefully through the dimly lit corridor; lab coat folded over one arm. Her steps were purposeful but unhurried— the walk of someone not trying to be invisible, just unremarkable.

She entered Lab 2C, a calibration room used only for select testbed equipment—high-frequency scanners and signal monitors. Rarely trafficked. Mostly logged by engineers on rotation.

Grace stepped inside. Closed the door behind her.

She walked straight to the equipment logbook — a thick blue binder on a side cart near the main terminal. Flipping back through the pages, she scanned recent sign-ins.

Three names repeated predictably—Raj, Allison, Darren— all maintenance staff.

Then:

"Levin, V.—4:16 PM—Diagnostic Pass on Oscillation Monitor #3"

Grace paused.

No one mentioned him running diagnostics here. Not even Jankowitz. And that timestamp was two hours before Rick flagged the Belgium signal anomaly.

She turned toward the oscillation monitor—silent now, wrapped in a plastic dust sleeve. She circled it slowly, crouched down, and checked the vent panels on the back.

A tiny magnetic clip hung just inside the grate. Empty. No markings. No internal sticker.

She didn't touch it. Just stared.

Grace stood again and returned to the binder. Slipped a small sticky note behind the page where Victor signed—not visible unless someone flipped it open deliberately.

On it:

Tag clip in OscMon #3. Entry pre-signal event. Watch this room.

She closed the binder, wiped her fingerprints from the cart with her sleeve, and backed out of the lab.

As she exited, she looked over her shoulder once—just a glance.

Then the door clicked shut behind her.

Grace entered the outer office where Sara, gym bag slung over one shoulder, was preparing to leave. She moved in silence, but not sneaking. Just enough for Grace to notice.

Sara said, "You've been staying late a lot lately."

Grace didn't look up.

"So have you."

"Yeah, but I'm not sneaking into calibration labs or combing through equipment logs when everyone else is gone."

That got Grace's attention.

She paused. Turned slowly. Met Sara's eyes.

"I'm not sneaking."

"You're quiet. Which is normal. But now it's a different kind of quiet."

Grace said nothing.

"I saw your note. In the binder. I didn't read it, just saw your handwriting."

Grace blinked. She looked away, then back. Her jaw tightened, just a fraction.

"I didn't want to accuse without evidence."

"You don't have to. But if something's bothering you—if something doesn't sit right—I want to know."

"I trust your instincts. Even when you keep them to yourself."

That softened Grace. She nodded once, then slowly sat down on the bench. Took a breath.

"Victor signed into Lab 2C two hours before the signal anomaly from Belgium. Said he was running diagnostics on an oscillator that didn't need diagnostics."

"You think he planted something?"

"No. I think he removed something. Or confirmed it was already in place."

Sara absorbed that. Sat next to her.

"You've been watching him?"

"Don't laugh but I've been reading spy novels. And intelligence manuals.

(half-smile)

"I know that sounds ridiculous.

"I didn't say anything because I would be the first one to make the 'Bring me moose and squirrel' jokes."

Sara reassuring her, "Not even a little. What's your gut say?"

Grace stared at the floor for a long moment.

Grace said without assertion, "My gut says he doesn't react like a man who's trying to survive here."

"He reacts like someone protecting a long game."

Sara looked down at the floor. Thoughtful. Then stood.

Sara said as a friend, "You're not alone anymore, Grace. We keep going, but we go together now."

Grace nodded again, quieter this time, relieved.

Grace's condo – night

Warm lamplight. Books stacked in thoughtful clusters. A whiteboard with no equations—just names, locations, timestamps, question marks.

Grace sat cross-legged on her couch, a large spiral-bound notebook open on the coffee table. Sara sat across from her, shoes off, a mug of black tea in her hands.

The notebook was filled with pages—half in Grace's precise handwriting, half sticky notes and printouts. Organized, logical, obsessively clear.

Grace turned to the first page marked with a blue tab.

"This is where it started. Day after the Belgium signal was flagged. Victor left early that night, no sign-in for the next morning. But I saw him in the parking lot—same clothes, different badge."

"Different badge?"

"One of the old security pass prototypes. I only noticed because I helped QA them last year. The magnetic strip was a half-millimeter off-center. The printer was misaligned."

Sara looked at her. Impressed.

"You remember that?"

Grace gave a small shrug.

"I remember patterns. Deviations stick."

She flipped the page. Diagrams. Lab schedules. "V.L." initials circled in red. Time notations. A sticky note with a list: "No phone. Minimal browsing. Never eats on-site."

Grace continued, "He's been invisible. Too invisible. He's careful not to generate noise, not just in a digital sense—socially, physically. No questions, no conflict. Just smooth surface. Like…

"Like a stone at the bottom of a clear river."

Grace looked up. Nodded once.

She turned to the final section—labeled:

FICTION → BEHAVIOR

"The novels helped. Not for the drama. For the rhythms. The long games." Grace explained. "I started mapping fictional agent behaviors to real-world anomalies."

Sara scanned the chart: fictional spies on one side, Victor's behavior on the other. A red line connected "Karla (TTSS)" to "Deliberate absence from social dynamics."

Another: "Kim Philby" to "Mirrors native ideology but doesn't participate emotionally."

Sara leaned back. Her brow furrowed in thought.

"This isn't paranoia, Grace. This is methodology. Discipline."

Grace said nothing.

"We need to protect this."

"You, this book—they're going to be key."

Grace looked at her notebook, then back at Sara. For the first time, she looked less alone. Less guarded.

"I was waiting for a snap."

"This might be it."

Soundproof walls. A whiteboard, a secure laptop. Early morning light filtered through vertical blinds.

Sara sat at one end of the table, arms crossed. Grace beside her, notebook open again—but now with several pages flagged for review.

Derek Wilshire entered, coffee in hand. His expression was curious but alert. He locked the door behind him before sitting.

"You said this couldn't wait."

Sara said, "It can't."

She nodded to Grace. Grace pushed the notebook forward.

Derek opened it—studied the first few pages. A flicker of surprise. He flipped to the red-circled lab logs, paused, then to the behavior columns. He leaned in.

"You tracked all of this on your own?"

Grace nodded.

"No unauthorized access. Just observations. Internal sign-ins, scheduling overlaps, public behavior."

"How long?"

"Since the Belgium signal. Maybe earlier, but that was when it aligned with the fictional patterns."

He looked up at her.

"Fictional?"

Sara cut in gently.

"She's been studying Russian espionage through novels and non-fiction. Le Carré, Philby, SVR doctrine. What started as personal curiosity turned into a behavioral mapping project."

Derek asked while reading, "Levin. You think he's compromised?"

"I think he's embedded." replies Grace.

Derek leaned back. Exhaled slowly.

"We've had anomalies in engineering logs from his lab— Rick and I flagged some inconsistencies last week. Missing buffer files. Weird checksum edits."

(pause)

"And this—this fits."

He tapped the notebook again.

"We can't go loud yet. But this changes our posture. We treat Levin as an active person of interest."

"And we use this quietly. Internal counter-surveillance." said Sara, "Tag his terminals. Eyes on his movements."

"And no sudden shifts." agrees Derek, "He can't know we're watching."

He looked at Grace.

"This… is exceptional work."

Grace didn't smile. But her shoulders eased—just a little.

"I can keep going. Track behavior against network access. I'll stay unseen."

"Rick and I will backstop you. No one else sees this yet. Not Jankowitz. Not the ops group.

"Let's bring this down like professionals."

Sara and Grace nodded.

CHAPTER THIRTY-THREE

Ghost Net

Fort Meade - Watchtower Conference Room 0815 Hours R

The air was tense, sharp with the sense of urgency that had been mounting over the last few days.

The door clicked open, and Derek, Sara, Rick, and Grace entered, each of them on edge. Grace clutched her notebook, still filled with her meticulous behavioral observations. Derek's brow was furrowed, and Rick's face was tight with concentration. They all knew what they were about to present would change everything.

Will didn't speak right away, instead motioning for them to sit. His voice, when it came, was calm and direct.

"Let's hear it," asked Will.

Rick took a deep breath, his finger tapping a tablet before him. He slid it across the desk toward Will. The screen displayed schematics of the Radiant Sentry EMP Shield,

Rick explains carefully, "We've tracked an internal breach. Victor Levin. Embedded as a lab assistant to Jankowitz. He's been accessing critical files—and not just any files. He examined

273

the Radiant Sentry EMP Shield's frequency matrix. The EMP's protective capabilities against certain high-frequency pulses."

Will's eyes narrowed as he absorbed the information, scrolling through the data on the tablet. The pieces began to fall into place. The Sentry was the all-important mission objective. Protecting its confidentiality and just as important maintaining the ignis fatuus (a false hope or delusion) offered by Operation Echo Mirage.

Morgan asked, "How long has he been compromised? And who else is involved?"

"It's hard to say, but we've traced it back to at least six months." Grace responds with nervousness, "Levin's behavior was suspicious from the start—inconsistencies in his work, odd sign-in patterns. But it wasn't until I started digging into Russian espionage tactics that the pieces clicked into place."

Will, nodding, "And now we've got a dangerous real live mole - not a doubled one like Sable - inside the most sensitive systems at LaserTech.

"We have always been concerned that Kir would be all over LaserTech and Radiant Sentry, and that meant that he would use as many sleepers and illegals as he could. Probably have half a dozen or more have penetrated in some way already. He'll be watching everything he can from any angle he can - low, high...in between.

"He is thorough and relentless. Just because we busted his D.C. illegals ring doesn't mean he is corralled. He will simply activate new ones after a quiet period. Hell, he may not even wait. Radiant Sentry is that important.

"We have to protect Sable's credibility – Operation Echo Mirage.

"We had hoped we had Echo Mirage under Gene's control with Sable planting plausible beguiling fraudulent information to keep them occupied. Now, to be sure they can trust Sable they are undoubtedly going to use Levin as some sort of backup, support or decoy."

He looked at each of them in turn.

"We have one shot at this. Levin has to be contained. No one can know about this, not the higher-ups at LaserTech--nobody. We're already behind on this—so we keep it internal and we move fast. The moment we alert the wrong people, it's over."

Rick asked, "What's the next step?"

Will stood, pacing slowly in front of the large windows behind him. Thunder rumbled in the distance. He paused, looking out at the storm as though drawing strength from it.

"We escalate the counterintelligence operation. Shadow Levin. No sudden moves. We use Grace's behavioral analysis to track him more closely. Every access point, every file, every movement—we're going to map it all.

"Z, Levin is a U.S. citizen so we will need authorization from the FISA court - please ask Guy to get a warrant for electronic surveillance. Sara, when we get the warrant, Cecil initiates active surveillance. Rick same with you when we get the warrant please coordinate with our friends at the NSA."

"Grace has drafted the decoy version of the Sentry specs. Same checksum, same data structure, but with false information buried in it," added Rick. "If Levin downloads it, we'll know for sure he's still active."

"We keep it tight," said Sara, "if anyone gets too close, we shut it down. Only trusted eyes see this."

Will gave a sharp nod. "Good. And one more thing—we don't let Levin out of our sight. I want his every step monitored. If he tries to bolt, we need to be ready to cut him off. No warning. No second chances. I'll call Cecil."

The room fell into a heavy silence as they absorbed Will's words. They all knew what was at stake.

He continued voice low, serious, "This is a war on two fronts. Our satellites. Our defense systems. And if we don't act decisively, we lose. Everything".

He turned to Grace, his voice softening, "Grace, keep your notebook tight. We'll need everything you've observed. But you stay out of sight—you're not just observing, you're in the field now."

Grace nodded, the weight of the responsibility settling on her shoulders.

"Everyone clear? We have to move fast. We can't let Levin or Moscow know we're onto them."

The team nodded in unison.

"Then let's get to work. This is bigger than anything we've handled before, and the stakes just keep getting bigger."

Will narrowed his eyes, flipping through the personnel file on Victor Levin. He leaned back in his chair, unconvinced by the significance of the man on paper.

"Levin's a lab tech. Mid-level clearance. He shouldn't be within reach of core defense systems, let alone capable of this kind of compromise. What's his actual value to the Russians?"

"That's the point. By himself, he's nothing." offered Grace quietly, but firmly, "But with the index file leak, they don't need him to be an expert. They know exactly what to ask Sable... and they can get double-blind confirmation from Levin."

Will turned to her, his interest piqued.

"He doesn't have to know what he's looking at. They feed him requests that sound like routine tasked — access this schematic, open that file revision—and all they're doing is cross-referencing. He's not analyzing. He's verifying."

"And with that index, they can match file hashes, track update histories—know which internal version is tied to what system. They can work backward to validate whether Sable is feeding them real data or feeding them lies," added Rick.

276

"It's a perfect compartment. Levin doesn't have to know he's being used for that. Just do his job, follow instructions. He thinks he's helping Moscow… but really, he's a litmus test. Pretty cunning if you ask me," said Sara.

Will sat forward now, the weight of it setting in.

"So, their thinking if Sable's been flipped… they'll catch it. And if she hasn't… they'll confirm every critical piece of Radiant Sentry in real time..

"Exactly.   And with the system proved and nearly operational—this is their last chance to either replicate it or undermine it before it's deployed." said Grace.

Will said in a stern tone, "Which makes Levin a dangerous kind of mole: the kind who doesn't know what he's worth."

A long silence.

Then Will stood.

"We can't spook him. Not yet. If he goes dark before Operation Echo Mirage can do some damage—they stay in the game.

He glanced toward the door, then back to the team.

"Stay on him. Every keystroke. Every move. If he so much as sneezes near a file with DARPA clearance, I want to know."

Sara and Grace say at the same time, "We're on it."

"As you suggested I will work with Thomas to update my behavioral profile. If he's under stress, we might catch a tell." said Grace.

"Good. Keep me posted. I want to fill in Ed and get his thoughts as well."

He looked around at the team, deadly serious.

"We are now in a live, active counterintelligence op. Containment. Validation. And disruption. All three, or we lose more than Radiant Sentry. I have never worked with a better team, so I like our chances.

"Great job, everybody - really great.

"Now get back to work." he said with a smile as he left the room.

They all looked at one another in feigned shock.

"What was that?" Z asked, expressing surprise at the compliment he just heard.

"That's the Gracie effect," teased Sara,. "

Gracie smiled as she rolled her eyes.

Still, as she watched him leave, her thoughts lingered longer than they should have. "There's something in the way he looks at me lately—like he's letting his guard slip, just enough for me to see the man behind the mission. It's subtle, but I feel it. In the quiet moments, the lingering eye contact, the softness that wasn't there before.

"He believes in me—more than just as an analyst or a strategist. I see it when he speaks to the team, but it's like he's speaking to me. Maybe he doesn't realize it yet. Or maybe he does, and he's just scared of what it could mean. God knows I am.

"But if this thing between us survives what's coming… then maybe it's real.

"We're in the thick of it now—no more simulations, no more hypotheticals. Real stakes, real targets. And Will's not just leading the mission—he's carrying something heavier than the rest of us can see. But if he believes in us... maybe we're exactly who we need to be right now."

She took a breath, steady and quiet. "Let's end this."

Fort Meade, Day 10 – Secure Briefing Room

Will Morgan stood at the head of the room, arms folded.

"The operation will continue through final Radiant Sentry testing," he said. "No contact. No confrontation. If SVR suspects he's burned, they'll send in a replacement—or worse."

Grace added, "He is to remain... alive, contained, and completely irrelevant."

"Status?" Will asked.

Rick responded without looking up. "He thinks he's still operational."

Will nodded once. "Then so are we."

Victor Levin's Condo – 0218 Hours R

Victor stirred in bed. Somewhere in his subconscious, something didn't seem quite right. Like the hallway lights at work were a half-shade dimmer. Like the new security guard knew his name too fast.

He stared at the ceiling. Thought of nothing. Rolled over.

Above his condo, the drone blinked once—just a flicker of infrared.

Then silence.

The Phantom Key

LaserTech 0718 Hours R

Victor Levin sat hunched at his desk, eyes scanning the schematics on his screen.

Tonight was different.

He'd waited. Weeks without access to anything of substance. A web of excuses, calendar errors, interdepartmental reroutes. A lesser agent might have panicked. Levin hadn't.

Because tonight, his access slipped. Just a crack. Just enough.

A test file. Titled RS_THRM_V17.dcf.

Not the full core sequencing algorithm—but something close. A mid-level thermal map for one of Radiant Sentry's pretest shell configurations. It was labeled internal-only, compartmentalized to Tier-3 clearance. Just enough to be valuable. Enough to pass along.

He downloaded it, encrypted it with his OTP, and embedded the data in a generic CAD container using his prearranged exfiltration tool.

Nothing pinged.

He plugged in a private USB key embedded in a car alarm fob. A subtle handshake to a private exploit chain that should bypass the LaserTech outbound filter.

He launched the drop.

To Victor, it looked like it worked.

Fort Meade – ACIC Cyber Division – SYBIL Command Interface

"Payload diversion intercepted. Live exfiltration attempt—origin: V. Levin."

"Payload flagged and captured. Rewriting target coordinates."

"Transmission routed to STYX Blackhole Node."

On screen, Victor's file was redirected to a dead-drop server located in Langley, buried in a burn-loop for foreign intelligence redirection.

A fake uplink confirmation was sent back to his terminal, mimicking Moscow's signal authentication.

SYBIL had done more than block the leak—she'd turned Victor into his own feedback loop.

Moscow – SVR Technical Center – Never Reached

Solovey's watch station received no signal. There were no alerts. The line remained quiet, unbroken. They assumed Victor had nothing to report.

The silence was perfect.

Victor exhaled. He'd been holding his breath.

The drop had worked.

He stood, walked slowly to the break room. Poured himself a stale cup of coffee. Eyes brighter. Chest less tight.

This, he thought, was progress. Finally.

Back in his condo later that night, he composed a short status update on the secure end of his burner phone. Ten words. Enough to let Moscow know he was back in the game.

"Drop successful. Key thermal sequence secured. Awaiting further tasking."

The message encoded. Transmitted.

Fort Meade – ACIC Comms Vault – 2337 R

"Intercept complete. Message spoof confirmation sent."

Back in Arlington, Victor's phone buzzed.

A reply appeared on screen as expected.

"Received. Maintain posture. Await validation order from channel Nyx."

Victor smiled. He didn't know SYBIL had written the reply. Or that channel Nyx no longer existed.

ACIC Briefing Room – 0916 Hours R

Will Morgan looked at the report on the display wall.

"This is textbook," he said, tone level. "We didn't just contain him. We fed him a tether."

Grace added, "SVR still thinks he's viable. We give them just enough to waste their time."

Rick nodded. "And if they escalate to a live meet?"

Will's eyes narrowed. "Then we choose the handler."

Encapsulation

Fort Meade ACIC Cyber Ops – 0342 Hours R

Victor Levin—codename Lynx—was no longer a threat.

Not because he'd been arrested. Not because he'd been confronted.

Because Rick Huang had activated Protocol Ghost Net.

Rick leaned over the console, eyes locked on SYBIL's command screen. Grace Roberts stood beside him, arms crossed. Zbigniew "Z" Zawadzki monitored the secondary feeds behind them, stone-faced. The room glowed in sterile blue light, humming with quiet, invisible power.

"Activate full encapsulation," Rick ordered.

SYBIL: "Affirmative. Lynx subject Victor Levin – surveillance protocol: RADIANT SHIELD. Execution timestamp 03:42:09. Operation live."

On the monitor, Victor Levin slept like a rock in his Arlington condo. A thermal Falcon drone feed hovered above the complex, relayed from a Q-Series microdrone mounted above the streetlight. Inside, six pinhole cameras embedded via false maintenance crews fed back continuous data.

No black bag team. No guns. No extraction.

He wouldn't know he was in a cage.

"What's happening?" asked Sara.

"We're putting Levin in a sandbox," answered Rick.

"How the hell can you do that?"

Rick leaned back from the console, a devilish smile consuming his face. "Okay, quick primer. Ghost Net encapsulation doesn't move data the way you think. There's no packet, no header, no handshake. Nothing for a scanner to grab onto."

He flicked a line of static across the monitor. "To the GRU, this looks like background hiss. Random noise. They can park every sensor they own on the fiber, and it'll just read as entropy."

Sara frowned. "So, what's actually happening?"

Rick's tone stayed flat, clinical. "Every bit is wrapped in randomized decoy states—think of it like nesting Russian dolls, but all painted to look like trash. Only the paired node knows which doll to crack open. Strip the noise, reassemble the payload.

"SVR's listening stack didn't detect the phantom GhostNet returned authentic-looking telemetry and used known SVR proxies."

Z gave a low whistle. "So even if they're staring right at it…"

Rick cut in. "They're blind. To them, the message doesn't exist. It's a whisper without air."

LaserTech – 0716 Hours R

Victor walked through the front turnstiles of LaserTech like it was any other morning. Badge scan beeped green. Coffee in hand. Calm, neutral expression. He nodded to the guards, checked his messages on his phone, and descended into Sublevel 3.

He didn't notice that every system he accessed was a sandboxed mirror of the real thing.

His terminal credentials now funneled him through a SYBIL-engineered shadow network. Emails returned plausible but irrelevant threads. Engineering documents contained the same headers, formatting, and formulas—but were scrubbed of anything classified within Radiant Sentry's architecture.

His calendar still functioned. His swipe card opened doors.

But everything he saw was an echo.

Fort Meade – Signals Node – 0803 Hours R

Rick Huang called it "surgical hallucination." The trick wasn't just keeping Lynx away from secrets—it was letting him believe he still had them.

Full NSA TECINT integration had already delivered a quiet patch to Victor's mobile OS—now a relay node feeding every call, every typed character, every heartbeat back to Fort Meade.

His laptop? Ghost-imaged every 11 minutes.

Wi-Fi signal? Proxied through a quantum-invisible packet filter designed by NSA SIGINT Analysts and two former Unit 8200 operatives.

Rick watched the feed, fingers laced. "If he tries to transmit anything real, it'll be junk. Every byte he touches is synthetic."

Z nodded. "What if Moscow tests him?"

"We're ready."

He tapped the key. One of Victor's outbound emails appeared—a coded phrase, lifted cleanly from a template SYBIL had injected hours earlier. It was perfect forgery, laced with the right jargon, the right metadata, the right sloppiness to pass as authentic.

"They want him to pass information?" Rick continued. "He'll pass it. But it'll be what we wrote. Garbage with just enough truth to keep him alive and keep them chasing shadows."

Z nodded slowly, the weight of it settled. Victor Levin thought he was still a player. Moscow thought they still had their man. But the board had shifted.

In reality, Lynx was nothing more than a puppet—and Watchtower held every string.

Yasenevo, Moscow – SVR Headquarters - 1520 Hours C

The Russian handler known only as "Solovey" received Victor's weekly signal burst. It was encoded in the usual OTP format, embedded in a steganographic PDF of technical specs.

They decrypted it. The data seemed valid.

U.S. energy calibration still aligned with ε^3. Thermo-structural stress limits lagged by 14%. Same as last month. No indication the Americans had made a breakthrough.

Satisfied, they shelved the file.

LaserTech, Day 3 – Sublevel 4

Victor grew a bit frustrated. His clearance requests were hitting unexpected delays. A scheduled sync with Dr. Kwon was rescheduled. Twice. SYBIL created perfectly mundane bureaucratic explanations.

He chalked it up to internal chaos. Shrugged. Waited.

He didn't know that Thomas had implemented Behavioral Drift Scoring (BDS). Every deviation from baseline—tempo of keystrokes, length of idle time, even the change in posture during lunch—was tracked in real time.

The BDS model Developed under an In-Q-Tel dual-track surveillance grant. In-Q-Tel was the CIA's venture capital arm— a non-profit strategic investor tasked with scouting, funding, and accelerating emerging technologies that serve U.S. intelligence and national security interests.

The Behavioral Drift Scoring (BDS) model was a hybrid behavioral analytics engine designed to detect subtle deviations from an individual's baseline cognitive, linguistic, and operational patterns. Originally intended for counter-radicalization tracking, the system was adapted by Thomas Carrone to flag embedded foreign assets undergoing mission-phase transitions specifically, Oleg Morozov, alias Victor Levin.

BDS uses historical biometric, linguistic, and contextual behavior records to establish a unique "cognitive fingerprint." In Levin's case, this included everything from keystroke cadence and email syntax to badge scan behavior, ambient conversation pitch, and facial tension under thermal imaging.

Victor had become a specimen in a glass box.

CHAPTER THIRTY-FOUR

Reconciliation

"Empathy is a necessary step for truth and reconciliation."

- Simon Baron-Cohen

Jayne Lin's apartment – New York City – night

The glow of her laptop screen illuminated Jayne Lin's worried face. Tabs were open to everything from Fort Meade's public affairs page to outdated staff directories. Nothing helped. She scrolled and typed, heart pounded.

A framed photo of her and Sara Brandt, taken years ago at a Hunter College High School event, sat beside her. Jayne glanced at it, jaw tightened.

Jayne murmured, "Come on, Sara... you said Fort Meade, but didn't say who. Who do I even call?"

She picked up her phone, hesitated, then dialed the number listed for Fort Meade's main base operator.

❖❖❖

Fort Meade – main operator desk – night

Operator. "Fort Meade switchboard, how can I direct your call?"

Jayne, "Hi, I'm... I'm trying to reach someone who supervises Sara Brandt. I'm sorry, I don't have a name. I just know she's... military intelligence. Army, I think?"

There's a pause.

Operator, "I'm afraid we can't give out personnel information. Do you have a unit or a command name?"

Jayne, "I just know she works in counterintelligence. Please—it's about her family. Her father's in a coma. Her mother's alone. I wouldn't be calling if it wasn't serious."

The line goes silent.

Then—

Operator, "Hold, please."

Fort Meade - Ed Perry's office– moments later

COL. Ed Perry, late 50s, composed but approachable, picks up a secure line. He's been working late, as always. He listens as the operator explains. His posture shifts at the mention of Sara's name.

Ed Perry, "Put her through."

Click.

Ed Perry, "This is General Ed Perry. You said you're calling about Sara Brandt?"

Jayne exhales—relief flooding her.

"Yes, sir. My name is Jayne Lin. I teach with her mother at Hunter in New York. I know this is... irregular, but I didn't know who else to call."

Ed Perry, "You did the right thing."

His voice is calm, grounding.

Ed Perry, "Sara's one of ours. And one of the best. Go ahead, Ms. Lin—tell me what's going on."

Jayne explains. The father's heart attack. The estrangement. The quiet despair of Sara's mother. As she talks, emotion slips in.

"I don't even know what I want from you. I just thought... someone should tell her, someone who cares. I figured if anyone does, it's whoever she works for."

A soft moment passes.

Ed Perry, "You're right. She deserves to know. And she does have someone who cares. I'll bring her team leader on the line. He's the one you're looking for."

Jayne blinked back tears.

"Thank you, General."

"You did a brave thing tonight; Ms. Lin. Risked a lot. I'll take it from here—but if you ever need me, I'm not hard to find."

He tapped his comm, leaned back into his chair, and called:

"Morgan, I need you on the line. It's about Sara."

Will Morgan came on the line and Ed Perry left the call. Will sat at his desk, tie loosened, posture tight. The phone crackled to his ear.

Jayne explained Sara' s father's heart attack and her mother's condition. She continued.

"—she hasn't spoken to them in years, Commander. Not since college. Her mother is... she's unraveling. I don't think she knows how to fix it."

Will listened, silent but engaged. His eyes darkened with concern.

Will, "And her father?"

"Still in a coma. They don't know if he'll pull through. Sara doesn't even know he had a heart attack. Her mother's too ashamed—or scared—to reach out.

Will exhaled, rubbing his temple.

"Ms. Lin—Jayne. Why come to me?"

"Because you're the one person I've heard her talk about with admiration. With respect.

"You know her. I don't. Not really. I've worked with her mother for many years. I just see a woman trying to be strong in front of students, while quietly falling apart. I had to try something. If this crosses a line, I'll take whatever fallout comes with it."

A long pause.

"You did the right thing."

Jane whispered, "Thank you."

Will hung up and sat in silence thinking. He opened Sara's personnel file—not to check clearances or operations. Just the photo. A younger, unguarded Sara. A flicker of defiance in her smile. He closed the file, stood, and left.

Fort Meads - Thomas Carrone's Office — minutes later

Thomas Carrone sat at his desk, reading a dossier when the phone rang and he answered. It's Will.

Will, "It's Sara."

Thomas straightened, alert.

"She okay?"

"Physically? Yes. Emotionally... I don't know."

Will paced as he relayed Jayne Lin's call. Thomas listened without interrupting—his expression unreadable but attentive.

"No contact since college. She came out and they shut her out. And now her father is in a coma, her mother's circling despair, and Sara has no idea. No siblings. No family beyond them."

Thomas leaned back and folded his hands.

"And you're asking if you should tell her."

"I'm asking if I have the right. And if I do—how the hell I'm supposed to do it without breaking her. She's holding so much right now. I don't want to add weight to that. But if I don't say something..."

"She might never get the chance."

Will said. "That's the fear."

Thomas is quiet a moment before he speaks.

"Will, I've seen her walls. They're precise. Engineered. She's brilliant at compartmentalizing pain - just like you. But you—she lets you close enough to matter. That's rare. So, if this comes from you... it won't be a wrecking ball. It might just be the first crack in something that needs to break."

Will absorbed that. Then:

"You think she'll hate me for it?"

"Maybe. At first. Or maybe she'll do what she always does— retreat. Deflect. But underneath that? There's a woman who's still that girl on graduation day, watching an empty row of chairs where her family should've been."

Will was silent. The image hits him harder than he expected. He knew it well.

"She deserves to know. And if it comes from someone she trusts—not out of obligation, but compassion—it might start something she doesn't even know she needs."

A long pause.

"Then I'll tell her."

"Good. And Will?"

"Yeah?"

"Be gentle. But be honest. She can handle it."

Will Tells Sara

Morgan's Office LaserTech - late night

The room is dim, lit only by the soft blue glow from a bank of monitors in sleep mode. The usual bustle of the ACIC has faded into silence, leaving only the quiet hum of security systems and the faint tick of the wall clock.

Will stands by the window, arms crossed, shoulders squared. He's been here a while—gathering the courage. When the door opens and Sara steps in, he turns slowly.

She eyes him, wary.

"What's going on?"

"Sit down, Sara."

Her brow furrows. She doesn't move.

"Are you pulling me from the investigation?"

"Of course not. This isn't about work."

That catches her off guard. She blinks, uncertain. Slowly, she sits.

Will sits opposite her. There's a pause—measured, careful. Then he exhales.

"I got a call today. From someone named Jayne Lin.

Sara's reaction is immediate—shoulders rigid, eyes flashing.

"How the hell does she know you?"

"She didn't. She reached out to Ed Perry, and he sent her to me. Said it was personal. And urgent."

He waits. She doesn't interrupt—but her guard is up. Impossibly high.

"Your father had a heart attack three days ago. He's in a coma."

Sara goes still. Breath caught mid-inhale. Her face—blank. Completely blank.

"Your mother didn't know how to contact you. She's alone. No siblings, no extended family. Just him. And now... just you."

Sara blinks. Swallows hard.

"You spoke to my mother?"

"No. Jayne did. She said your mom's not herself. Falling apart. Waking up to some things too late. She's scared. Ashamed. And she wants to see you."

A heavy silence settles. Sara looked down, her jaw clenched tight.

"I haven't spoken to them in over ten years. Since college."

"I know."

"They didn't bother to call when I graduated. Not one word. Not even a text."

Her voice breaks on the last word. She forces it back.

"And now I'm supposed to drop everything because she's decided to feel something?"

Will leans in slightly—not to push. Just to stay close.

"I'm not telling you what to do. I'm just making sure you know the truth. Before it's too late to decide for yourself."

Sara looks away, jaw clenched. The silence this time is longer.

When she finally speaks, her voice is small.

"She didn't want a daughter like me."

"Maybe not then. But people change, Sara. Sometimes... pain wakes them up."

Another long pause, Sara stood suddenly and turned away. Her arms crossed tightly over her chest. Her whole body was trembling. Not rage. Not fear. Something deeper. The ache of something unresolved and buried too long.

"I don't know if I can do this."

"You don't have to do it alone."

She turned back to him. Her eyes are rimmed red, but she doesn't cry.

"Why are you always the one who shows up?"

Will didn't answer. He just met her eyes.

"I don't trust many people. But you...I trust you with everything. Even this."

Will rose, slowly.

"Then let's figure this out together."

Sara took a step closer. Then another. She pressed her forehead against his chest—not romantic, not needy. Just safe.

Will wrapped his arms around her. Holding her.

And for the first time in over a decade, Sara Brandt lets someone hold the weight she'd carried alone.

Sara's Apartment, Odenton - 2320 Hours

Sara sat at her small kitchen table, the lamp casting a pale circle of light on the paperwork she wasn't reading. Her phone lay face-down beside an untouched cup of coffee gone cold.

She'd been like this for an hour. Maybe two.

A coma.

A heart attack.

Her mother asked for her.

She ran a hand through her hair, exhaling hard.

"What am I supposed to do?" she said under her breath.

Go see him? After ten years of silence? After being told she was a disgrace—an embarrassment to the family name? After the slammed door and the line that never reopened.

Her throat tightened. She swallowed it back, the way she'd learned to do. Suppose she went, and he didn't wake up. Suppose he did and turned his head away. Suppose it made everything worse.

Will's voice lingered in her mind—calm, steady, maddeningly patient.

You don't have to do it alone.

She almost smiled at that. Typical Will. Always framing pain as a mission you could plan around.

Her eyes drifted to the window. The reflection showed someone she barely recognized—older, harder around the edges, but still that same girl who'd walked out of her parents' house with a backpack and a stubborn belief that love shouldn't have to be negotiated.

Now here she was, debating whether to walk back into that same house—or at least into the shadow of it.

She pushed the phone away, then pulled it back. Tapped the screen awake. Her mother's number glowed. She hovered over call.

And didn't.

Her hand trembled once, then steadied.

She whispered to the quiet apartment,

"If I go... what do I even say?"

No answer came. Just the soft hum of the refrigerator and the rain starting against the glass.

Sara leaned back, staring at the ceiling. The truth was simple and unbearable.

She wanted to go.

She was terrified to.

When the tears finally came, she didn't bother to stop them. They weren't loud. Just silent proof that the past hadn't disappeared—only gone dormant, waiting for a moment like this.

She wiped her eyes, closed the phone, and turned off the light.

Tomorrow would decide itself.

Grief and forgiveness

New York City apartment – Brooklyn – next day

The door opens slowly.

Sara steps into the foyer of the apartment she hasn't seen in over a decade. Nothing's changed—the same muted wallpaper, the framed black-and-white photos from summer vacations, the old coat rack with its wobbling hook.

It smells like furniture polish and dust and something floral. Familiar. Painfully so.

Will lingered a step behind her, quiet, giving her space. He doesn't touch her, doesn't speak. Just there.

From down the hall, footsteps approach.

Sara's mother, Linda Brandt, appears on the threshold to the kitchen. Her gray-streaked hair is pulled back into a practical bun. Her eyes—tired, worn—search Sara's face like it might vanish.

Neither moves.

Linda, "Sara."

It's not an apology. Not a plea. Just her daughter's name— like it hurts to say, like it heals to say.

Sara's throat tightens.

Sara, "Hi, Mom."

A pause. And then Linda closes the distance.

There's a strange, stuttering pause where both hesitate— frozen by everything unsaid. And then, finally, Linda wraps her arms around her daughter. It's an awkward embrace at first, stiff with years of silence.

But Sara doesn't pull away.

She closes her eyes.

Lets it happen.

Lets it matter.

Behind them, Will remains still—watchful. A guardian standing outside the circle of grief and forgiveness.

Linda pulls back, her hands on Sara's arms.

"I didn't know how to reach you. I... I didn't know what to say."

"You didn't have to say anything. You just had to try."

Linda nods—ashamed, but grateful. She looked at Will, eyes misted.

"Thank you. For bringing her."

Will gives a small nod.

"She brought herself. I'm just the ride."

Linda manages a trembling smile before she turns away.

"Come on. Let's go see your father."

Mount Sinai Hospital – Cardio ICU – early evening

The room is bathed in dim artificial light, sterile and too quiet. Machines beeped, and a monitor flickered with steady vitals. Sara's father, Stephen Brandt, lies unconscious—pale, thinner than she remembers, a ventilator fixed to his mouth, IVs in both arms.

Sara freezes in the doorway.

Her mother walks ahead and settles in the chair by the bed. Reaches for his hand like it's something she's been doing every hour.

Sara doesn't move.

Will steps up beside her, still silent.

Then he leans toward her.

"You've faced worse. Just… breathe."

Sara nods, imperceptibly. Her arms folded across her chest—like she's trying to keep something from spilling out.

"He was never cruel. Just… absent. Checked out. I thought Mom hated me more than he did. But maybe he just didn't know how to show up."

"You showed up."

Sara swallows hard, then steps forward.

She approaches the bed with quiet, tentative steps. The ventilator wheezes gently. Her father doesn't stir.

She stands over him for a long moment.

Then—

"Hi, Dad."

Her voice cracks.

"I don't know if you can hear me. Or if you want to. But I'm here."

She didn't reach for his hand. Not yet.

Instead, she stood between the past and the man in the hospital bed and waits—like the rest of her life was holding its breath.

Will watched from the corner.

He said nothing.

Did nothing.

But Sara felt him there—solid, unwavering.

And for now, that's everything she needed.

New York City – Central Park – night

The city hummed around them. Streetlights glowed through a thin mist as Sara and Will walked side by side beneath the skeletal arms of leafless trees. The silence between them was unhurried—neither awkward nor expectant. It just was.

The chill in the air made their breath visible, like ghosts of words not yet spoken.

Sara's hands were jammed into her coat pockets. Her shoulders hunched. She didn't look at Will as she spoke.

"When I left for college, I told myself I didn't care if I ever saw them again. That if they couldn't accept me, then I didn't need them."

"I said it so many times I started to believe it."

"You almost made me believe it."

Sara half-laughed, eyes down.

"Yeah. But walking into that apartment… it was like time just stopped. And I was fifteen again, hiding the way I dressed until I got to the subway."

Will glanced over, letting her speak without interrupting.

"I didn't come back for them, you know? I came because I needed to know. If he'd changed. If she still hated me. If there was anything left to save."

She kicked a loose pebble off the path. Watched it skitter into the dark.

"And then I saw her face. Just… raw. Like something finally broke through. And I didn't know what to do with that."

Will kept walking, slow and steady.

"You don't have to do anything with it. Not tonight."

She exhaled slowly.

"You're always like this at the big moments. Calm. Like you're made of stone or something."

"It's a trick. I'm made of bourbon and anxiety."

She smiled. For the first time in hours, it reached her eyes.

"You flew to New York without asking if I wanted company. Just showed up."

"Didn't think you'd ask. Thought I'd save us both the trouble."

"And what if I told you to go back?"

"I'd be on the next train. But first I'd sit outside the hospital to make sure you didn't change your mind."

She stopped walking and turned to him. The park was quiet—just the sound of wind in the trees and a distant siren. Sara studied him.

"You're the only person who's never made me feel like I had to explain who I am."

"That's because you never did."

He shrugged.

"Besides, I think I'd know the real you anywhere. You're loud, irreverent and guarded...and brilliant and... you make people better, even when you don't mean to."

She's quiet. Something about that landed harder than she expected.

After a moment, she reached out and hooked her pinky through his.

It wasn't romantic. Not theatrical.

Just true.

They stood there like that for a moment before they continued their walk—two shadows moved through the city, tethered not by need, but by choice.

LaserTech - morning

The hallway hummed with quiet urgency. Analysts and agents moved with purpose. Voices murmured through glass-walled rooms. Familiar terrain—sterile, precise, secure.

Sara stepped off the elevator. Same badge, same weighty mission file in her hand.

But something was different.

Her gaze was clearer. Not lighter, but more anchored. As if something loose inside her had settled into place.

She crossed the threshold of the bullpen. Grace Roberts looked up from her screen and nodded.

Gracie, "You're back."

"You say that like I was gone for a year."

"Time's relative. Also, we ran three surveillance sims and two network audits without you, so yes, a year."

She smirked but doesn't reply. Just headed for her desk.

Will was already there—reviewing the latest intercepts, half a coffee gone cold beside him. When he saw her, he straightened a little. Met her eyes.

"Everything okay?"

Sara nodded.

"No. But it's better."

Will gave her a long look, then gestured toward the empty chair across from him.

She dropped into the chair, flipped open her file, and started organizing her notes—calm, methodical. But her hands moved slower than usual. There was thought behind each gesture.

Will watched her for a moment. Then, "How's your mom?"

Sara paused.

"Trying. I don't know where it'll go. But she held my hand in the hospital. And that's more than I thought I'd get."

"Sometimes... trying is everything."

She didn't answer, but a small nod gave her away.

They got back to work. The hum of the office continued around them. But for Sara, the silence inside was different now. Not gone—but not hollow.

For the first time in years, the past felt... survivable.

CHAPTER THIRTY-FIVE

Black Sky

Colorado - Peterson Space Force Base x - 0035 Hours T

The cavernous Joint Operations Center (JOC) hummed with the buzz of servers; its muted lights cast a twilight glow over endless flickering screens. A massive display of outer space dominated the front wall, its high-resolution imagery providing an unbroken view of the heavens. Inside the darkened command center, dozens of Guardians worked at their stations, silently monitoring the silent ballet of satellites and debris orbiting far above Earth.

At her console, a young Guardian leaned closer to her monitor. On one of her three large screens, she saw two objects—one much larger than the other—edging closer in a grave dance. A bloom of debris erupted across her screen, tiny markers scattering like fireflies. A satellite had just disintegrated. Her heart slammed against her ribs, her academy drills echoing in her mind: Stay sharp, lives depend on it. She zoomed in, watching the cloud of metallic fragments expanding, influenced subtly by atmospheric drag.

She understood the importance of what she had just witnessed. She had been trained well and knew how to respond. It was a Black Sky Alert, a space military emergency.

Hands steady but mind racing, she thought stay calm do this by the numbers - identify the killer.

She moved her cursor over the surviving object. A label popped up: ASAT Cosmos 2576, a Russian anti-satellite weapon.

Breathing sharply, by the book - she slammed her hand down on a red button fixed atop her console, a crimson light began blinking. The Shift Leader's boots echoed as he hurried to her console, eyes locked on the blinking crimson light.

"Report!?"

She pointed urgently at the chaotic screen.

"Kosmos 2576 just took out an Oko-class satellite. Debris field's spreading fast."

The Shift Leader squinted at the spiraling chaos.

"Did this just happen?"

"Yes sir, less than a minute ago. It appears that Kosmos two five seven six destroyed an old Oko class."

Without hesitation, the Shift Leader spun on his heel and briskly marched to his command desk. He lifted a red telephone handset—one that, when lifted, automatically rang the JOC Duty Officer's line.

"We have a Black Sky Alert sir."

Moments later, the JOC Duty Officer burst through the sliding doors, his uniform straightened with haste, eyes drawn to the towering display. The area of the debris field had already grown visibly larger in the brief time it had taken him to arrive.

The Duty Officer asked, "I see. How old is this?"

"Only moments old sir."

The Duty Officer nodded. He reached for the orange phone headset hanging by the console, pressed the button, and dialed.

"We have a Black Sky Alert sir."

He hung up without another word.

National Military Command Center (NMCC) 0300 Hours R

Deep in the labyrinthine heart of America's defense nerve center, a call was made.

Miles away, in a darkened bedroom, Major Will Morgan stirred. His secure-line phone blared, its encrypted chime vibrating against the nightstand's bare wood. He fumbled for the phone, squinting at its harsh blue glow."

"What time is it?"

The voice on the other end was clipped and official.

"Sir, it's oh three hundred hours Romeo. We have a Black Sky Alert, Major."

Will sat up a little straighter, adrenaline beginning to seep into his veins.

"Just now?"

"Yes sir. A car is waiting outside for you, sir."

He swung his legs over the side of the bed, already reaching for the duffel bag he kept packed for just such emergencies.

"Very well. I'll just be a minute."

"Sir, I'll wait on the line until you get into the car."

Dragging his fingers through his hair, Will struggled for presence of mind.

"I want to pick up Grace Roberts, my satellite systems expert..."

"Sir, that won't be necessary we have a car waiting outside her condo now as well. Sir, would you like me to notify her, or would you rather do it?"

Will smiled grimly.

"I better do it. She's not military and is not used to this procedure. We don't want to have her screaming off into the night."

"Sir, of course, sir."

Will ended the call, his mind fully alert now. He moved with methodical speed: a fast shower, a clean uniform, a check of his gear. Within minutes, he slipped into the crisp pre-dawn air, the weight of a potential orbital catastrophe pressing on his shoulders."

Glen Burnie, MD - Morgan's Condo - 0318 Hours R

A new black Cadillac sedan idled at the curb, its leather interior sharp with polish. Behind the wheel sat a silent driver; beside the rear door, a Marine in full dress blues stood at attention.

Will approached, nodding.

"Good morning Marine."

"Good morning sir."

"Do we have a secure phone?"

"Sir, yes, sir."

Without further ado, Will ducked into the back seat. He flipped open the armrest, revealing a secure phone nestled inside. He dialed Grace Roberts.

As Will's car sped off across town, in her condo, Grace Roberts jolted awake to the shrill ring of her phone.

Grace rubbing sleep from her eyes, "Hello?"

Will's voice, steady despite his racing pulse, reassured her.

"Gracie, Will, there is a car with a Marine guard outside your door. Do not be alarmed. This is standard Pentagon procedure."

Still in pajamas, Grace stumbled toward her window, peeking out through the blinds. Sure enough, there it was—the black sedan, the Marine guard. Her heart pounded with confusion and fear.

"3:20 in the morning! Standard procedure for what?"

"Sorry for the time and the procedure - its standard. I'm calling you on a secure phone from the car and am already on my way. I will call you and explain on the secure phone in your car. Do you have the go bag we asked you to prepare in your instructions?"

Her mind still foggy with sleep, Grace, testy, replied.

Grace Roberts (cranky) "Yes, I am a scientist. I know how to follow instructions. Where are we going? Oh yeah, you'd have to kill me, right?"

She hung up before finishing the thought, muttering to herself as she threw on clothes.

Back in Will's car, the Marine Guard spoke up.

"Sir, I have the Space Command JOC on the line for you. Just pick up the handset, sir."

"Morgan, who do I have here?" asked Will.

"Sir, this is the JOC Duty Officer Elijah Brown at Peterson, sir, "we have had an event. The Russians have destroyed an old Oko class with what appears to be an EMP from ASAT Comos 2576, sir."

"Thank you Duty Officer Brown. Keep me posted please." Replied Morgan.

Marine Guard said, "Sir, Professor Roberts is now secure. We have her on the line. Just pick up the phone, sir."

Will blinked in mild surprise.

"Thank you."

He picked up the handset again.

Glen Burnie, MD - Gracie's Condo - 0320 Hours R

"Gracie?"

"You were expecting someone else?"

Will let the comment slide without taking the bait.

"Space Force Command declared a Black Sky Alert. That is code for a crisis condition. In this case, the Russians have vaporized one of their old satellites in a successful test of their Anti-Satellite Attack System...threatening our orbital network. I assume everybody who is anybody all the way up to POTUS will know in a few hours if they don't know already. Professor, I wouldn't have woken you at such an early hour for anything less."

There was a brief pause on the line before Grace's voice softened.

Grace Roberts (sheepishly), "Oh."

"We are headed to Fort Belvoir to meet with Owen Edwards the Commanding General of the United States Intelligence and Security Command (INSCOM) and whomever he chooses to get out of bed." explained Will.

Her voice is more alert now, "It's going to be a long day."

And so, it would be.

Fort Belvoir - INSCOM Commander's Conference Room

The heavy oak door sealed with a soft thud. Around the polished table sat Will Morgan, Owen Edwards, Guy Zarelli, Judd Lockwood, Grace Roberts, and Sara Brandt—assembled under the cold weight of a Black Sky Alert.

Major General Owen Edwards stood at the head of the table, eyes sharp, voice low.

"Russia's test changes everything. Expect a full press on Radiant Sentry."

The room went still.

307

"Grace," Edwards said, "technical readout."

Grace straightened, her calm intellect filling the silence. "They're using electromagnetic pulse. It can't be blocked—but it can be redirected."

She outlined the options in clipped precision: "Shielding—Faraday containment to neutralize electric charge. Hardening—make systems resistant to EMP damage but won't stand up to nuke powered. Redundancy—backup systems, though those will just be targeted next."

Will leaned forward. "So Radiant Sentry is a Faraday system?"

Grace hesitated. "Can't confirm specifics, sir. But if we scale it right—it changes everything."

Edwards nodded grimly. "Then we buy time for LaserTech to finish it. Ideas?"

Lockwood's grin was thin. "Feed the Russians junk intel. Let them choke on it."

Guy Zarelli added, "Possible, but the ops teams can't decode the science. We'll need a translator. Someone to work with Genevieve Larsson."

Grace smiled. "That would be me."

A rare spark of humor lit the room. Edwards turned to her. "Welcome to the circus."

Will broke in. "They've got our file index. They'll press hard. We need to keep them chasing ghosts."

Grace leaned back. "What if we invent our own jargon—fabricated acronyms, pseudo-science terms? They'll waste weeks trying to decipher nonsense."

Sara laughed. "Weaponized gibberish. I love it."

Will nodded. "Keep the backdoor open in LaserTech's system. Don't spook them."

Guy added, "And Sable stays under ACIC, not FBI. Full control."

Edwards concluded, "Good. Grace, draft an op concept by end of day. Will—vet it."

Grace smiled. "He'll have it in ninety minutes."

Edwards allowed himself the faintest grin. "Helen will loop in CIA, FBI, and Perry. For now—need to know stays razor tight."

The meeting ended with a quiet scrape of chairs—each officer heading out to wage a war no one else knew had begun.

I-95 N - 0320 Hours R

The rumble of the highway filled the silence in Morgan's government-issued sedan as they made their way back toward LaserTech. Sunlight streamed through the windows, casting a golden sheen across the dashboard. In the back seat, Sara Brandt leaned her shoulder lightly against the door, a subtle smile tugging at her lips as she turned to Grace Roberts.

"I guess we'll be seeing a lot of you from now on," Sara said, her voice light, teasing.

Grace, sitting in the middle seat, chuckled and lifted her hands in a half-hearted surrender. "Yes! Never thought I would be a spook," she replied, her tone bemused, the unfamiliar title still tasting strange in her mouth.

Sara laughed. "We're all called spooks except for the FBI. Those tight asses call themselves agents." She glanced over at Will, who was focused on the road but couldn't quite hide his amusement. "I think the boss is at a loss for words."

Will Morgan glanced briefly in the rearview mirror, his lips curving into a grin. "Welcome to the NFL. We're lucky to have you," he said with warmth. "You just have to promise that the two of you won't gang up on me."

Sara gave a mock look of innocence. "It's best if you disabuse yourself of that notion," she said, making Grace snicker.

Will gave a mock groan and checked the time on the dashboard. "Right about now Owen is talking to Ed," he mused aloud, "and my phone should ring in a few minutes."

On cue, the phone mounted on the dashboard lit up. It automatically connected to the car's Bluetooth, and Will held his index finger to his lips in a gesture for silence. Sara and Grace exchanged amused glances.

The voice of Edwin Perry filled the car's interior, gruff and unmistakable.

Ed began, completely ignoring Will's presence.

"Commander Edwards just told me that instead of a big fat decoration for the department," Ed continued, his sarcasm sharp, "we now have an expensive ongoing operation."

Sara stifled a giggle behind her hand.

"And we have a new high-priced consultant," Ed added, his tone dripping with mockery. "The only saving grace is not that she is apparently a stunner with a smile to die for—no, it's that she is about ten times smarter than you."

Grace raised her eyebrows, exchanging an impressed glance with Sara.

"At least I'll have that to enjoy," Ed finished. "Now, if you can manage to stay out of trouble for the next couple of hours, see me when you get back."

"Just a cost of doing business... Sir," Will replied dryly and ended the call.

Sara let out laughing, shaking her head. "In Ed Perry speak that means 'great job guys, great addition to the team, and I have already figured out how to stick Owen with the tab.'"

Will smirked, steering them off the highway toward Fort Meade.

The afternoon sun filtered weakly through the high windows of Fort Meade's secure offices, casting muted stripes across the polished floor and the piles of documents that littered Will Morgan's desk.

The air inside his office carried the faint hum of electronics and the sharper buzz of tension. Grace Roberts, Sara Brandt, and Will himself were gathered in a loose semi-circle, the weight of the next phase of their operation settling heavily around them.

Will leaned forward, elbows resting on his knees, studying Grace intently.

"Gracie, how difficult is this for you to do?"

Grace exhaled, running a hand through her dark brown hair, her face set in concentration.

"Very. But between Gene and I it's doable."

Will nodded thoughtfully, tapping a pen against his knee. His voice was steady, practical, as always.

"Grace will have to work out of Fort Meade and deal remotely with Gene in Maryland."

The realization seemed to hit Grace mid-thought. She sat upright, blinking as the emotional implications surfaced.

"Oh my, I just realized that when we leave LaserTech Derek will be devastated to lose Sara."

A small, rueful smile played across Will's face. He glanced sideways at Sara, who looked momentarily stricken.

"And you. The two of you have been wonderful with him."

Sara swore under her breath, folding her arms tightly across her chest, as if bracing against the guilt that was already creeping in.

"Crap. Crap. Crap."

Will shrugged, the pragmatist to the core, his voice gentle but firm.

"Can't be helped he doesn't work for us."

There was a pause—the kind of silence heavy with the unspoken. Will broke it with a sly half-grin.

"Do you want me to break it to him? We don't need you two flooding the place with tears."

They all chuckled, but the sadness underneath lingered, like a slow leak in a sealed room.

CHAPTER THIRTY-SIX

Operation Echo Mirage

Fort Meade - Watchtower Conference Room - Two Days Later

The conference was packed, humming with subdued energy. Around the oval table, Sara, Grace, Z, Cecil, Rick Huang and Thomas Carrone, a Profiler sat paying apt attention. On the large screens mounted at the front of the room, Gene, Gus, and Judd joined remotely, their images pixelated but clear enough to capture their focused expressions.

Will Morgan stood at the head of the table, sleeves rolled up revealing a tattoo "9.11.01", a presence of quiet authority.

Will welcomes everyone, "The gang's all here so let's get started. This is a meeting to discuss Operation Echo Mirage."

Sara shot him with a mischievous grin, leaning back in her chair, "We'll dispense with the secret handshake?"

A few chuckles echoed around the room.

"Gene and Gracie are working on fake feeds to give the Russians. We need to establish protocol for vetting these ideas and the manner in which they are delivered. Gracie..."

Grace clicked a remote, bringing up a series of dense diagrams and scientific model on the Vibe whiteboard. She spoke with the surety of someone who lived in the intricate labyrinths of advanced engineering, "Well, if we're the Russians the thing we would be focused on is eddy currents. Bear with me..."

She paced, pointing to the screen, the room falling silent as they followed her.

"Supercomputer simulations can visualize and analyze the eddy currents, which are induced electrical currents, that flow within the conductive walls of a Faraday cage. These eddy currents play a key role in blocking electromagnetic fields."

She clicked again. New slides appeared, filled with graphs and electric field mappings.

"Currently, they may not be completely effective against low-frequency magnetic fields or very high-frequency electromagnetic radiation. EMPs involve electromagnetic radiation encompassing a broad range of frequencies, including high-frequency ones."

She paused to let the gravity of the vulnerability sink in.

"If we can get them to think we have made significant advances in the range of electromagnetic frequencies in which eddy currents can be made effective, they could spend considerable time and resources chasing their tails."

A murmur of approval stirred around the room.

"If the Russians move away from trying to steal physical files to interrogatories based on file names in the index, we can rather quickly develop false file names designed to direct their inquiry where we would like them to go."

Sara's voice broke in, bright and wry, "If not, we can always say that security has been tightened and that physical files are no longer possible."

From the screen, Gene's voice came through with a gravelly edge.

"For example, a file named 'Probe Configurations for fluid dynamic eddy current testing' would be loaded into the system with access limited to the author as if a draft. Answering Russian inquiries regarding this topic would be relatively easy. This paradigm would allow us to create many new files to bog down the iterative process for months."

Grace gave a small nod of agreement, adding another layer to the plan.

"An additional benefit is that their questions may give us some insight as to where they are."

Will looked around the room, sweeping his gaze over the faces that were now lit with interest and purpose.

Thomas Carrone spoke up.

"Will, I think we can anticipate a strong reaction from Moscow. I'm guessing they will go on the offensive to try and discredit Radiant Sentry as a fanciful waste of money and perhaps take a shot at a disinformation campaign blaming intelligence agencies for everything including the 1956 World Series."

Z chuckled and chimed in, "That's a cheap shot at my New York Yankees for those of you unfamiliar with New Jersey inferiority syndrome."

Smiling but ignoring Z, Carrone continued, "They will feel the need to ramp up the pressure on LaserTech, DARPA and Space Force.

"They took their shot, pardon the pun, and missed so they are left with few choices. The go to for them is misinformation."

"Anyone have any thoughts?"

The silence that answered him was not hesitation, but agreement—the kind of stillness that precedes action.

Will lingered behind, reviewing simulation outputs and quantum modeling predictions. He confides in Edwin Perry:

"I used to build investigations from data analysis, physical surveillance, travel records, and analysis of communications.

315

Now we're betting lives on statistical ghosts and entangled particles. I don't trust what I can't interrogate."

CHAPTER THIRTY-SEVEN

The Resonance Riddle

"Success is stumbling from failure to failure with no loss of enthusiasm."
—Winston Churchill

Linthicum Heights, MD – LaserTech Labs

For nearly two years, the promise of Radiant Sentry had hung in limbo, caught between breakthrough and breakdown. The system worked—mostly. In test after test, it demonstrated precise, near-instantaneous disruption of high-energy kinetic threats and focused EMP pulses. But always with one infuriating caveat: its shielding and detection capabilities faltered at the outer edges of the electromagnetic spectrum. Some frequencies passed through untouched, like knives slipping through gaps in chainmail. The team called it "the resonance riddle," though it felt more like a curse.

Every possible solution had been tested—modular phase shifting, quantum oscillation dampeners, brute-force harmonic

317

flooding. Each attempt either introduced new instabilities or failed to expand the spectrum envelope.

It wasn't that they didn't know what was wrong—it was that no one could figure out why every answer fell just short. The failure wasn't due to incompetence; it was due to complexity. Nature, it seemed, was refusing to cooperate with theory. And behind every simulation crash, hardware failure, or inconclusive result, the stakes loomed: without full-spectrum coverage, Radiant Sentry was vulnerable—and so was everything it was meant to protect.

Now, after hundreds of millions spent and a mountain of redacted memos and exhausted whiteboards, the final barrier remained unbroken. Until one unexpected spark—born not of design, but of intuition—changed everything.

Linthicum Heights - Derek Wilshire's Condo 1900 Hours R

Derek sat alone in his apartment tending his aquarium and reflecting on his life.

Numbers make sense in a way people don't.

For someone with Asperger's—and a mind tuned to mathematical precision — the world runs on a hidden syntax. Equations don't lie. Patterns follow rules. Prime numbers never cancel plans or pretend to like you. They either fit the sequence or they don't.

People, on the other hand, are noise.

Their smiles don't always mean happiness. Their words often mean the opposite of what they say. Eye contact is like trying to stare into the sun—too much information, all at once. You learn, early, that your honesty can be misunderstood as rudeness. That your long explanations sound like lectures. That your quiet isn't mystery, it's "weird."

So, you retreat—not because you want to be alone, but because every social encounter feels like defusing a bomb with invisible wires.

You crave connection, like anyone else. You just don't know the choreography. You don't intuit the pause in a conversation that signals it's your turn to speak. You miss the inside jokes. When you do speak, you might go on about number theory or fractal geometries while others glance at their phones, make excuses, or shift away politely.

Eventually, they stop inviting you.

And so, most of your friends are abstract—theorems, proofs, elegant structures that don't drift away or grow cold. You live in your own cathedral of logic. It's beautiful but echoing. Solitary.

The few who do stay—the rare ones who see you behind the awkward phrasing and encyclopedic focus—are precious. But they're rare. Most days, it's just you, the equations, and the silence.

And still, in that silence, you solve problems others can't see.

Because while the world might misunderstand you, you understand the world — deeply, structurally, beautifully. You see the fault lines beneath the surface. You map what others miss. And in that, even in loneliness, there is meaning.

Derek liked the work at LaserTech. The problems were interesting, the pay was certainly good, and the scientists were friendly enough. They treated him with respect — always polite, sometimes deferential. He was valued for his skills, no question about that. Especially George Lee, the boss, whom he liked a great deal.

He hoped he could help George solve his Radiant Sentry resonance riddle problem. He had been thinking a lot about it but needed to see it in a live test.

But he didn't feel a part of anything.

They gave him puzzles to solve—tightly scoped, always compartmentalized. Rarely with context. He'd patch a

319

vulnerability, trace a logic flaw, optimize a recursive compression routine... and never be told what it connected to. No one explained what the code meant beyond the surface. It was like contributing to a machine without ever seeing what it did. A cog in an invisible engine.

That was fine. It had always been fine.

He'd grown used to loneliness over his thirty-four years. Not the melodramatic kind, just the quiet, steady absence of common ground. He didn't mind eating alone. He liked tropical fish more than people. He'd accepted—long ago—that while others paired off into friendships and lunch cliques, he was the guy who fixed problems from the inside and then went home to an aquarium and a silent apartment.

Until Will's team showed up.

The first time he met Sara Brandt was in the cafeteria. He was eating his usual plain tuna wrap, bottle of water, tablet open beside him—when she asked if she could join him. She didn't ask what he did. She already knew. She asked about his aquarium. Mentioned that she heard he had reef fish. She knew the names of a few species.

That alone would have stunned him.

But then Grace Roberts joined them. And they invited him to eat lunch with them the next day. And the day after that. Eventually, it wasn't an invitation—it was routine. He followed them like a satellite. They started calling him their shadow partner.

And he liked it.

He had never been anyone's partner before. But now, for the first time, he went everywhere they went. He had all the code-level clearances—more than they did—so when Sara asked if he could sit in on one of Will's meetings, Will just nodded and said, "Of course." Will took him to dinner like one of the team.

Later, Derek had asked Grace about it, wondering if he was overstepping.

320

"Will lets Sara bring anyone she wants," she said with a smile. "He allows just about anything Sara wants."

But when he asked Sara directly, she shook her head.

"It's not that," she told him. "Will just likes surrounding himself with smart people."

Smart people. Not freaks.

That phrase stuck in his head for days. Not because it was flattering—though it was—but because it felt like someone had finally drawn a line between him and the part of himself he'd spent a lifetime hiding. Like maybe this was the group he belonged to. Like maybe the thing he had always thought made him different was the thing that made him welcome.

When he uncovered the line of rogue script buried deep inside LaserTech's production code—the line that explained the breach—he was elated. Not because he'd solved another puzzle. But because he'd been useful. Because Will had trusted him. Because Sara had believed in him. Because he could finally return some of what he'd been given. And he wanted to do more. He would try. Every day.

This—this was the best time he'd ever had in his working life. The most alive he'd ever felt. And though he didn't say it out loud, not to anyone, the thought of the team leaving made something tighten in his chest. He didn't want to go back to being a shadow with no one to orbit.

Not now.

Not after this.

Linthicum Heights, MD – LaserTech Labs – May

Project Director George Lee hunched over the oscilloscope, eyes darting between waveform spikes and diagnostic overlays.

The cage hummed in the background, sealed, shielded—supposedly.

"Shield integrity at ninety-eight percent," the system chirped.

George grumbled, "Then why the hell is telemetry jittering?"

He watched as a clean pulse distorted into a slow smear, dragging like syrup through the signal. Low Frequency bleed—again. He swapped in a manganese ferrite lining and rebooted.

Same result.

He scrubbed a hand through his hair. "It's not failing. It's whispering." He leaned in. "Whatever's leaking... it knows how to duck."

High End Collapse

LaserTech Secure Clean Room Chamber – June

The test rig howled as a gamma spike cracked through the system, burning through three layers of shielding like flash paper.

George winced. "Goddammit!"

He hit the shutdown. Smoke curled from the inner cage housing—again.

Across the room, a junior tech watched nervously. George waved them off. "It's not the material. It's not the grounding." He kicked the metal base. "It's the physics laughing at me."

He stared at the waveform decay. The low end crept. The high end smashed. The middle held.

He whispered to no one, "It shouldn't be possible for both ends to fail differently... unless they're not failing."

Dead Spectrum

LaserTech - George Lee's lab Labs – August

George sat alone, surrounded by shattered ceramic composites and half-disassembled panels. The whiteboard was a maze of notes, circled and crossed out. His coffee was untouched. Cold.

He tried layering silver mesh with vapor-deposited polymer. The simulation showed promise—until the pulse test.

The system flatlined. Zero shielding above 120 GHz.

George slumped in his chair.

He whispered to himself, "We're not shielding a signal. We're shielding a war."

The screens glowed with defeat. He didn't delete the data. He let it sit. Like a wound.

Derek's Echo

LaserTech – George Lee's lab – late afternoon

After three more expensive failed tests and, more importantly, sixty more days, Grace Roberts visits George Lee in his lab in the vain hope that she can perhaps be a catalyst to the insolvable frequency problem plaguing Radiant Sentry.

The hum of active processors filled the lab like a distant storm. On George's massive workstation, spectral analysis data poured across half a dozen screens—fast, dense, and angry with color. Radiant Sentry's latest performance logs blinked in warning amber: signal degradation, edge-case failure, EM scatter.

Her eyes moved between the scrawled formulas crowding the whiteboard. Only George or Gene Larsson had lived with these dead ends long enough to sense where the pattern bent and where it broke. And yet, as she stared, she wondered—sometimes it took someone untouched by all those false starts to spot the first crack in the wall. Maybe a fresh pair of eyes can jump start something.

George ran a hand through his hair and exhaled hard. "We've isolated the mainband integrity, but the extremities are still trash," he said, eyes fixed on a scrolling diagnostic trace. "The cage holds at midrange, then falls apart. Low-frequency interference bleeds through like syrup—inductive coupling through every cable spine. And the gamma bursts—" he waved at a line of jagged peaks "—just laugh at our shielding."

Grace, arms folded, leaned over the console. "We accounted for lateral bleed through all nine sectors. Redundant routing, decoupled pathways. Still corrupted?"

George nodded. "Still corrupted. And if SISTER's waveform starts feeding that junk into the interpretive stack, it's going to start drawing false correlations."

She frowned. "Which means Radiant Sentry starts hallucinating threat vectors."

George nodded again. "Like seeing enemies in clouds."

Derek stood off to the side, head cocked, eyes half-lidded. He wasn't only watching the numbers—he was listening. The hum wasn't static to him; it was rhythm, a stubborn mathematical melody threaded under the machinery.

He closed his eyes.

Low frequencies weren't leaking. They were calling back. He heard it like a bass note struck too close to a drum, the vibration folding, echo feeding echo. Not chaos—choir.
Inside his head, he ran the steps of his peculiar dance:

- Overlay the pulses, not in sequence but in harmony.
- Feel where one wave bent into another, the fold where symmetry became feedback.
- Stop chasing failure—follow the music.

The hum became a metronome. The metronome became a song. In his mind's ear it wasn't shielding collapsing—it was resonance, two notes locking into sympathy until the cage itself sang back.

His eyes snapped open, breath sharp.

"Stop. It's not a breach—it's an echo. The low end isn't leaking, it's feeding. Sympathetic pulse from the high side. Look at the timing—it's folding over itself. A loop. The cage is resonating, not failing."

George froze, staring at the trace. Derek's finger jabbed at the waveform, excitement breaking through his calm.

"Don't solve the shield. Solve the feedback."

For George it was data. For Derek it was mathematical music resolved into harmony. The hum in his skull, the math on the screen—finally, the same note.

"It's not a breach—it's an echo. The low end isn't leaking. It's feeding. Look at the timing—folding over itself. A loop."

George glared at the trace. At first—chaos. Then, like a lens snapping into focus, the pattern clicked. Not collapse— resonance. The cage itself sang back.

George said, "...Solve the feedback, not the shield."

Derek pushed off the wall, eyes lit with clarity. His hands cut through the air, sharp, urgent.

"Exactly. Kill the sympathetic pulse. Tune the harmonic. Insert damping material here—no, there, on the high side. Shift the timing two microseconds. Do it now." Derek said.

George's fingers flew over the console. For the first time in days, the problem didn't feel like weight—it felt like momentum, like running downhill with the wind at his back.

The cage steadied. The spikes began to smooth, the hum softening into balance.

George shot Derek a look, equal parts disbelief and admiration. Derek only grinned faintly, the echo still ringing in his head. "Told you. It wasn't noise. It was music."

The monitors stayed flat. The cage was sound.

And for the first time in weeks, the impossible felt possible.

George leapt from his stool so suddenly he nearly knocked it over, grabbed Derek in a spontaneous bear hug that lifted him half an inch off the ground.

"We couldn't do this without you, Derek. you're irreplaceable. Full Stop!"

Derek flinched, startled and stiff, blinking like he'd been struck. Grace smiled—a real smile, deep enough to crease her eyes. A Duchenne smile.

Derek gave a shy, half-formed one back, awkward and self-conscious.

George, already spinning back toward the keyboard, was muttering calculations under his breath.

Grace tugged Derek's sleeve. "Come on. Let him cook." Derek repeated, "Let him cook."

They left the lab, leaving George to the storm of discovery he loved best — the kind that came from the quiet voice no one else heard.

LaserTech – George Lee's lab – early morning

The sun hadn't quite cleared the ridge, but the lab was already glowing with the cold blue of monitors running endless loops of simulation data. The air was stale with overnight brainwork—half-drunk coffee, the faint ozone tang of overheated circuits, and George's signature lack of ventilation protocol.

George was slumping over his desk, head on crossed arms, snoring. One screen blinked Simulation Complete.

Grace pushed the door open, carrying a coffee tray, followed closely by Derek holding a stack of printouts and a breakfast muffin balanced on top.

She took one look and sighed affectionately. "George. Good morning, sleepyhead."

No response. Just another snore and a twitch.

Derek cleared his throat. "Hey George, we brought you some coffee."

Nothing.

Derek looked at Grace, shrugged, and — with perfect timing — dropped the thick file folder to the floor with a loud thump.

George jerked up with a snort, eyes bleary and unfocused. "Wha—what? I wasn't sleeping, I was... running parallel analyses..."

Grace arched an eyebrow. "Uh-huh."

George blinked a few times, then caught sight of Derek and broke into a wide grin. "Derek, you bloody genius. It works. At least on the computer—but it works!"

Derek tilted his head. "You validated it overnight?"

"Damn right I did." George rubbed his face, grabbed a cold cup of yesterday's coffee, thought better of it, then took Grace's offering instead. "I reran the pulse timing with your resonance model layered in. The low-frequency tail collapses—just like you said. And the gamma noise dampens along the fold line. It's stable."

Grace was already scanning his primary monitor. "You added active cancellation in sector eight?"

George nodded. "Only way to stop the harmonic self-feed. Once the pulse loop is neutralized—"

"Radiant Sentry sees cleanly," Derek finished.

George snapped his fingers. "Is Jankowitz in yet?"

Grace shook her head. "Not that I've seen."

George was already on his feet, jittery with momentum. "Never mind. Let's go find him."

Just then, the door opened.

Gene Larsson walked in, sharp-eyed, tablet in hand. "What's going on in here? I could hear George from the hallway."

Before anyone could answer, Marcus Liebowitz stepped in behind her, sipping from a thermos. "The gang's all here. What'd I miss?"

George looked around, counting heads. "Except for John. Where the hell is John?"

Without missing a beat, Derek tapped a few keys. One of George's larger screens flickered, showing a closed-circuit feed from the lab next door. John Jankowitz, head materials physicist, hunched over a scope, tweaked a circuit array without looking up.

Derek, deadpan: "Where he always is."

George squinted at the feed. "Wait, is that live?"

Derek nodded. "Time-stamped. He's two minutes into a recalibration cycle."

George was already halfway out the door. "Perfect."

The group chuckled and followed as George burst out of the lab and veered into the next room.

--*Jankowitz's lab – continuous*

John looked up, startled, as George barged in.

"John! You're gonna want to hear this. It works."

John blinked. "What works?"

"Derek's fix. The resonance riddle theory. Clean signal. We're scheduling an all-hands systems test — as soon as you're ready."

John's eyebrows lifted. "Seriously?"

Grace, stepping in behind George, nodded. "Seriously. And it holds up under triple-layer scrutiny."

Marcus leaned against a counter, grinning. "Well damn. Someone finally broke the ghost loop."

Gene was already tapping notes into her tablet. "I'll get the scheduling block cleared. SYBIL will need to run a precheck."

John set down his tools, already shifting gears. "Give me an hour to refresh Sector Nine, then I'll be ready."

George beamed, slapping Derek on the shoulder. "You may have saved the project. You matter more than you know.."

Derek gave a faint, embarrassed smile and stared at the floor.

Grace elbowed him. "Try not to collapse the laws of physics before lunch."

Derek blinked once. "No promises."

The team spread out around the lab, energized, coordinated—a hive igniting around a breakthrough. For the first time in months, Radiant Sentry wasn't on the defensive.

It was waking up.

Echo Chamber

Linthicum Heights, MD – LaserTech Labs

The lab buzzed with quiet triumph. Derek's harmonic resonance breakthrough had just pierced the final layer of Radiant Sentry's shielding anomaly. SYBIL confirmed it: a viable method for detecting signal leakage without breaching the containment protocols. They had a path forward.

Virtually everyone was on hand for the test. Anticipating a long-awaited moment of triumph.

Gene gave Derek a nod across the table. Rick clapped twice and went back to cataloging the waveform archives.

Then the lights flickered.

Just once. Hardly noticeable.

George asked, "Did anyone else see that?"

"Voltage dip," Gene replied. "Transient. SYBIL?"

"Spike detected in auxiliary monitoring subsystem. Source: Console 4."

Marcus blinked. "Nobody's been using Console 4 for weeks."

Derek turned toward it. The screen had come alive.

Not from login.

From execution.

Lines of code were scrolling rapidly—dump routines, silent wipe commands, system-level intrusion paths.

"A breach! Oh my God, someone is sabotaging the system," exclaimed Cathy Wang.

Derek's voice was ice. "SYBIL, identify user session."

"Active session mask in place. Console 4 is operating in root-level isolation."

Sara had already moved. She drew her weapon and covered the console, on the far West wall.

"Get me the room log," she snapped. "Visuals, movement history, who was at that station in the last six hours?"

"Last confirmed user: VLEVIN."

Everyone looked at Victor.

Victor Levin—codename Lynx—sat at Console 4, his fingers moving with deceptive calm. Onscreen, command-line windows blinked with lines of code, the kind designed to melt through safeguards and exfiltrate deep architecture without a trace. He thought he was winning.

Every path he took looped back on itself, yet he walked on, untroubled—like a man pacing circles inside a prison he couldn't see.

Across the room, Rick Huang monitored telemetry in real time, his jaw clenched. "SYBIL, report console integrity status."

"Encapsulation integrity: holding. GhostNet scaffold: stable. Sabotage vectors contained within sandbox."

Rick turned to Sara. "He thinks he's burning down the system. In reality, he's just poking a simulation."

Sara folded her arms, watching Levin frantically input escalation commands. "He's thinks he is working on the actual system as if that'll trigger a failover." She shook her head. "It's adorable."

Derek Wilshire leaned in closer to his screen, running a real-time delta comparison against the live system. "No penetration past the decoy environment. None. It's brilliant."

SYBIL's interface flickered, not from damage—but in mimicry, simulating the very destruction Levin believed he was unleashing.

Levin's fingers paused. His smugness evaporated as he realized the failure cascade he'd triggered… wasn't cascading. The interface hiccupped, rebooted, then returned to nominal status.

Rick finally broke the silence. "SYBIL. Confirm: was the encapsulation in GhostNet successful?"

"Affirmative. User access was quarantined in engineered shadow net. All system-level intrusions contained. No breach of mission-critical assets."

Sara stepped forward, arms still crossed, a bemused look on her face, weapon still pointed at Levin. "You mean to tell me… you really didn't understand you've been encapsulated this whole time? Sandboxed in a SYBIL-engineered shadow network?"

Levin said nothing. His eyes darted across the screens, still trying to make sense of the reality collapse around him.

Derek shook his head admiringly. "He bought the theater. All of it."

"System reboots complete." SYBIL's voice was calm, clinical—unbothered.

"System-level intrusions quarantined. Would you like to initiate full-spectrum simulation again?"

Sara broke into a laugh. It echoed in the chamber like a cracked bell—half incredulous, half entertained. "She's trolling him now."

Levin slumped back in his chair.

The room, once electric with tension, settled. But no one let their guard down. They had caught a mole. They had watched him try—and fail.

And SYBIL, watching over all of them, was already preparing for the next game.

Linthicum Heights, MD – LaserTech Labs - Moments later

The door hissed open with a hydraulic sigh that instantly silenced the room.

Major Will Morgan stepped in, unhurried.

Black field jacket, clean-shaven, unreadable as stone. His boots made no sound on the polymer floor, but the weight of his presence turned everyone toward him like a magnet.

Victor Levin—the mole, the saboteur, the sleeper—looked up from Console 4, pale and blinking, his lips parted like he might still have something to say.

Will said nothing. He didn't need to.

Sara stepped aside wordlessly. Derek straightened. Rick backed away from his screen. SYBIL dimmed the ambient lighting subtly, the system instinctively mirroring its master's tone.

Will came to a full stop five feet from Levin.

"You did well," he said, his voice quiet. Controlled. "You stayed buried for years. Learned our systems. Bled just enough information to stay useful, not suspicious. Textbook."

Levin started to speak—perhaps to defend, perhaps to stall—but Will cut him off with a single raised finger.

"But you made a mistake."

He took a slow step forward.

"You underestimated the people in this room."

Another step. Levin flinched.

"You thought SYBIL was code. You didn't understand she's instinct."

Will's eyes narrowed. His voice dropped half a register.

"And you thought I wouldn't come down here myself."

Now face to face, Will stared into Levin's eyes with such stillness it seemed to freeze the air.

"You don't need to know what happens next, Mr. Morozov."

Levin blinked.

Will allowed himself the smallest smile.

"That wasn't a question."

He turned to Rick. "Secure all traffic. No external comms. No movement until SYBIL sweeps every drive from his last sixty logins."

"Already started," Rick replied.

To Derek: "I want a psychological pattern map of his syntax over the last three weeks."

"On it."

Will stepped back toward the exit, never once looking over his shoulder. "He's no longer an internal threat. He's an opportunity. SYBIL will take it from here. Let's learn from him before he disappears."

Sara raised an eyebrow. "Disappears?"

Will paused at the threshold. "No one hears about this. Not yet. He's going to help us—just like he helped them."

And then he was gone.

The door sealed behind him.

Levin sat in his chair, sweating through his collar. The weight of the silence crashed down again—until SYBIL spoke, from every wall.

"Victor Levin has been neutralized. Simulation node active. All actions henceforth monitored and preserved. Welcome to containment."

Sara gave Levin a sympathetic shrug. "Could've just transferred out. But no—had to go full sleeper agent."

She turned and walked away, Derek trailing behind her, shaking his head.

Levin said nothing.

There was nothing left to say.

LaserTech Radiant Sentry control room – later that day

The control room at LaserTech's secure compound felt like the brainstem of a living machine. Glass walls, glowing consoles, floor-to-ceiling screens running diagnostics and waveform visualizations. A soft hum of servers surrounded everything—a pulse of power and anticipation.

Grace, George, John, Derek, Marcus, and Gene had taken their stations, joined by a few key engineers. The air was taut, but focused. Every motion was deliberate.

SISTER, DARPA's integrated AI system, spoke through the overhead speakers in her neutral contralto:

"Diagnostic grid aligned. Power thresholds green. Initiate full-spectrum simulation?"

George Lee said, "Do it."

A mechanical whir kicked in. Radiant Sentry's core systems began powering through their calibration sequences. Electrostatic field harmonizers locked into phase. External shielding arrays aligned with projected orbital threats.

Grace tapped through a rolling matrix of equations. "EM shield responding."

John squinted at his screen. "Pulse entry in ten seconds. Gamma spike staged."

SISTER

"Warning: Gamma-edge pulse entry. Cascade sequence pending."

Derek, calmly: "Counter-phase damping initiated."

A moment passed. Nothing shorted. Nothing cracked.

SISTER

"Pulse neutralized. System integrity: stable."

George straightened up. "Did anyone else see that delta shift?"

Marcus swiveled in his chair. "It didn't just hold. It corrected in real-time. That's adaptive resonance."

Grace leaned forward, breath shallow. "Wait for it..."

The screens flickered—and then everything locked into place.

SISTER

"Radiant Sentry coherence level: 99.84%. System is fully operational."

The room froze.

For a breathless second, no one spoke. Then George gave a choked laugh and threw his hands in the air.

George said, "We're live. She's seeing everything."

John, stunned: "Stable at full load... I never thought I'd see it."

Gene, smiling said, "The D.C. brass is going to have heart attacks when they get this report."

Marcus clapped Derek on the back. "Hell of a morning for a systems breakthrough."

Derek blinked slowly, then looked to the main screen — a clean, flowing visualization of Radiant Sentry's detection grid. For once, no interference. Just clarity.

Grace, gleaming with pride: "You did it, Derek."

Derek answered without looking away. "We all did."

The room quieted, each person watching the steady rhythm of a system that had once teetered on the edge of chaos. Radiant Sentry now pulsed like a living sentinel—aware, awake, and unbreakable.

SISTER

"Awaiting mission directives."

The room erupts in cheers, hollers, high-fives and fist bumps.

Linthicum Heights, MD – LaserTech SCIF

The secure line crackled once, then went dead silent—a perfect channel.

George Lee stood alone in the SCIF, his badge clipped to his collar, a classified data cube glowing soft blue in the reader behind him.

Across the secure video feed, the Director of DARPA, Helena Quinn, 55, appeared—shoulders squared, her gray hair pulled back tight, eyes sharp with that distinct combination of brilliance and impatience that George had learned to respect from a distance.

Her presence alone shifts the air in the room: calm but not soft, composed but never disengaged. Her voice is measured, low, and surgical in tone, as if each word is selected and tested before release. A physicist by training, and a battlefield psychologist by instinct, Helena earned her reputation not just through innovation, but through calculated survivability — in bureaucracy, in black budgets, and occasionally, in policy warfare.

To her staff, she is both oracle and scalpel — visionary, but capable of cutting loose anything that compromises operational integrity. Her background in materials science and autonomous systems gives her an edge in technical conversations, but it's her grasp of the political chessboard that makes her dangerous to underestimate.

She walks the line between scientist and strategist with unnerving precision.

She wears tailored suits with the simplicity of someone who has outgrown the need for fashion statements.

"Talk to me, George. Your message said urgent priority—Radiant Sentry status update?"

Knowing her impatience for useless preamble, he didn't waste her time.

"We've achieved full-spectrum shielding," he said. "As of 0900 hours this morning, the EMP matrix withstood both low-frequency and high-frequency electromagnetic attacks in continuous spectrum sweeps without data loss, penetration, or degradation. Containment held. No latency. No phase bleed."

Helena blinked once, slowly. "You're telling me the cage finally works."

"I'm telling you; it reacts. We're not just deflecting anymore—we're transforming. The new matrix uses a proprietary material—filament-doped ruthenium interwoven with nanocarbon graphene. The result is a tunable phase-harmonic interface at the material level. Incoming energy isn't absorbed or blocked—it's dispersed through controlled photon scattering. What hits us gets unraveled, refracted, and harmlessly scattered across the spectrum."

"Uh—you want to give that to me in a form a Senator can understand, please," asked Helena.

"I'm not sure that's humanly possible," said George, now feeling his oats, "How about this.

"What we've developed doesn't just block energy — it changes how energy interacts with the material itself. Using an advanced synthetic mesh of ruthenium and graphene, we've created a surface that can redirect harmful energy through a process called photon scattering. Instead of taking a direct hit, the energy gets broken apart and safely scattered as harmless light. It's not absorption, and it's not deflection — it's controlled dispersion."

Helena leaned forward, interest sharpening into intensity. "And you can scale it?"

"Yes," George said. "We've already begun adapting the matrix for mobile defense platforms. Aircraft bays. Satellite command relays. We believe we can extend this to hardened field operations within sixty days, assuming DARPA priority support and supply chain clearance."

"Who else knows?"

"No one outside my team and Deputy Director Larsson. You're the first outside call."

Helena sat back, folding her hands. The room around her was dark, illuminated only by the screen's glow. George could practically see her mind calculating strategic implications.

"This buys us time," she said.

"It buys us survival," George corrected.

"Has NSA validated the threat window from the Kosmos array?" she asked.

"We're assuming worst-case," George replied. "Russian orbital activity suggests they're prepping another dry run— another near-Earth flyover. And we have credible intel indicating their new burst-mode is higher frequency than anything we've encountered."

Helena nodded. "Then this breakthrough didn't come a day too soon."

George hesitated. "We'll need a classified deployment framework before word leaks. This doesn't stay in a lab, Helena. It can't."

"It won't," she said. "You'll get your framework. And you'll get it fast."

There was a beat of silence between them. The kind shared by people who knew what was at stake.

Finally, she leaned closer, voice dropping an octave.

"You just leveled the playing field, George. Don't let it tilt again."

The screen blinked off.

George stood there for a moment, alone in silence. He exhaled and turned back toward the data cube, already thinking ahead—deployment logistics, shielding retrofits, continuity of government shelters. The weapon in the sky still existed.

But now, for the first time, they had something to stand against it.

CHAPTER THIRTY-EIGHT

Showdown

Moscow 1300 Hours C

Beneath a fortress of concrete and rebar, a private chamber buzzed with the faint hum of jamming equipment. Every wall here was built to deflect signals, to smother electronic whispers before they could escape.

Sergei Malenko Director of the Radiative Pulse-Activated Resilience Protocol (RPARP) sat at the command table, flanked by Major Elena Grishin, Georgy Markova and Kir Smirnova. Behind them, a digital board glowed with the outline of a new American satellite system: RADIANT SENTRY-NOVA: SHIELD PLATFORM.

Malenko's voice was dark with anger—and something colder still.

"So, the American mole—Sable—was feeding us a dream. Let's return the favor."

Grishin leaned forward, her eyes glinting like a blade catching a sliver of light.

"We leak a false vulnerability. Make it look like we've cracked their shielding matrix. They'll scramble to patch a problem that doesn't exist.

"We can simulate a breach in their orbital logs. Make it look like we took down one of their satellites. Trigger anomaly alerts in their own system—remotely. Just enough to make them think we've seen through the veil."

Malenko nodded slowly, his expression one of grim satisfaction.

"And in the chaos, we test our real weapon."

He let the words hang heavy in the air before turning his gaze on Markova.

"You're sure our cloaked platform can deliver?"

Markova allowed a tight, confident smile. "The Tselina-9 drone is in orbit now. EM-silent, fully automated. If they believe we're attacking in one direction... they'll never see the real blade coming."

Grishin raised an eyebrow.

"What's the target?"

Malenko shrugged.

"A test, nothing vital. One of their classified comsats. The kind they'll notice... but can't acknowledge publicly."

Malenko's smile grew colder, amused. "A ghost hit. Like their own. Poetic."

Behind them, on the giant screen, one of the American satellite icons blinked, faltered... and faded away.

S-91 just blinked out

Colorado Springs,CO - Peterson Space Force Center

The soft ping of alarms broke the usual low murmur of conversation. In a single synchronized movement, a dozen operators straightened in their chairs, eyes darting to their screens.

At the entrance, Lieutenant Ty Harris, tall and fit, strode into the room, a coffee cup steaming in his hand. He was an intuitive and experienced officer who had witnessed just about everything in the last seven years. saw the tension instantly and set the cup aside.

"Talk to me," he barked.

A tech officer turned, his face pale.

"S-91 just blinked out. No debris, no trajectory change. It's just... all gone."

Harris stiffened.

"Shield breach? Ghost hit?"

The tech shook his head frustrated.

"Unknown. We were running a diagnostic when it vanished. But there's no spike. No pulse. Nothing. Clean silence."

Harris grabbed the comms headset and keyed into a secure line.

"Contact the Pentagon watch commander. And tell them the Russians might've just learned to whisper."

The hum of the room grew electric as operators leaned into their screens, searching for a threat that had left no trace.

Smoke and Mirrors

LaserTech Radiant Sentry Control Room

Red alerts flare across the upper band of the wall-to-wall interface. Monitors stacked three deep show orbital telemetry, Radiant Sentry's satellite matrix, and diagnostic sweeps. A low hum of stress permeates the room—keyboards clicking faster than usual, voices clipped.

SYBIL:

S-91 satellite telemetry offline. Probable kinetic impact. ASAT trajectory confirmed—vector: Barents Sea.

George Lee under his breath mutters, "That's a hit. They took the shot."

"How the hell did they target it?" Gene Larsson wonders out loud, "Radiant Sentry shielding should've masked the signature."

John Jankowitz approaching console.

"SYBIL, run a deep-spectrum footprint on the shielding matrix. Cross-reference with decoy latency across S-82 through S-92."

SYBIL (V.O.)

"Anomaly detected. Orbital signatures suggest partial matrix breach—originating from S-85 node cluster. Leak vector: high-band IR flux."

Gene exclaims, "No. That's impossible. That node's hard isolated."

"They didn't break the matrix." said George, "They just made it look like they did."

Gene eyes narrowing

"Smoke and mirrors. A ghost hit."

"They want us to scramble." Adds George, "Patch a vulnerability that doesn't exist... while they watch how we respond."

SYBIL (V.O.)

"Confirming: simulated breach logs injected at 04:12:07 UTC. No actual shielding compromise detected."

A beat of silence. The operators stop typing, glancing toward the center of the room.

Grace Roberts stepping in from the adjacent SCIF.

"Joint Space Command's flagged it too. Ghost data. Russians want to see if we flinch."

George said to the room, "We don't flinch. We verify. Strip everything down, full forensic pass. No assumptions."

Radiant Sentry Ops Control Room – Six Hours Later

Gene stands in front of a translucent HUD, streaked with orbital paths and data overlays. George reviews the final logs with Derek and Grace.

"Every node clean. No infiltration, no telemetry deviation." said George, "Radiant Sentry is airtight."

Sara quietly, resolute said, "Then we go live."

She reaches for the encrypted console key, plugs it into the system port.

Sara said, "SYBIL, prep for final integration and activation. Operation: Threshold Prime.

SYBIL (V.O.)

Confirmed. Radiant Sentry is ready for final test deployment.

Radiant Sentry - The big shield

The sun beat down mercilessly on the high-tech sprawl of the testing grounds, a glimmering mirage against the endless desert.

Inside a cavernous hangar, a structure the size of a football field gleamed under industrial lights.

Suspended from a complex lattice of support, the prototype satellite core floated mid-air—a marvel of layered alloys and Faraday-grade shielding.

Lieutenant Lane, dressed in a radiation-shielded suit, walked alongside Dr. Kira Valentine. The hiss of filtered air filled their helmets.

Lane whistled in awe.

"So, this is it. Radiant Sentry - The big shield."

"Radiant Sentry doesn't sleep. It doesn't blink. Like the falcon, it waits in silence, one talon hovering over the kill switch."

Valentine, ever composed, adjusted the tablet in her gloved hands.

"Version 3.6. Triple-layered with dynamic wave modulation. When the pulse frequency changes mid-strike, the lattice compensates."

Lane grunted.

"And if we're wrong?"

Valentine allowed herself the faintest of smiles.

"Then we get to see a $2.4 billion blackout live on national defense TV."

Ahead, a control panel blinked to life, a red button shielded beneath a glass cover labeled: SIMULATED STRIKE – CLASSIFIED LEVEL 6.

Lane tapped his comms.

"All teams report. Initiating Project Radiance Sentry live-fire EMP simulation in T-minus 60 seconds."

Krasnoznamensk, Moscow Oblast

The Russian team watched in tense silence. Grainy satellite footage fed through an encrypted line, the resolution low, the distance vast.

Georgy Markova I senior military analyst for strategic space operations leaned over the operations table, scowling. "All we can do is watch?"

Svetlana Korolevd head of orbital defense division shook her head.

"Our last infiltrator was burned last month. DARPA's files are airtight. The encryption—quantum-layered."

Grishin's voice was heavy with bitterness.

"We spent two years chasing shadows. They fed us a maze, and we walked right in."

Markova snapped, slamming a hand on the table.

"Then we build our own. From scratch."

Svetlana sighed.

"That could take years."

Kir Smirnova looked at the screen as the countdown ticked lower.

"Then we make sure they never get to use theirs before we do."

Yes!

Vandenberg Space Force Base CA

The countdown hit zero.

A low-frequency hum filled the vast hangar. From a specialized emitter, a contained EMP wave burst forth, slamming into the shielded core with a crackling roar.

Sensors screamed. Sparks flew.

346

And when the light faded—the satellite remained standing. Operational. Untouched.

Dr. Valentine, staring wide-eyed at the live readouts, grinned in disbelief.

"Power integrity 100%. No data loss. Thermal signature clean."

Lieutenant Lane allowed himself a rare, satisfied smirk.

"Yes! Our shield just held up to the hammer."

Around them, a cheer came up from the technicians, though one near the back watched a side-screen nervously—a small alert flashing: OUTSIDE OBSERVATION DETECTED.

Yasenevo, Moscow -SVR Headquarters -1815 Hours C

The night outside was still, the city cloaked in icy darkness.

Inside, Svetlana Korolevd poured two fingers of dark vodka into a crystal glass and handed it to Malenko and one to Smirnova. They stood in silence for a moment; the flicker of satellite feeds still reflected in the windowless walls around them.

Malenko's voice was low, reluctant.

"It worked, didn't it?"

Smirnova took a slow sip before answering.

"Yes. We have no way in to LaserTech. No weakness. For the first time in two decades, we are blind."

They clinked glasses, toasting not to victory—but to the cold, bitter acknowledgment of defeat.

"We consider this absolutely imperative. If the Americans develop a counter to our space weapons systems, we will be defenseless for decades. We must know how it works so that we can develop a counter."

Kir's voice dropped to a whisper.

"We are well aware of the stakes."

Sergei Malenko leaned forward.

"This is a zero-sum game that we must win."

Yasenevo, Moscow Directorate S / Kir Smirnova's Office

The city was a steel heart beating under ice. From his window, Kir Smirnova watched the faint shimmer of snow drift across the inner courtyard—the same view he'd had for seventeen years.

To anyone else, it might have looked lifeless. To Kir, it was precision—discipline made visible.

He poured tea from a small, chipped porcelain cup—an heirloom from his mother, who had fled Leningrad during the siege and never stopped boiling water before dawn.

The habit stayed with him. So did her warning: "In Russia, my son, survival is not a gift. It is a calculation."

He lived by that. Not ideology. Not patriotism. Calculation.

Patriotism was for speeches and funerals.

Duty was for the naive who hadn't yet learned that the State devoured its own with the same appetite it showed its enemies.

No, what moved Kir Smirnova wasn't duty—it was symmetry.

Order from chaos. Predictability from deception. The quiet beauty of a world where every secret had a cost and every betrayal a ledger.

When Zakharov died, Kir hadn't felt anger—only imbalance.

A destabilizing variable in an equation he had spent decades balancing.

Someone had tipped the scale, and that was intolerable.

He stared at the file spread open across his desk: Genevieve Larsson—"Sable."

A phantom asset turned liability.

Brilliant. Unpredictable. Human.

He almost admired her—the same way a surgeon admires a tumor for how perfectly it hides inside living tissue.

He whispered, almost to himself: "Intelligence is not the pursuit of truth. It is the art of useful lies."

The Americans had begun to play his game.

That was dangerous—and fascinating. He picked up his pen, elegant, Soviet-era steel, and signed the new order.

A single word scrawled in Cyrillic across the page: ликвидация—liquidation.

His subordinates would interpret it as ruthlessness.

But to Kir, it was mercy—a form of closure, restoring equilibrium.

He looked once more at the snow outside; the reflection of his own face ghosted on the glass.

If anyone had asked why he did what he did, his answer would have been simple:

"Because someone must maintain the illusion that the world still has rules."

CHAPTER THIRTY-NINE

Senate Hearing

"When they call the roll in the Senate, the Senators do not know whether to answer 'Present' or 'not guilty'.

— Theodore Roosevelt

Washington, DC U.S. Capitol – 1630 Hours R

The air is thick with tension. A long mahogany table glows under the recessed ceiling lights of the Sensitive Compartmentalized Information Facility. Around it sit the members of the Senate Select Committee on Intelligence, stone-faced, notebooks open but untouched.

At the head of the room:

Senator Voss (D-CA) quietly, but firm, "Let's be clear: if Radiant Sentry can't hold up under simulated pressure, we're not just behind—we're bleeding."

Edwards in a calm,, diplomatic voice said, "Radiant Sentry is a space-based defense matrix—a next-gen orbital firewall designed to detect, deflect, and neutralize kinetic and electromagnetic ASAT threats from near-peer adversaries. ... China and Russia chief among them.

"It's not yet operational, not fully deployed—but components have been under test for six months."

Lewis holding his hands said, "While your concern is breach vectors, mine is human. We believe at least two foreign assets made contact with personnel linked to LaserTech's signal propagation team."

Mansky glanced at her file. "We have chatter suggesting Moscow viewed Radiant Sentry as an existential threat—and they've thrown their sharpest Cyber knives at it."

A moment of silence. Senators jot notes. Then—a staffer entered, passed Edwards a folded slip.

Edwards read it, then glanced up and asked, "Mr. Chairman, I need to request a temporary recess. Ten minutes. I must verify something... significant."

Senator Voss with a curt nod. "Ten minutes."

After ten minutes, the doors closed again. Edwards reentered his posture subtly different—composed but electric.

Edwards sat, cleared throat. "Apologies for the interruption. I've just received secure confirmation from our uplink at Vandenberg Space Force Base.

"The latest Radiant Sentry module—successfully intercepted and neutralized a live kinetic kill vehicle during today's covert orbital test.

"First live intercept. Confirmed."

A beat of stunned silence. Senator Ryland leaned forward.

Senator Whitlock said, "So it's no longer theoretical."

Edwards replied, "It's real. And it's awake."

The news of Radiant Sentry's successful intercept hung in the air like a seismic aftershock. The committee, momentarily stunned, now snapped back into gear—questions sharper, tones less forgiving.

Senator Ryland (R-TX) said, "Congratulations, Commander. But I need to know—if this thing works, what's to stop Moscow or Beijing from stealing the blueprint and building their own?"

"That's why this breach is existential. Radiant Sentry isn't just hardware—it's sovereign advantage. If they duplicate or reverse-engineer even part of it, we're not talking about parity— we're talking about losing first-strike deterrence."

Senator Voss (D-CA) said, "Eleven assets, Commander. Eleven Russian operatives either embedded at or targeting LaserTech. That's not infiltration, that's occupation.

"How did that happen on your watch? Should LaserTech's contract be revoked?"

Lewis replies in a stern voice, "LaserTech's vulnerability was exploited before Radiant Sentry entered operational prototyping. But I won't sugarcoat this—they failed to detect sleeper activity early. The breach points were varied: technical staff, contractors, off-site data syncs.

We've neutralized the eleven confirmed Russian assets—all tied to SVR and GRU. One remains under federal custody. The rest... are no longer threats."

Senator Whitlock (I-CO) asked, "Who uncovered them?"

Lewis glanced at his notes, then to Edwards.

"ACIC—with internal support from LaserTech's embedded security and a small operations unit. They leveraged behavior models, irregular access logs, and SIGINT intercepts. A pattern emerged. Then the hammer came down."

Mansky (CIA) added, "The operation was codenamed Iron Echo. It was... clean. Discreet. But the Russians know we know. Their chatter went dark within hours."

Senator Ryland asked, "And DARPA? What steps are being taken to prevent this again?"

Edwards replied, "We've transferred oversight of all quantum-core designs and frequency modulation libraries to an air-gapped, zero-trust enclave. Personnel vetting has shifted to a continuous monitoring model.

"We've also deployed SYBIL—ACIC's AI—to enforce dynamic privilege access on classified projects. No more static credentials. No more predictable targets."

Senator Voss leaned forward.

"I want a classified report on Radiant Sentry's architecture and full summary of the Iron Echo op.

"I want names. And I want a clear answer: Can you guarantee the next genius with a clearance won't be another goddamn double?"

Edwards exhaled slowly.

"No, Senator. But I can guarantee they won't get anywhere near Radiant Sentry again."

Silence returned—but this time, it's not disbelief. It's the sound of calculus: weighing threats, accountability, and the cost of secrecy.

Senator Voss (D-CA) asked, "Eleven Russian assets. A project compromised. And we're supposed to believe this is still under control?'

Edwards responded, "Senator, with respect—Gene Larsson was our double, not theirs."

Staff whispered. One aide dropped a pen.

"She played them. Fed the SVR falsified schematics and theoretical dead-ends. It cost her everything—but it slowed them down. It gave our team the time they needed."

Senator Voss asked, "Are you saying this woman deceived a Russian directorate solo?"

"No. I'm saying she outmaneuvered them—for years. And it worked."

The weight of that lingered.

Senator Whitlock (I-CO) asked, "General Edwards. Let's talk about the breakthrough. In layman's terms. What happened? And... who made it happen?"

Edwards took a breath and replied, "Radiant Sentry required broadband survivability—from ultra-low interference that bled into the cage, to gamma-spectrum cascade events from orbit. Shielding failed at both extremes. Every fix at one end broke the other.

"The breakthrough came from someone who doesn't think like the rest of us—and never pretended to.

"Derek Wilshire. One of our junior analysts. Asperger's diagnosis, yes. But he's a savant with patterns. He saw a temporal correlation in the system noise—something no machine learning model caught, and no physicist even thought to look for."

Senator Voss asked, "An intern solved the problem?"

"Not an intern. A savant with islands of genius. An extraordinary talent in certain areas.

"He redefined the signal envelope—gave us a shielding model that re-routes catastrophic frequencies into dampened sacrificial pathways. It works. On paper. In sim. In live test.

"He saved Radiant Sentry. Maybe more."

A long, respectful silence. Even the usual cynics on the committee sat straighter.

Senator Whitlock asked, "Derek Wilshire?"

"Yes, Senator."

Senator Whitlock said, "I'll try not to sound like his aunt, but... let the record show, we owe that young man our thanks. And more."

Senator Voss paused and then nodded—the closest thing to a concession she ever offered.

Senator Hale added, "And this brave young lady Gene Larsson." "

"Derek Wilshire. And Gene Larsson. One saw what no one could. The other risked everything to slow down the enemy."

The hearing resumed, but the air had shifted: what was doubt had turned to reverence. Radiant Sentry had its first quiet heroes.

Moments after adjournment

The chair's gavel had barely echoed before aides moved to collect binders and tech briefcases. Senators filed out in murmuring clusters, the air still crackled with adrenaline, suspicion, and classified gravity.

Commander Owen Edwards gathered his notes, nodded to Jennifer Mansky and William Lewis as they moved toward the exit.

A quiet voice stopped him.

"Owen"

Senator Grace Whitlock, stone-faced and cool-eyed, stood across the room. She didn't raise her voice. She didn't need to.

She gestured once, toward the well of the chamber—the narrow floor space between the senators' crescent desk array.

Edwards followed her. Neither said a word until they stood shoulder to shoulder beneath the sharp LED lights and sound-muffling acoustic panels.

Whitlock glanced at the security cameras. Still running. Still red-lit.

He leaned in. Voice low. Too soft for any mic to catch. "What the hell really happened to Nikita Zakharov?"

A pause. Long enough to let the question bloom. Edwards didn't blink. He didn't even sigh. He just turned his head and said: "Fancy Bear took care of business."

Whitlock's face didn't move, but something colder entered her eyes. "Jesus."

A beat passed. The implication hung in the silence like a guillotine on hold.

Edwards turned away first, buttoned his coat he replied, "Sometimes, Senator, the Russians bury their own bones. They knew we were on to him as Sable's handler and they couldn't take the chance we might be able to turn him. They needed him silenced, not just out of the way."

Whitlock didn't stop him as he walked off. But she didn't move either — not for a long moment.

Then she exhaled, the sound of a woman who'd already made too many compromises.

And followed.

Fort Meade - Watchtower Conference Room - 1530 Hours R

The air in Will Morgan's office buzzed with a taut, celebratory energy. His entire team was gathered around, the close-knit group that had weathered storms together now sharing a rare moment of anticipation. Paper lay stacked on Will's desk, computer monitors blinked behind him, and through the tall windows, shafts of late morning light sliced into the room.

Will stood near his desk, arms crossed, a natural calm radiating from him even in these weightier moments. His desk phone rang, the old-school, secured landline flashing with a name that straightened his posture.

General Owen Edwards.

Without hesitation, Will reached out and lifted the receiver, his voice steady and respectful. "Good morning, Commander Edwards."

Owen's voice, rich and commanding even over the line, filled the phone. "Will, the Undersecretary asked me to convey his personal thanks to your team."

Will's mouth twitched into a faint smile. He turned, glancing at his team—Sara, Z, Derek, Grace, Cecil, Thomas, Cathy—all waiting, curious. His voice held a touch of warmth now.

"Thank you, sir, but if you would like to tell them yourself, they all happen to be right here."

"I sure would."

Will tapped the speaker button, his hand steady, and spoke clearly.

"Go ahead, sir. You're on speaker."

The room grew still. The only sounds were the quiet hum of the air conditioning and the faint rustle of someone shifting in their seat.

Owen's voice rang out, full of unmistakable pride.

"You are all here because you love your country and you are the best at what you do."

The team exchanged brief, embarrassed glances—private smiles, small nods.

"Your great work is a testament to what inter-agency teamwork can accomplish."

Owen paused, letting his words land.

"The Undersecretary has asked me, on behalf of the nation, to thank you for your devotion and skill. Personally, I couldn't be prouder to call myself your countryman."

There was a thick moment of silence, the kind that said more than words ever could.

"God bless America."

The speaker clicked as the call ended, but the weight of the moment hung in the room like a tangible thing—shared, respected, deeply felt.

Will Morgan lingered at the table after the others had gone, fading into silence. He still carried himself with the same quiet authority, the same watchful calm. But something in his eyes had shifted—harder, sharper, as if the line he always measured against had drawn closer.

He thought again of strengths and shadows, how easily one slid into the other. Resolve could calcify. Loyalty could blind. Even clarity could narrow into cold detachment.

That was the price of the work: learning to live where the line blurred, to hold steady while knowing you could cross without ever meaning to.

He rose at last, straightening his jacket, and left the room. The team would follow him into whatever came next. They always did. And he would carry the compass he'd earned the hard way—never forgetting how thin the line really was.

Fort Meade - Watchtower Ops - 0600 Hours R

Morgan stood slowly, stretching the tension from his muscles. He called out to the team milling just outside his office.

"Anyone for dinner? I'm buying."

Sara Brandt smiled but shook her head.

"Can't tonight, boss, but I'll take a rain check."

Everyone knew: if Sara wasn't going, Derek wasn't either.

Grace Roberts slung her bag over her shoulder and grinned.

"I'm in. How about a real restaurant this time?"

Morgan chuckled to himself as they headed out—a moment of peace before the next storm.

Odenton, Md - Orchard Cafe - a "Real" Restaurant

The restaurant was dim, tucked into a quiet corner of the city where the clinking of silverware and the murmur of conversation seemed miles away from the world they both inhabited. A rare moment of peace stretched between Will Morgan and Grace

Roberts as they sat across from each other, their table tucked near a window that framed the darkness outside.

Gracie leaned forward, a half-smile playing at her lips as she toyed with the stem of her wine glass.

"That kind of praise must make you feel good," she said, her voice gentle but knowing. "I sense you respect Owen a great deal so coming from him, it matters."

Will shifted in his seat, the corners of his mouth tugging in a restrained smile.

"Yeah, of course," he said. His voice was steady, but there was an edge of weariness there, like a soldier too long at the front. "But remember—this game never stops."

He leaned in a little, his eyes sharpening.

"Right now, our adversaries are watching everything. The Russians. The Chinese. All of them."

For a moment, the restaurant's soft lights caught in his gaze, giving him a far-off, battle-worn look.

"It's like the NFL—they're all watching film. These plays don't work for very long."

He paused, letting the words settle between them like dust on old ground.

"They figure out counters. Neutralize or destroy effectiveness."

A dry smile tugged at the edge of his mouth. It didn't quite reach his eyes.

"You know what you call 53 guys watching the Super Bowl?"

Gracie's smile grew, sensing the rare hint of humor from him.

"What?" she asked.

Will's face stayed deadpan.

"The New York Jets."

Gracie chuckled, the sound soft and real. Yet Will's expression didn't change, steady as a mountain under siege by years of storms.

"And why do they keep losing? Even with talented players—some years, as good as anyone?" he asked.

She considered him, her smile still lingering.

"Culture?" she guessed.

"Bad culture," Will said. His voice carried the weight of hard-earned experience.

"We've stayed ahead because our culture is better than our enemies'."

He turned, glancing out the window into the night beyond—dark and unyielding.

"If that ever changes... it's all over but the shouting."

A long beat of silence fell between them, broken only by the soft clink of dishes in the distance. Gracie studied him, reading the lines etched into his face by battles seen and unseen.

"If I may say—you are a curious and complicated man," she said, a warmth threading through her words. "Someone fondly described you to me as a curmudgeon with a heart of gold."

Will gave the slightest smirk, fleeting and shy.

"Your team doesn't just respect you—they revere you," Gracie continued, her tone softening even further. "And that's something else altogether. Something earned."

She let the silence stretch, her gaze fixed on him, weighing the lines of his face as though she might catch some hidden flicker. The corner of her lip twitched, part smile, part hesitation. Finally, her voice slipped into the quiet.

"But no one really knows you, do they?"

Will's smile faded, leaving only the hardened mask behind. Gracie pressed on, her voice never rising above a whisper.

"Sara comes closest. But she doesn't share. You two have a bond—trust, mutual respect. I envy that."

She hesitated, searching for the right words.

"Z told me his story. I heard about your doctor."

Her voice was heavy with understanding.

"Tells me a lot... but I think there's more buried deep down."

Her gaze didn't waver.

"Do you ever let it out?"

For a moment, Will didn't answer. He stared into the dark beyond the window, the weight of his past anchoring him in place. When he spoke, his voice was low, fragile in its steadiness.

"I had a tragic event in my life... and ever since, I've buried myself in the work."

He didn't look at her. Maybe he couldn't.

"When you find out the people closest to you have lied to you—not once, not in passing, but for a lifetime—it changes something."

The words sat between them, heavy and unmovable.

"Trust becomes... hard. Elusive. Impossible."

Finally, he turned to her, his eyes carrying the silent echoes of old betrayals.

"The work—and the faith I have in my own character, my own ability—that's been my shield."

The silence that followed wasn't awkward. It was real, two people standing at the edge of a chasm neither had expected to cross tonight.

Gracie nodded, the barest motion of respect.

"That's a heavy shield to carry... but I get it," she said.

She stepped closer, her presence not invasive, just there—solid, steady, true. She thought to herself, the guarded heart pays a quiet cost.

"It's not weakness to be wounded by betrayal," she said, her voice gentle but firm. "It's proof you had the capacity to trust—to love—in the first place."

She let that hang there, a balm offered without expectation.

"People survive that kind of pain in different ways. Some run. Some destroy."

Her eyes shone with quiet admiration.

"You built something—something that protects people. That matters."

Will looked at her, something flickering behind his guarded eyes—a spark, brief and unguarded.

"And personally... I don't think you're hiding behind your shield," Gracie continued, voice unwavering. "You're not that guy."

"I think you've just been waiting for someone... someone who won't swing at it when you lower it."

Will chuckled, a rare sound, warm and human.

"You talk like you've known me for years," he said.

Gracie smiled, the type of smile that saw straight through a person.

"Maybe I just recognize the armor. I've worn a version of it myself."

Will nodded slowly, a few seconds passing between them. Then:

"I don't open doors easily, Gracie. Most people don't even bother knocking."

His voice was rough, but there was no mistaking the gentleness underneath.

"But you... you ask real questions. You listen."

Finally, he truly met her gaze, the walls still there but thinner, transparent now.

"Maybe I've been waiting. Or maybe I just didn't notice the right person when they showed up."

There was a softness in his voice that few had ever heard.

"You're good at seeing people, Gracie. Even the ones who'd rather stay unseen."

Gracie's smile deepened, her heart aching just a little.

"Maybe that's the secret—seeing what people don't show."

Will nodded, the ghost of a smile touching his mouth.

"And not using it against them."

The night held them there, suspended between the past and something fragile, something new.

Glenn Burnie, MD - Gracie's Airbnb late evening

Grace sat cross-legged on her couch, a thick throw blanket curled around her shoulders, her laptop dark and untouched beside her. The only light in the room came from the floor lamp in the corner, casting a soft glow over the bookshelves, her notes, and a half-finished mug of green tea.

She hadn't planned to replay the entire conversation with Will in her head—but there it was, looping again in slow motion. His voice, careful but unguarded. The rare softness in his eyes. The honesty that slipped through when he wasn't shielding himself.

"I don't open doors easily, Gracie. Most people don't even bother knocking."

"But you... you ask real questions. You listen."

It had landed harder than he realized.

Grace leaned back against the cushions and closed her eyes, the words pressing gently on her chest like a weight both welcome and terrifying. Will Morgan was not a man who gave himself away. He didn't just guard his emotions—he ran a fortified city around them. And yet, in the quiet of that conversation, as the evening slipped away, something shifted.

She'd seen it. Felt it. A door had creaked open.

The rational part of her warned against reading too much into it. Will was a master at compartmentalizing—he could very well wake up tomorrow and file the whole moment into a locked drawer, never to revisit it again. She wouldn't blame him. She understood trauma when she saw it. And Will wore his past like an old fracture—he'd healed, sure, but he still favored the limb.

Still, there was a thread of something in his voice. An ache. A hope. A possibility.

She reached for her journal on the coffee table and flipped it open to a blank page. No title. No structure. Just thoughts, unedited:

It's strange how someone so composed can feel so fragile up close. He doesn't hide who he is—he hides who he used to be. There's a difference. And maybe he's not afraid of me seeing it… maybe he's afraid of what I'll think once I do.

She paused, pen still.

There's a part of me that wants to reach out and pull him closer… and a part that knows how easily he could shut the door and lock it again.

He said he doesn't open doors easily. I believe him. But he opened one tonight. Even if just for a second. And maybe— maybe that's all I need to keep showing up.

Her phone vibrated on the table. A message.

"G, until next time–Will"

She stared at it for a long moment.

A small smile tugged at her lips. Not much. Just enough to say he meant it. Enough to say this wasn't nothing.

Grace tucked the journal back into its spot on the table and pulled the blanket tighter around her. She didn't need all the answers yet. She didn't even need a label for what this was.

But she knew how to recognize a man trying. And tonight, Will had tried.

That was enough.

The West Wing Walk

The White House – West Wing -1830 Hours R

The White House was quieter than usual—no press, no handshakes, no spectacle. Just six names on a discreet manifest, ushered through the Northwest Appointment Gate under armed escort.

They moved together, not in formation, but in gravity. Each had been summoned, though no one had explained precisely why.

Will Morgan walked ahead, his eyes scanned every camera, every hallway. Grace Roberts walked at his side, her expression poised but unreadable. Gene Larsson stayed close behind, shoulders back—a quiet defiance in her gait. George Lee and Sarah Brandt kept step with each other, whispering about whether this was some kind of reprimand or recognition.

At the tail of the group, Derek Wilshire ambled with his usual uneven pace, head turned up toward the intricate plasterwork of the West Wing ceiling.

Derek murmured to himself, "They tuned the air-handling system differently here. Whisper mode. Probably to reduce HVAC rumble during secure meetings…"

General Ed Perry waited for them in the Oval Office doorway.

"Evening. You won't be here long—just long enough for the right people to look you in the eye and say thank you."

He opened the door. Inside, folders lay closed on the table. Small brass nameplates waited.

"You won't find any press release. No citations. No ceremony. But make no mistake—what you did changed the equation. You didn't just protect a weapons system. You protected the illusion of invincibility."

Ed turned toward Derek. "And Derek, the breakthrough... they want it in your own words. For the record."

Derek blinked. "My own words" often felt like the wrong size tool for what he saw in his head.

Derek said, "I noticed the harmonic reflection curves weren't asymptotic. They had a double saddle. That implied—"

Will interjected, "He saw something the rest of us didn't. And he acted on it. That's all they need to know."

Ed smiled. "That's good enough."

Gene, using her own last name as if to make a point, asked, "And Larsson?" Ed met her gaze.

"You played a dangerous game. You fed Moscow delay loops and invalid code. How long do you think before they figure out it was you?"

"They already suspect. But they'll never be certain. Not now."

Ed nodded slowly. "We'll make sure you're not on your own."

From down the corridor, a uniformed liaison appeared and gave Ed a nod.

Ed said, "The President is ready. Come with me."

As they turned the corner past the West Colonnade, the last of the sunset burned orange through the glass. The moment felt surreal—as if they'd stepped into the part of history usually scrubbed from the record.

They entered the Oval. A quiet gesture. No flags, no press. Just President Stratton, sleeves rolled, standing in front of his desk with a stack of handwritten notes.

He didn't offer them seats.

President Stratton said, "No cameras. No stage. Just this. My thanks."

He looked at each of them, one by one.

"Gene Larsson—you walked a knife's edge and turned it back against the hand that held it. You slowed a nation and bought us precious time – just enough."

President Stratton, to Derek. "Derek Wilshire—you saw a flaw in our armor no AI or analyst ever found. You patched the breach and didn't ask for credit."

President Stratton to Will and Sara. "Will. Sara. You held a team together through deception, danger, and paranoia. The system may be autonomous—but the victory was human."

President Stratton to George and Grace. "George, Grace — you gave the system its bones. You kept it from collapsing under the weight of its own ambition."

He stepped closer.

"There are things this country cannot afford to acknowledge. This was one of them. But it will not be forgotten. Not by me."

He held out a single envelope to Will.

"This contains personal commendations. One for each of you. No medal. But something more durable. Something sealed."

Will took the envelope. A rare flicker of emotion crossed his face.

The President nodded to Ed, who opened the door again.

President Stratton told them, "You'll exit through the West Lobby. No escort. No spotlight. But tonight, you walk out of here as the firewall that held and protected a nation."

They filed out in silence.

As they stepped into the warm night, Grace turned to Derek.

"Hey. That was a lot for you. You okay?"

Derek replied, "I liked the ceiling. And he didn't blink when I said 'double saddle.' That was cool."

George clapped him with fondness on his shoulder.

They didn't say another word until the black SUV doors closed behind them.

And somewhere, miles above, Radiant Sentry drifted on in silence — no longer blind. Standing guard.

Fort Meade Morgan's Office

The office was a small island in a sea of operations, cluttered with classified files, old coffee mugs, and two decades of battle fatigue.

Morgan sat alone, the dim light throwing shadows across his face. He watched SVR communications unraveled line by line on the AI decryption monitor.

Then he saw it. "Sable CONFIRMED – INITIATE PHASE TESTING."

A quiet smile touched his lips as he leaned back, exhaled through his nose. "That's check," he said to the empty room. "But not mate. Yet."

Later, he spoke into a secure line with Rick Huang, his most trusted technical officer.

"How are we going to best isolate the code to prevent further intrusion without revealing our knowledge of the breach?" Morgan asked, spinning a pen absently between his fingers.

Rick's voice crackled through the speaker, calm as always. "We know how they originally got in and can monitor those gateways. We will also know the questions asked and the file names to which they refer. Hopefully, we can craft answers and stay on theme. I don't think any more needs to be done."

Morgan allowed himself a rare moment of relaxation. At least on that front, they were ahead.

CHAPTER FORTY

China - It Never Ends

Former CIA Director Michael Hayden on China's campaign as "breathtaking in its scale, breadth, and sophistication,"

Fort Belvoir, VA – Commander's Office - 1930 Hours R

The room is quiet except for the soft ticking of an antique wall clock and the low hum of an encrypted comms console idled in standby. Floor-to-ceiling bookshelves held titles on foreign intelligence services, counterespionage theory, and decades of DoD white papers. A framed photo of Owen shaking hands with a former Secretary of Defense sat behind him. The air carried a faint hint of strong coffee and chilly air from the overworked HVAC system.

Owen Edwards, methodical and cerebral, sat at his desk in his shirtsleeves, scanned a digital threat matrix displayed on a secure tablet. The outline of Chinese strategic programs glowed in red and gold. Across from him stood Ed Perry, Will Morgan's commanding officer at ACIC—hard-edged, practical, and mission-first.

Commander Edwards looking up from the tablet. "We're seeing irregular data signatures coming out of Qinghai and Sichuan. The MSS is getting bolder. They're no longer just stealing schematics—they're mimicking operational patterns. Near-perfect ones."

"That means they've got someone on the inside," Ed said,

Edwards nodded. "Someone close. Embedded in a DARPA subcontractor. Not necessarily LaserTech—but someone in the same ecosystem."

After a momentary pause, he continued: "After Sable wraps, I need Will's team in place. I want a parallel mole hunt. Deep work, layered."

Ed Perry considering. "You'll have them. But I'll need more personnel. Mandarin and Cantonese linguists—real field-grade. Not language school grads. If we're dealing with MSS tradecraft, we need cultural fluency, not just translation."

"I've got two candidates from DIA I'll float over. One's ex-NSA, cross-trained in SIGINT and HUMINT. The other's fluent in Hakka dialects—spent three years embedded in Taiwan's cyber fusion cell."

Ed Perry nods approvingly. "That works. But Grace Roberts..."

Shaking his head Ed Perry said, "I can't guarantee she's available. She's nearing burnout. If Sable ends ugly, she might pull back."

Owen leans back. "She's good. But she was always a scalpel, not a hammer. And you need hammers now."

He paused, then with deliberation said, "What about Gene Larsson?"

Ed Perry deadpan. "You mean Geneiac?

"If she wanted to, she could be running LaserTech. But she doesn't care about status—only the science. Will trusts her. She has the edge of someone who can see ten moves ahead and doesn't have to prove it to anyone.

"I'm sure you remember half the place wanted her in jail until Will put his foot down."

"Exactly," said Edwards, "we can't afford only temporary consultants. We need someone embedded, consistent. Someone who isn't going to walk when the hours get brutal.

"And thank goodness for Will. Ed, I was expecting a call from you asking for support, which I was more than willing to provide." He chuckled. "Guess Will didn't need it."

"Can you make the case to DARPA?" asked Edwards, "Or do I need to call in a favor?"

Ed Perry said, "I'll make the call. But she's worth it. She may not love moving into government structure, but if Will asked her, she'll listen. She respects his integrity. She's one of the few who can see past his armor."

"And he'll need someone like that. Especially if we're about to start the Chinese chapter of this war." replied Edwards.

They both fall silent for a moment, the magnitude of what lay ahead stretching out between them like an open field filled with mines.

Ed Perry asked, "How long do we have?"

"Not long. The Chinese have already tested a fractional orbital bombardment system. The next strike won't be experimental. It'll be decisive."

"Then we move now. I'll prep Will."

Commander Edwards nodded once. "Good. Let's get it done."

CHAPTER FORTY-ONE

Lessons Learned

"A wise man once said: 'An error doesn't become a mistake until you refuse to correct it.'
— *John Fitagerald Kennedy*

Fort Belvoir, MD - secure conference room

The INSCOM operations center at Fort Belvoir felt like a bunker—no windows, white noise, LED glare.
Ed Perry, Commander of ACIC, stood at the head of the table, voice hard.

"Eleven Russian assets tied to LaserTech—two moles, two swallows, three sleepers, and a four-man kill team. DARPA's vetting failed. Our team was compromised on arrival, just as Will predicted. Without experience and luck, some of us would be dead. FBI's Hostage Rescue Team neutralized the kill team. We may not be that fortunate next time."

William Lewis of FBI nodded, jaw tight. Said, "We had SIGINT fifteen hours ahead. We were lucky."

A stir around the table. Helena Quinn of DARPA bristled. "We run polys every five years. But no lab is immune to deep-cover placement. If CIA flagged him a decade ago—"

"Maybe we would have—if DARPA's HR hadn't redacted half the files," said Mansky.

Owen Edwards Commander INSCOM lifted a hand. "Enough. The question is what we do now."

Will Morgan leaned forward. "Start with subcontractors. Vendors. Access logs. Anyone with Tier Three or above."

Lewis said, "And reinvestigations every two years, not five."

"You want to re-poly 6,000 researchers every two years?" asked Helena.

"You want to gamble national security on a budget line?" replied Will.

The silence that followed ended the debate.

Edwards said, "I'll form a task force. Perry, Mansky, Quinn—your chiefs get invites today. CI overhaul in a week."

"Let's hope we're not already behind the next Lynx," said Mansky.

Edwards pressed further. "Russia isn't the only threat. China's academic infiltration, AI poisoning. North Korea using criminal syndicates. We've already seen backdoored firmware in DARPA supply chains."

"ACIC and NSA link a scholar program to anomalous exfil. Malware matches Chengdu '21 signatures," said Perry.

"And North Korea?" asked Lewis.

"Contracting. Less ideology, more cash," said Perry.

"So what—chase ghosts across continents?" asked Will.

"We replicate Iron Echo. Force them to move. Then strike," answered Perry.

Edwards said, "Unanimous. Full-spectrum CI audit. ACIC leads. All foreign-born personnel reviewed, affiliations revalidated. Fast."

The air thickened. Pages turned. Pens clicked.

Finally, Will spoke again, calm but final. "My team's a scalpel, not a garrison. We exposed a network, not just a mole. Radiant Sentry is operational. Mission complete. Long-term defense isn't our role."

Edwards nodded. "And I agree. Radiant Sentry transitions to DIA oversight. Embedded CI advisors, live telemetry across all Tier One labs. Your team is rotated out—quietly—before the next kill team gets a second shot."

"You'll be on call for surgical work," said Perry. "But we're not burning out a precision asset in trench warfare."

Will rose, voice steady. "You want a perimeter; you build a wall. Just don't ask my people to be bricks in it."

No one argued.

Fort Meade Secure Briefing Suite - That Day

The room was smaller than they were used to. No screens, no maps—just a scarred table, burned coffee, and fatigue etched into every face.

Will Morgan sat at the head, his team stretched along either side, all looking like they'd come off a battlefield no one could see.

Ed Perry entered with a folder under one arm. He looked more like a weary professor than ACIC's commander.

"I won't keep you long," said Perry. "No medals, but the report upstairs won't pull punches. Two moles exposed. Network dismantled. Radiant Sentry live. And not one civilian casualty. That's historic."

Silence. Sara leaned back, Derek studied his hands, Gracie pushed her glasses back.

"What's the shelf life on our cover?" Will asked.

"Twelve hours. You'll leave staggered, commercial, no trace. Relocation packages ready. For now—you're ghosts again."

He set the folder down. "Sleep. Breathe. Vanish. One month. You've earned it."

The door clicked shut.

Thomas broke the silence. "Two years of prep. Seven months embedded. A mole, a double agent, a shootout—and it ends with coffee and a manila envelope."

Sara allowed a half-smile. "Welcome to counterintelligence. Fireworks on the way in. Exit through the gift shop."

Derek looked up and asked, "Think Radiant Sentry will hold?"

"Long enough. Long enough for the next trap. That's the work." Answered Will.

Grace leaned forward. "You think Lynx was the last?"

"No. But he's the last one we didn't see coming."

Sara stood, slinging her bag. "Headed to the city."

Grace followed. "Someplace warm. Any recommendations?"

Will smiled faintly. "Now, there's a thought."

Thomas sighed. "Me? Sleep for a month. Then maybe pretend I'm a writer again."

One by one they left. Will stayed behind, exhaling only when the door closed.

He opened the envelope. Eight commendations, hand-signed. One for each of his team, plus Gene Larsson, the one he insisted on. And beneath them, a single sheet:

REDEPLOYMENT OPTIONS – CLASSIFIED (EYES ONLY)

Will stared, then slid the envelope shut. He didn't tear it up.

LaserTech – Gene Larsson's Lab – Later that Night

The polished lab counters are now mostly cleared of their usual clutter. The digital readouts on the diagnostics bench hummed. Gene Larsson is alone, a black Michigan hoodie pulled over a white tee, sleeves bunched at her elbows. Her ponytail is coming loose, and a half-eaten protein bar sits next to her untouched coffee.

The knock at the glass door is soft, but distinct. She looks up.

Will Morgan steps in. Quiet, as always. The kind of quiet that doesn't mean small. His fatigue is visible, but so is the gravity of purpose. He closes the door behind him.

"You've got a minute?"

Gene leans back in her chair, arms crossing, eyes sharp. She studies him before answering.

"You don't do social calls. So, I'm guessing this isn't a Michigan recruiting update."

"It's not. Something's brewing. China, this time."

"DARPA subcontractor ecosystem. Another potential mole. We're redeploying the team after Sable wraps. Probably a longer haul."

Gene's eyes narrowed. The shift from curiosity to analysis is immediate.

"LaserTech?"

"Not necessarily. But somewhere near the nerve center. Could be optical payload contractors. Could be a rival lab in Reston. DCSA wants someone internal. Someone who doesn't rotate out when things get hard."

"I asked about you."

She stares at him for a long moment This isn't a surprise— but it still lands with weight.

"You sure they'll even approve it?

"Wasn't long ago I had to prove I wasn't the damn mole myself."

"And you did. I never doubted it.

"You stayed. When you could've run. You kept working. When they whispered. That mattered."

Her eyes drift toward the far wall where a framed NASA patch hangs next to a worn Wolverine pennant. She thinks for a moment, then turns back.

"I don't do politics. I don't file reports to make generals happy. And I'm not going to start calling people 'sir'."

"You won't have to. You'll still be a civilian. The truth, period. Same thing you've always done."

Gene slow nod. "And Grace?"

"Might not be coming with us this time – at least not full-time. She's earned a break. But I need someone with steel, Gene. Not just brains. Someone who understands how deep this hole can go."

Gene exhales, slow and controlled. She looks down at the half-eaten bar, then back up.

"You know I trust you, right?"

Will gives a single muted nod. It's all she needs.

"Fine. I'm in. But I pick my own lab space, I bring my own data structure, and if anyone calls me "Geneiac," they answer to me."

"Deal."

Gene smirks, "And I want a new coffee maker."

"Now you're pushing it."

They share the smallest flicker of a smile. In Gene's world, that's as close to loyalty as it gets.

Fort Meade - Watchtower Conference Room – One Month Later

The recessed lights reflect off the steel-gray walls and polished surface of the round conference table. Digital monitors hum with secure feeds, red-tagged folders stacked neatly beside tablets. Will Morgan stands at the head of the room, calm, hands behind his back. The team is gathered—Sara, Derek, Thomas, Cecil, Gene, Grace, Z and Rick, each with their own brand of alert posture, waiting.

Will starts the meeting,

"Welcome back, everyone. Hope you're all rested because we're at it again."

"Sable's wrapped, and Command wants us pointed toward the next breach—this time, China. Operation Sino Protocol."

The room stills. Derek tilts his head, already thinking three dimensions ahead. Sara folds her arms, gears shifting internally. Thomas raises an eyebrow.

Rick asked, "LaserTech again?"

"Unknown. It could be anywhere in the DARPA subcontractor matrix. Optical payload systems. Quantum encryption. They're not sure yet—but they think there's a mole. Possibly embedded. Long game." Will responds.

"You're saying we're flying blind?" asked Cecil.

Will... "No. We're flying lean."

He turns to the touchscreen panel behind him, taps a name onto the monitor:

Dr. Gene Larsson – Mission Specialist, Systems Integrity – Permanent Assignment

Will continues, "Gene Larsson's coming with us. Officially this time. She's been cleared for a standing position in our group."

Sara leans forward, eyes sharp. "That's a big move. She trusts us?"

"She trusts me," said Will. "She'll soon learn she can trust the team."

He paused searching for a thought.

"She stayed on when others backed away. Took heat without flinching. And she knows the scientific ecosystem better than anyone we've worked with—cold starts, funding streams, tech gaps, all of it."

Derek comments, "She's the only person I know who can cross-check a classified budget against photonic emissions signatures from memory."

Thomas said, "Also, the only one who made Grace stop talking mid-sentence."

Cecil chuckles, "Hell of a résumé."

Sara chuckles to herself, "China - we're gonna need a bigger boat."

Will firmly. "She's mission essential. And she's one of ours now."

Will's voice is steady, but something unspoken runs underneath it—something only this group, forged in pressure and fire, can pick up on.

"A new war is coming. A new enemy. Same team.

"We start transition protocols soon."

The team nods, a quiet understanding passing among them like current.

CHAPTER FORTY-TWO

A Next Chapter

"The only Limit to our realization of tomorrow will be our doubts of today."
— *Franklin D. Roosevelt*

Pentagon E Ring Conference Room –1840 Hours R

The light through the windows is blue-gray, the chilling cold that settles behind closed doors in Washington when secrets are being decided.

Present:

Will Morgan, Major ACIC, Fort Meade

Ed Perry, Commanding General ACIC, Fort Meade

Owen Edwards, Commanding General INSCOM, Fort Belvoir

Helena Quinn, Director DARPA (listening in virtually)

A secure, windowless room in the inner corridors of the Pentagon. A large table, dark wood. SYBIL's secure access screen is on standby. Silence has weight here.

Will Morgan straightened a dossier, then looked up." I want Derek reassigned to Fort Meade. Full clearance. Full integration."

The room froze. Ed Perry lifted an eyebrow. Owen Edwards didn't respond for the longest moment. He leaned back, arms crossed, calculated.

Owen Edwards still, even. "You want Derek Wilshire?"

"Yes."

Ed Perry said, "Will, I respect your instincts, but you're asking to rip the heart out of the Radiant Sentry problem-solving loop. That kid just cracked the frequency bleed issue that stalled us for six months. He's practically the reason we even had something to demo for the Senate."

"I'm aware."

Owen said, "Then you know what you're asking. LaserTech's CTO is already waving red flags. DARPA's not thrilled either. Derek's a tactical genius—but he's also an asset with limited bandwidth. He belongs where he can finish what he started."

"He already has."

A pause. Perry looked at him, surprised. Owen narrowed his eyes.

Will said, "Radiant Sentry will always evolve. But the bottleneck we faced was conceptual, cognitive. Derek shattered it. Now you want him to manage code merges and patch cycles? That's like asking Gauss to babysit an abacus."

"So, what exactly do you think he should be doing?"

"Pattern acquisition. Anomaly isolation. Counter-deception modeling. With SYBIL fully online, his mind is the only one I've seen that thinks like it does. He doesn't just understand the system—he intuits it. He speaks its language."

Ed Perry said, "SYBIL's a neural lattice AI. Are you suggesting Derek has a synthetic mind?"

"I'm saying he mirrors it. Or it mirrors him. I don't care which came first. I care that in an era of fifth-domain warfare - cyber warfare, Derek Wilshire is the closest thing we have to a sentient pattern firewall. With what's coming out of China and North Korea—quantum-hardened polymorphic malware, electro-optic decoys, command spoofing, Derek isn't just useful. He's necessary."

Owen said, "DARPA won't release him without a fight."

"Then fight. Or kick it upstairs."

Ed Perry asked, "To whom?"

"National Security Advisor or SecDef. Let them decide if they want our best mind tucked in a corner... or placed on the front line where it can turn the tide."

Silence.

Perry leaned back in his chair. He looked at Owen, then at the live terminal, then at Will.

Ed Perry said, "Well, if we're going to break a dozen turf agreements and offend half of northern Virginia, we might as well do it clean. I'll call Maddox at NSC."

Owen sighed. "I'll draft the provisional release memo. But I want assurance: Derek isn't thrown into some black vault where he gets used until he breaks."

"He'll be with me. He won't break."

Roosevelt Room – White House Next Day - 1610 Hours R

Golden light casting long shadows across the polished table. Secure phones off-hook. Coffee untouched. No press. Just the truth.

Present:

President Jonathan Stratton – calm, sharp, reading everything between the lines.

Robert Maddox – National Security Advisor.

General Arthur Kelman – Secretary of Defense.

Elena Raine – Director, National Security Agency.

Julia Branson – Junior White House Aide, former cyber policy analyst.

Kelman said, "Mr. President, we support the reassignment. Wilshire belongs with Will Morgan's team."

President Stratton skeptical, "I thought Wilshire was critical to the DARPA/LaserTech integration? You're telling me now he's more valuable in counterintelligence?"

Raine added, "He already is, sir. Even before we realized it."

Maddox, sat forward, said, "Derek didn't just patch Radiant Sentry. He saw the breach when no one else did. The code line injection? The recursive feedback loop? That wasn't luck. That was pattern recognition that outpaced our best AI alert systems by 36 hours. He saved us—and we didn't even know it yet."

"Will Morgan figured that out. He knew Derek wasn't a lab tech. He wasn't a code monkey. He's a battlefield instrument—just not on a battlefield we can see." said Kelman, "Will pulled him into the room early. No red tape, no drama. Just instinct. His team didn't flinch. Sara Brandt befriended him and she and Grace Roberts let him follow them everywhere - even sat in on Morgan's meetings."

President Stratton asked, "And LaserTech didn't object?"

"They didn't have time. Derek had already spotted the flaw. The same flaw their Tier 1 analysts missed. And Will's people— Brandt, Roberts, Huang—they embraced him like he belonged there all along," said Raine.

"Morgan didn't slot Derek where the org chart said he should go," said Kelman, "He let him wander—shadow the team. That's how we found the leak in the Radiant Sentry sandbox. That's how we got ahead of the ASAT spoofing from the Russians. And that's how we managed to obfuscate the Lynx mole without tipping Moscow off."

A pause. The President drummed his fingers on the table.

President Stratton asked, "I don't doubt his mind. But what you're describing sounds like a one-man wild card. What if he burns out? Melts down?"

Julia Branson quietly, from the back—then louder. "Sir... he won't. That team is the reason he's still functioning."

All eyes turned to her. She stepped forward, voice calm but passionate.

"Morgan's team is unconventional - they only care about results. They never treated him like a freak. Never locked him out of rooms or drowned him in protocol. They gave him purpose. Direction. More importantly, they trusted his instincts—and he rose to meet that trust again and again."

She glanced at Kelman and Raine for permission—they nodded subtly. She continued.

"Think about this: the person who spotted the Russian code siphon... who intuited the dead drop hidden inside Radiant Sentry's own defense shell... who predicted the satellite drift anomaly from memory—was never officially assigned to the case."

The room went still.

"He was just tagging along. And they not only let him they embraced him."

She looked directly at the President.

"Imagine what happens when we let him lead."

"What's the pushback?" asked President Stratton.

"A few contract officers who want to protect the brand," replied Raine, "but the adults in the room see the math."

"We've already kicked it to Maddox. He signs off, we greenlight it," said Kelman, "But we thought you should hear it first. Because you'll be the one defending it when something bigger than Lynx shows up."

President Stratton considered, then nodded. "Approved. On one condition.

"Will Morgan keeps him close. I want a report every 72 hours for the first month. If that kid ever goes dark, I want Morgan in my office before the lights finish flickering." said President Stratton."

"Done." said Maddox.

"He won't go dark, sir. Not with Morgan's team." Said Raine, "Derek is the one place he truly belongs. He will thrive."

President Stratton said "Good. Then let's move. I want the paperwork on my desk before NSC tonight."

Branson exhales, Kelman signs the pre-authorization, and Raine walks out dialing Fort Meade. Across the river, in a secure room, Will's phone begins to buzz.

Fort Meade - Watchtower Ops

The hammering had stopped. No more pounding, no more drilling, no more drywall dust clinging to coffee mugs.

The long-awaited expansion of Team Watchtower's office was finally complete—on time, mostly—and scheduled to open Monday morning.

The renovations were simple in theory but hard-won in execution. A wall had come down to connect to the adjacent suite. In its place: a corridor leading to six new offices and a central bullpen housing four cubicles arranged in a tight tactical diamond. Two of the new offices were oversized, built to accommodate the tech division's gear-heavy reality. One already had Rick's name—VECTOR—plastered on the frosted glass, and he'd moved in over the weekend with something approaching religious joy.

The second oversized office? Unassigned. Blinds drawn. Locked.

That mystery was already generating whispers.

With the expansion, Will Morgan had taken the opportunity to reconfigure seating as well. Genevieve Larsson (VERITY) took Rick's old office next to Sara Brandt (VESPER), a move few missed the significance of. Cathy Wang was placed directly across from Sara in the front cubicle, her first real desk assignment—no more couch in the corner with a loaner laptop.

Grace Roberts (no code name yet) was assigned an office next to Will's for when she was on-site, though she split her time between UM and Fort Meade.

By 0800 Romeo, everyone was in.

Rick was already wired in, two keyboards clicking in tandem, a mug that read I void warranties perched beside a tangle of cables and an empty Red Bull. The rest of the team filtered through the new corridor, murmuring appreciation and calculating line-of-sight advantages. But eyes kept drifting toward the locked door next to Rick's.

Black vertical blinds.

No key.

No answers.

A nameplate gleamed on the glass in ACIC-standard typography: RESONANT.

Everyone knew Will had insisted on code names only on nameplates, a security policy that turned out to be more than just a formality. Sara was VESPER. Rick, VECTOR. Will himself was SENTINEL. But RESONANT?

That was new.

Will wasn't saying.

The curiosity spiked when Ed Perry, Commanding General of ACIC, stepped into the corridor just past 0810, crisp in a civilian-cut suit and carrying two steaming coffees. He handed one to Will, took a long look down the new hallway, and said:

"Not bad for a basement."

Will smiled. "We're above a motor pool - a step up."

Rick leaned into the corridor. "Hey, boss—anyone ever going to open Resonant's door? Or is that a containment chamber?"

Sara crossed her arms. "I'm starting to think there's a body in there."

Ed made a show of fishing his phone out of his pocket. "Guess we'd better call maintenance."

As if on cue, a maintenance tech already in the hall stepped forward with a keycard. He tapped the panel. The door unlocked with a discreet click.

The blinds rolled up.

Derek Wilshire stood inside, grinning under soft LED light, surrounded by screens, cables, and—most impossibly—a floor-to-ceiling aquarium, glowing with bioluminescent coral and small darting fish.

"Surprise," Perry said dryly. "Meet your new analyst."

There was a stunned moment of silence—

—and then Sara, Grace, Genevieve, and Cathy all screamed in unison, startling the fish and causing Rick to spill half his coffee on his lap.

Derek opened his arms like a magician at curtain call. "Miss me?"

Genevieve and Sara strolled over to Genevieve's new office. Inside was a brand-new Terra Kaffe TK-02 Espresso Machine.

Sara exclaimed, "You kidding me, that's a two grand coffee machine,"

They looked at each other and at the same time said, "The Gracie effect."

Finally, a normal day at the office. The low hum of computers filled the outer office, blending into the soft clatter of keys in the bullpen area. Sara was working diligently in her office when Z strolled in.

"Hey Sara, got a minute?"

"Sure."

There was a pause, just long enough to hint that Z was winding up for something more than a routine check-in.

"What's up with the boss? Happy birthday messages, cakes, enthusiastic praise, nicknames and now pulls rank to acquire Derek. What's with him?"

Sara smiled, a knowing curve to her lips. She clicked through a few files on her screen, already anticipating where this conversation was heading.

Sara nodded over his shoulder towards Grace, who was still focused intently on her monitor in her office across the room. "I'm looking at it."

Z turned and glanced across the room.

"Huh?"

Sara's smile deepened. She repeated, more pointed this time. "I'm looking at it."

Realization dawned in Z's voice, quick and teasing.

"Oh, Gracie? Interesting. Is there something there?"

Sara's eyes flicked briefly to Grace, then back to her screen. She kept her voice even, but there was a certain warmth she couldn't hide.

"Seems to be the case."

Z let out a low whistle.

"Mutual ya think?"

Sara considered it. In this line of work, reading between the lines wasn't just a skill—it was survival.

"I suspect so. Hard to read two peas in a pod. Fingers crossed."

There was a pause, then a softer tone from Z, unusually gentle.

"You're really fond of her aren't you."

Sara's answer came easily, no hesitation, no guardedness.

"Yeah, really am. A lot."

"So am I."

Then silence between two friends who understood more than they ever said out loud.

Fort Meade Campus 1500 hours R

The campus stretched wide and open around them, the autumn air crisp but still warmed by the afternoon sun. Leaves crunched lightly underfoot as Sara and Grace walked side by side, their steps unhurried.

Around them, the secure compound of Fort Meade pulsed with quiet activity. Analysts and officers passed by, most locked in their own private worlds, badges catching the light.

Grace tucked a stray strand of hair behind her ear, glancing sideways at Sara with a mixture of amusement and bewilderment. "Will has been in a particularly good mood, especially for him. What do you think is with him?"

Sara shot her a sidelong look, a sly glint in her eyes. "I'm walking with it."

Grace slowed frowning in confusion. "What? Wait... really?"

Sara nodded, her expression the picture of certainty. "Really. You mean you haven't noticed."

Grace's mouth opened and closed, her mind racing through memories, trying to piece together a picture she had half-seen but never fully acknowledged. "Well... I... uh..."

Sara stopped walking, planting herself firmly on the path. She turned fully to Grace now, her voice low but certain. "Gracie,

I have worked with him virtually morning, noon and night for fifteen years under the most stressful conditions."

Sara's voice softened, her words carrying weight, sincerity. "I know him better than anyone on this planet, which I know isn't saying much... but..."

She shrugged, helpless to explain how some truths were felt more than proved. "Since you arrived, he has stepped out of character more than in all the time before."

Sara started ticking off points on her fingers, one by one, her tone half playful, half grave. "Birthday messages, nicknames, enthusiastic praise, fish tanks, good mood all the time—either someone else has taken over his body or he's smitten."

The wind stirred the golden leaves around their feet, swirling them in lazy eddies.

Sara locked eyes with Grace, willing her to understand. "At work he focuses like a laser beam on what's in front of him. When he talks to us, he doesn't bother to look up."

She let the statement hang for a moment, then added softer still. "Except when you're in the room. Then he can't take his eyes off you."

Grace stared at her, stunned into silence. For a long moment, the world around them seemed to fade away.

Grace finally managed, in a voice decibel above a whisper. "I don't know what to think."

Sara gave her a small, knowing smile, a hint of mischief in her voice as she delivered the final blow with a wink. "I do— you're a consultant, not an employee, if you get my meaning. I'll leave it at that."

The wind stirred again, carrying away the last of the conversation—but the meaning lingered, undeniable, between them.

Grace walked on slowly, processing, while Sara followed, a small, satisfied smile playing at the corner of her mouth.

"Don't think I can. Don't want to."

Fort Meade Campus - 1900 Hours R

Fort Meade's campus had begun to quiet for the night, most buildings settling into their amber evening glow. Grace and Will walked along one of the winding outer pathways, the hush of the evening folding around them like a soft blanket. The scent of drying leaves and late-summer warmth floated on the breeze.

Grace tucked her hands into her jacket pockets, stealing a sideways glance at him—half admiration, half something she still didn't dare name out loud. Sara's teasing words from earlier drifted back to her, unbidden:

He looks at you differently, Gracie. Don't pretend you haven't noticed.

She had noticed. God help her, she had noticed. And now she was trying not to overstep a line she desperately wanted to cross.

"You're an interesting man, Will Morgan," she said at last, voice lighter than she felt.

He huffed a small breath, almost a laugh. "Interesting usually comes right before *complicated*."

"It can," she agreed softly. "But with you... it's different. You have this significant capacity to handle all sorts of complicated, difficult or painful things."

Will's hands were tucked neatly behind his back—his habitual posture when he was thinking instead of deflecting.

His mouth twitched, not quite a smile, but something close. "Learning how to close chapters in my life without removing them altogether became a useful personal shield throughout my life. he said. "One I've relied on more than I care to admit."

The words weren't boastful; they were simple truth, spoken with the quiet gravitas of a man who had lived them.

Grace nodded, absorbing it. They walked for several quiet

steps, the wind whispering through the trees above them. Their strides matched without effort—something that startled her with how natural it felt.

She risked a teasing smile, soft but aimed with intention. "So… is tonight another one you will be filing away in your emotional archives as well?"

Will shook his head slowly, a shy smile tugging at the corner of his mouth. "Don't think I can. Don't want to."

Something warm unfurled in her chest, unexpected and frighteningly hopeful. *Sara might actually be right,* she thought. *God help us both.*

But hope came with danger. She didn't want to push him. Didn't want to misread what he was offering. Didn't want her eagerness to be the thing that made him retreat behind every fortified wall he had rebuilt.

We both suck at this, she thought, half-laughing at herself. *Two brilliant people completely useless when it comes to each other.*

"A next chapter…" she said carefully, allowing just enough feeling to show without letting it spill over. "That would be… sweet."

His blue eyes flickered toward her—uncertain, but not unwilling. The look struck her somewhere unguarded. A moment hung between them then, neither of them brave enough to reach for it, neither of them willing to walk away from it.

They kept moving, close but not touching, two silhouettes cut against the last streaks of orange and pink along the horizon.

The path ahead stretched wide and open before them.

Possibility—quiet, fragile, and hopeful—lay somewhere along   it.

And for once, neither of them turned away.

Kir Smirnova's secure phone pings. Unmarked sender. He opens it. A single message: K, until next time – Will

The End

INDEX

INDEX

Russian Space Weapons Capabilities	
Kinetic ASATs	Russia has launched satellites, such as Cosmos 2576, equipped with the ability to intercept and destroy targets in orbit.

Polyus Project	Legacy Soviet-era programs. Polyus was designed to house a laser weapon.
Almaz Project	Almaz, an orbital weapons platform equipped with a rapid-fire autocannon.
Cosmos 2543	"Demonstrated a non-destructive ASAT test—believed to be a precursor for more aggressive capabilities."
Nesting Doll "Matryoshka"	Inspired by traditional Russian nesting dolls, involves one satellite releasing a smaller satellite, which in turn releases another, and another. Demonstrated in 2019 by releasing a smaller satellite from a larger one, which then performed maneuvers near a US satellite.

Chinese Space Weapons Capabilities

Direct-Ascent ASATs	China's SC-19 missile successfully tested in 2007—destroying one of their own defunct satellites with a kinetic kill vehicle. Modified ballistic missile platforms provide the delivery systems.
Co-Orbital ASATs	Developing satellites capable of maneuvering close to targets—either for surveillance or direct engagement. Some may be equipped with robotic arms for physical manipulation or sabotage."
Electronic Warfare and DEWs	Systems to jam satellite communications and navigation signals. Directed-energy systems for sensor blinding and permanent damage to satellite optics.
Proximity Operations (RPO)	Chinese RPO-capable satellites have been conducting surveillance or probing defenses of U.S. and allied assets.
Cyber Capabilities	actively developing cyberattack strategies targeting satellite command-and-control systems, uplinks, and terrestrial support networks.
Other Capabilities	China's long-term objective is full-spectrum dominance of space."

US Intelligence Agencies

The US intelligence and counterintelligence community is a network of eighteen agencies and offices. These include the Central Intelligence Agency (CIA), the National Security Agency (NSA), and various elements within the Department of Defense (DoD) such as the Defense Intelligence Agency (DIA) and the intelligence components of the military services. Other key players include the Department of Homeland Security (DHS), the Department of Justice (DOJ), and the Department of Energy (DOE).

Independent Agencies:

Office of the Director of National Intelligence (ODNI): Oversees and coordinates the activities of the entire intelligence community.

Central Intelligence Agency (CIA): Focuses on foreign intelligence and conducting covert operations.

Defense Intelligence Agency (DIA): Provides military intelligence to warfighters, defense policymakers, and force planners.

National Security Agency (NSA): Specializes in signals intelligence (SIGINT) and cybersecurity.

National Geospatial-Intelligence Agency (NGA): Provides geospatial intelligence (GEOINT).

National Reconnaissance Office (NRO): Designs, builds, and operates the nation's intelligence satellites.

Intelligence elements of the military services: This includes the Army, Navy, Marine Corps, Air Force, and Space Force.

Other Departments and Agencies:

Department of Homeland Security (DHS): Includes the Office of Intelligence and Analysis and Coast Guard Intelligence.

Department of Justice (DOJ): Includes the Federal Bureau of Investigation (FBI) and the Drug Enforcement Administration (DEA).

Department of State: Includes the Bureau of Intelligence and Research.

Department of the Treasury: Includes the Office of Intelligence and Analysis.

Department of Energy: Includes the Office of Intelligence and Counterintelligence.

Foreign Intelligence Agencies

A foreign intelligence service is an agency tasked with gathering intelligence outside its own country's borders. Several countries have prominent foreign intelligence agencies, including the CIA (US), MI6 (UK), Mossad (Israel), and DGSE (France). These agencies play a crucial role in national security by collecting information on foreign governments, organizations, and individuals.

Here is a list of some notable foreign intelligence services:

Acronym	Name	Country	Responsibilities
ASIS	Australian Secret Intelligence Service	Australia	Australia's foreign intelligence service
DGI	Dirección de Inteligencia	Cuba	State intelligence agency
BND	Bundesnachrichtendienst	Germany	Germany's foreign intelligence service
CSIS	Canadian Security Intelligence Service	Canada	Foreign intelligence service and security agency
DGSE	Directorate-General for External Security	France	France's primary foreign intelligence agency,
FSB	Federal'naya sluzhba bezopasnosti Rossiyskoy Federatsii	Russia	Federal Security Service
GRU	Glavnoye Razvedyvatel'noye Upravleniye	Russia	Military intelligence; counterpart and rival to SVR.

ISI	Inter-Services Intelligence	Pakistan	Pakistan's premier intelligence agency
MI6	Secret Intelligence Service	United Kingdom	Foreign intelligence agency
MOSSAD	Institute for Intelligence and Special Operations	Israel	intelligence gathering and covert operations,
MSS	Ministry of State Security	China	China's main intelligence agency
RAW	Research and Analysis Wing	India	India's external intelligence agency
SVR	Sluzhba Vneshney Razvedki Rossii	Russia	Russian foreign intelligence service

Five Eyes

Originated during World War II from a U.S.–U.K. signals-intelligence (SIGINT) sharing pact known as the UKUSA Agreement (1946). The alliance formalized deep cooperation in the collection, analysis, and exchange of intelligence—especially electronic and communications intelligence—among the five countries.

Core Characteristics
1. Scope: Primarily signals intelligence (SIGINT), but extended to human intelligence (HUMINT), cyber defense, counterintelligence, and surveillance coordination.
2. Integration: The member nations maintain joint databases, shared collection networks, and interoperable classification standards—allowing analysts to access and cross-correlate intercepted communications under shared protocols.

Agencies Involved
3. United States: NSA (National Security Agency)
4. United Kingdom: GCHQ (Government Communications Headquarters)
5. Canada: CSE (Communications Security Establishment)
6. Australia: ASD (Australian Signals Directorate)
7. New Zealand: GCSB (Government Communications Security Bureau)

Function

Five Eyes countries divide global monitoring zones, exchanging raw intercepts and analytic outputs almost in real time. They also cooperate on cyber operations, encryption standards, and counter-espionage investigations.

This alliance forms the foundation of the Western intelligence-sharing ecosystem, later expanded through partnerships such as:

- ◆ Nine Eyes (adds Denmark, France, Netherlands, Norway)
- ◆ Fourteen Eyes (adds Germany, Belgium, Italy, Spain, Sweden)

Military Time Zones (NATO)

The U.S. military uses time zone letters from the NATO phonetic alphabet. Spelling: "Alpha" replaces Alfa; "Juliet" replaces Juliett.

The letter J is skipped in sequence.to prevent confusion with "I" and because some alphabets lacked it.

Special Designations: Z (Zulu): Greenwich Mean Time / Coordinated Universal Time (UTC ± 00:00). J (Juliet): Local time at the observer's position.

Usage Example: 0600 R = 6:00 a.m. in UTC − 5. Pronounced "zero six hundred Romeo."

Letter	Time Zone	UTC Offset	Location Example
A	Alpha	UTC+01:00	Berlin, Paris, Madrid, Rome
B	Bravo	UTC+02:00	Athens, Cairo, Helsinki, Kyiv
C	Charlie	UTC+0300	Moscow, Riyadh, Baghdad
D	Delta	UTC+04:00	Dubai, Baku, Yerevan
E	Echo	UTC+05:00	Islamabad, Karachi, Tashkent
F	Foxtrot	UTC+06:00	Almaty, Dhaka, Bishkek
G	Golf	UTC+-7:00	Bangkok, Hanoi, Jakarta
H	Hotel	UTC+08:00	Beijing, Singapore, Perth
I	India	UTC+09:00	Tokyo, Seoul, Pyongyang
J	Local	Local	Observer's Local Time
K	Kilo	UTC+10:00	Sydney, Vladivostok, Guam
L	Lima	UTC+11:00	Honiara, Nouméa, Magadan
M	Mike	UTC+12:00	Suva, Anadyr, Funafuti

N	November	UTC-01:00	Azores, Cape Verde
O	Oscar	UTC-02:00	South Georgia and South Sandwich Islands
P	Papa	UTC-03:00	Buenos Aires, Montevideo, Nuuk
Q	Quebec	UTC-04:00	Caracas, Halifax, Manaus
R	Romeo	UTC-05:00	New York, Bogotá, Lima, Miami
S	Sierra	UTC-06:00	Mexico City, Chicago, Guatemala City
T	Tango	UTC-0700	Denver, Phoenix, Calgary
U	Uniform	UTC-08:00	Los Angeles, Vancouver, Tijuana
V	Victor	UTC-9:00	Anchorage, Gambier Islands
W	Whiskey	UTC-10:00	Honolulu, Papeete
X	X-ray	UTC-11:00	Pago Pago, Niue
Y	Yankee	UTC-1200	Baker Island
Z	Zulu	UTC-00-00	London, Lisbon, Accra

U.S. Military Defense Conditions

Defense Condition (DEFCON) levels are a five-tier system used by the U.S. military to signal readiness for national security threats, ranging from **DEFCON 5** (normal peacetime posture) to **DEFCON 1** (maximum readiness for war). The scale runs in reverse—lower numbers indicate higher alert status. The U.S. military is currently at **DEFCON 5**.

Level	Readiness	Exercise Term
DEFCON 5	Normal readiness	Normal (Peace)
DEFCON 4	Increased readiness	Round House
DEFCON 3	Enhanced readiness (Air Force ready to mobilize in 15 minutes)	Fast Paced
DEFCON 2	High readiness (forces ready to deploy in under six hours)	Round House
DEFCON 1	Maximum readiness (war is imminent or underway)	Cocked Pistol

The Core Divide: Title 10 vs. Title 50

Aspect	Title 10 (U.S. Code)	Title 50 (U.S. Code)
Who operates under it	Department of Defense (DoD): Army, Navy, Air Force, Marine Corps, Space Force	Intelligence Community (IC): CIA, NSA, DIA, NGA, NRO, and DoD intelligence components when doing "intel activities"
Nature of authority	Military operations-overt, uniformed, governed by the Law of Armed Conflict (LOAC)	Intelligence & covert operations-clandestine or covert, often deniable
Chain of command	President → SecDef→ Combatant Commanders	President → Director of National Intelligence (DNI) / CIA Director (depending on activity)
Legal oversight	Congressional Armed Services Committees	Congressional Intelligence Committees
Disclosure	Usually public or at least declared to Congress	Can be classified "Findings" notified only to the Gang of Eight
Typical examples	Combat deployments, JSOC raids, cyber defense ops, uniformed collection in theater	Espionage, foreign HUMINT, SIGINT intercepts, covert action, influence ops